Advance praise f

"For ancient cultures, stories—some rooted
to passing on wisdom and knowledge. One thinks of the Bible for the Hebrews, the *Epic of Gilgamesh* for the Sumerians, the *Iliad* and *Odyssey* for the Greeks, and the *Aeneid* for the Romans. This fictional account of one of David's Mighty Men, Benaiah, takes the small amount of history that we know about this ancient Jewish warrior, found in the cycle of stories about David in the Old Testament, and weaves a convincing story about what he might have experienced and what he might have been like. A book imparting wisdom and pleasure at the same time—it does not get much better than this!"

—Michael A. G. Haykin
Professor of Church History
The Southern Baptist Theological Seminary

"*Benaiah: Mighty Man of God* demonstrates that an author need not rely on the sort of unrestrained embellishment that characterizes many works of historical fiction in order to present a subject in vivid colors. Throughout this thrilling story, Thompson's high view of Scripture is evident as she connects the dots to show us the life and mission of one of the central characters in King David's administration. Even better, she skillfully reveals the central character in the Bible's storyline: the promised Messiah. Readers of this book will find themselves reveling in the gospel of grace and glorifying the God of mercy."

—David N. Theobald
Pastor
Grace Baptist Church

"In *Benaiah: Mighty Man of God*, P. H. Thompson fleshes out a little-known character in the Bible, a soldier during the reign of David whose exploits rivaled—and sometimes surpassed—those of the king he served. Drawing on Biblical references and her knowledge of the time and historical events, Thompson paints a fascinating portrait of a man who dedicated his life to his king and his God, and who was immortalized in the pages of Scripture as a result."

—Sara Davison
Author of the award-winning *Seven Trilogy*

"In *Benaiah: Mighty Man of God* we experience the life and times of King David through the eyes of Benaiah, one of David's Mighty Men. Benaiah's quest for redemption drives his loyalty, but also leads to inner conflict when David orders him to do unconscionable things. A character list, Bible quotes headlining each chapter, and a set of discussion questions add clarity and value to this well-written biblical fiction. Thompson delivers a fascinating and worthwhile read."

—Violet Nesdoly
Author of *Destiny's Hands*

BENAIAH

BENAIAH

MIGHTY MAN OF GOD

P. H. THOMPSON

BENAIAH: MIGHTY MAN OF GOD
Copyright © 2019 by P. H. Thompson

ISBN: 978-1-4866-1807-1

Word Alive Press
119 De Baets Street, Winnipeg, MB R2J 3R9
www.wordalivepress.ca

WORD ALIVE
—PRESS—

Cataloguing in Publication may be obtained through Library and Archives Canada

To Benaiah, son of Jehoiada;
a mighty man,
a man of character.
I can't wait to meet you
in Heaven
to see how close I got
to your real story.

CONTENTS

"…Behold, to obey is better than sacrifice, And to heed than the fat of rams."
—1 Samuel 15:22

ACKNOWLEDGMENTS

To my husband, Gary, who supported my writing even before he read this book.

To my mom, Leena, my daughters, Hanna and Leah, and my son-in-law, Rony, for waiting patiently for the "first book" to become a reality and for photo-documenting the journey.

Thanks to the team at Word Alive Press: Sylvia St. Cyr, Marina Reis, Kyla Neufeld and the graphic design department. This whole process has been a pleasure. Thanks for helping me check another goal off my bucket list.

Thanks to Kathy Ide for doing the first round of edits during the years that I was too sick to move the project forward. You were very patient with this newbie writer and gave so many helpful suggestions.

Thanks to my friends who were willing to read the unpolished versions of Benaiah's story, warts and all. And a shout-out to my grandchildren, who can read this when they are older.

Thanks to Rony Mikhael for creating my author website.

Thanks to all the pastors and teachers I've had over the years, who have instilled in me a love for the Bible and its characters.

Finally, thank you Jesus, for saving someone like me and for blessing me with an opportunity to follow my dreams. May You receive all the glory.

CHARACTERS IN ORDER OF APPEARANCE

Benaiah son of Jehoiada Main character. A mercenary soldier known for three notable deeds (killing a giant Egyptian, fighting two Moabite ariels, and killing a lion in a pit on a snowy day), who joined with David while he was a fugitive from Saul. He became one of David's mighty men (elite, special forces soldiers), who was in charge of a third of the army for three months, and then became David's personal bodyguard, in charge of the Cherethites and Pelethites (executioners and runners/couriers). Finally, he was put in charge of the entire army of Israel under King Solomon. Married, father of at least two sons: Ammizabad (also a soldier) and Jehoiada (a counselor to Solomon after Ahithophel).

Ammizabad 1) Benaiah's brother (fictional).
2) Benaiah's first son, who was also a soldier.

Dinah★ Benaiah's mother (Ima/mama).

Rizpah★ Benaiah's younger sister, also the name of one of Saul's concubines, whom Abner took from Ishbosheth, Saul's son.

Yael★ Benaiah's younger sister.

Shua★ Female servant of Jehoiada and Dinah.

Yemima★ Benaiah's younger sister.

Mikhael ben Kenan*	Benaiah's best friend from Kabzeel, who also became a mercenary soldier.
Benjamin and Orpah*	Friends of Benaiah's family.
Simeon*	Former soldier who trains Benaiah and Mikhael as children.
Jehoiada	1) Benaiah's father (Abba). 2) Benaiah's second son, who became a chief counselor to Solomon in place of Ahithophel.
Itamar*	Bully, brother of Abijah.
Shallum*	Benaiah's elder brother, already a priest in Kabzeel.
Mariah*	Benaiah's wife, mother of Ammizabad, Jehoiada, Maytal and Sela.
Netaniah*	Mikhael ben Kenan's wife (daughter, Azubah).
Sebni*	Egyptian giant defeated by Benaiah.
Abiathar	Son of Ahimelech, son of Ahitub of the town of Nob, priest, formerly under Saul, then David, exiled and demoted by Solomon.
Eleazar ben Zichri*	A former servant and guard of Saul, fled during the massacre at the town of Nob.
Doeg the Edomite	Servant of King Saul, chief of his herdsmen, who betrayed Ahimelech the priest of Nob to Saul, involved in the massacre of the town of Nob.
Saul	First King of Israel, King David's father-in-law through his daughter, Michal.
Tirhanah*	Mariah's father (Abba), Benaiah's father-in-law.

Zibeah*   Mariah's mother (Ima), Benaiah's mother-in-law.

Uriah the   One of David's mighty men, husband of Bathsheba, son-in-law
Hittite   of Eliam (another of David's mighty men), killed by order of
                 David.

David   Seventh son of Jesse, second king of Israel, and King Saul's son-
                 in-law. Reigned seven years in Hebron, thirty-three years in Je-
                 rusalem. From Bethlehem. Wrote many psalms.

Joab   Nephew of David, son of David's sister Zeruiah, brother of
                 Abishai and Asahel, one of the top three of David's mighty men,
                 general over David's army, then the whole army of Israel, mur-
                 derer of Abner and Amasa. Took the city of Jerusalem from the
                 Jebusites. Loyal to David until he sided with Adonijah. Executed
                 by Benaiah on Solomon's orders.

Abishai   Brother of Joab and Asahel, nephew of David, one of the top
                 three of David's mighty men, co-conspirator in Abner's death,
                 but not Amasa's.

Asahel   Brother of Joab and Abishai, nephew of David, killed in battle
                 by Abner, General over Saul's army.

Zeruiah   David's sister, mother of Joab, Abishai, and Asahel.

Ittai the   One of David's chiefs, one of the top three mighty men, along-
Gittite   side Joab and Abishai.

Eliam   1) Elder brother of David; soldier with Saul.
                 2) Father of Bathsheba, one of David's mighty men.

Michal   Younger daughter of King Saul, first wife of David, married off
                 to another man while still married to David.

Palti   Son of Laish, married to Michal, Saul's daughter, while she was
                 still married to David.

Merab Elder daughter of King Saul, promised to David, but then married off by Saul to another.

Ahinoam David's second wife after Michal, from Jezreel; mother of Amnon.

Nabal Wealthy landowner in Carmel, husband of Abigail, scoundrel, struck down by God.

Abigail Widow of Nabal, from Carmel, David's third wife, mother of Chileab (Daniel), known for her wisdom.

Abner Son of Ner, Saul's uncle; commander of Saul's army, appointed commander of David's army under a united Israel, but murdered by Joab in retaliation for the death of his brother, Asahel.

Amasa Son of Jether, commander of the army of Judah. Revolted, along with his cousin Absalom. Cousin of Joab (their mothers were David's sister and half-sister), and nephew of David, murdered by Joab, who was envious that David appointed him commander-in-chief after Absalom's rebellion.

Achish Philistine king. Lived in Gath, gifted David with the city of Ziklag in return for his loyalty. Duped into believing David was loyal to him.

Rei Trusted soldier of both David and Solomon.

Mahasham★ Rei's wife.

Shammah One of David's soldiers.

Eliab One of David's soldiers.

Nebit★ Egyptian servant of an Amalekite.

Ishbosheth Saul's youngest son, king after Saul's death, murdered by two scoundrels, Rechab and Baanah.

Maacah   Daughter of Talmai, king of Geshur, wife of David, mother of Absalom and Tamar.

Haggith   Wife of David, mother of Adonijah.

Abital   Wife of David, mother of Shephatiah.

Eglah   Wife of David, mother of Ithream.

Maytal★   Benaiah and Mariah's first daughter. Means "Dew Drop."

Ahi★   Servant of David in charge of the Court of the Women (wives and concubines).

Rechab   Brother of Baanah, son of Rimmon the Beerothite, of the tribe of Benjamin, murderer of Ishbosheth, son of Saul.

Baanah   Brother of Rechab, son of Rimmon the Beerothite, of the tribe of Benjamin, murderer of Ishbosheth, son of Saul.

Ahithophel   David's chief counselor, then traitor under Absalom, father of Eliam, grandfather of Bathsheba.

Nathan   The prophet, sent to confront and comfort David.

Uzzah   A man who was struck dead by God for daring to touch the ark to steady it during its transportation to Jerusalem.

Shemaiah   Also called Sheva, David's scribe.

Jehoshaphat   David's recorder, or equivalent of Secretary of State.

Ziba   Servant of Mephibosheth, father of ten sons, former servant of Saul, steward of Mephibosheth's property, betrayer of Mephibosheth.

Mephibosheth   Son of Jonathan, grandson of Saul, lame in his feet, adopted by David.

Bathsheba Wife of Uriah; daughter of Eliam (one of David's mighty men), granddaughter of Ahithophel (David's chief counselor), David's wife; mother of King Solomon.

Ashima* Bathsheba's female servant.

Milka* Benaiah and Mariah's female servant.

Zadok High priest, along with Abiathar, then after him, during the time of David and Solomon.

Absalom Son of David and Maacah, grandson of Talmai, the king of Geshur, brother of Tamar, murderer of his half-brother, Amnon; known for his vanity and his hair; instigated rebellion and treachery against his father; killed by Joab.

Tamar Daughter of David and Maacah, granddaughter of Talmai the king of Geshur, sister of Absalom, raped by her half-brother, Amnon.

Amnon Son of David and Ahinoam, David's second wife; raped his half-sister, Tamar; murdered in retaliation for it by his half-brother, Absalom.

Jonadab Son of David's brother Shimeah; cousin and friend of Amnon and Absalom; known to be very crafty.

Shimei son of Gera A Benjamite, of the house of Saul, who cursed David as he fled from Absalom, later came down to meet David to apologize and pledge his faithfulness to him. He was placed on house arrest by Solomon, then executed by Benaiah on Solomon's orders for violating the terms of his sentence.

Barzillai A rich Gileadite, who, at the age of eighty, gave provisions to David and all who were with him when he fled Absalom. Also one of the first to greet him when he returned across the Jordan. David offered to care for him in return, but he declined, sending his son in his place. Later his descendants were provided for by Solomon.

Machir The son of Ammiel, lived in Lo Debar, and sheltered Mephibosheth from the age of five to adulthood. Came with Barzillai the Gileadite to provision David.

Sheba son of Bicri A Benjamite who started a rebellion against David, during which time Joab murdered Amasa, son of Jether. Sheba was beheaded after negotiations between Joab and a wise woman in Abel of Beth Maachah.

Sela* Benaiah's second daughter. Means "Rock."

Jair* Benaiah's son-in-law. Means "He Shines."

Gad The prophet sent to encourage David while he was on the run from Saul, and to confront him after his unlawful census.

Merari* Mariah's sister's husband; died in the plague after the census.

Ornan The Jebusite who owned the property God chose for David's sacrifice after the unlawful census, and the site Solomon chose on which to build the first temple. Also known as Araunah.

Solomon Israel's third king; son of David and Bathsheba, known as Israel's wisest and richest king. Reigned forty years in Jerusalem. Built the first temple. Had seven hundred wives and three hundred concubines. Wrote many songs and proverbs.

Adonijah Son of David and Haggith; attempted to usurp the throne of David from Solomon while David was yet alive; paroled then executed by Benaiah on Solomon's orders when he asked for Solomon's concubine, Abishag.

Abishag A young Shunamite virgin, chosen to keep David warm in his last days. He did not know her intimately. Adonijah wanted her, but she was Solomon's once he became king.

*fictional name

CHAPTER ONE

"Benaiah was the son of Jehoiada, the son of a valiant man from Kabzeel, who had done many deeds…"

—2 Samuel 23:20

Benaiah skidded around the corner of Mikhael's ben Kenan's house and surveyed the vast grove of olive trees behind their large home. Mikhael's father was an olive merchant. As he stood there panting to catch his breath after his long run, he spotted his friend sitting on the low stone wall skirting their property. He bounced off when he saw Benaiah approach.

"What took you so long?" Mikhael grumbled, as Benaiah sprinted up to him. "Simeon is not going to appreciate us showing up late."

Benaiah rolled his eyes, "My Ima made me bring my little brother along."

Mikhael peered around Benaiah, as if ten-year-old Ammizabad might be hiding behind him.

"So where is he?"

"I sent him on an errand," Benaiah winked. "By the time he's done, we'll be long gone. And since he won't know where we went, he'll go back home, to the women."

Mikhael laughed, "Well done." He grabbed his friend's arm. "Let's go."

The two boys jogged towards their destination, the home of an old soldier's from King Saul's army, who offered to teach them some basics of soldiering. Being from the tribe of Levi, Benaiah was expected to become a priest like his father, but it held no appeal to him. He wanted the thrill of fighting the enemies of Israel, the Philistines. They had been trying to take over their land and make the Israelites their servants for centuries.

A few years ago, a Philistine giant named Goliath had challenged the army of Israel morning and evening for forty days. If he won, the Israelites would have to become slaves to the Philistines. No one in the army would accept the challenge, not even King Saul himself, who was head and shoulders above most men. But then, a young shepherd boy named David ben Jesse volunteered to fight. Everyone was surprised when King Saul approved it, since David wasn't even a professional soldier. And then he actually won! He defeated the giant with a well-placed stone from his slingshot to Goliath's forehead.

Benaiah and Mikhael often re-enacted the battle, each one wanting to be the hero, David. But because Benaiah was larger than Mikhael, he would play Goliath. Now they would learn how to fight for real, but Simeon might cancel altogether if they couldn't even be counted on to arrive on time. The boys picked up their pace.

"How'd you manage to sneak away?" Mikhael asked.

"I told my Ima I was coming to your house. It was true, even if it was just a stopping point. I was almost out the door when she told me to take Ammiz along. But I was afraid he'd report back to her about what we really did, so I sent him on a side trip."

"Good idea. I'm sure Simeon wouldn't appreciate if we showed up with more people than he expected."

Benaiah couldn't reach his thirteenth birthday soon enough. Then he would be viewed as a man in his parents' eyes, and he could make his own decisions without reporting to them all the time.

After an arduous trek up a slope on the outskirts of Kabzeel, in southern Judah, Benaiah and Mikhael arrived at the home of the old warrior. Mikhael knocked on the heavy wooden door and then glanced over at Benaiah and smiled. He looked as excited as Benaiah felt.

Several moments later, an elderly female servant answered. After learning their names, she led them into the front courtyard, which spanned the width of the four-room home. Then she disappeared into one of the two rooms to the right of the central hallway.

To their left, stone steps led from the courtyard to the flat roof, which typically functioned as more outdoor living space for the family. Benaiah wondered if Simeon had a family. He didn't see anyone or hear any voices. Perhaps that woman was his mother rather than a servant?

Suddenly, a massive man stood in front of them. Benaiah judged him to be at least forty since he had so much battle experience. He stroked his beard as he perused his new trainees.

Uncomfortable with the silent scrutiny, Benaiah cleared his throat. "Sir?" he squeaked out. Then he tried again and managed to say it in a less pathetic voice.

"When you arrive somewhere, you state your name and business," Simeon bellowed.

The two boys straightened.

"Benaiah ben Jehoiada, reporting for training, sir."

"Mikhael ben Kenan, reporting for training, sir."

Benaiah glanced at Simeon as he paced back and forth in front of them.

"Keep your eyes front when speaking, trainees. You don't ever have an eye-to-eye conversation with a superior officer."

Benaiah affixed his gaze to a crack in the wall beyond Simeon as they answered, "Yes, sir!" in unison.

When Simeon stood directly in front of them, Benaiah could feel the heat of his glare on the top of his head.

"You're late!" Simeon's breath moved Benaiah's hair.

He gulped. "That was my fault, sir. I had an errand to run for my Ima." Benaiah hoped he wouldn't ask if he had accomplished that mission.

The man paced in front of them, limping slightly. His hands were clasped behind his back, and his muscular chest strained his tunic. He nodded his approval. "Your parents are your top priority at this point. They are your commanding officers. For now."

Benaiah didn't share that he had delegated his errand to a lower-ranking soldier, his brother.

"Up to the rooftop," Simeon shouted. "Go, go, go, go, go!"

As the boys scrambled up the stone staircase, Benaiah thought he caught a ghost of a smile on the old warrior's face, even though he wasn't supposed to be looking.

On the rooftop, they stood at attention as they waited for Simeon. Like most rooftop living spaces, there was added seating, a table, an herb garden and plants, as well as a small fig tree in a large clay pot. They waited while Simeon slowly made his way up the steps. It sounded like he was taking a step and then following the first leg up with the second, like his little sister, Rizpah, did because the steps were too tall for her. Benaiah wondered what had happened to him to cause the limp.

"Can we learn to fight with swords?" Mikhael dared to ask.

Simeon drew a sword out from behind the fig tree. "Like this?" He swished the thick, double-edged sword in front of him effortlessly, as if it was a common kitchen utensil.

The boys nodded, wide eyed.

"No."

Their shoulders slumped.

"Iron weapons like this are scarce in Israel because the Philistines have forbidden us from making them. They fear an uprising. We must go to them even to sharpen our tools, and then pay them for the privilege." He sneered. "The only people with real swords are King Saul and his sons. And anyone who can take a sword from a defeated enemy."

Benaiah imagined Simeon taking the sword in his hands from a fallen soldier. Perhaps that was when he acquired his limp. "Can we touch it?" Benaiah asked, even as he reached toward it.

Simeon withdrew the sword. "Not yet. A soldier needs to train his body first, then learn how to fight hand-to-hand, before attempting to wield a sword. Even then, he must always use his most powerful weapon: his mind."

Benaiah's mouth dropped open. He hadn't thought of that. He assumed physical strength was all that was required.

"A soldier has to anticipate his opponent's next action and act quickly. He needs to know his enemy's weaknesses and exploit them. He must be bold. There can be no hesitation."

This man knew so much about warfare. How privileged they were to be here, learning from someone who knew what it was like to fight other real soldiers.

Benaiah smiled inwardly. This was the best day ever!

★ ★ ★

Ammiz stared at the neighborhood around him. Benaiah had told him to take the loaf of fig bread their mother had made to Benjamin and Orpah, their family friends. Ima had told Benaiah to do it, then insisted he take Ammiz along. But as soon as they neared Mikhael's house, Benaiah had ordered Ammiz to complete the errand while he went to meet his friend.

Ammiz thought he knew where he was supposed to go. But since he had only gone to their home once with his parents, he hadn't paid much attention to the landmarks.

He hugged the warm fig loaf to his chest, the smell of it giving him some comfort, as if Ima was nearby.

As he wandered the hard packed dirt streets, trying to remember which door belonged to his parents' friends, he froze at the familiar voice of his enemy behind him, mocking his stutter.

"Look everybody! It's A-a-a-miza-b-b-bad!"

He turned to see Itamar and three other boys striding toward him. The passersby kept about their business, as if they didn't notice anything out of the ordinary.

Before Ammiz could run away, Itamar was standing over him, blocking the newly risen sun, glaring down at him.

"What do you have for me there?"

Ammiz pulled the loaf closer to himself, in a futile attempt to preserve the gift. In an instant, Itamar tore it out of his arms and unwrapped it, tossing the striped blue and white cloth to the ground. He inhaled the aroma of the bread.

"Mmmmm. How did you know I was hungry?" Itamar laughed, then looked around at his friends, who also laughed.

Ammiz had no choice but to get through whatever humiliation they would heap on him, and then he would be safe. Until the next time.

Itamar tore off a section of the warm loaf and shoved it in his mouth. "Hey, this is good." He shared the bread with his friends. "Did you make this yourself... with your Ima?" He spat out the last word.

"G-give it b-b-back," Ammiz whispered. "It's not for you."

It was too late now. The loaf was almost gone.

He should go back home and tell Ima what had happened. But he knew he wouldn't. Instead, he would claim he tripped and it fell onto the road. She would be angry with him at first, and he would have to accept her punishment. But at least he wouldn't have to relive the shame of telling her he'd been teased about his stutter. Again.

This wouldn't be happening if Benaiah had gone with him. There's no way Itamar would be so bold if Benaiah was near. But even if Ammiz could get away and find his older brother, Benaiah wouldn't be happy that he hadn't completed his errand.

Itamar wiped the last crumbs from his lips. "Ah, that was good. Do you have anything else?"

Ammiz lunged to the right but Itamar's arm flew out across his chest to stop him.

"Where do you think you're going?"

Ammiz raised his arms to push back, but Itamar grasped him by both shoulders. Ammiz looked beyond him to the other boys, hoping to find even one ally who would stand up to Itamar for him, but they all looked away.

"I have a project for you," Itamar sneered.

"A p-p-project?"

"I want you to get me a pomegranate from the marketplace."

"But I... I don't have any m-money."

Itamar leaned closer to Ammiz and spoke slowly and deliberately. "I said *get*, not *buy*, you dummy!"

"I'm not going to steal for you!"

"Oh, yes, you are," he hissed.

Ammiz considered his predicament. Perhaps he could go along with it, until he could run away or ask for help. He nodded almost imperceptibly.

Itamar released his shoulders. "That's more like it. Now, let's go. I'll point out which market stall I want you to take it from. There's a man I don't like, who is always shooing me away like I'm an annoying fly."

Itamar grabbed Ammiz's arm and propelled him along the road. Ammiz tried to pull away, but Itamar's grip was too strong.

★ ★ ★

As the two soldiers-in-training walked toward home in the waning sunset, they practiced some of the defensive moves Simeon had taught them. "I can't wait to learn how to use one of Simeon's clubs," Benaiah said.

"I could barely lift that thing, let alone swing it," Mikhael said as held an imaginary club over his head.

"I want to try to make one. Then I can practice at home."

"You'd need to find some dense wood."

Benaiah wondered where he could find some. He couldn't very well ask his Abba for help. Jehoiada, a priest, was so different from Simeon. "I can't imagine ever being as confident as he is. His presence just shouts, 'I dare you.'"

Mikhael laughed. "I know! And I wouldn't dare."

By the time Benaiah arrived at home, his father was returning from his duties. Jehoiada put an arm around his son and they entered the house together. Benaiah wished his Abba wouldn't embrace him while the neighbors could see them. He wasn't a child anymore.

"How was your day, Son?"

"Good." Benaiah didn't offer any details. His father wouldn't understand his desire to be a soldier. He might even be angry with Benaiah for considering it. Five-year-old Rizpah ran into the courtyard to greet Jehoiada and Benaiah. Jehoiada scooped her up into his arms. "Abba, my doll went on a journey today. She went all the way to Gibeah to see King Saul."

"Did she now? And did she get a glimpse of him?"

"Yes, and he was wearing a beautiful crown with colorful jewels. And the queen was there, and the little princes and princesses all said we could play with their toys. They have very nice toys."

Benaiah tugged on her pigtails. "I'll bet they do."

Benaiah's mother, Dinah looked up as they entered the eating room. "Where is Ammizabad?"

Benaiah's eyes widened. "Isn't he here?"

She rose to her feet, her needlework falling to the floor. "Of course not. He left with you this morning." She advanced toward him.

Jehoiada turned to Benaiah. "What happened today, Son?"

Benaiah couldn't imagine where Ammiz could have gone. It was a simple detour. "We were going to drop off the loaf for Benjamin and Orpah, like Ima asked us to, and then meet Mikhael at his house. But then..."

"But then what?" Dinah asked.

"Mikhael was waiting for me at his house, and I was late, so I told Ammiz to drop off the loaf instead."

"You sent a little boy off alone?" she shrieked.

Little Rizpah's wide eyes darted between Benaiah and their parents. Shua, their servant picked up baby Jael, who had started to cry, from her basket and tried to soothe her by bouncing her and patting her on her back.

"Their home wasn't far away when we split up. And he was supposed to meet me at Mikhael's house afterward."

"And did he come there?" Jehoiada asked.

Benaiah hesitated. He lowered his gaze. "I don't know."

"What do you mean?" Color drained from Dinah's face.

"We didn't stay at Mikhael's house."

"Where did you go today?" Jehoiada spoke in measured tones.

Benaiah knew he'd be in trouble, but his brother was missing. He took a deep breath. "Mikhael and I went to Simeon's house, to learn how to fight like soldiers."

"Who is Simeon?" Jehoiada asked.

"A soldier."

Dinah sank onto the bench. "I told you to look after him!"

If Ammizabad was hurt, or worse, it would be Benaiah's fault. He hadn't thought about his brother once the whole time he was playing soldier.

Jehoiada reached for an oil lamp as he looked to their servant. "Shua, stay with the girls. Dinah, come with me. We'll check the path between here and Benjamin's house, and then between there and Mikhael's house. Benaiah, take a torch.

P. H. Thompson

It'll be dark soon. Search wherever else you think he may have gone. And may Yahweh help us to find him unharmed."

CHAPTER TWO

"…To obey is better than sacrifice…"

—1 Samuel 15:22

Benaiah searched every road and yard between Mikhael's house and Simeon's, but his efforts were pointless. Ammizabad wouldn't have gone home—he would have tried to find Benaiah and Mikhael.

He went back to the spot where he had abandoned his brother and checked every alleyway, half hoping to find Ammiz and half hoping to not. The best-case scenario would be to return home and find his little brother there, safe and happy.

It would be dark soon. Benaiah imagined his brother alone, afraid, possibly hurt… or worse. All because of his desire to prove he was a man.

Please, God, help us find him. Benaiah walked purposefully through the dirt streets of Kabzeel, checking all the places he knew Ammizabad might frequent.

His mother's words reproached him with each step. *"I told you to look after him!"*

What a horrible person he was. The worst brother in the world! If he could find Ammiz alive and well, he would take his punishment gladly and learn his lesson. He just wanted his little brother back.

Getting desperate, Benaiah searched neighborhoods beyond where he thought Ammiz might have wandered into.

In a narrow street between a row of houses, he spotted a piece of blue-and-white-striped cloth in the middle of the road. He snatched it up. It had been run over by a cart or two, but Benaiah recognized it as the cloth his mother wove on her loom. He held it to his nose. It still held a faint aroma of fig loaf.

Ammiz had been here.

Praying for direction, Benaiah tucked the striped cloth into the sash around his waist and scrambled toward the central market. He asked everyone he saw if they had seen a young boy alone. No one had.

As the vendors began closing up their shops for the day, Benaiah asked the same questions, describing Ammiz and his clothing.

One vendor gave him a shred of hope. "Yeah, I saw that scoundrel. He and his friends tried to steal from me! Lucky for them I can't run as fast as in my youth. I chased them off in the direction of the creek."

Ammiz would never steal. And he didn't have any real friends. Yet, this was all Benaiah had to go on. He thanked the man and walked toward the creek.

With each step, he grew more fearful that Ammiz would not be found this night. He could go home, hoping his parents had found him. But the anxious feeling in his gut told him the news would not be good. He had to continue searching until Ammiz was found.

At the end of the street of market stalls, he heard a faint whimpering. Benaiah stopped and strained his ears to locate the direction of the sound. It was coming from his left. He hurried around the corner into a narrow alleyway.

Ammiz sat against the stone wall, holding the side of his head. Benaiah rushed to his side. "Ammiz! Are you all right?"

"M-m-my head hurts," he mumbled.

A pool of dried vomit lay on the ground beside him. Benaiah crouched in front of his brother. "Look at me," he commanded.

Ammiz slowly raised his eyes, but they did not focus. Benaiah examined his scalp. He saw no blood, but he could feel a lump. "Can you stand?"

"I th-think so."

Benaiah helped him up, then caught him as he swayed.

"I'm a little d-d-dizzy."

Benaiah scooped Ammiz into his arms and started toward home. "What happened? How did you get hurt?"

"I was trying to d-d-do what you told me," he began, but tears cut off his words.

Ammiz seemed more upset that he didn't do as Benaiah had ordered than that he was injured.

"Never mind that now," Benaiah soothed.

"Then Itamar and his friends saw me."

"Abijah's brother?"

Ammiz nodded. "They grabbed the loaf and ate it. Then they t-t-tried to make me steal fruit for them, but I wouldn't do it. I knocked over a b-b-basket instead, and the man chased us off." Ammiz' eyes drifted closed.

Benaiah walked as quickly as he could without tripping. His brother was much heavier than Benaiah expected, but he gladly bore this burden.

"Did those boys hurt you?" Anger rose in Benaiah's chest at the thought.

"The m-m-man in the market recognized Itamar and threatened to tell his father. Itamar told me it would be my fault if his father p-p-punished him. He came toward me, and I knew he was going to try to hurt me. So I ran. But they chased me."

Benaiah pressed his lips together. When Ammiz was better, he would find Itamar and teach him to never come near Ammiz again. Yet, even as he hoped to shift the blame, he knew none of this would have happened if Benaiah hadn't sent Ammiz off by himself.

"I think I fell and hit my head. I don't r-r-remember what happened next. When I looked around, they were gone. I t-t-tried to go home, but I couldn't remember where it was, and my head hurt so much."

The terrain began to slope downward, which should have been easier, but it made Benaiah's footing less sure.

"D-d-do you think Ima will be angry with me for losing the l-l-loaf?"

"No. They'll just be happy that you're okay. And they'll be proud that you didn't steal. None of this is your fault. It's those boys. And me. Ammiz, I'm so sorry. I never should've sent you off by yourself."

Ammiz smiled weakly. "It's okay. I know you didn't want me to play with you and Mikhael. N-n-no one else wants to play with me either. I'm used to it."

Tears blurred Benaiah's vision. He blinked them back. He had to accomplish this new mission of carrying his brother home to safety, but his brother's easy acceptance of rejection broke Benaiah's heart.

Poor Ammiz! He couldn't help his stutter.

"What d-d-did you and Mikhael do today?" Ammiz asked sleepily.

Benaiah wasn't sure if rest was the best thing for him or if he should try to keep his brother awake. He decided to talk with him because it scared him whenever Ammiz' eyes drifted closed. "We went to see a man named Simeon. He's training us to be soldiers."

Ammiz's eyes opened wide. "Like David and Jonathan?"

Benaiah smiled. "Yes."

"Aren't you going to be a p-p-priest like Abba?"

"No. I want to fight."

"You'll be a good soldier."

"I hope so. Because I think that's what Yahweh wants me to be."

"You'll fight giants, too."

Ammiz felt heavier with each step. Benaiah grunted, readjusted his burden, and carried on.

Their stone house finally came into view. Many torches lit the yard, held by neighbors who had come to help in the search or to support the family.

Their father rushed forward to take Ammiz from Benaiah's arms and carry him into the house. Benaiah felt surprisingly empty without his brother.

"Ammizabad!" Their mother ran to him and followed him as he took Ammiz into their sleeping room and laid him on a palette. She stroked her younger son's forehead and kissed his face. "I was so worried. Are you hurt?" Her voice quavered.

"What happened?" Abba asked Benaiah.

"He told me he fell and hit his head. He's dizzy and he was sick."

Abba felt his son's scalp. "There's no cut. But there is swelling here." He looked into Ammiz's eyes. "Son, can you tell me what day it is?"

Ammiz slowly lolled his head and tried to open his eyes. "The first d-d-day of the week?"

Their parents exchanged worried looks. It was the fifth day.

Abba pointed at Benaiah without taking his eyes off Ammiz. "Who is that by the door?"

Ammizabad looked at his brother and smiled. "He's the one who b-b-brought me here."

"Yes, but what is his name?"

His head tilted to the side. "I d-d-don't know."

Ima cried out.

Ammiz's eyes darted between his parents. "What's wrong?"

"Nothing, Son," Abba said, patting his hand.

"I'm tired," Ammiz whispered.

"Rest then." Abba covered him with a blanket.

When Ammiz was sleeping soundly, Benaiah updated his parents on what had happened. Ima stroked her son's forehead, but turned away when Benaiah stepped close. He wished she would yell and tell him how angry and disappointed she was, but that wasn't her way. She would torment him far more with her silence.

Benaiah wanted to stay up with Ammiz, but his parents sent him to his sleeping room. When he reached the doorway, he looked back. Both of his parents sat next to the palette, their eyes closed and lips moving in silent prayer.

Benaiah couldn't sleep, his worry for his brother's health, and guilty thoughts tormenting him through the night.

A few hours later, a scream from his mother startled him. "Do something! He can't breathe!" The baby started to cry.

Benaiah ran to his parents' sleeping room. Dinah stood a few paces from the palette, wringing her hands, Jehoiada was kneeling next to his son, attempting to stabilize Ammiz' jerking limbs. His red face was contorted into a grotesque mask, his eyes fixed open. Foam seeped from his mouth through clenched teeth.

Benaiah longed to look away from the horrific sight, but he couldn't. He backed up until he felt the cool wall behind him.

Ammiz's complexion changed from red to bluish gray. The jerking continued so long. Benaiah had never seen such an event, and it scared him. What did it mean? Jehoiada rolled him over to his side. Nothing he did seemed to stop it.

Suddenly, Ammiz went limp and very still. His eyes seemed to stare transfixed at the ceiling.

"He's not breathing!" Ima screamed.

Abba put his ear to his son's chest. After several moments, he began to weep. "Oh, my son. My son!"

"No!" Ima cried. "My little boy can't be dead! He can't be!" She fell to her knees beside the bed and shook his shoulders.

Abba took her hands and stilled them. "Don't," he said gently. "He's gone."

Benaiah stood rooted to the stone floor. It couldn't be true. His actions couldn't have led to this: his brother dead.

But it had. And all because Benaiah had disobeyed.

★ ★ ★

His brother was buried the next day. The sound of his mother's wailing broke his heart. Nearby relatives and friends came to support the family. Not surprisingly, the boys involved in the incident were absent, although their parents were in attendance. Jehoiada chose not to confront them at this time, but Benaiah already had plans to search them out. Benaiah answered any questions about what happened with vague answers, happy when their supporters knew enough not to push for details while their grief was still fresh. After a week of mourning, their supporters went home and the family was left to carry on.

At mealtimes, Benaiah stared at his food. He had no appetite, but his parents expected him to appear at the table. Ima stared at the empty bench Ammiz used to occupy, tears filling her eyes.

At breakfast several days later, Rizpah again asked, "Why isn't Ammiz here?"

P. H. Thompson

Abba got up from the bench and came to kneel by his daughter. "Rizpah, honey, Ammizabad fell and got hurt, and Yahweh took him to be with Him. Remember we told you?"

Confusion showed in her face. "But who will play dolls with me?" Ima sobbed and covered her mouth with her hand.

Benaiah squatted down beside his sister. "Would it be okay if I played dolls with you instead?"

"Will you make their voices high when they talk, like Ammiz always did?"

"Of course." Benaiah would do anything to help his family adjust to their loss.

★ ★ ★

After a second week of awkward silence and tears, Benaiah's father motioned for him to follow him to their rooftop. "We need to talk about what happened with your brother."

Benaiah prepared himself to accept the blame he deserved.

They climbed the stone steps leading from the courtyard to their flat rooftop. Benaiah felt as if he were a condemned man walking to the gallows.

They sat down on a bench near the herb planter. Benaiah noticed the soil in the herb garden was dry. Caring for the garden had been one of Ammizabad's chores. Benaiah inhaled the fresh smell of mint and determined he would take over that responsibility.

Abba gently laid a hand on his shoulder. "Son, why did you go to Simeon's house that day?"

Benaiah expected his father would focus on his actions that day, not his motives. Benaiah wasn't ready for that conversation. He stared at his hands. "Father... I believe Yahweh wants me to be a soldier." He looked up, expecting anger or a lecture. Instead, Abba asked, "Why do you think this desire is from Yahweh?"

"I know I'm expected to join the priesthood when I turn thirty. But I don't feel drawn to caring for the tabernacle, teaching the law, assisting with sacrifices, accepting tithes, making long prayers."

Realizing it sounded as if he were insulting his father and spurning the great privilege of the priesthood, he added, "I know all those things are important. But God has given me a desire to do something for my country. I want to fight in Saul's army against the enemies of Israel."

Abba's long silence unnerved him.

"Perhaps I can be a soldier first, and if Yahweh calls me to it, I can still become a priest when I'm older." It seemed like a reasonable compromise, especially since thirty felt like a lifetime away.

"You don't require a special calling to be a priest. Being born a Levite, and especially an Aaronite, qualifies you and compels you to be what Yahweh designed our tribe to be. Even though your older brother is already serving, you are still expected to fulfill your priestly duties. You have been consecrated to the service of God from birth."

"But I have such a strong desire to do this. Surely it's from Yahweh."

"Perhaps. But a real man can protect and care for the people he loves in other ways than soldiering."

His father's gentle words cut him to the heart. All the skills he could learn as a soldier would mean nothing if he didn't use them to protect those God had entrusted to him. And he had already failed to protect his brother.

"Ammiz wanted to be just like you. Did you know that?"

Benaiah hung his head. He did not deserve the respect his brother had for him.

"Can I tell you a story?"

Benaiah nodded. Jehoiada was a natural storyteller. Abba stroked his beard, as he did whenever he was instructing his family. "Samuel has shared this story with the priests, so we'd know what God has planned for our country's future. A few years after Saul began his reign, the Lord told him that He wanted to punish the Amalekites for ambushing God's people on their way up from Egypt all those years ago. They picked off the weak ones and the stragglers at the rear ranks, when they were tired and weary. The Lord vowed then that he would blot out the remembrance of them from under heaven, once we were established in the land. The Lord commanded him to utterly destroy the Amalekites and all they had. But Saul spared their king, Agag, as well as the best of the sheep, the oxen, the fatlings, the lambs."

Benaiah had heard of the Amalekites, but he didn't know about this incident in Israel's recent history.

"The Lord told the prophet Samuel that He greatly regretted installing Saul as king, because he had disobeyed a direct command. Samuel was grieved by this announcement and cried out to God all night on Saul's behalf."

Benaiah was shocked to hear God changed His mind about the king He had anointed over Israel. "The next day, when Samuel went to see Saul, the king said to Samuel, 'Welcome, brother! I have done as the Lord commanded.' But Samuel said, 'If you have, then why do I hear sheep bleating and oxen lowing?'"

Benaiah could relate to Saul's excuse. He also thought he would get away with secretly seeing Simeon, but then his disobedience was discovered.

"Saul protested, saying, 'But I *have* obeyed God and gone on the mission He sent me.' He blamed the people, saying that *they* had kept back the best of the animals. He added that they were for sacrifice, as if that made it all right."

Benaiah could see through Saul's excuses. Were his own as flimsy?

"Samuel asked Saul, 'What do you think? Does the Lord take as much delight in burnt offerings and sacrifices, as in obedience to His commands? No, but to obey is better than sacrifice, and to listen is better than the fat of rams. Because to God, rebellion is as bad as the sin of witchcraft, and stubbornness is as bad as idolatry.'"

Was Benaiah's disobedience a sign of rebellion in God's eyes?

"Samuel added, 'Because you have rejected God's word, He has rejected you as king.'"

Benaiah bolted up. "What? Saul won't be king of Israel anymore?"

"That's how it seems. We don't know when it will happen, but God will appoint another man to replace him. Perhaps Prince Jonathan."

Benaiah had heard good things about Prince Jonathan. "My point is, Son, Yahweh is greatly displeased when we disobey Him. We priests do the tasks He has prescribed, but He is far more pleased when He sees the attitude of our hearts. He is more concerned that we do what He commands than that we go through the motions with ritual."

What does God see when He looks at my heart? Benaiah wondered. He sat back down on the bench. His father took his hands in his and looked intently into his young son's eyes.

"Regardless of what I want for your life, or what you want for your life, if you have an obedient heart, Yahweh will lead you into your life's work, and you will serve Him well."

Was it too much to hope that his father's position was softening?

"Perhaps you can spend a few years with me, learning God's law and seeing what is involved in the service of Yahweh. When God replaces Saul with a new king, if you still feel He is leading you to be a soldier, I will not stand in your way."

Benaiah wondered if he could manage spending the next few years training for the priesthood, knowing that if he did, he might have his father's blessings to serve as a soldier. Besides, didn't the story his father just told him confirm that God preferred obedience to sacrifice? There were plenty of priests to offer sacrifices and incense to God, including his older brother, Shallum, who was already married and established as a priest in Kabzeel. Benaiah could obey as a soldier. Surely that was better.

"Who knows? Training for the priesthood may even make you a better soldier," Jehoiada added.

Benaiah stood and pulled his father into an embrace. "Thank you, Abba. I promise, I will always obey you and God."

CHAPTER THREE

"When a man has taken a new wife, he shall not go out to war or be charged with any business; he shall be free at home one year, and bring happiness to his wife whom he has taken."

—Deuteronomy 24:5

Benaiah followed his nose into the cooking room, enticed by the aroma of his favorite lamb stew. "What's the occasion?" he asked.

Dinah glanced at him, and then looked away quickly. She taste-tested the broth, nodded her approval and answered, "Tirhana and Zibeah are coming over for dinner."

"Do I know them?"

"You must have seen them at worship, but perhaps you haven't been formally introduced to their family."

"Their family? Who else is coming?"

Benaiah was beginning to suspect this was probably another one of his parents' awkward attempts at matchmaking. Now twenty, Benaiah had resisted his parents' pressure to marry because he saw it for what it was: an attempt to keep him in Kabzeel forever. He was sure they thought, once he was tied down to a family, he'd abandon his dreams of soldiering. So, they'd been inviting friends over to share meals... and those guests brought along their marriageable daughters.

So far, the young women he'd been introduced to were nice enough, but some were rather naive. Others seemed desperate. Some didn't appeal to him physically. Others seemed uninterested in his future plans and were most likely to want to settle in Kabzeel and have babies, whereas he couldn't wait to leave this town on his great adventure.

Over the last seven years since Ammizabad's death, by which he marked the passage of time, all of his friends had gotten married and settled down. Even

Mikhael had a wife, Netaniah, and a one-year-old daughter. He worked in his father's olive grove, like a regular, responsible adult. But on the rare occasions when he could get away from his responsibilities to spend some time with his childhood friend, the two men spoke of their shared ambition to leave town and become soldiers in the army of Israel. Having a family made it more difficult, but not impossible.

"Let me guess," Benaiah said as he threw his head back in exasperation. "They have a daughter of marrying age who is coming along with them tonight?"

"Yes, Mariah is a lovely young woman," Dinah said defensively, "Please try to be reasonably polite, for our sake. Please, Benaiah."

Benaiah sighed. "All right, Ima. But only because you made my favorite meal tonight." He kissed her cheek.

Benaiah heard their guests call out a greeting outside the courtyard. Jehoiada ushered them in and introduced them to Benaiah. He did recall seeing the parents somewhere. They had three children with them, he guessed ranging in age from eight to about eighteen.

Ima joined them and exchanged embraces with their friends. As he greeted them politely, Benaiah noticed the young woman, Mariah, was unlike the others he had met over the years. Not only was she stunning—with shiny black hair partially hidden by a veil and brown eyes that sparkled with amusement—but when his gaze locked with hers, three things happened simultaneously: his mouth fell open in surprise, the four parents exchanged a knowing glance and Benaiah realized that his parents had just found a reason for him to never leave Kabzeel.

The meal should have been like any other, but Mariah unnerved him. He didn't usually feel nervous, but this time he actually cared what she thought of him. He had no interest in appearing rude or arrogant; he wanted her to approve of him for some reason he couldn't understand. When she asked for the bread to be passed, Benaiah nearly knocked over his cup scrambling to get it for her. He was excited when their fingers accidentally brushed against each other as he passed it to her. But what pleased him even more was that she seemed to feel the same attraction and stole glances at him as the conversation droned on around them. How he longed to ask her to join him on the rooftop so he could find out more about her. Was this just a physical attraction or was it possible they could be compatible in other ways? What did she dream about? How would she feel about his future plans? Why did he care? Why was he thinking about such things within the first hours of meeting her?

Would she be disappointed to learn he would not be a priest like his father, which she no doubt expected? Most of the girls his parents have tried to set him up with seemed delighted with the prospect of becoming the wife of a priest. Since the priest's family lived on the offerings of the people, they lived well and never went hungry. And priests hardly ever went off to war. On the rare occasions when they were called to go, they remained behind the soldiers, safely praying.

Benaiah heard himself being addressed by Mariah's father, Tirhanah. He gave himself a mental shake to return to the moment. "I'm sorry, sir. Can you repeat the question?"

"I was wondering how your training for the priesthood is going? It must be about the time you begin your duties. You're twenty, isn't that correct?"

"Yes, sir, I am." Benaiah noticed Mariah cringe slightly. Did she feel for him, as if her father was just beginning his interrogation? He looked at his parents, who were now intently interested in their stew. They were leaving it to him to explain. Oh well, he wasn't ashamed.

"I'm not going to be a priest," he blurted out.

"Not going to be a priest?" Tirhanah repeated incredulously. "How can that be?" He looked at Jehoiada, as if to check whether such a thing could possibly be true. Benaiah looked over at Mariah to gauge her reaction and she seemed as surprised as the other adults. She stopped eating to hear his answer. Only the two younger children seemed not to care.

For seven years, Benaiah had done his best to learn the priesthood, tried to imagine himself in the role everyone expected him to fill. But his dream of becoming a soldier had never died. On the contrary, keeping it inside seemed only to fan the flame of his passion.

"No—I—well, I feel God calling me in another direction."

Tirhanah cleared his throat. "Not everyone is cut out for the priesthood. It is a lofty calling, after all. But I've never heard of an Aaronite being anything but a priest. That's why God set them apart."

Did Mariah's father think Benaiah was unworthy? Why couldn't anyone see that becoming a soldier was as much a "calling" as becoming a priest?

"Yes, that's what is usually expected. Thankfully, our elder brother, Shallum, is already well established as a priest here in Kabzeel, so it's not like our family isn't represented."

Tirhanah turned to Jehoiada. "Perhaps... Jehoiada, I could train your son to be a merchant. He could work in my shop as an apprentice."

Why was he not asking Benaiah what his plans were? He was a man, not a boy dependent on his father's direction anymore. Benaiah noticed his mother was silent. He knew she was disappointed with his decision to become a soldier. Did she fear for him? Or, did she think her matchmaking plans would be dashed if Tirhanah didn't approve of the direction Benaiah would go in his life? Benaiah had no intention of spending the rest of his life making and selling pottery.

Mariah looked at him, intent on hearing his response. Was she hoping he'd accept the offer to become a merchant? Was she looking for a safe, secure future? Only one way to know for sure.

"Actually, sir, my intention is to become a soldier."

"A soldier!" Tirhanah's bushy eyebrows lifted in surprise.

To his surprise, he didn't feel the typical thrill of victory that had always come when he successfully thwarted his parents' matchmaking efforts. Even the usual relief over not having to settle down was mixed with a new emotion: a touch of disappointment and a slight stab of irritation at the thought of this lovely young woman marrying someone else.

Benaiah glanced at Mariah to see if she was as shocked as her parents, or as disappointed as his parents. Instead, she looked momentarily surprised, and then seemed to be processing the information, as if readjusting to a detour on a journey. Perhaps she didn't understand what being a soldier's wife would entail. Was that good or bad?

"Isn't Saul's army stationed at Gibeah with the king?" Tirhanah asked Benaiah. At least he was addressing him again, man to man.

"Yes, that's the main location. But there are skirmishes in various regions," Benaiah said.

The topic of conversation made everyone but the youngest children seem to forget to eat. They carried on, noisily slurping their stew while the adults processed this news.

"I think it's an admirable profession, to guard the king and to fight Israel's battles," Mariah said. The parents all looked shocked at her bold statement, but Benaiah felt ready to burst with pride at her support of him.

"There are also rumors that Saul won't be on the throne much longer. That his young son-in-law, David, has become quite popular and is a competent soldier, fighting the enemies of Israel. Wouldn't it be something to be aligned with such a man? This was the one who defeated the giant when he was just a youth," Benaiah added. He admired David from afar, even as he lost respect for King Saul after the stories he heard from his father.

Tirhanah looked between Benaiah and Mariah, no doubt wondering at the conversation they seemed to be having to the exclusion of others at the table. Dinah stood suddenly, "More stew, anyone?"

"I'll have some, Ima," Benaiah said without taking his eyes off Mariah. Probably best to end the conversation there, let everyone consider the implications of it and draw their own conclusions. As Benaiah ate his second bowl of lamb stew, he marveled at Mariah and was captivated by her intelligence and apparent support of his unorthodox career choice. Could she be the one who would allow him to have the best of both worlds: a family to care about and a career as a soldier?

Dinah began to clear away their dishes and asked Benaiah to take Mariah to the rooftop herb garden to gather some mint leaves for tea. He knew there were plenty in the cooking room, but since he had been hoping for such an opportunity to be alone with Mariah, he agreed heartily and waited for her to rise from the table. She looked to her parents for approval, they nodded and she followed Benaiah to the bottom of the stone stairwell leading to the rooftop veranda. He followed her up the stairs.

Then, Benaiah noticed his mother had sent their servant, Shua, to accompany them at a discreet distance. The younger children asked permission to play outside, including twelve-year-old Rizpah and seven-year-old Yael, and the men went out for a walk. The women headed to the cooking room. Did they really want these mint leaves? Benaiah wondered.

"Do you really approve of such a life?" Benaiah asked, as they gathered mint leaves. He feared she would change her mind and shatter the faint hope he felt. He was already considering what life with her would be like. If he agreed to marry Mariah, they could build a house near her family so they would be close by while he was away fighting. His mother would be happy to see them more often than if they lived in Gibeah full time while he fought in Saul's army. Perhaps he could fulfill his dreams after all—at least a slightly revised version of them—while still making his parents happy and even having a wife and family.

Mariah looked up into his eyes, resolve and admiration evident there. "Yes, I do."

Benaiah released a breath and smiled. "Then I'll talk with my father."

★ ★ ★

Benaiah squinted as he attempted to sew the blue-and-white striped fabric to a sling of braided leather. *How do women do this?* After numerous failed attempts to thread the needle he'd borrowed from his mother's sewing basket, he'd finally managed to push it through the thin fabric into the thick leather—a few times. But his stitches were loose and uneven, and the edges of the cloth were beginning to fray.

The striped fabric, which had last been used many years ago to keep a loaf of bread warm, would surely stand out against his neutral-colored battle clothing, but Benaiah didn't care. He'd kept it for seven years, ever since his brother died, and he wanted to make something permanent out of it, as a constant reminder to him of the cost of disobedience.

Discouraged with his lack of sewing skills, he wrapped the needle and thread up in the cloth and tucked it into the pocket of his tunic. Though it stung his pride to do so, he needed to ask for help. Shua would have done it, but this would make a good excuse to see his betrothed.

He found Mariah at the town well, helping an older woman fill a small bucket. Then, she took a dipper of water to a beggar before drawing some for herself.

When she started to heft a heavy-looking wooden yoke to her shoulders, he hurried to her side. "Let me help you."

Her eyes sparkled when she grinned at him. "I have been doing this since I was a little girl, Benaiah. I am perfectly capable of fetching water for my family."

"I know." He grabbed the two full buckets at her feet. He attached them to the wooden yoke and placed it over his back and shoulders, careful not to slosh the water out.

"Thank you, Benaiah." They started toward her home. "What brings you to the well today?"

"Do I need a reason to see my future wife?" He asked with a wink.

"Of course not." Mariah met his gaze. "Abba will be very happy to see you. With a house full of women, he craves male companionship. He loves to talk about politics, but never does so with me. He seems to think all women are either uninterested or uninformed."

Benaiah was surprised at her response. "How did you become interested in politics?"

Mariah lifted her chin. "I listen when the men speak. And if anyone ever asked for my opinion, I'd give it."

He raised an eyebrow. "Well, when we're married, I'll be sure to include you in every political conversation I have."

She chuckled. "I wouldn't want you to be scorned by the other men for having an opinionated wife." A blush colored her cheeks. "But I'd be happy to share my thoughts when we're alone."

Benaiah felt blessed to be marrying an intelligent and considerate woman.

He longed to take her into his arms and kiss her. Their families had been making plans for their wedding to take place the following harvest season, but Benaiah didn't know if he could wait that long to make this incredible woman his bride.

He cleared his throat. "There was another reason I stopped by the well today."

"Oh?"

"I need help sewing something."

She tilted her head. "Do you need a garment mended?"

"No, no. Shua and Ima take care of that. It's more... personal. Something I need for my soldiering."

She tilted her head. "If you bring it by the house, I'll be happy to take a look at it."

"Actually, I have it with me. May I show it to you?"

Mariah gestured to a grassy area under a leafy sycamore tree. Benaiah set the water buckets down carefully so as not to lose any precious water. They sat on the grass in the shade as he fished his sewing project out of the pouch at his waist.

Mariah examined the bundle of fabric and the leather strap. "What's it supposed to be?" She laughed.

"That leather strap will be attached to my belt and hold my club. I wanted to cover it with the fabric my brother had in his hands the day he died."

Mariah let the project fall into her lap. "Oh, Benaiah. That is so touching. Of course I'll help you."

He pointed to the section he'd attempted to sew. "My stitches aren't very straight or close together."

"That's not the only problem." Mariah loosened the stitches Benaiah had tried to make since they weren't knotted. She stretched out the fabric and folded it, then laid the strip of braided leather on it. "Is this the direction you want the stripes to go?"

Benaiah had not even considered such a thing. Did it matter? "I guess so."

"If you sew the material with the right sides together, then flip it inside out, the stitches won't show."

Benaiah shook his head. "That makes perfect sense."

"If it's going to hold something as heavy as a club, you'll want to leave about a finger's width of space on the other side of the seam and make a second row of stitching, so it won't unravel easily when there's pressure on the edge. After you turn it right side out, thread the leather braiding through the center and stitch the ends closed."

"I never would've figured out all that. You're so smart."

Mariah shrugged. "You've just never been taught. And you have other skills I don't have. That's what marriage is, you know. Each partner supplying what the other one lacks."

Benaiah set the sewing project aside and took her hands in his. "You're going to be a good helper for me in many ways, Mariah." He leaned closer, inhaling the fresh scent of her hair. "I just hope there are ways I can benefit you as well."

An elderly couple passed by. Benaiah quickly pulled away from Mariah, then smiled and greeted them. After they passed, he leaned in for their first kiss.

Harvest time could not come soon enough.

CHAPTER FOUR

"And he [Benaiah] struck down an Egyptian, a handsome man. The Egyptian had a spear in his hand, but Benaiah went down to him with a staff and snatched the spear out of the Egyptian's hand and killed him with his own spear."
—2 Samuel 23:21, ESV

"And he killed an Egyptian, a man of great height, five cubits tall. In the Egyptian's hand there was a spear like a weaver's beam; and he went down to him with a staff, wrested the spear out of the Egyptian's hand, and killed him with his own spear."
—1 Chronicles 11:23

It wasn't a difficult decision for Benaiah to become a mercenary soldier, rather than a member of King Saul's army. Not only had he lost respect for the king because of what his father had told him about his disobedience, but Benaiah heard stories of the king's melancholy and suspicious attitude towards his son-in-law, David. Because David was successful wherever he went, the women who composed victory songs praised David over Saul, attributing victory over thousands to Saul, but tens of thousands to David. Whether it was literally true or not, Benaiah didn't know. But the king had supposedly made several attempts on David's life as a result.

Such a king was not worth following. Yet Benaiah wanted to fight the enemies of Israel. As a mercenary soldier he could do this. They were paid handsomely with any spoils they acquired. He and about twenty other soldiers would go on raids in regions hostile to Israel. Sometimes they actively sought out the enemy, and other times, like today, they stumbled upon them.

As Benaiah stood on a hill and looked down towards the massive Egyptian soldier standing in the valley in front of him, his hand grasping a spear the size of a weaver's beam, he felt like young David from the story his father had told him about Goliath. He and eight other mercenary soldiers were returning from a skirmish against the Philistines. He had not expected to run into this group of Egyptians, much less to be challenged by the one the others called Sebni. Since no one else in his company volunteered to fight the man, Benaiah prayed for wisdom and strength and stepped up to the competition.

Mikhael had tried to convince him to take some more substantial weapons to use against the man. Mikhael's weapon of choice was a javelin, and Benaiah marveled at the distance and accuracy with which his friend could attack a target. While Benaiah was most comfortable with his club and dagger—both weapons more suitable for hand-to-hand combat—he chose a staff to attack the soldier, a staff he could probably snap in two with ease. The Lord had been with young David and had given him a resounding victory over Goliath. Benaiah prayed the God of David would perform a similar miracle through him.

The man stood five cubits tall. Benaiah had always thought his own four cubits was intimidating, as he rarely had to look up to any man. But even standing uphill from this fully armored Egyptian, he felt almost like a child. And Benaiah was not nearly as adept at using a slingshot as young David had been.

Sebni was uncommonly handsome, with dark, wavy hair and a smooth, face, a square jaw and intense eyes. He seemed ill-suited for such a rough profession. He should be surrounded by soft linens, servants and the finer things of life, not glaring at Benaiah.

"Hebrew!" He spat.

Benaiah was surprised at the use of the old term. While technically true, now that they were settled in Israel, a country named after the patriarch Jacob, most of their neighbors and enemies referred to them as Israelites, or even as servants of Saul. Personally, Benaiah wanted no association with King Saul, which was why he had chosen to fight as a mercenary instead of with the armies of Israel.

The Egyptian looked past him to the small group of Israelite soldiers standing well behind him—Mikhael among them.

"Just one of you has the courage to challenge me?" He snarled. "I could take on all of you at once."

Benaiah didn't doubt it. The man's upper arm was as thick and solid as his own thigh. But he could not allow the taunts of his enemy to go unanswered. He was the son of Jehoiada, after all.

Benaiah remembered Simeon telling him and Mikhael that a soldier must be aware of his enemy's weaknesses and exploit them without hesitation. But what if an enemy didn't have any weaknesses? He should have asked Simeon that question, he thought wryly.

"Sebni!" The giant's armor bearer called to him and extended an arm to offer alternate weapons. Sebni shook off the suggestions and planted his feet into the rocky terrain, an immovable, unconquerable object if Benaiah had ever seen one. But then he recalled what he'd heard about the famous battle where Saul's son Jonathan and his armor bearer defeated a large number of Philistines. They were outnumbered, tired from climbing uphill and exposed, yet he said, "God can save whether there are many or few."

Standing straight and tall, Benaiah called out, "God can save whether there are many or few!" His voice sounded braver than he felt.

Sebni laughed. "The Lord? Do you still believe in that invisible god of yours instead of the one that shines on us every day and gives life to all?"

The Egyptians worshiped the sun god, Ra. Yet this pagan soldier had perfectly described the God worshiped by the Israelites, the Creator of all things, including the sun. "Our God, who defeated your paltry gods quite soundly before Israel left Egypt, is the one who gives life," yelled Benaiah. "Yet you do not acknowledge Him. Therefore, He will this day take it from you."

With a final prayer for wisdom and strength, Benaiah charged down the hill. In order to make use of his staff, Benaiah had to get up close to Sebni. Benaiah kept his eye on the giant's hand to see if he would launch the massive spear in his direction or go for the dagger attached to his side. Benaiah darted to his right so that if the giant did launch his spear, he'd have to pivot, giving Benaiah an additional blink of an eye to dodge it.

Sebni closed the gap between them, squinting against the setting sun almost directly behind Benaiah's head. Benaiah smiled. The Lord was using His creation, the man's own god, against him.

Then, in a single, fluid movement, Sebni bent his knees and hefted the spear to rest on his right shoulder. As quickly and effortlessly as if he were nocking an arrow, he aimed it at Benaiah.

Benaiah skirted left and sprinted around the man. Sebni whirled around. With his weapon still hoisted on his right shoulder, he bent his knees, holding his left arm out in front of him for balance. He pulled his shoulder back to launch the spear, but the movement caused the small, round rocks beneath his feet to roll. He faltered, and Benaiah scrambled behind him.

When Sebni turned to face Benaiah, he lost his balance on the uneven ground and was blinded by the setting sun. Benaiah took advantage and thrust his staff into the opening under Sebni's metal elbow plate, the only part not protected by armor.

P. H. Thompson

Benaiah heard the crack of breaking bone. Sebni winced and dropped his spear. As he bent to grasp his weapon, Benaiah struck his helmet with a loud clang.

Sebni's head lolled from side to side for a moment, and then he fell over, landing with a great thud.

Benaiah fetched the spear, lifted it with some difficulty and carried it back to Sebni, who was moaning on the ground. Benaiah shoved aside the man's breastplate, hoisted the heavy spear up over his head, and, with a grunt of supreme effort, thrust it into his chest. A cheer rose up from his compatriots, who rushed up to Benaiah and patted him on his back.

Benaiah stood over the fallen giant, drawing in deep breaths. He was more exhausted than he'd ever felt in his life, but he thanked God for giving him the victory.

Benaiah rocked the weapon back and forth a few times to dislodge it. When it pulled free of the dead man's chest, blood poured out of the wound and soaked the ground around him. Benaiah tossed the spear to the ground and walked away from the bloody corpse. The few remaining Egyptians, seeing the battle was now against them, turned and fled.

"What are you going to do with the spear, Benaiah?" Mikhael asked as his companions took a closer look at the corpse at their feet.

Indeed, what could he possibly do with a spear the size of a weaver's beam? Perhaps Mariah would like him to build her a new loom. He smiled. "I suppose I will keep it as a reminder of the faithfulness of the Lord in defeating our enemies."

Mikhael laughed. "Our challenge will be bringing this massive thing back home." His friends looted the corpse of its armor.

Benaiah chuckled. "No one else will fit into that, you know."

Mikhael cocked an eyebrow. "Perhaps we can melt it down to make a few iron swords?"

The men all looked to Benaiah. What happened with the spoils of his enemy was his decision to make.

"Yes, take them."

As they departed toward Kabzeel, two men hoisted the spear off the ground with great effort and positioned the giant's armor atop it. Benaiah withdrew the giant's dagger from his waist and examined its fine workmanship.

As he took one last look at the man on the ground, he remembered his brother's words as he carried him back home, *"You'll fight giants too."*

CHAPTER FIVE

"And the king said to Doeg, 'You turn and kill the priests!' So Doeg the Edomite turned and struck the priests, and killed on that day eighty-five men who wore a linen ephod. Also Nob, the city of the priests, he struck with the edge of the sword, both men and women, children and nursing infants, oxen and donkeys and sheep—with the edge of the sword."

—1 Samuel 22:18–19

Benaiah never thought he'd be happy to be returning to Kabzeel. But then, he didn't usually have a wedding to look forward to. Mariah, his betrothed, was in her home, waiting for him to come whisk her away for a week of celebrations, and then begin their new life together. He couldn't get to his hometown fast enough.

Benaiah and Mikhael had just finished yet another successful battle against their long-time foe, the Philistines, who lived west of Israel along the coast. The fight had gone so well, their commander had approved their request to return home, to see their families and refresh themselves before the next skirmish.

When they were just a few miles from Kabzeel, they saw two men approaching over the rise. One was dressed in priestly robes, the other as an Israelite soldier. The priest identified himself as Abiathar ben Ahimelech ben Ahitub of the town of Nob. The other claimed to be Eliezar ben Zichri, a former guard of Saul.

Benaiah had never heard of someone defecting from armed service to the king. And Eliezar was much too young and healthy-looking to have been voluntarily released.

Curious as to why a priest would be traveling with a member of the king's guard—and why that guard was no longer in the king's service—Benaiah asked, "And where might you men be headed?"

"We are running from King Saul," Eliezar explained.

"In fear of our lives," Abiathar added, his hands trembling.

"Why?"

Abiathar looked behind him, as if they were being pursued even now, "David, the son of Jesse, came to see my father, Ahimelech, the priest."

"You've met David, the son-in-law of the king?" Benaiah asked. Oh, that he would have the privilege of someday meeting the famous giant-slayer!

Abiathar nodded. "David told my father that he was on the king's business and that he and his men were hungry. My father had no food, except for the holy showbread, which was just being switched out for fresh bread, so it was, in effect, common. After confirming that the men had kept themselves from women, my father gave David the showbread."

Benaiah had never heard of anyone who wasn't a priest eating the holy offering. It was forbidden. Perhaps Abiathar recognized in David the anointing of God?

"After they ate, David asked if there were any weapons on hand. My father gave him the sword of Goliath the Philistine, whom David killed in the Valley of Elah. It was kept in Nob behind the ephod."

That seemed fair. Though that would certainly irritate Saul, if he heard of it. The king's unreasonable envy of his son-in-law's military success no doubt began when the young man saved Israel from Goliath and the Philistines. That sword represented all of David's victories.

"A servant of Saul, Doeg the Edomite, who happened to be there that day, overheard the exchange. He must have slipped out and ran to tell the king."

Eliezar took over the story from there. "I was with Saul in Gibeah when he heard the news. He bellowed to his servants, 'I'm surrounded by conspirators! That son of Jesse has betrayed me, and no one will inform me.' Even though David had done nothing that Saul should consider treacherous."

Benaiah put a hand on Eliezar's shoulder to calm him. Clearly there was more to this story than a king's words of wrath, or these two men would not be fleeing from him. "What did Saul do next?"

"He summoned all of the priests of the Lord who were in the town of Nob. When they were all assembled before the king, he charged the priests with conspiring against him, based on the report he heard from Doeg: that Abiathar the priest had given David bread and a sword, and had inquired of God for him."

"That was only partially true!" Abiathar protested. "He did give him bread and the sword, but David did not ask him to inquire of God for him. My father protested as much and didn't understand why Saul was worried about his son-in-law, who was faithful to the king. But the king wouldn't listen, and sentenced my father and our whole family to death."

Eliezar added, "Then he told us guards to kill them because their loyalty was with David."

"What? How could he order such a wicked thing?"

"We knew nothing at all about what he planned to do," Abiathar added. "We just came because we had been summoned by the king."

Eliezar closed his eyes and shook his head. "We did not wish to strike the priests of the Lord, even though we knew we could be killed if we disobeyed the order. When the king saw our hesitation, he ordered Doeg the Edomite to do it. Doeg killed eighty-five priests that day. Then Saul further ordered the execution of all the inhabitants of the city of Nob, men and women, children and nursing infants, oxen and donkeys and sheep."

What an evil man this Edomite was, trying to ingratiate himself to the king, first by reporting on David's actions, then by carrying out this slaughter. Benaiah couldn't imagine such an atrocity. These were fellow Israelites, priests and innocent families, not their enemies.

"Some of Saul's guards tried to defend us that day," Abiathar said. "But Doeg killed them too."

How could Saul kill his own people? And why would he do such a terrible thing?

"I managed to escape with Abiathar. Saul ordered his men to capture us, but when they caught up, they did not harm us. They urged us to escape and said they would tell Saul they couldn't find us."

Benaiah knew if David had gone to Kabzeel to ask for help from Jehoiada or Shallum, instead of to Ahimelech in Nob, Benaiah's father or brother would have given it. Then his family and community would have been massacred. Including Mariah.

He had to get home, marry his beloved and leave Kabzeel with her immediately. He would try to convince their families to accompany them. But whatever they chose to do, his job was to protect her.

Perhaps he should find David and join his group. He would have to live on the run for as long as it took David to secure his rightful place as the next king of Israel, but at least he would have his wife by his side, under his protection.

"My friends," Benaiah said to Abiathar and Eliezar, "we are headed to Kabzeel. Come with us. You will be safe in the home of my father, Jehoiada the priest. You must tell this story throughout the land."

P. H. Thompson

"Thank you," Eliezar said, "but our presence would only bring danger to your people. We must find refuge with David. We will only be safe with God's anointed."

"I could not agree more, but I urge you to take the short trip to Kabzeel with us. I plan to marry as soon as possible upon my arrival. After that, we can search for David together."

"I will go with you as well," Mikhael said.

Benaiah tilted his head at his friend. "Do you think your wife will be favorable to living a nomadic existence?"

Mikhael raised an eyebrow. "I believe she will be as amenable to it as your wife will."

Benaiah hadn't even considered that Mariah might not come with him. Convincing her parents might be difficult, however. Perhaps this was too much to ask of her.

"Trust me, brothers, we will all be safe," Mikhael said, clearly sensing the doubt and fear in the air. "Benaiah here killed a giant whose spear was as thick as a weaver's beam. And he went up against two Moabite ariels and defeated them single-handedly.

Eliezar's eyes widened. "That's forty men against one!"

Mikhael held up a hand to show he wasn't yet done. "He also killed a lion. In a pit. On a snowy day!"

Benaiah didn't like anyone to boast about his victories with men outside the military. But the spark in Abiathar's eyes assured him that Mikhael's tales had changed the priest's perspective.

"In that case, I suppose a stop in Kabzeel would fit into our plans," he said.

CHAPTER SIX

"Therefore a man shall leave his father and mother and be joined to his wife, and they shall become one flesh."

—Genesis 2:24

Benaiah introduced their traveling companions to his parents, forgetting that Abiathar already knew his father. After they told the horrific story to his parents, Benaiah gave them the good news.

"I returned only to take my bride and then we will find David and fight with him against Saul."

Dinah squealed. It took a moment for Benaiah to realize she was more excited for the prospect of her son's imminent wedding than the thought of losing them soon after. That realization would hit soon enough.

"A wedding! Beginning today?"

Benaiah nodded. "Yes, mother. Today."

"Girls! Shua! Come quickly!" she shouted as she left the men. She gave Benaiah a quick kiss on the cheek before she ran off to begin the food preparations. Shua, Rizpah and Yael left soon after with Dinah to purchase food at the marketplace.

Jehoiada was more subdued, obviously overwhelmed by the grim news of the massacre.

"Father, will you also leave this place, as Abiathar is doing? It could've happened here just as easily."

"I know, Son." He closed his eyes in a brief prayer. When he opened them, he looked at the men resolutely. "No, we will stay. Our times are in His hands. Our place is here."

Benaiah wondered if his father thought he was being cowardly or faithless by choosing to leave. He hoped not, because he felt as sure of his own decision as his father did his.

"If the political situation gets more unstable and you have any concern at all, come with us to David. You'll find acceptance and safety."

Jehoiada nodded his agreement, then attempted a smile.

"Today is a day of joy. My son is taking a wife!" He stood and started to the door. "We have much wine to buy, Son, and wedding garments for you. We can't let the women enjoy all the preparations."

Benaiah stood. "I'll join you at the marketplace shortly. First, I need to go to speak with Mariah's father about our change in plans."

Jehoiada slowly shook his head. "I don't envy you that task, my son."

★ ★ ★

Benaiah felt it was only fair to speak with Mariah's father, to let him know they would not remain in Kabzeel once they were wed, but would leave immediately after their marriage week to follow after David, away from Saul.

Benaiah knew Mariah would have already heard the news that he'd returned to Kabzeel and was certain she was preparing for their wedding day. Hearing of his meeting with her father would only confirm it in her mind.

Benaiah smiled. *Good. Let her anticipate this night as much as me.*

Tirhanah met Benaiah in the marketplace. They walked as they talked, since Benaiah told him the wedding festivities would begin that day, and there was still much to prepare.

"Please give Zibeah my apologies for the suddenness of my return."

Tirhanah brushed away the comment. "Think nothing of it. She's been anticipating this day for months. If she could have found a way to preserve the food all this time, she would have began cooking and baking the day of your betrothal to our daughter," he said with a laugh.

"I feel so blessed to be marrying your daughter, sir."

Tirhanah tilted his head to Benaiah in surprise.

"Why so formal? You are our son. Call me Abba."

"Yes, sir. I mean, Abba." It felt strange, since Benaiah hadn't even referred to his own father with the sentimental term since he was a child.

"So, what did you want to speak with me about, since it's obvious you're not having second thoughts about the wedding itself."

"Nothing like that, sir... Abba." Benaiah corrected. It was hard to change from thinking and acting as a soldier to a civilian. "But I needed to let you know about a change in our plans for after our marriage."

"What kind of change?" Tirhanah asked warily.

Benaiah relayed the awful story of the massacre of the priests of Nob, and his desire to follow after David and bring his wife along. Tirhanah listened intently, shocked at the story and yet obviously not pleased with the idea of losing contact with his daughter so soon.

"Life alongside a fugitive soldier is not what I expected for my daughter," Tirhanah said as he rubbed a hand over his thick beard.

"I know, Abba," Benaiah said. "But she is my responsibility, and I promise I will keep her safe. That is, she will be my responsibility, unless you refuse to give her to me as my wife."

Benaiah waited, wondering why he even suggested such a thing. He did not want to leave Kabzeel without Mariah. *His wife.*

Tirhanah studied Benaiah a few moments. Benaiah straightened beneath his scrutiny, hoping to demonstrate a confidence he did not feel.

"No."

Benaiah sucked in a breath.

"No, I won't refuse you, but I will speak with Mariah about this and let her decide for herself if she's ready for such a life."

Benaiah exhaled. It was all he could ask. He was sure Mariah loved him and would follow his lead. Wouldn't she?

"I won't speak with Zibeah until after Mariah has made the decision. I know she'd try to convince her to stay close to home. She'd tell her it's safer here."

"If that was true, I'd convince her of it myself, but after what happened in Nob, I don't trust she'd be safe anywhere but by my side."

"Well, Son, you are the hero of Kabzeel. When that giant's spear was carried into town, we were very proud to say you were to be our son. That visible reminder of God's blessing on your chosen profession only added credence to the other fantastic stories we heard of your exploits."

Tirhanah stopped by a market stall to purchase two sacks of almonds. He handed one to Benaiah.

"Thank you," Benaiah said as he accepted the snack.

"No, Son, I have no doubt you can protect my daughter. We'll leave the final decision with her, but I know you're a fine man. Even if your only asset was that you were the son of Jehoiada, it would have been enough. The son of a priest is a man of character."

Benaiah couldn't hear any more praise. Tirhanah obviously hadn't heard the circumstances of Ammizabad's death, or he would not be praising Benaiah's stellar character. It seemed that no matter how noble his deeds since then, Benaiah couldn't dislodge the guilt of that day from his conscience.

"I am proud to be his son," Benaiah said. "He has taught me much about being a man." That much Benaiah could say truthfully. He had learned to be a protector. Never again would someone under his care suffer at the hands of others.

"I promise I will protect Mariah, Abba."

The men embraced.

"I believe you will, Son." Tirhanah stepped back, but kept his hand on Benaiah's shoulder as he looked up at him. He smiled and added, "Now, let's make some purchases. We have a wedding celebration to prepare for!"

★ ★ ★

Mariah's mother, Zibeah, finished adjusting the veil covering her daughter's head, then secured the ring of coins across her forehead, Zibeah turned Mariah slightly to face her. Tears shimmered in her eyes. "You're beautiful, my dear one. This is such a happy day."

Mariah realized then that her Abba hadn't yet informed his wife about the change in plans. She wouldn't be happy to hear she would be losing a daughter so soon after gaining a son, but for now, Mariah decided her Abba was right in letting her enjoy this day. She'd been dreaming of it for years.

"And to think that you're marrying such a fine man, a hero and the son of a prominent priest in Kabzeel!"

"Yes, Ima. Benaiah is a wonderful man. And I know he has deep feelings for me, as I do for him. I'm so happy this day is finally here."

Mariah could hardly believe it herself. In the year since their betrothal, Benaiah had truly become the hero of Kabzeel. His valiant exploits against the Egyptian giant, the lion in a pit on a snowy day and against two entire ariels of Moabite solders made her so proud to be his wife.

Was anyone in all of Israel as brave as her husband-to-be? Perhaps David ben Jesse, the King's son-in-law, who killed the giant, Goliath of Gath when all the soldiers in the army of Israel cowered in fear. Surely he was brave, as a youth against a seasoned soldier. But the Lord was with Benaiah ben Jehoiada as well, and he was her hero. Her admiration had grown quickly to love during their betrothal year as she began to know him better.

Her Ima's expression grew solemn and she motioned for the servants to leave the room.

"What is it?" Mariah asked.

Her Ima pulled her to sit beside her on a stone bench. She took her daughter's hand and held it between both of her own. Mariah could see that her Ima seemed disturbed by whatever it was she needed to say. She couldn't imagine what it could be, since she had just praised Mariah's husband-to-be.

"My dear daughter," she began, not raising her eyes from her daughter's hands. "I haven't yet spoken with you about a woman's responsibilities to her husband."

"Of course you have, Ima. You've taught me all I need to know to manage a home."

Zibeah pressed her lips together and shook her head.

"No, Mariah, I'm referring to your marriage week, and what will happen when you two are alone in the marriage tent."

Mariah pulled her hand away. This was awkward.

"Do not trouble yourself about that, Ima," Mariah said, standing up. "I have an understanding of what happens. We'll be fine."

"How do you know?" Her mother's eyes widened in alarm.

"My friends have married sisters. They tell them and my friends tell me." She adjusted the head piece and crown of coins although they didn't need adjusting.

"Besides, I'm sure Benaiah has been told what he must do." She was sure her betrothed would be gentle with her, but she didn't need to share that with her Ima.

"Well, if you're sure," Zibeah said with obvious relief in her voice.

"I'm sure, Ima. But thank you for thinking of talking to me."

* * *

That evening, as the oil lamps were burning, Mariah could hear the shouts of joy and merriment outside her home. Through the latticed window, she could see the light of the torchbearers' approach. The musicians played, and Benaiah's family and friends sang familiar songs of love. Mariah and her family and friends waited, twittering with excitement as the wedding processional approached and the sound of joyful singing grew louder. Mariah smiled nervously, awaiting the voice of her bridegroom.

Then she heard it and her heartbeat pounded heavily in her chest. This was it!

"Mariah, my sweet! I have come to take you as my bride and make you my wife. Do not delay in coming to my side while I declare my love to you in the midst of this great company," Benaiah's voice carried through the window.

Her younger brother held open the door as her family and friends filed through it. Although she couldn't see, she knew her father would approach her new husband and embrace him. Mariah took a deep breath and stepped through the door.

P. H. Thompson

There stood her bridegroom, so tall and handsome, his beard freshly trimmed, his dark, almond brown eyes fixed only on her. He stretched out his hand toward her and she placed her own hand in his. He gave it a squeeze and smiled at her. Then he lifted her up into the carriage that would bring them to his parents' home, where the ceremony and feasting would begin. They'd be crowned king and queen of the festivities, and the singing, feasting and entertainment would last a week.

But tonight, at some point, Benaiah would whisk her away to the wedding tent to consummate the marriage. Once he emerged from the tent to declare that they were truly man and wife, the celebrations would be elevated to greater levels of joy and merry-making.

They would have a week together. Only one week to become familiar with her new husband and the mysteries of the marriage-bed, before they would begin a life among the nomads following David. What of privacy then? What of comfort and making a home with her husband, enjoying all the wedding gifts they'd received? She had so little time to pack today, what with preparing herself for her wedding celebration—washing, perfuming, dressing and decking herself in jewels—that she couldn't really imagine even a week into her future when her life would change. Although she didn't hesitate when her father told her of the change in plans, as she didn't want to lose Benaiah, she did have misgivings about such a life. How would she manage when that world would be so different from what she had known?

For now, she wanted to just enjoy her day, look into the eyes of her beloved husband and anticipate the night when he would love her with more than words.

CHAPTER SEVEN

"And everyone who was in distress, everyone who was in debt, and everyone who was discontented gathered to him. So he became captain over them. And there were about four hundred men with him."

—1 Samuel 22:2

After a week of traveling, slowed down by the women and child in their company— Benaiah and Mariah, Mikhael son of Kenan and his wife, Netaniah, along with their two-year-old daughter, Azubah, Abiathar the priest and Eliezar the guard—found David and his men in the mountains in the wilderness of Ziph. They heard there had been a falling out between King Saul and his son-in-law. It was no mere squabble or misunderstanding, for King Saul was now actively searching for David to kill him. He and many soldiers who had fought alongside him in the army of Israel had chosen to take a stand with David, even against the legitimate king. Some hinted that David would make a good king. He was well loved, and accomplished great exploits against many of their hostile neighbors, especially the Philistines to the west.

While still on the perimeter of the mountains, out of nowhere, a man blocked their path, who they would later learn was Uriah the Hittite. He looked them up and down, and seemed to decide they were not a threat. He then asked Abiathar to state their business, out of deference to his age and position.

After Abiathar told his story, Uriah turned to the soldiers.

"And you? Why are you here?" Uriah asked Mikhael.

Mikhael straightened up. "I am Mikhael ben Kenan. My friends and I are mercenary soldiers who want to fight with David. We learned of the massacre in Nob from Abiathar and Saul's guard here, Eliezar, son of Zichri," he said, motioning to the other soldier, "and we cannot imagine serving under such a wicked king."

"What massacre?"

· Benaiah was shocked to find they had not heard about it yet.

"We will tell David all about it," Eliezar said.

"And the women, and the child?" he asked, nodding in Mariah and Netaniah's direction. As if in response, Azubah cried, but Netaniah shushed her quickly.

"They are our wives. I am Benaiah, the son of Jehoiada, a priest of Kabzeel. My wife, Mariah, and Mikhael's wife, Netaniah, can help with daily life in the camp. I assume there are other women there?" Benaiah asked hopefully.

"There are. Quite a few, in fact. Children, too." Uriah circled the three soldiers, as if sizing them up. They kept their eyes forward, hoping they'd be accepted. They had nowhere else to go.

"As for the men who are joining David," Uriah continued, "it seems they fall into one of three categories; they are either in distress, in debt, or discontented." He leaned in to Benaiah, seeming not in the least intimidated that Benaiah was a head taller than he. "Which one are you?"

Benaiah straightened even more. "I am determined. I will serve David with my life."

One side of Uriah's mouth quirked up. "Follow me."

★ ★ ★

Next they were brought before David. Benaiah didn't have to be introduced to know he was in charge. David was the obvious leader. He had a ruddy, but handsome appearance, with dark, curly hair and a trim beard. His military bearing spoke for itself.

Benaiah couldn't believe he was finally meeting the hero of Israel. David had been on a pedestal in Benaiah's imagination, from his childhood.

Uriah the Hittite whispered in David's ear. Then they were allowed to approach.

Abiathar told his story first. David's anguish was apparent. He seemed especially upset to hear the name of Doeg, the Edomite.

"I remember him from my time in the palace in Gibeah. I didn't trust him, even then. I knew that day, when Doeg the Edomite was there in Nob at the same time, that he would surely tell Saul. My actions have caused the death of all the persons of your father's house."

He sighed deeply, and then said to Abiathar, "Stay here with me and don't be afraid. Saul, who seeks my life, will now seek yours as well, but you'll be safe with me."

David then noticed the orther men, who were clearly not priests. The women and baby stood nearby.

"Who are these?" he asked Uriah. Uriah nodded to them to speak for themselves.

The three soldiers stepped forward and stated their names, their fathers and their hometowns.

He looked to Uriah.

"What is your impression?" he asked.

"I believe they are trustworthy and valiant, sire," he answered.

"Very well. I'll meet with the men individually later. Dismissed."

Benaiah, Mikhael and Eliezar were then accepted into David's fold of four hundred men, and attached to the troop of soldiers who traveled with him while he was on the run from Saul.

* * *

Asahel ran back to Davd's camp after surveying the large group approaching from the west. He was the fastest runner Benaiah had ever seen. "My lord, Saul and his army are headed this way. It looks to be about three thousand men," he reported to David.

"If God is pleased, they will just pass by," David said.

Benaiah assessed their situation. They were out on patrol in the Wilderness of En Gedi, near its famous spring, just David and a handful of his most trusted soldiers, three of them his own nephews: Joab, Asahel and Abishai. They were near the Rocks of the Wild Goats. The road that passed by them was near the sheepfolds. They were far enough away from their ever-expanding group of soldiers, women, children and livestock so Benaiah didn't fear for their safety. They were all sheltered back at the Stronghold, a town on top of a giant natural tower with only one way up, well protected and provided for while David's men kept watch for Saul's imminent return. He only left off his pursuit of David when the Philistines invaded the land. Benaiah supposed he should be impressed that in this case, Saul put national security ahead of his personal vendetta against David.

More and more mercenary soldiers were joining David every day. Many had lost respect for King Saul after the massacre of the priests at Nob. Benaiah definitely had. Whether it was madness or a vindictive spirit that drove him, many felt Saul was not ruling in righteousness.

There were only a handful of them here now. Even if their whole company of soldiers was with David, they would number only four hundred soldiers. What were they compared with Saul and three thousand men, intent on capturing or killing David and anyone aligned with him?

Benaiah thought of Mariah and remembered the warmth of her body against him as he awoke that morning. If Saul did capture David, would he also kill everyone associated with him, out of spite, for aiding him? Benaiah already knew the answer. Saul was unstable and vindictive.

Other than one cave among the sheepfolds, the countryside had low hills of green grass for the sheep, as well as streams, but no natural hiding places. "If we try to head back toward camp, they'll clearly see us and overtake us. I don't want to lead them back to our families. They're safe now. If Saul does capture us, then we will be the only ones to die," David decided.

Benaiah was inclined to agree. As much as he would rather not die—today or any day—he would rather lose his own life, knowing his wife was safe.

"Let's take cover in the cave," David ordered.

They quickly ducked into the mouth of the cave, their eyes adjusting to the half-light of the cave several minutes later. The musty smell was strong, but not intolerable. They dared not light a fire, as both the light and smell of smoke would give their position away. As they crept further into the darkness, they found that the cave was larger inside than it appeared from outside, and there were plenty of hiding places in the recesses of it.

They had not been there long, when the sound of a multitude could be heard approaching along the road. The soldiers marched while the king would be riding his royal donkey. They passed by too close for Benaiah's liking.

Then Benaiah heard voices, faint at first, then louder. "Here, let me help you, Sire."

Benaiah heard of huff of annoyance. He froze and looked at the other men in the half-darkness of the cave. They knew it, too. King Saul, himself was coming in to the cave!

Yahweh be praised! This was too good to be true! David had been on the run from Saul for far too long now. He could not win if he fought Saul's army with his own, but now Saul's great numerical advantage had been turned on its head. They now outnumbered him, at least in here, and Benaiah knew that with their rage against him, it would only take one of them to end the wicked king's life.

Although they would undoubtedly lose their lives after they killed Saul, Benaiah considered it would be worth it to avenge the death of the priests and people of Nob, and to free David from his tormentor. How like Yahweh to arrange this circumstance and deliver David's enemy right into his hand!

Benaiah watched David's expression change from surprise to consternation. Perhaps he was considering whether to order one of them to do it, or take care of the matter himself. Benaiah hoped David would just issue the order to him. He wouldn't hesitate to rid the earth of King Saul.

"I'll make sure it's safe first, my lord," Benaiah heard the voice of one of Saul's soldiers say. So there were at least two other soldiers nearby, as well as Saul, Benaiah concluded. Since David's men outnumbered them they could dispatch them quickly.

Benaiah's hand was already on the hilt of his sword, anticipating that the soldier would inspect the back of the cave. He listened as the soldier seemed to make only a cursory inspection of the main cavern in the cave, but did not venture into the areas where David and his men were hiding in the shadows. If he didn't know better than to be silent, Benaiah would've snorted with disdain at the soldier's lack of thoroughness. What kind of bodyguard was afraid of the dark?

"It's all clear, my lord," they heard the soldier falsely report on his way back out of the cave.

Benaiah used this opportunity to speak his mind.

"Here's your opportunity to avenge yourself on your enemy. God clearly arranged the circumstances for you to do it." Benaiah whispered to David. The other men nodded their agreement, encouraging David forward. They rose to standing silently, hands on swords, as they heard Saul enter the cave.

David motioned for the rest of them to remain where they were as he crept into the outer room. So he had decided he would do it himself, Benaiah concluded.

Benaiah had never seen the king in person, and here was his first encounter with him, with the king relieving himself. Benaiah listened as David crept near the king, waiting for the sounds of death he had become accustomed to, but they did not reach his ears. A few moments later, David returned, Saul exited the cave, and began making his way back to his waiting army.

When it was obvious they were safely out of Saul's hearing, his men exploded with their questions.

"Why did you let him go?" Abishai hissed, his voice rising in pitch with exasperation.

"He was delivered up to you by the Lord, to avenge the priests and people of Nob!" exclaimed Asahel.

"You'll never have another opportunity like that!" Benaiah added.

"You could have struck him down with one blow, and the whole nation of Israel would've thanked you for ridding them of that man!" Joab said with obvious disdain.

David held up what seemed to be a small piece of fabric. Benaiah strained his vision in the semi-darkness to confirm what he was seeing.

"What's that?" Benaiah asked.

David's head and shoulders dropped. "It's a corner of the king's robe. I cut it off without his knowledge."

Benaiah was incredulous. A piece of cloth! He got up that close to Saul? He had a chance to take the head of his enemy if he wanted, and all he did was take a piece of cloth! How was that vengeance for the people of Nob? How did that end their time on the run? How did that keep their families safe?

"I shouldn't have done it," David confessed.

Benaiah looked from one man to the next over David's bowed head. He felt guilty about taking a scrap of fabric? What could a piece of cloth possibly do to a man's conscience?

Even as he asked the question in his mind, his hand slipped to the rough fabric holding his club to his waist. *Ammiz.* Benaiah sighed. It's what the fabric represented. Taking a sword to the king's robe was as if he had taken the king's life. He could understand that, but then David should have ordered one of them to kill Saul instead, if he couldn't bring himself to do it.

"God forbid that I should do such a thing and strike down the king, since he is the Lord's anointed."

"One of us can do it for you, my lord. It's not too late, even now. We can make sure he won't trouble you anymore. Please, let me go," Benaiah asked.

"No, I won't allow it, even on my orders. If the Lord wants my enemy to pursue me my whole life, and even kill me, then so be it. But I won't touch the Lord's anointed. If the Lord wants to free me from Saul, He will deliver me another way."

Benaiah thought it was obvious the Lord *had* just hand delivered Saul to him, but he held his tongue, since he saw the other men weren't protesting anymore. As much as Benaiah disagreed with David's decision, he remembered his vow and was determined to obey, as a good soldier. *To obey is better than sacrifice,* he reminded himself.

Although it hadn't ended the way Benaiah had hoped, at least they were alive and able to fight another day.

David took another look at the triangle of Saul's royal robe in his hand, pressed his lips together in resolve and strode with purpose out of the cave into the sunlight. Benaiah and the others gaped at each other, not quite sure what was happening at first. Why would David go out so soon? Saul and his army were still too close. They would surely see him.

They scrambled out after him, squinting as their eyes adjusted to the bright afternoon sun. Would there yet be a battle? David strode boldly to the middle of the road as Saul was being helped onto his donkey.

David called out to him, "My lord the king!"

Benaiah was incredulous. If it wasn't bad enough that David let him go, now he was surrendering without a fight! They would all be executed.

Saul looked behind him as David bowed with his face to the earth. Benaiah saw the look of surprise and concern register on the faces of Saul's guards. He wondered how the king would deal with their incompetence.

Benaiah observed David's other men. Joab was practically snorting with anger, his hand on his sword, awaiting the battle to the death that was sure to come. The others appeared equally resolved, though no doubt confused as to their leader's behavior.

But David appealed to Saul, actually trying to reason with the mad king. "Why do you believe those who say that I am trying to harm you? You can see for yourself that the Lord delivered you to me in the cave. Someone even urged me to kill you, but I had pity on you and spared your life, because you are the Lord's anointed."

David lifted the triangle of cloth up to show Saul. "And see the proof! I was close enough to you to cut off a corner of your robe." Saul turned to look down at his robe, picked up the hem and examined it. He looked up at David with wonder.

"Since I only cut your robe, and did not kill you should prove to you that I mean no evil or treachery against you." David paused and then added, "Yet in spite of this, you hunt me to kill me. I'll let the Lord judge between us and avenge me on you, if He desires. But I won't use my sword against you."

Saul couldn't seem to stop gazing between the tattered robe in his hand and the corner of the robe in David's hand. David continued, "The ancient proverbs say that wicked acts are done by wicked people, but I won't do such a thing. Why do you pursue me? I'm nothing but a flea or a dead dog, no one of importance. I'll let the Lord judge between us and plead my case, and deliver me from you."

"Is that really you, my son, David?" the king asked.

Benaiah watched as Saul was overcome by emotion as he considered what almost happened and what David confessed. He held his torn robe in both hands and wept. Then he turned to David and confessed, "You've proven yourself more righteous than I because you've rewarded me with good when I've rewarded you with evil. You've demonstrated it today by not killing me when the Lord gave me into your hand."

Saul shook his head in wonder. "For what person finds their enemy and lets him get away? May God reward you for your mercy towards me this day."

Benaiah was trying to make sense of what had just happened. The Lord delivered Saul, David's enemy into his hands. But David showed mercy and didn't kill him or even allow his men to do it for him. He not only let his enemy escape, but went after him to surrender, and confessed to his "crime" of taking a corner of Saul's robe. Then he pleaded with Saul and told him the reason he didn't kill him was out of respect for his office, since he was anointed by the Lord. Unbelievable!

Yet Saul had no regard for the office of the priests of Nob, who were also anointed by the Lord! He killed all eighty-five of them, along with everyone else in town, including the women and children! These were the people of Israel! Yet as his father had told him, Saul didn't carry out the order to destroy the wicked Amalekites, who were enemies of Israel. Saul was an evil king, and Benaiah couldn't understand David's reasoning in sparing Saul. Did David think that if he killed Saul, he'd be no better than him?

Surprisingly, Saul seemed to soften towards David, at least for now.

"Now I have to admit what I've feared all along, that you will surely be king after me, and that the kingdom of Israel will be stronger with your leadership."

Benaiah couldn't believe what Saul was saying. Saul knew David would eventually be king? Is that why he pursued David all this time? Out of jealousy?

"So promise me, please, by God, that you won't kill my descendants or destroy my reputation when you finally take the throne."

Saul seemed to acknowledge that he knew David would not take the throne from him by illicit means, but neither did he seem willing to step down from it now.

He was asking too much! Benaiah wondered how far David's mercy would go. It was one thing to spare the life of a reigning king, but if David ascended to the throne of Israel, it would be in the best interests of the security of his throne to remove all rivals. Yet, David surprised him yet again.

David nodded his assent. "I swear by the Lord that I'll neither destroy your descendants nor your name when God finally grants me the throne of Israel."

Saul sighed with relief and bowed his head in acknowledgment. Benaiah waited. What now? Would they embrace like old friends and go back to the palace for a meal together? Was their time on the run really over? Would he and Mariah settle in a real home, enjoying time together as a couple? Benaiah had to admit he liked that idea, even though he'd grown accustomed to the life of a soldier. There was probably a reason why God told Moses that, when a man takes a wife, he should not go to war for a year. What would it be like to know some semblance of a normal life?

Benaiah watched David as he and Saul studied each other for a long moment, as if unsure what to do next. In spite of the remorse, the confessions, admissions and vows they just shared, it seemed neither one seemed willing to change the current arrangement. They had a truce, but not real peace. Saul nodded once towards David, was helped onto his donkey by his servant, and headed back toward Gibeah. David turned his group back toward the Stronghold, still clutching the corner of Saul's robe.

CHAPTER EIGHT

"But the Lord said to Samuel, 'Do not look at his appearance or at his physical stature, because I have refused him. For the Lord does not see as man sees; for man looks at the outward appearance, but the Lord looks at the heart.'"
—1 Samuel 16:7

Benaiah sharpened his sword and placed it next to his club. While they were in the Stronghold, he didn't wear his weapons. But they were headed out on patrol today, and they were likely to venture into areas where they would encounter their enemies, so he gird his sword to his waist and tucked his dagger into the sheath on his right calf. His club was still secured by the sling made of the blue and white cloth his brother was holding the day he died.

So far, the cloth holding up well, but Benaiah knew it wasn't as secure as a leather sling, like the other soldiers wore. He had reinforced it with a band of leather several times. He would never part with it.

Uriah the Hittite had questioned him about it once, and Benaiah only answered that it reminded him of the cost of disobedience. The look he gave Uriah after he said it silenced any further inquiry. Let them wonder. Let them think him moody. Benaiah didn't care.

He knew that he had learned his lesson and would never question orders again. He would be the most loyal soldier David had. David would never have to wonder if Benaiah was trustworthy, faithful or loyal.

As Benaiah tapped the club dangling at his waist, he exhaled heavily. *To obey is better than sacrifice*, he repeated soundlessly.

★ ★ ★

A messenger arrived at the Stronghold, his robes torn, ashes on his head as a sign of distress. He approached David and gave him the sad news that Samuel, the prophet, had died. "The Israelites have gathered together and lamented for him. He has been buried at his home in the town of Ramah."

David tore his robes as a sign of grief.

"Oh, my friend! Oh, Samuel! You were a faithful prophet in Israel, giving us the Word of the Lord in these dark days. This is truly a sad day in Israel."

Later, when David seemed ready to talk more of Samuel, he shared with Benaiah that Samuel had anointed him as king when he was yet a young boy still tending sheep.

"It was right after the incident when Saul did not follow through on the slaughter of the Amalekites." David explained.

"I heard about that from my father," Benaiah said.

"Samuel was so disappointed in him and said he continued to pray for Saul and mourn over him. The Lord said to him, 'How long will you feel sorry for Saul? I've rejected him as king of Israel. Fill your horn with oil and go to Bethlehem. I am sending you to Jesse who lives in Bethlehem, because I have chosen one of his sons to be the new king.'"

Benaiah heard the rumors that David would surely be the next king of Israel, and even Saul's acknowledgment of it, but he was surprised to learn that it was decided long ago, back when Samuel said those famous words that Benaiah now lived by, *To obey is better than sacrifice*, and made official by the anointing with oil by a prophet of the Lord.

"What was it like," Benaiah asked, "when Samuel came to your home?"

David laughed.

"I had no clue. I was out with the sheep, as I usually was, when I was summoned to the place of sacrifice. I didn't know that he had already been introduced to each of my six older brothers. As each one passed him, Samuel said he was sure that he was the one God had chosen, because they seemed like natural, charismatic leaders, like Saul. But the Lord told him, 'Do not look at his physical appearance or size, because I've refused him. For the Lord doesn't see as man sees; because man looks at outward appearances, but the Lord looks inward, at the heart.'"

Benaiah considered David's words. He was always awed whenever he heard the very words of God Himself. It was interesting that God said He had provided Himself a king, when Saul had been given to the people as king. They demanded one so they could be like the other nations around them. They weren't content to have God alone as their king.

Saul's tall stature and handsome features had been key factors in his popularity, as the people wanted a king that would look good in the eyes of the countries round about them. Now, Benaiah was hearing that God wasn't concerned with outward appearance, but with inward character. David far surpassed Saul in that regard. He was a man of character as well as a tender spirit. Around the fire, he would play the instruments he'd made himself and sing psalms of praise to God that he'd written.

David continued, "So, when I arrived at the place of sacrifice and saw my whole family and the town elders there, all staring at me, I looked behind me, thinking there must be something else drawing their gazes in my direction." He demonstrated by slowly looking behind him. "But there was no one else behind me."

David laughed at the memory. He shook his head in disbelief, and continued, "Then Samuel approached me with a horn of oil. I fell to my knees before him. I didn't know who he was or even what was happening, but I felt compelled to kneel. He poured the oil on my head and said the favor of the Lord was on me and He had chosen me to be the shepherd of His people, Israel. I'm sure my mouth was hanging open in shock.

"Then I saw the look in the eyes of my brothers, particularly my three eldest, who were already old enough to fight in Saul's army, and I knew they thought there must have been some mistake. I was thinking the same thing. I didn't really understand what this ceremony was all about, seeing as I was still so young, and obviously not ready to be king. This was even before I defeated Goliath, so to my brothers I was just a little boy.

Since Saul was still in power, I kept it in mind, but then I went back out to the sheep, and did what I always did. And here we are years later, and I'm still not king. When I was living in the palace I could imagine it would happen soon. Even Jonathan thought it. But, instead, here I am, in the middle of nowhere, running for my life."

Benaiah couldn't argue with the facts, but he wanted to encourage David.

"God's timing isn't the same as ours. And perhaps He has things to teach you now that you could not learn in any other circumstance. To trust Him, like Joseph when he was wrongly accused of assaulting Potiphar's wife and was thrown into prison for ten years. I'm sure he wondered if those early dreams God had given him of him being in a place of authority were really from God, or his own imaginings. But we all know it happened: in God's perfect timing."

David smiled and patted Benaiah on his shoulder. "Thank you, Benaiah. I do believe you are right. Even my days as a shepherd were not wasted years. Like Moses, I had to learn how to lead sheep before I could lead people."

"Weren't your brothers at least impressed by you when you killed Goliath and delivered Israel?" Benaiah asked.

"That happened later. But when I came to the battlefield to bring food from my father, and to bring back word to him about my brothers and the battle against the Philistines. I got there just when Goliath came out. He had been challenging the army of Israel daily and defying our God to act. I was incensed! I asked, 'What reward is offered to the man who kills this Philistine and ends the shame of Israel? Who does this uncircumcised Philistine think he is to defy the armies of the living God?'"

Benaiah was in awe, hearing this story from David directly. He had heard different versions of it from those who were there that day, but now he was hearing it from the hero of Israel himself.

"They told me that the man who kills Goliath would be given great riches by the king, as well as his daughter to wed, and his family would be exempt from taxes in Israel. I couldn't see why no one else had volunteered. It was not the reward that spurred me to action, but the gall of this Philistine, who dared to mock and taunt our God, as if He was one of their idols, like Dagon, their fish-god.

"But Eliam was angry with me. He said, 'Why are you even here? Aren't you supposed to be with the sheep in the wilderness? Now they're unattended, no doubt.' I couldn't even answer him before he told me what he really thought of me. He said, 'I know it's just your pride and impertinence that made you curious to come and see the battle for yourself.'"

"He was resentful that God had chosen you over him?"

David nodded. "I just shook my head at him. I said, 'What have I done now? Is there not a cause for anger? Someone needs to confront this challenge!'"

Benaiah smiled since he knew the end of the story. "Did he eventually respect you?"

"Not at first. I couldn't seem to get any of the soldiers to agree with me. They were all terrified of Goliath. He was almost twice my size. But then word got back to King Saul that someone was willing to stand up to challenge the giant from Gath. He summoned me before him. When I arrived, he looked beyond me to see the person I must have been there to announce, much like I did when Samuel anointed me."

David laughed at the memory.

"I could see Saul was disappointed to see me. I tried to reassure him. I said, 'There's no need to be afraid of this man. I, your servant, will go and fight this Philistine.' But he protested, 'You can't possibly fight him, because you're only a youth, whereas he's been a soldier since he was your age. Besides, have you seen him?'" David smiled and his bright brown eyes sparkled at the memory.

"I told him, 'As the keeper of my father's sheep, there were times when a lion or a bear came and tried to take a lamb out of the flock. I'd go out after it, strike it, and save the lamb from it. When it would turn on me, I would attack and kill it. Since God gave me victory over such ferocious enemies as both lions and bears, this Philistine will also be just as they were, and even more so, because he has dared to defy the armies of the living God.'"

"And that's when you married his daughter, Michal?"

"Some time afterwards. At first I was to marry Saul's elder daughter, Merab. But at the last minute, Saul gave her to another. Michal was quite in love with me; I knew that already, from the few times I'd met her, but Saul wasn't concerned about her desires. He seemed to think something about her character would vex me. We were quite happy together, which in turn vexed the king."

David picked up his leather shield to oil it.

"You already know the rest of the story, but the best part of that day wasn't when I dropped him with one well-placed stone to the forehead from my sling-shot, or when I took Goliath's head off his shoulders in triumph. It was when my brothers lifted me on their shoulders, parading me through the ranks after our victory, claiming it was their brother, David ben Jesse, who delivered Israel."

"But then your brothers joined the fight alongside you, against Saul," Benaiah said.

"I wouldn't say we fought together against him as much as we ran from him, but yes, they eventually joined me, once I fled. It wasn't safe for them to stay in Saul's army anyway, since he would surely have questioned their loyalties because they were related to me. It was good to have my family with me, even though our circumstances weren't great, living in caves and strongholds. They eventually saw that Samuel wasn't mistaken when he anointed me, and in spite of how it appears at the present time, they also know I will eventually be king in Israel. But for their safety I sent them to Moab, as the king there respects me and we still have family there, from my great grandmother, Ruth."

"May the Lord make it so," Benaiah added sincerely. If he had any concerns that he may have made a wrong decision in becoming a soldier over a priest, or any qualms about fighting against the current king of Israel, they faded away as

Benaiah listened to the stories David told. Samuel the prophet heard directly from God that David would be king. What better place could there be for Benaiah than here with the future king of Israel, defeating their enemies, obeying all that David commanded him?

Yes, he was meant to be a soldier. Even his father, Jehoiada would understand it eventually, when David was a true king, as God promised.

CHAPTER NINE

"Now these were the men who came to David at Ziklag while he was still a fugitive from Saul the son of Kish; and they were among the mighty men, helpers in the war, armed with bows, using both the right hand and the left in hurling stones and shooting arrows with the bow. They were of Benjamin, Saul's brethren."

—1 Chronicles 12:1–2

Benaiah, Mikhael and Eliezar spent their days training with David's other men in the Wilderness of Paran. It felt good to belong. Benaiah had never fought in a real national army, but chose the life of a mercenary soldier. While many of the men who joined with David were formerly discontented, indebted and distressed, as Uriah had said when they first arrived, with him they found purpose. Benaiah was especially surprised to find many of Saul's clan, the Benjamites, had defected to David.

Although it was true many of them came for the personal gain associated with the life of a mercenary soldier, there were nevertheless many men with whom Benaiah was impressed. Whenever he heard of their exploits, none of the stories ever came firsthand, as the men were as humble as they were valiant. Each story came from someone who had witnessed the battles.

There was Jashobeam the Tachmonite, who single-handedly killed hundreds of men. When the others arrived to help, his muscles were still so tense his hand was stuck to his sword and the other soldiers had to pry it out of his hands. All that was left for them to do was to plunder. The Lord had brought about a great victory that day.

Abishai, David's nephew, fought against three hundred men and killed them. He became one of the captains. Others stood their ground in the center of a field of lentils and fought off the Philistines.

They watched as the new men trained. Benaiah was amazed to see their ability to shoot arrows or hurl stones from a slingshot with equal skill using either hand. Not an easy feat. That kind of finesse was not a gift he had been given. He had brute strength, able to wield his club with deadly effect. He obtained his sword from among the slain enemies of the Lord, as most of the men had. It didn't take long for him to learn to use it, as he had against the two ariels of Moabite soldiers. He could also use his wits, and he possessed surprising agility, which was necessary in his fight against the giant Egyptian. But the reason any of them triumphed over their enemies was because the Lord was with them, of that he was sure.

Benaiah emerged from his tent to see David storming through camp, kicking over pots. He looked to Uriah the Hittite with a question in his eyes. He came near to Benaiah and spoke quietly.

"He just received word about his wife, Michal."

"What of her?"

"Saul has married her off to someone named Palti, son of Laish."

"But they are not divorced."

"Precisely. David knows Saul did it only to cause more grief and show his power over him. He did something similar when he gave his elder daughter, Merab, to another, when she was promised to David for killing Goliath."

Benaiah recalled that David had told him about that. He could only imagine how frustrated David must feel. Marriage to another man was not something that could be undone without consequences. He must also be grieving her loss. From what David had told him, he did love Michal. He had to leave her behind when he fled for his life. She had even helped him escape through a window, while she claimed he was sick. David was told she had made an image of him under the covers so they'd think he was in his bed. Saul must have been furious to have been so deceived by his own daughter.

Benaiah wondered what David would do now. Many of his men had their wives with them. He must have felt his own loneliness keenly. Benaiah knew that many kings took more than one wife; perhaps David would begin to search again. But he didn't know how well that would work out. Being on the run in the wilderness was not the best place to find a suitable wife.

★ ★ ★

Soon after, fifty of David's men were again in the wilderness, near Carmel. They were helping the shepherds of a man named Nabal, from Maon, who had business in Carmel. They spent several weeks encamped with the shepherds, helping to guard Nabal's extensive flocks.

"So, what's there to see in Carmel?" Mikhael asked one of the shepherds one evening as they sat around a fire warming themselves.

The shepherd laughed as he added another log to the fire. "The same thing you'll see in every other hamlet in the country. Unless you count the monument King Saul set up for himself in the center of town."

"He didn't!" Mikhael exclaimed.

"It's true. It says he's the first king of Israel, which is true enough, names his sons, and then lists his exploits in battle, especially his victory over the Amalekites."

"Unbelievable! That was the episode of disobedience that sealed the loss of his kingdom. Why would he boast about that?" Benaiah exclaimed.

"Someone should add his murder of the priests and people of Nob to that monument," Mikhael said wryly. "That's what he'll be remembered for."

Benaiah nodded his agreement. He felt nothing but disdain for the king. A monument, in his honor, lest the name of Saul be forgotten? Benaiah felt the urge to spit at the thought of him.

★ ★ ★

David's men returned to him in the wilderness of Paran and reported that Nabal would begin shearing his sheep. Apparently, Nabal was quite wealthy with three thousand sheep and a thousand goats. David's personal history as a shepherd gave him an understanding of what was involved. He sent Benaiah and nine others back with him to assist Nabal's servants and to ask him for some provisions in return. Shepherding wasn't really something Benaiah was familiar with, but when David said go, Benaiah went.

They found the man himself in the midst of the sheep shearing. It was a grand event with feasting and dancing. Nabal looked over his shoulder and saw them approaching, but turned up his large nose at them and then issued orders to his servants, as if their arrival was of no consequence. Benaiah wondered that he wasn't intimidated by the sight of ten men approaching, who were quite obviously soldiers.

They stood by, awaiting the moment when Nabal would acknowledge their presence. Finally, he turned to them with a disdainful expression.

"Yes? Who are you and what do you want?" he sneered.

Benaiah bowed before Nabal and the men with him followed his example.

"My lord, we greet you in the name of our master, David, son of Jesse, son-in-law to King Saul. Peace be to you, peace to your house, and peace to all that you have!"

Nabal's slight smile revealed his approval of their recognition of his importance enough to bow before him.

"I've heard of Saul, of course, but who is David? What is it he wants? He does want something from me, doesn't he? Doesn't everyone?" He laughed at his own joke. His servants were wise enough to laugh as well.

"My lord, our master, David says, 'I've heard that you are in the midst of shearing. Your shepherds were with us, and we protected them and guarded all that was with them. You can check with them to see if these things are so. Therefore, we ask for a kindness to be shown to my men since it is a feast day. Please give whatever seems good to you.'"

Benaiah waited. And waited. He waited so long, he wondered if Nabal would even answer. When he finally did, Benaiah was shocked.

"Who is David, and who is this son of Jesse? There are many servants nowadays who break away each one from his master. Yet, he expects *me* to take *my* bread and *my* water and *my* meat, which I have killed for *my* shearers, in order to take it and give it to men when I don't even know where they're from?"

Nabal practically shrieked at them, "He can't be serious! Tell him to beg elsewhere." With that he turned away from them and issued more orders to his servants, the matter apparently settled.

Benaiah recovered from his shock quickly, stood and bowed once more to Nabal. He caught the shocked and apologetic expressions on the faces of the servants. Benaiah shot them a look of warning and then turned on his heel and marched away, pondering the arrogant response from the scoundrel. In spite of his comments, he no doubt had heard of David. Did he have no common sense enough to fear this man?

It took Benaiah the length of time to return to camp to put his finger on what exactly annoyed him most about Nabal. It was his bully-like demeanor. He hated bullies. Hated how they put others down so they could feel superior. How they used force and intimidation to get what they wanted.

Like the boys who had a part in Ammizabad's death.

David had been so respectful to Nabal, more than he deserved, apparently.

More than this, he wondered how David would respond to this insult.

CHAPTER TEN

"Then David said to Abigail: 'Blessed is the Lord God of Israel, who sent you this day to meet me! And blessed is your advice and blessed are you, because you have kept me this day from coming to bloodshed and from avenging myself with my own hand."

—1 Samuel 25:32–33

B enaiah didn't have long to wonder how David would respond to Nabal's rebuff. As soon as they returned and reported Nabal's rude response to him, he sprang from his seat, reaching for his sword.

"Every man gird on his sword," he ordered. "Assemble four hundred men. That should be more than enough to deal with this rascal. The other two hundred can stay behind and guard the women and children."

Benaiah could easily have remained, since they had been away for weeks now, guarding shepherds. He missed Mariah, but he couldn't even spare time to greet her when he was needed by David. Besides, Benaiah didn't want to admit it, but he was energized by the thought of a new mission. No, he would not be found lounging by the fire with his wife when he had an opportunity to follow David on a mission. He had to admit that he wanted to see David put Nabal in his place.

As they marched toward Carmel, Benaiah reflected on the situation. He could understand David taking offense at Nabal's harsh response to his request. It had been worse to hear it in person. The man was harsh and rude. He was filled with his own self-importance and didn't recognize how David's men had truly been as a wall of protection to Nabal's men both day and night.

But he wondered what David would do in response. Surely four hundred armed soldiers were too many if all he wanted to do was display a show of force and intimidate the man?

David was still seething; his anger did not dissipate as they journeyed toward the home of Nabal.

"My protection of this man's servants and property was all for nothing. He has returned disdain for my kindness."

It was true, Benaiah thought, but then David surprised him.

"I swear that not one male among his family and servants will be alive by morning light," David said.

Benaiah wondered at David's harsh response. He hadn't really considered what David's actions would be when they first set out. Now it seemed more like personal revenge than a tongue lashing on Nabal for his insult.

Was David justified in his actions? Was it out of proportion to the offense? Benaiah considered it, but chose to trust David. Benaiah fingered the sling of his club, remembering Ammizabad. When it was a matter of obeying or questioning orders, Benaiah would obey. To do otherwise, Benaiah knew all too well, could lead to disastrous results.

No, he was not the one making the decisions. He was the soldier; David was their leader. He would obey. He trusted David. The Lord was with David.

But the unrestrained fury he could see in David's eyes concerned Benaiah. Would he really kill Nabal's family and servants for his lack of hospitality?

More importantly, would Benaiah be a willing participant in the slaughter?

These were not the enemies of Israel or even the armies of David's enemy, Saul.

This was a family and its servants.

In Israel.

He had spent weeks with these harmless shepherds. Would David now order his men to kill them without mercy? Would Benaiah obey?

While he wrestled with this dilemma, someone pointed out a group of men approaching. As they came closer, Benaiah could see they were leading many donkeys, which were loaded down with sacks.

When they were close enough to be heard, David asked, "Who are you?"

They answered, "We are servants of our mistress, Abigail, wife of Nabal. She sends this gift to my lord, David. She follows behind."

Benaiah couldn't believe it. It was similar to when Jacob was going to meet Esau after many years apart. He sent wave after wave of gifts on ahead of him to appease his brother's anger. Could it be that the scoundrel, Nabal had a change of heart? He hoped it was so. He didn't want to do what he knew in his heart was wrong.

After the donkeys stopped, the men's eyes sparkled in anticipation of the great feast. Abigail had sent bountiful provisions of bread, raisins, wine, five dressed sheep, roasted grain and cakes of figs.

Soon after, the woman herself approached, riding a donkey. When she drew close, she dismounted quickly and fell on her face on the ground before David.

"Let the blame fall on me for this wickedness that was done to you!" she cried out.

Was she taking the blame for what Benaiah knew to be her husband's fault?

The woman—Abigail, her servants had called her—was very beautiful. She was clearly much younger than her husband, Nabal.

Poor woman. Benaiah didn't often consider what women felt when they were placed in these arranged marriages. Most seemed happy enough. He and Mariah were happy. But this woman had to live with a harsh and unreasonable man! Benaiah felt sympathy for her.

"May I try to explain what happened?"

David stepped forward. "Please stand." He reached out his hand and helped Abigail to stand before him.

She exhaled and began, "Please disregard that scoundrel, Nabal. Just as his name suggests, he is a fool, and he acts like one."

Benaiah had to smile. Nabal meant "Fool." Who would name their child a fool?

She continued, "But I, your maidservant, did not see the young men of my lord, whom you sent."

That was true. She wasn't there. The servants who were there must have reported the exchange between himself and Nabal to her.

"Now, since no action has been taken yet, and no blood has been shed"—she took a deep breath—"instead of avenging yourself, may your enemies be confounded."

She motioned to the gift of food laid out before him, "And may this present that I've brought be given to you and your servants. Please forgive my oversight. For I have heard of you, and know for certain that the Lord will establish you and your house, because you fight the battles of the Lord, and there has been no wickedness in any of your dealings to this day."

Benaiah was amazed at this woman. Her estimation of David was as right as her husband's opinion was wrong. She had obviously heard of David and his exploits and recognized that the Lord was with him. She seemed to be hinting at the difference between his military battles and this personal vendetta. If David followed through with it, he'd be little better than Saul, when he massacred the inhabitants of Nob. What an insightful woman this Abigail was!

"And even though you now have an enemy who is seeking to kill you, your life will surely be safe in the hands of God, whereas your enemies will be thrown out, like stones out of a sling."

Benaiah liked this woman more each time she spoke! She seemed to be aware of Saul's pursuit of David, and she knew just the right thing to say to David, using the image of the sling to remind him of his battle with Goliath: that it was the Lord who delivered him from his enemies in an unexpected way.

Benaiah could see David's expression soften with her words and his posture relax.

"And in that day when you are established as the ruler of Israel, as God has promised, then your conscience will not rise up to convict you that you have shed blood for no reason, or that you have avenged yourself."

Benaiah was astonished at Abigail. She was well informed about David and the rumors about him one day becoming the king of Israel. She was encouraging him to leave his personal insults to the Lord, so that he would not live with regret.

Benaiah could see the tension leave David's shoulders as he considered Abigail's words.

Then she added, "After God has blessed you, please remember me, your maidservant."

She seemed to be finished speaking. She bowed again.

David threw his head back and laughed.

Abigail seemed as surprised as Benaiah. Was it a laugh of derision or delight? Would David accept the gift?

David reached forward as if to touch Abigail, but then pulled his hand back to his chest.

"Thank God for sending you to meet me today! And for your sage advice, because it has kept me from avenging myself over your husband's behavior. Because I assure you, if you hadn't hurried here to intercept me, I was determined that Nabal would have no male heirs or servants by morning!"

Abigail's features showed relief, but until that moment, she may not have been aware of the extent of the revenge David had been planning.

Benaiah was relieved as well, but he chided himself for not being the one to speak out. If Abigail had not come, would he have blindly followed David's order to kill the family and servants of Nabal? It was shocking to him that he couldn't answer the question. Was he going to wait and decide at that moment?

Why wasn't he bold enough to speak out, like Eliezar and the other servants of Saul who refused to carry out his wicked orders to kill the priests of Nob?

It was obvious to everyone that what David was planning was wrong. Yet, the wisdom did not come from David's friend, Benaiah, the son of Jehoiada the priest, who should have known better, but from a woman!

A woman rescued him from an action that would have surely grieved him his whole life. Benaiah already had enough regrets in his own life. He had great respect for Abigail, but her words only made him think of his own inaction and cowardice.

David gave orders for the food to be removed from the donkeys, but Abigail insisted he take the donkeys as well. David accepted the generous gift with a nod to Abigail.

"You may return safely to your home," he said with a smile. "You've convinced me not to act on my anger."

Abigail again bowed low to the ground and then departed with her servants. David's gaze followed her until she disappeared behind a hill in the distance.

"That was one incredible woman," David commented.

"Very discerning," Benaiah remarked.

"And beautiful," David added. He led one of the donkeys back toward their camp.

"And married," Benaiah cautioned.

David sighed. "Yes, married. But very beautiful."

★ ★ ★

David married a woman named Ahinoam of Jezreel. He had met her on their travels and sent for her with a proposal of marriage. Benaiah wondered if it was in response to the news of Michal's remarriage, or his frustration over meeting Abigail and finding she was already married.

Soon after, another messenger arrived with news that Nabal had died. Right after Abigail told him about David's plans for revenge and how she averted disaster, his heart died within him and he became as a stone. He died a week later. David praised God.

"Praise God, because He has intervened on my behalf and has answered Nabal's insults with His own rebuke. He has brought Nabal's wickedness back on his own head while keeping me from personal vengeance."

Benaiah was thankful as well. He still shuddered when he thought of how events could've unfolded.

David called Benaiah to his side.

"Benaiah, take a few men with you and go to Carmel, to Abigail, the widow of Nabal. Tell her I am proposing marriage to her."

Benaiah smiled at David. He was like a little boy, anticipating a new toy. He could not deny that he was happy for his friend, although he wondered how life in the camp would change now that David would have two wives to please, after so much time without even one wife. He also wondered how David's other wife, Ahinoam, would feel about the new arrival, so soon after their wedding.

How would Abigail feel hearing a proposal through a messenger? Perhaps she'd understand it revealed more about David's importance than his lack of concern for romance. Benaiah could understand how David's loneliness, coupled with the recent news of Michal's re-marriage, would make him make this step now. Abigail seemed to hint her interest when she asked David to remember her.

Perhaps the wilderness was a good place to find a wife after all!

★ ★ ★

When they arrived at the large home, they were invited in by the servants. Abigail approached them and bowed before them. She looked even more beautiful now in this refined setting and in her costly, pale yellow gown.

"My lord," she said to Benaiah.

Benaiah wasn't accustomed to such deference to him. The woman was so gracious to show respect to anyone associated with David. He decided to be direct.

"David sent us to you, to ask you to become his wife."

If she was surprised by the proposal, she didn't show it. She hesitated only momentarily, then bowed her face to the earth and said, "I am his humble servant, here to wash the feet of his servants."

She then summoned her servants, who packed some of her things, and followed Benaiah and the other messengers. Abigail rode on a donkey, followed by five of her maidservants. She was obviously a woman of means, who was accustomed to luxury. How would she feel about sleeping in caves and tents, traveling for long periods with no promise of a stable home life in the near future? Would she resent having to share David with Ahinoam, his other recently acquired wife?

She seemed willing to try, offering to become as a servant of servants, but Benaiah suspected it was David who appealed to her most. He was a handsome man, a natural leader, a fierce warrior and future king. He would appeal to any woman who was now without the protection of a husband. And to leave a life with a scoundrel of a husband like Nabal and going to one like David was probably something she never dreamed could happen.

So Abigail became David's wife.

CHAPTER ELEVEN

"And Benaiah the son of Jehoiada was a valiant man of Kabzeel, a doer of great deeds. He struck down two ariels of Moab. He also went down and struck down a lion in a pit on a day when snow had fallen."

—2 Samuel 23:20, ESV

"David has asked to see you, Benaiah."

He couldn't imagine why David would want to single him out. He put down his sword. He'd sharpen it later.

Benaiah found David around a fire, talking with Joab. He rose when he saw Benaiah approach. Benaiah felt uncomfortable at the role reversal. David was their leader and yet he was so humble.

"My lord," Benaiah said.

"Benaiah, walk with me a moment." He motioned away from the camp. They passed a group of soldiers sparring, and some women going about their daily chores in their current camp.

When they were alone, David said, "I've heard of your exploits, Benaiah."

"My lord?"

David laughed and patted Benaiah on the shoulder. "Come now. You didn't think I'd hear about it? It's been the talk of the camp. I know something about slaying giants myself, you know."

Oh, that's what this was about, Benaiah thought. The fight with the Egyptian. He would have to talk to Mikhael about his loose tongue.

"So, how did you do it? He was not only six cubits tall, but armed with a spear. Quite a thick spear, too, as large as a weaver's beam, from what I'm told. And you had only a staff."

"He was overconfident, so I used that against him. I also used his weight. You know, the bigger they are, the harder they fall."

David laughed. "Yes, I do know that. It sounded like thunder when Goliath came crashing down."

"He was bigger than me, but not as agile because of his armor. I outflanked him when the sun was in his eyes used my staff to wrest the spear out of his hands. Then, I found a weak point in his armor and hit him on the head to stun him. I used his weight to throw him off balance."

"And then you used his own spear to kill him?"

Benaiah smiled wryly. "It seemed fitting."

David laughed. "So, you got yourself a souvenir out of it?"

"That's about all it is. It's too unwieldy for me to use."

"I know. That's how I felt when Saul tried to send me out to fight Goliath in a suit of armor. I had to be tactful and just say, 'I haven't tested them.'"

Benaiah laughed. "You were just a boy going up against a seasoned soldier, armed with only a sling. Now that's an exploit."

"I wasn't armed with only a sling and five stones. I had the God of Israel on my side. As did you. That's how we defeat our enemies."

Benaiah nodded his agreement.

"But I've heard more. You also went up against not one, but two Moabite ariels."

"I didn't go looking for trouble, my lord, but when they were suddenly in my path, I had to act."

"It was very brave of you to fight when you were so greatly outnumbered, Benaiah. Some men would have run."

"The Lord was with me that day."

"So it seems. But the most impressive thing I've heard about you was when you killed a lion in a pit on a snowy day. And that you went down after it. It's not easy to be the aggressor with an animal that is so territorial."

Benaiah looked out over the edge of the hill. Somewhere out there, Saul's troops were still hunting them.

"It was necessary. This lion had already killed two people in town. Once they get a taste for human blood, they need to be stopped."

"I've killed lions and bears when I was guarding my father's sheep," David said, "but an angry lion in an enclosed space on slippery ground? That's the worst enemy in the worst circumstance, under the worst conditions. A lion can crush your skull with one swipe of his paw, and that's not even accounting for his teeth and claws."

"Those things did cross my mind at the time, my lord," Benaiah said wryly.

"And on a snowy day, your fingers would be numb, which would make it difficult to handle weapons. And the snow would make your footing treacherous and slippery."

Benaiah nodded. "All those things were true."

"But you stayed focused. How did you do it?"

"I prayed, very fast. I remembered how Yahweh protected me in the past, and I trusted Him to do it again."

David smiled. "So He has."

As they turned back toward the camp, David said, "Benaiah, you've been a valiant soldier, an obedient servant and a good friend. Some would say that those three challenges you faced helped build your character. But I think they only proved what kind of man you already were. It's evident the Lord is with you."

Benaiah didn't know what to say to that, so he remained silent and David continued.

"I would like to assemble a small group, say thirty elite men. They would be my main bodyguard and oversee the other troops and go on special missions. I trust you with my life, Benaiah. Would you consider this position?"

Benaiah bowed low. "My lord, I would be honored to serve you in any role. I know the Lord is with you and you will one day sit on the throne of Israel."

"I would like to see you there with me, Benaiah." David helped him to stand. He clapped Benaiah on the back as they returned to camp.

* * *

Benaiah considered his conversation with David. He felt honored and humbled at the same time. He had worked hard to become a soldier. He knew Yahweh was with David and, therefore, wanted to be associated with him. He was especially honored that David would trust him enough to place him with such a select group of men.

Some Gadites also joined with David. They were mighty men of valor, men trained for battle, who could handle shield and spear. Benaiah was glad they were on David's side. He would hate to come up against such men in battle.

Yet, he knew what he was. He knew what his disobedience had cost him: the life of his brother. With each battle, with each challenge, Benaiah wanted to prove himself. Prove he would never again leave someone he cared about unprotected, never let bullies push people around. He wanted more than anything to be, in reality, what he dreamed of in his mind: an obedient soldier, a protector, a guard.

Could he somehow undo the guilt of his actions, the disappointment in his parents' eyes whenever they looked at him? Would he ever do enough noble deeds to outweigh that one that still plagued him?

Benaiah found his wife with the other women. He was excited to share the good news with her, that David respected him enough to include him among his elite soldiers. It was an honor he never expected.

He took Mariah by the hand and led her away from the others so they could share his news in private and sneak a kiss as well.

Mariah giggled at Benaiah's obvious delight.

"What's happened to make you so happy? Usually you're serious: training and drilling, or going on missions."

"David took me aside. He's heard about some of my battles, from before I joined him. He is putting together a group of elite soldiers whom he trusts explicitly, to go on special missions with him."

Mariah hugged him. "I'm so happy for you. I'm glad he finally sees in you what I do." Then a slow smile spread across her face. "I have some news, as well... I'm pregnant."

Benaiah picked her up and spun her around. "A baby? I'm going to be a father?"

Mariah laughed. "Yes, that's how it works." After a few moments, Mariah's smile faded, and she frowned.

"What's wrong?" Benaiah asked.

"This is hardly an ideal place to give birth. And I'm away from my family. And what if you die in one of your battles. What will we do then?"

Benaiah tucked her under his chin and stroked her hair. "I know. But you've seen babies being born here already, and there are many soldier's wives to support you. I know it's not the same as being back home near your mother, but perhaps we'll soon be in a different circumstance where we'll be safe and have a sense of normal life. I promised your father we won't always live out here."

Benaiah felt even more determined to protect his wife and child.

"But you do understand how important it is for me to be who God made me to be, and to serve God by serving David? I belong here, with these soldiers I admire so much. And it is such an honor that David chose me."

"Benaiah, I understand that about you, I do. It's one of the reasons I love you. But I worry about you already, and now you'll be taking more risks, volunteering for dangerous missions to impress David even more. He sees you as a warrior, but you're also my husband and the protector of your family. I know you, Benaiah, you can't help it. You live to prove yourself, but what will I do if something happens to you?" Mariah turned away and covered her eyes.

"Don't cry, my love." Benaiah kissed the top of her head. "I know you worry. I appreciate that you're there waiting for me when I come back. It gives me something to fight for. It makes me careful. I promise you I won't take any unnecessary risks. I want to come home to you. But you have to trust that God will keep me safe, just as I have to trust God to keep you safe when I'm away."

"I understand. I don't want you to change. You need to be the man God made you to be. Just remember that we're your family, and we'll be here long after you've stopped being a soldier. I will try to trust that God will keep you safe so you can keep us safe."

Benaiah hugged her again. "Thank you."

Benaiah kissed his wife, and then said cheekily, "Now, how about we go celebrate our exciting news in private?"

CHAPTER TWELVE

"So David took the spear and the jug of water by Saul's head, and they got away; and no man saw or knew it or awoke. For they were all asleep, because a deep sleep from the Lord had fallen on them."

—1 Samuel 26:12

The spies David had sent out returned with the news that Saul, who was still pursuing David, and three thousand chosen men of Israel were nearby, encamped in the hill of Hachilah, opposite Jeshimon, by the road. David went out to a ledge himself and saw the place where Saul was encamped. Saul lay in the center of the camp, with the soldiers circling him for protection. So David returned to the camp and asked, "Who will go with me to Saul in the camp?"

Benaiah knew what he was asking. It was beyond bold. It was crazy. Two men against three thousand? Yet the appeal of it was irresistible to him as a soldier. Then Mariah's news replayed in his mind. He knew she wouldn't want him to take too many chances with his life with a baby on the way.

But, while he was contemplating what he should do, Abishai, David's nephew and Joab's brother, stepped forward and spoke up: "I will go down with you."

Benaiah regretted his hesitation. A soldier should obey quickly. He should not be second-guessing himself. He should've been the one to go with David. Instead, he'd be back at camp, wondering what was happening, feeling he was not where he should be: protecting David.

David and Abishai left at nightfall. How Benaiah longed to go, to be doing instead of worrying! He vowed he would not hesitate again.

After a restless night with little sleep, Benaiah watched for their return, pacing through the camp. He berated himself for his earlier indecision and worried about the outcome. Would they return safely, or would they be captured or killed by Saul's forces? And why was David going himself?

Finally, Benaiah could make out the form of two men approaching on foot in the distance. As they drew nearer, he saw one seemed to be carrying something in his hand. Benaiah smiled with relief. It was David and Abishai. Praise Yahweh for His protection!

Men crowded around David and Abishai as soon as they came into camp, eager to hear what had happened. David deferred to Abishai to tell the story. He sat nearby and smiled at the eagerness in Abishai's voice as he recounted their adventure.

"We arrived late at night and saw they were again sleeping in the same manner as the night before, with Saul in the midst of the camp, and thousands of soldiers around him." He drew concentric circles on the ground as he explained. "We began to creep into the midst of the sleeping soldiers, every moment fearing one would awake and kill us. No one stirred. In fact, the sound of their snoring masked any noise we may have made. It's as if the Lord caused a deep sleep to fall on the entire camp! I've never seen anything like it! Not even a sentry was awake. When we realized this was of God, we didn't even bother to whisper, yet still no one woke up."

Benaiah and the other men listening shook their heads in amazement. Truly God was with them!

"So we arrived in the center of their camp without incident, and there was Saul, sound asleep, with his ever-present spear in the ground near his head. It was just begging for me to take it and finish him. His general, Abner was next to him, snoring loudly, oblivious to the danger to his king.

"Then I said to David, 'This is it! God has delivered your enemy to you. Look how He arranged things!' It was obvious to me, with the miraculous way we'd made it so far. So I said, 'Please let me do the honors and pin him to the ground with his own spear. I won't have to do it a second time!'"

At this, the men let out a loud cheer. Benaiah felt envious at the opportunity he missed. He would have offered to do the same.

"Good for you, brother!" Joab praised. "I would have dispatched him myself."

Abishai looked to David, as if unsure how to tell the rest of the story. David arose and came into the midst of the eager soldiers.

"He didn't do it," David announced.

The men groaned.

"Because I wouldn't let him."

Benaiah shouldn't have been surprised by this, yet he was. Not just surprised, but disappointed. It was just like in the cave! David had demonstrated undeserved mercy to Saul yet again. Unbelievable!

"I said to Abishai, 'No, don't do it. No one can touch the Lord's anointed and get away with it. I know that either God will strike him down, like Nabal, or he will die naturally, or he'll be killed in battle. But God forbid that I should do such a thing.'"

"So that's it, then?" Benaiah asked.

"I took Saul's spear from was near his head, and this water jug, and we left. No one stirred as we left, either," David said.

This was all too familiar to Benaiah. David had a chance to kill his enemy; Yahweh engineered miraculous circumstances; David's conscience was pricked; he forbade others to do the job, claiming Saul is the Lord's anointed; then he took a memento to prove he was there. All this story needed now was to have David wake Saul up to confess to what he'd done, and it would be exactly the same.

Abishai picked up the rest of the story.

"Then this morning, we were over on a hill opposite Saul and his army, with a valley between us. David called out to Abner, but he wouldn't answer. So David said, 'Don't you hear me, Abner?'"

Benaiah threw his head back in disbelief. It was the same! David confronted Saul!

"Then Abner answered, 'Who do you think you are to presume to speak to the king?'"

Abishai smiled as he remembered the exchange.

"So David said to Abner, 'Even though there is no one with your status in Israel, you are proving yourself to be a mere man. Why haven't you guarded your sovereign?' He let Abner consider that for a moment, and then added, 'For while you slept, someone came in with the intention of killing the king.' He didn't let them know it was David himself in their camp. Then he said, 'This is not a good situation. As his general, you deserve to die for not guarding him properly. Look around you and see if you can find the king's favorite spear, or the jug of water that was next to his head as he slept.'"

Benaiah marveled at David's bold words to Abner. He could only imagine how that must have stabbed at Abner's pride as a soldier!

"But Saul recognized him and he said, 'Is that you again, my son, David?'"

Benaiah felt he could have told the rest of the story himself. Saul was responding in the same way as at the incident at the cave.

Abishai confirmed his suspicions. "Then David said, 'Yes, it is I, my king. Why do you still pursue me? What is my crime against you? Please listen. If God Himself has incited you against me, He will accept an offering for willful sin in my place. But if it's a person, then may God curse them, because they have driven me out of the land of my people, to a land of idolaters.'"

Benaiah understood David's meaning. By forcing him to be on the run, he was among the idol-worshiping Philistines. Although David wouldn't worship idols himself, he was indicating his desire to once again worship with the people of God.

"He said, 'Please don't let me die for no reason. The king is hunting insignificant prey.'"

"Then Saul said, 'I am in the wrong. Come back, my son, David. I won't harm you anymore, because you've proved for the second time now that you are not trying to kill me. Instead, I've been foolish and am the guilty party here.'"

"He always says that, but it means nothing. You can't trust him!" Benaiah argued.

David motioned for Benaiah to calm down. "I know, that's why we kept our distance," David said. "I pitched the spear towards them from the hill and said, 'Here is the king's spear. Have someone retrieve it. Let God be the judge who is right or wrong. He again gave you into my hand to test me, but I wouldn't take the opportunity, because you are His appointed leader. Because of that, I value your life, as I hope my life is valued in God's eyes. He'll deliver me out of all my troubles.'"

Abishai added, "Then Saul said, 'Bless you, my son, David. I know you will continue to do great things and succeed in the end.'"

Benaiah said, "He knows it in his mind, but won't do anything to make it happen."

David agreed. "True, he isn't ready for that. He may never be. But regardless, it will still happen as God has decreed."

Abishai concluded, "So Saul went his way, and we returned here—" he hoisted the jug— "with a royal jug!"

★ ★ ★

A week after he returned from Saul's camp with the jug, David gathered his mighty men together. "I'm so weary of being hunted by Saul. In spite of his assurances to the contrary, I don't trust that he'll ever stop pursuing me. There have been too many close calls. The only option I can see is to hide out in Philistine territory until he tires of the chase. I know he won't venture outside of Israel to find me. This way we can escape and hopefully have some semblance of peace."

Benaiah was surprised to hear David so depressed. How could that be after such a miraculous deliverance?

"Do you think the Philistines will accept you and the rest of us? After all, there are now six hundred soldiers with you, as well as our families. They may be intimidated by that," Joab asked.

"Not to mention that you are the one who killed their hero, Goliath," Abishai said.

"And you've slain thousands of Philistines since then," Benaiah added.

"Nevertheless, it's also known throughout the land that Saul seeks my life. Achish, the king, may believe we are united against a common enemy, and therefore trust me. I also think it would be best to have our families finally settled into a city," David said.

Benaiah was of two minds about David's decision. He couldn't imagine living among the pagan Philistines, and he knew Mariah wouldn't like it either. As the son of a priest, he knew how much God detested idol worship, and how it could be a snare to the hearts of the people. But he also knew Mariah's mind about being in the wilderness while she was pregnant.

He also wanted to get settled. Women and children should be in homes, not out in caves, tents and strongholds, awaiting their men to return from military raids. He guessed David's two new wives had some influence on his decision. Regardless of his feelings in the matter, Benaiah would obey David, trusting that God was leading them, even into the heart of Philistia.

★ ★ ★

Mariah was nearing the end of her pregnancy.

Benaiah wondered if they would have a son, and if he'd be a good father. Would he allow the child to follow where Yahweh led? Would it matter to him if the child became a priest or a soldier, or even a cart maker? He didn't think so. He had learned from his own life struggles that sometimes, in spite of one's tribe, Yahweh had a different direction planned. Benaiah didn't regret his own decision to become a soldier over a priest. He was right where God had called him to be, at David's side, even if it was among Israel's enemies, the Philistines.

Ironically, they had first settled in Gath, the very hometown of the giant, Goliath, whom David slew. It was one of five royal cities in Philistia, and David soon established his reputation militarily, gaining the trust of King Achish.

"You seem distracted, Benaiah. Is all well?" David asked. Benaiah never allowed personal issues to interfere with his duties in the past, and he chided himself for letting his emotions show now.

"I'm fine, my lord."

"Is it Mariah, then? She's due to have your child soon, isn't she?"

"Yes, she started to have some pain during the night. She assured me it was normal, and insisted I go to work as usual."

"Ah, I see, but you can't stop thinking about her?"

Benaiah dropped his head. "Yes, and she has no family here to help with the delivery and the care of the baby when it comes."

"Yes, a woman needs her mother, especially with the first child. Only a woman can help another woman at times like that. I sometimes think I want to be there to support them, but when my sister gave birth and I heard her screams of agony through the wall, I headed in the opposite direction. I don't know how they bear it."

Benaiah appreciated that David was trying to be helpful, but his talk of women screaming in the pangs of childbirth only made him worry even more for Mariah, in spite of the fact that she wasn't alone; the other soldier's wives would help her.

David regarded Benaiah with what he could only read as sympathy. "Go on home. Make sure all is well. I'll see you tomorrow."

Benaiah straightened even more. "I'm fine, my lord. I'm sure she's fine."

David laughed. "Yes, I've no doubt you're fine. But you'll be better when you check on your wife, and when you can pace outside the room and hear the first cries of your son or daughter."

Benaiah smiled at the thought, but didn't want to leave his post. He didn't move.

"Go, Benaiah, that's an order. Send me word when your child is born, it doesn't matter the hour." Benaiah was surprised at the personal gesture from David.

Benaiah looked around the room a moment. "Yes my lord, I'll... I'll find someone to replace me. Thank you, my lord. Thank you." Benaiah hurried out of the room to the sound of David chuckling.

* * *

The shrill cry of a newborn broke the silence of the early morning. Benaiah let out a breath. Mariah's long, hard labor was over, and their child was born.

Mahasham, Rei's wife, opened the door to their room. She looked exhausted, so Benaiah could only imagine how Mariah felt. She gave Benaiah a weak smile when she saw him.

"She's fine, Benaiah. The midwife is just finishing up. Soon you can go in to see them."

"I heard the baby. It's fine?"

Mahasham patted Benaiah's forearm. "Yes, Benaiah, he's fine."

"He?" Benaiah's face split with a grin. "I have a son?"

"Yes, a fine son. Blessings."

Benaiah grasped Mahasham's shoulders and spun her around. She laughed in surprise at his happy response.

"A son! I have a son! When can I see him?"

"Just a moment."

After what seemed like much more than a moment, Benaiah was allowed into the room. Mariah opened her eyes when she heard him. Her hair was matted to her forehead with perspiration and she looked thoroughly worn out, but he didn't think he had ever seen her more beautiful, except perhaps on their wedding day. She pulled back the covers on the baby to reveal his little scrunched up reddened face.

"Here's your Abba," Mariah said to the baby by way of introduction.

Benaiah's eyes filled with tears as he looked between his son and his wife. He felt so blessed. He felt protective of his little family. He didn't want them to ever be in danger. He thought of his little brother and suddenly understood his parents' fear when he was missing and imagined their grief when he died.

"Welcome, little one." Benaiah stroked his little cheek and the baby turned toward him and opened his tiny mouth.

"He's looking for his first meal, already," Mariah said.

"Born hungry?"

"Like his father." Mariah smiled.

Benaiah caught her eyes. "Thank you," he said and kissed her.

"I'm so glad you were able to be here. It was worse than I expected, even with so many experienced women and the midwife here. I'm so thankful he's safe and healthy."

"I know we won't give him his name until he's circumcised, but I already know what I want to name him. Ammizabad."

"After your brother who died?"

"Yes. Ammiz should have lived a long life, but because of me he was killed by those boys. That won't happen to this boy. I will protect him. He can be the man my little brother never was."

"Ammizabad it will be then."

CHAPTER THIRTEEN

"So David and his men came to the city, and there it was, burned with fire; and their wives, their sons, and their daughters had been taken captive. Then David and the people who were with him lifted up their voices and wept, until they had no more power to weep."

—1 Samuel 30:3–4

Benaiah couldn't believe the sight before him. From far off, they could see smoke rising from what had been the city of Ziklag. It was the city where they had left their families and livestock, assuming them to be safe while the men were on military raids.

As they raced towards the city, Benaiah's heart repeated one name over and over: *Mariah.* His wife and son, whom he promised his father-in-law he would protect. Tirhanah didn't want his daughter taken away to live a nomadic existence, in harm's way. She should've been in a home in Kabzeel, close to her parents, safe from harm, caring for their son, not here among the Philistines.

But after so much time in the Stronghold or wandering throughout all Israel and Philistia, they were finally settled in a real city of their own. It set Benaiah's mind at ease, knowing Mariah was living in a home, near the wives of the other soldiers, enjoying a normal life for the first time in their marriage. Ammizabad was now a year old and brought such joy to their lives. It was as it should be. Mariah didn't like living among pagans, but since Ziklag was a city of David, it was populated with only their own people.

But now his worst fears were realized and it was all his fault. What would he find? Burned corpses? Mariah's abused body? His little boy's remains? How could he ever face her parents with the news? He would see that look again, the one he saw on the faces of his own parents when he let them down and they lost their son.

I told you to look after him! Even after all these years, he could still hear his mother's voice, see the accusation in her eyes, when he had abandoned his brother. Now he would experience it again from Mariah's family.

None of the men said anything during the frantic run towards the city. They were all lost in their own thoughts, hoping they wouldn't find their worst fears realized: their families murdered.

He had failed again, failed to protect those he loved. Was Yahweh punishing him for becoming a soldier rather than a priest? Hadn't he been doing the right thing? Wasn't he right where Yahweh wanted him to be? Benaiah wasn't being disobedient this time, and yet the consequences were the same.

Mariah! Ammiz!

The men ran through the gates of the city. Charred remains of carts littered the streets, but, thankfully, they didn't see any dead bodies. They went to their own homes, afraid of what they would find, but needing to know the fate of their families.

Benaiah stepped through the open door of his burned out house, stepping over shattered clay pots and burned chairs. In the distance he could hear the wailing of the other men. What had they found? What would he find? His eyes searched through the rubble, his vision blurred with tears.

Mariah? Please don't be here. I couldn't bear to think of you suffering like this, dying like this. Mariah. Ammizabad.

Benaiah couldn't find anyone in the rubble, so he made his way back into the central square, where the other men were also stumbling back.

"Did you find anything?" Benaiah asked.

"No. They're gone," Rei said.

"Everyone?" David asked.

"Yes. All gone."

"Who could have done this?" Eliab asked.

"My guess is the Amalekites," David said, walking into the square. "This is their handiwork. It makes them feel they have a hold over me. They knew this was my city. They were trying to take revenge on me for destroying their cities. They think to add to my anguish by taking my two wives, Ahinoam and Abigail, and all that I hold dear, rather than killing them outright. If it had been the Philistines, the Geshurites or the Girzites, they wouldn't have left them alive."

Benaiah sank to the dust and ashes, adding his voice to the sound of the other men, keening and sobbing. Each one had suffered loss. They wept until they had no strength left.

David also wept, but Benaiah heard him thank God.

"How can you thank Him for this? Our wives, our sons and our daughters are all gone," Jezliah asked.

David answered, "I'm thankful that they are not here dead at our feet. They were taken, and Yahweh may be pleased to keep them safe and lead us to them."

"How can you say that?" Shammah exploded at David. "You, yourself, know how the Amalekites have always been towards our people. They attacked the children of Israel when they left Egypt and were wandering in the dessert. They picked off the weak and vulnerable at the back of the line. Now, they've done the same by stealing our women and children!"

"Who knows what they'll do to them? What they may have already done to them!" Eliab said, giving voice to their worst fears.

"All in retaliation for your attacks on them. This is your fault, David!" said another.

At this, several men picked up stones. They needed a scapegoat for their anger and fear, so David became their target. In spite of his own grief, Benaiah stepped in front of David, blocking him from an attack, a look of challenge in his eyes.

"We can't turn on each other. It won't help get our families back," Benaiah said.

The men softened somewhat, but Benaiah felt he still needed to get their attention off David.

"If you want someone to blame for this, blame Saul."

"Saul? What has he got to do with this?" Rei asked.

"My father Jehoiada, who is a priest, told me that God had commanded Saul, through Samuel, to utterly destroy the Amalekites as punishment for their attacks on Israel from the very beginning. Saul disobeyed, sparing the king and the best of the flocks, making the excuse that the people with him were the ones who disobeyed and kept the animals alive for the purpose of sacrifice. But Samuel told him the Lord was displeased with him, and that to obey was better than sacrifice.

"Samuel told Saul, 'The Lord has torn the kingdom from you, and has given it another, who is better than you. God, who is the Strength of Israel, will not lie or change His mind, because He is not like a mere man who would do such a thing.' Because of Saul's failure to obey the voice of the Lord that day, the Amalekites remain and have troubled Israel yet again."

One by one, the stones dropped to the sand.

David, who sat on the ground absorbing the accusations like blows from his enemies, now stood and wiped his eyes with the back of his hand. Seemingly energized by Benaiah's reminder about the wickedness of the Amalekites, God's promise to give him the kingdom, and the need to obey the Lord's command, David wiped a hand over his face as if washing away his earlier discouragement. He called out, "Abiathar!"

"Yes, my lord?" answered Abiathar, son of Ahimelech.

"Please bring the ephod here to me."

So Abiathar brought the priestly garment, which contained the Urim and the Thummim used for discerning the will of God, to David. Since Abiathar, the only surviving relative of Eli, fled with the sacred lot when he came to David at Keiliah, King Saul was left without a way to discern the will of God.

"Inquire of the Lord if I should pursue them and if I'll find them."

Abiathar used the Urim and the Thummim and, with a smile, he reported, "Pursue them, for you will surely overtake them and recover all that was stolen."

The men who overheard the Lord's response looked at each other, mouths open in surprise. Benaiah laughed with joy. Could it be possible that God would lead them to the enemy, give them the victory and, best of all, reunite them with their families?

David clapped a hand onto Abiathar's shoulders and gave it a squeeze. "Thank you, my friend." Then he addressed the men.

"We are assured of victory in our quest. We will recover our families and belongings. That is the word of the Lord to us. We have nothing left to do but to obey. Although we do not know where they are, they are known to the One who sees all. He will lead us to them. Let's move out."

Benaiah was encouraged by David's words and the assurance that Yahweh would give them the victory. He would see his family again! Even those who were angry enough at David to stone him now marched with purpose. They arrived at the Brook Besor, where two hundred more of their number were waiting, seated around fires or stretched out in sleep, still exhausted from the last campaign.

David updated them on the situation in Ziklag and the plan to pursue the enemy.

"We cannot join you, my lord. Many are wounded from the previous raid from which we returned, but most of us are worn out. We can stay by the remaining supplies so they won't be looted as well, lest we be left with nothing at all to sustain the troops," one offered.

David stroked his beard as he considered this. "Very well. These are all the provisions we have since the town was destroyed. There are still four hundred of us. That should be enough to pursue the Amalekites. As Jonathan said, the Lord can save by many or by few."

David prayed for direction and studied the ground to determine which way they headed. He chose to go northeast. As they marched, Benaiah recalled his promise to Mariah's father to protect her. He assumed she'd be safe with him. How often had he explained his need to her to be who God called him to be: a soldier, a guard, a protector? What kind of protector had he turned out to be? *Please keep them safe, Lord!*

After traveling for half a day, they spotted a young man in the field, and he was brought to David. He was dressed in the tunic of a servant. His mouth hung open, his lips cracked, his tongue parched. David ordered a drink to be given to him. After drinking more than half the skin of water, he was able to close his mouth. Then, they fed him a cake of figs and two clusters of raisins. His eyes brightened with the sweetness of the food. He finished the water and sighed with relief.

"When did you last eat?" David asked.

"I've had no food or water for three days."

"Where are you from, and whose servant are you?" David asked.

"I'm an Egyptian who serves an Amalekite general. Three days ago I became ill, so he left me behind."

"Where was he up to that point?"

"We were in the territory of Judah and the southern area of Caleb, as well as the area of the Cherethites where we invaded. We also set fire to Ziklag on our way through."

David closed his eyes in thanksgiving. "Praise be to the Lord," he breathed.

"Can you lead us to them?" David asked the young Egyptian.

The man's eyes widened in fear, but then he answered, "If you can promise me by your God that you won't kill me or turn me over to my master, then I'll take you to where I know they were headed."

David promised him, and the Egyptian pointed towards the east. Benaiah couldn't believe it. They were already going in the general direction of the Amalekites. Yahweh led them on this detour, to find this man, who would lead them directly to the enemy, and their families. Benaiah thanked God for His sovereignty.

After another day of travel, they came to a ridge at twilight. They heard the sound of a great company of people, as well as music and laughter. They crawled to the edge and peered over into the bowl-shaped valley.

"There they are," the Egyptian announced.

"Thank you. You are free to go," David told him.

The servant fell to the ground before David. "But sir, I have nowhere to go. Please let me serve you, for you have shown me the mercy of God in sparing my life."

David studied the man. "Very well. What is your name?"

"Nebit, my lord."

"Nebit, you may fight with us or refrain. We will find a place for you among our people," David promised.

"Thank you, my lord. I would like to refrain. I still am not well," Nebit said, standing up.

"Very well. Guard our things," David ordered. Nebit bowed and made his way toward the heap of supplies. He was given a weapon.

Benaiah surveyed the scene before him. In the basin below them, a great multitude was spread out. Surprisingly, they were not preparing for their next battle, but eating, drinking and dancing. There were several fires aiding with visibility, which would fade in the twilight.. They could make out that the spoil the Amalekites had captured from Ziklag and other towns of the Philistines and Judah: the people and livestock at the edge of camp. They were being guarded by just a handful of soldiers, who no doubt were not happy about being excluded from the celebrations.

They didn't put the prisoners in the middle of the camp, as Benaiah would've expected, but instead assumed the valley wall behind the prisoners' tents would be a sufficient rear guard. Benaiah surmised this would make them easier to rescue and less likely to be hurt in the fighting. He thanked God for those seemingly small details.

One of the benefits of living among the Philistines and supposedly fighting the battles of the Philistine king was that they now had access to more weapons. A few years earlier, in Israel, only the king and his sons had weapons. Ever since Benaiah was young, the Philistines forbade blacksmiths in Israel, lest they make swords or spears. Israelites even had to go down to the Philistines to sharpen their plowshares, axes and sickles—and this for a charge, as Simeon had told them. But now, not only did they have weapons made for themselves, but they also plundered more from the Philistines and other groups they attacked.

David divided his men, most to be involved in fighting the Amalekites and a smaller number to rescue their families. Benaiah was a fighter, and that's where he was expected to be, but one part of him would've liked to be the one to rescue Mariah personally, to ensure she and Ammizabad were safe, and kiss her soundly.

David stationed his finest archers, those that could shoot with either the right hand or left hand with equal accuracy, along the rim of the bowl. They had a great vantage point from which to target the enemy or concentrate their arrows. Those who were skilled with a slingshot were next to them.

They awaited David's signal to attack. When it came, the archers sent their volley of arrows into the midst of the unsuspecting warriors. Immediately following the first volley of arrows, the slingshots were fired.

The music ceased and the Amalekites looked about in confusion in the semi-darkness. Once they realized they were being assaulted from all around them, they scrambled to get to their weapons, which they had removed during their festivities. By that time, David's men had poured over the sides like insects. The smaller group of twelve soldiers under Eliam's leadership headed straight for the prisoners.

Benaiah had to focus on the fighting at hand. The Amalekites were fierce warriors, outnumbering David's men, and, in spite of the element of surprise and God's assurance of success, they would still need to do the hard work of fighting.

The Amalekites recovered quickly to mount a defense, but David and his men were highly motivated. They wanted their families back. The fighting was fierce, mostly one-to-one, warrior against warrior. Benaiah preferred to use his club, for the most part, but drew his sword or dagger when he was up against a soldier armed with one as well.

The battle lasted from twilight that day until the evening of the next day. Not all the Amalekites chose to stay and fight. When they realized the battle had turned against them, about four hundred fled on camels. David's men did not even attempt to go after them, since they had arrived on foot.

Benaiah was amazed at the odds. They came down against this great troop of soldiers with only four hundred men. After a great slaughter, four hundred Amalekites still managed to escape. How many soldiers had each man fought to recover all that was lost? Benaiah was too exhausted to count the bodies.

But he couldn't rest. His thoughts were on Mariah and Ammiz.

Benaiah directed his steps toward the area where their families had been held. He stepped over dead Amalekite soldiers, his desire to see Mariah with his own eyes propelling his heavy steps. By now, many other men had also concluded the battle was over and there were no more enemies to fight, and were all streaming in the same direction. He could hear shouts of joy, saw children clinging to their fathers' legs, husbands and wives embracing.

Then he saw her. His own sweet wife, slightly disheveled, but so beautiful to him. So healthy, so alive.

"Mariah!" he called. She looked up from where she sat, stood and ran into his arms.

"Benaiah! I knew you'd come! I prayed and prayed."

Benaiah embraced and kissed her soundly He pulled back, looked down into her face and drank in the sight of her.

"Ammiz?"

"He's fine. I'll show you soon. He's sleeping."

"I'm sorry. I'm so sorry I failed to protect you. I love you, Mariah." He rained kisses over face and head.

"Shh, it's okay. I know you love me. I knew it even when we were taken away. I never doubted it. Yahweh was with us, even though we were surrounded by our enemies. They didn't hurt us. We all had such a profound feeling of peace, I can't even describe it. We knew you'd come."

Benaiah kissed her again, then Mariah led him to the tent where Ammiz was sleeping. Benaiah was so happy to see him alive and well, he picked him up to shower him with kisses. The baby woke up and rewarded Benaiah with a wide-mouthed smile. Benaiah blew raspberries on the boy's belly, and Ammiz erupted in giggles.

They joined the others who were assessing their situation. There seemed to be no battle losses at all on their side. Amazing! Everyone who had been taken by the Amalekites were safe and unharmed. Even the spoil taken by the Amalekites was untouched, along with plunder from previous raids: great flocks and herds. David lost nothing of all their people and possessions, just as God promised, and they left with even greater riches and livestock as spoil.

David was reunited with his two wives. Benaiah couldn't imagine a divided reunion like that. He was happy with his one wife. She was enough. He was blessed.

Benaiah thanked Yahweh for His goodness. He was truly with David, in directing him to Nebit, in giving him such a great victory over the Amalekites, and mostly in restoring their families to them safe and sound.

After posting guards around the perimeter, in case of a desperate counterattack, they celebrated their reunion and the goodness of the Lord. They rested well that night in the tents of their enemies, and then gathered up the spoils of war and drove their herds ahead of them.

As they returned to the Brook Besor, the men who had guarded the supplies came to meet them. David greeted them while many others began to tell of the great victory the Lord had given them. Some of those soldiers were also reunited with their wives and children.

When they inquired about the multitude of animals with them, David said, "This is David's spoil. We will divide it up among us."

Benaiah heard murmuring from some of the soldiers who returned with him from battle.

David heard it too. "What is your concern?" he asked them.

Several men stood together. "Because these men didn't go with us to fight, we don't think it's fair that they get to share in the spoils we recovered." Then, as if realizing how harsh it sounded, they offered, "They can take their wives and children, and go."

Benaiah wondered what David's response would be. Would he penalize those who didn't fight with them? Would he be angry with these men for their selfishness, or would he think they were right about it not being fair for those who stayed behind to benefit from a battle in which they did not fight?

David answered calmly, "My brothers, you can't do such a thing with what the Lord has given us. He miraculously led us to our enemy, and gave us this great victory. We didn't win this battle in our own strength.

"You won't find anyone who'll agree with you on this. I've made my decision; there will be equal share of spoils for those who go to battle, and those who stay by the supplies."

Benaiah could see the men who brought the complaint weren't pleased with David's judgment, but then they were wicked and worthless men. They weren't following David because they admired him and were looking forward to one day seeing him as king over Israel. They were greedy men who realized that if the spoil was divided between a greater number of men, it would mean less for them. They were true mercenaries, fighting with David only for personal gain.

"Moreover," David added, "this will be a statute and ordinance from now on. All my soldiers are equal in value."

Once they returned to Ziklag, they sorted through the ruins, trying to salvage what they could. They realized they could not live in this place any longer.

David sent some of the spoil to the elders of Judah, to his friends, in all the places where David and his men had roved, with the message, "This gift is from David, taken as spoils from the enemies of the Lord."

Benaiah's respect and admiration for David continued to grow as he saw the wisdom of his leadership and the blessing of God on his life. That night, as Benaiah wrapped his arms around his wife and son, he again thanked God for His protection. Truly God had led Benaiah to be here, serving David, who did what Saul failed to do.

To obey was better than sacrifice.

CHAPTER FOURTEEN

"How the mighty have fallen in the midst of the battle! Jonathan was slain in your high places."

—2 Samuel 1:25

On the third day after they had returned from the slaughter of the Amalekites, a young man was brought to Ziklag before David with his clothes torn and dust on his head as a sign of great mourning. He fell to the ground and prostrated himself before David. Benaiah stood at David's right hand.

"What is your report?" David asked him.

The man answered, "I have come from the battle between Israel and the Philistines in which the king and his sons were fighting."

David leaned forward, "Tell me everything you know."

"The Israelites have retreated from battle, many people have been killed, including Saul and his son, Jonathan."

David flinched as if he received a physical blow to his middle. Then he schooled his features and asked, "How do you know that Saul and Jonathan his son are dead?"

The man seemed to brighten as he began to retell the story of the defeat of David's enemies. "By chance I was on Mount Gilboa when I saw King Saul leaning towards his upraised sword. He was looking over his shoulder at the advancing chariots and horsemen. He must have known he could not escape. Then he saw me and motioned for me to come to him. Then he asked who I was. I told him I was an Amalekite. Then he surprised me by saying, 'Please kill me before those Philistines get here and torture me.'"

David showed no emotion as the man continued his account of Saul and Jonathan's deaths.

"So I did as he asked and killed him, because he didn't have long to live anyway. He had been severely wounded by the archers. Here is proof that it was really the king." He drew a crown and arm bracelet from a sack and laid them at David's feet.

When David saw Saul's crown and bracelet before him, he stood and took hold of his own clothes and tore them in grief. Benaiah and all those present did the same. They wept, fasted and mourned for King Saul, Prince Jonathan and the soldiers of Israel until evening.

In the evening, David summoned the man before him again. He asked him to retell his story, and then said, "How could it be that you weren't afraid to take the life of the king, the Lord's anointed? Since you admitted it yourself, in fact, you boasted about it, you have sealed your judgment."

Then David turned to Benaiah and said, "Execute him!"

As Benaiah approached the Amalekite, he cried out, "I didn't do it! He was already dead when I found him! I only said it for a reward! I didn't kill Saul!" But Benaiah silenced him with one stroke of his sword.

The lamentations continued well into the week. It had been such an emotional week, having returned from battle to find Ziklag burned and their families gone, pursuing the enemy and fighting them for a whole day, and then traveling back to their burned out homes, only to hear the news about Israel's defeat and the death of the king and his three sons.

Benaiah recognized the judgment of God on Saul and his descendants, and what this would mean in clearing the way for David to become king over Israel, as God had promised. While he had no personal affection for Saul, he did respect Jonathan and recognized him as David's friend. He had visited David in the forest in the Wilderness of Ziph and encouraged him. He wasn't at all threatened by David, but even as the heir to Saul's throne, Jonathan recognized that David would one day be the next ruler of Israel. Benaiah even overheard Jonathan once tell David, "Don't be afraid of my father, Saul. God won't let him find you. I know you'll be the next king of Israel, and I'd be honored to serve next to you."

Prince Jonathan was an extraordinary man, and Benaiah heard he had protected David and interceded for him with his irrational father many times, warning him to flee when he determined that Saul meant to harm him.

Because of that, Benaiah mourned his loss.

That evening David wrote a song of lament for Saul and Jonathan and shared it with the company. He called it the Song of the Bow.

"The beauty of Israel is slain on your high places!
How the mighty have fallen!
Tell it not in Gath,
proclaim it not in the streets of Ashkelon—
lest the daughters of the Philistines rejoice,
lest the daughters of the uncircumcised triumph.

"O mountains of Gilboa,
let there be no dew nor rain upon you,
nor fields of offerings.
For the shield of the mighty is cast away there!
The shield of Saul, not anointed with oil.
From the blood of the slain,
from the fat of the mighty,
the bow of Jonathan did not turn back,
and the sword of Saul did not return empty.

"Saul and Jonathan were beloved and pleasant in their lives,
and in their death they were not divided;
They were swifter than eagles,
they were stronger than lions.

"O daughters of Israel, weep over Saul,
who clothed you in scarlet, with luxury;
who put ornaments of gold on your apparel.

"How the mighty have fallen in the midst of the battle!
Jonathan was slain in your high places.
I am distressed for you, my brother Jonathan;
You have been very pleasant to me;
your love to me was wonderful,
surpassing the love of women.

"How the mighty have fallen,
and the weapons of war perished!"[1]

Benaiah couldn't help but marvel that David was so gracious toward the memory of Saul, his enemy, who had pursued him these many years, seeking his life. He was truly an extraordinary man.

Soon after hearing about the death of Saul, instead of rebuilding Ziklag, David inquired of the Lord, asking if he should go up to any of the cities of Judah. They had lived with the Philistines for a year and four months. The Lord directed him to go to Hebron, so David and his company and their households went to Hebron. David also took his two wives, Ahinoam the Jezreelitess, now very far along in her first pregnancy, and Abigail, the widow of Nabal the Carmelite.

Then, the men of Judah, David's tribe, came and anointed David king over the house of Judah. They informed him that the men of the town of Jabesh Gilead were the ones who had buried the bodies of Saul and his sons. They were loyal to the king because he had once saved them from an attack by the Ammonites. They were the ones who had found him and his sons slain, their heads removed, their armor stripped and placed in the temple of the Ashtoreths. Their bodies had been fastened to the wall of Beth Shan in a grisly display.

These valiant men traveled all night and brought the bodies back to Jabesh Gilead to burn them. Then they buried their bones under a tamarisk tree and fasted for seven days of mourning.

David was impressed with the men of Jabesh Gilead, in that they realized it was shameful to leave the dead unburied. He sent messengers to them, saying, "May God bless you for the kindness you've shown to your lord, Saul, in burying him. I will surely repay you for this kindness. Since Saul has died, you should know that the house of Judah has anointed me king over them."

Benaiah understood the intent of this message was to show the Gileadites he held no malice toward the now deceased king, and it was setting the stage for his own leadership over them.

★ ★ ★

Mariah kneaded the dough on the floured table. Benaiah smiled at the scene. She was so petite, and yet she attacked the dough as if she were defending her child from a wild beast.

"Is there any threat to David's throne from Saul's other son—what was his name—Ishbosheth?" she asked.

Benaiah tilted his head. He liked discussing politics with Mariah.

"Not an imminent threat. But Saul's general, Abner, has installed Ishbosheth king over Israel. For these two years he's kept his distance from David, and there have been no hints of war. His hold over the country is only as strong as his alliance with Abner. It's essentially a military leadership, and Ishbosheth well knows it. He's a weak leader and would not remain in power without the aid of Abner."

"That's good to know. I'd hate to see any fighting between Israel and Judah, since we're brothers." Mariah pushed on the dough one more time with the heel of her hand, pulled half of it towards her, then turned it out into a clay bowl and covered it with a towel to rise.

Benaiah rose and took his wife in his arms, despite her sticky, floury hands and her protests. He kissed the top of her head.

"Let's pray we can have a period of peace and rest from all our enemies."

★ ★ ★

Once they were established in Hebron, David took even more wives, who bore him many children.

His firstborn son was named Amnon, and he was the son of Ahinoam. Abigail, the widow of Nabal, bore him a son named Chileab, who was sometimes called Daniel. His third son was Absalom, by his wife, Maacah, the daughter of Talmai, king of Geshur, a territory north of Ishbosheth's shaky realm. His fourth son was Adonijah, by his wife, Haggith. The fifth was Shephatiah, by his wife, Abital. The sixth son was Ithream, by his wife, Eglah.

Benaiah understood the custom of kings taking many wives for political reasons, but as the son of a priest, he knew that the people of Israel were not to be like the nations around them. Yahweh had warned them that, when they had a king, he was not to multiply horses or wives, or enrich himself with silver and gold.

Yet, David now had six wives, and even more concubines. Benaiah respected most everything David did, but this caused him some consternation. He saw the example of the patriarchs, Abraham and Jacob, who had children by more than one woman. It caused strife among the women and children, as the parents inevitably chose favorites. Surely it would not bode well for David when the time came when all these darling children were adults vying for his throne.

Benaiah couldn't imagine the strife in a house with more than one wife. He found it enough of a challenge to please one wife. But the thought of Mariah brought a smile to his face. Yes, he'd like this day to be over so he could hurry home to please her.

CHAPTER FIFTEEN

"Now it was so, while there was war between the house of Saul and the house of David, that Abner was strengthening his hold on the house of Saul."

—2 Samuel 3:6

The common room trembled with excitement when David was told that Abner and twenty of his men had requested an audience with him. David already knew what this meeting concerned, as Abner had sent messages beforehand, saying, "It's well known that the land of Israel is now yours to rule. Make a formal agreement with me and I'll use my influence to bring the rest of Israel under your leadership as well."

Although Israel consisted of twelve tribes, they seemed to distance themselves. The ten tribes in the north referred to themselves as Israel, while Judah and Benjamin in the south seemed to band together.

Would Abner really switch sides and now support David, or was it a trick? Saul's only surviving legitimate son, Ishbosheth, had given no indication that he would step down from the throne of Israel to make way for David.

Benaiah wondered what Abner's motivation could be. At present, Ishbosheth wasn't much more than a puppet king, while Abner, in control of the military, was the actual leader of Israel. He had installed Ishbosheth to power, transferring his support and allegiance to him rather than David immediately after Saul died. It made no sense for Abner to forsake that kind of power. What could he hope to gain? Did he expect to be the general over the territories now ruled by David as well? That must be it. But how would David's ambitious General Joab feel about that?

Benaiah was determined to be more vigilant in his protection of David. He respected Abner as a valiant warrior, but was wary of him because of his unwavering loyalty to the house of Saul in the past.

General Joab wasn't present when Abner met with David. Although Joab didn't seem to harbor ill feelings toward Abner for the recent murder of his brother Asahel, Benaiah still wondered. Joab didn't seem to be the forgiving sort, if Benaiah knew the man at all. It was prudent to be as wary of Joab as he was of Abner. He was ambitious and wily.

Abner arrived with his men and some representatives from Israel. The men were divested of their swords before they entered the common room, and Benaiah also ensured that there were three times as many guards on duty.

Abner had brought with him Saul's daughter, Michal, David's first wife. Saul had married her off to another man, even though she and David hadn't been divorced, to hurt David when he was on the run. Now, she was being returned as a sign of goodwill on Abner's part, for the covenant to which David had agreed included Michal's return.

David's message in response to Abner had read, "I will make a formal agreement with you as you suggested, on one condition. I will not meet with you in person unless you bring Saul's daughter, Michal, when you come."

It was now reported to David that she had come, but she didn't enter with Abner. She was taken directly to the Court of the Women. Benaiah wondered how David's first wife, a daughter of a king, would feel about being lumped into a community of wives and concubines and children, all vying for the king's attention and favor.

Benaiah also couldn't figure out David's request to get his wife back. Surely it was political, to demonstrate his power over the house of Saul, especially since he had demanded it of Ishbosheth, who obviously didn't have enough strength to refuse David. He may have loved Michal at the beginning, and would have remained true to her. Yet, now that she had lived with another man as his wife, it wouldn't have been right for David to take her back as a wife in every sense. Or would that even apply, since the marriage had been involuntary? Benaiah would have to ask Abiathar, the priest. How complicated these royal marriages were!

Benaiah heard that Michal's new husband, Paltiel, was heartbroken at having her torn from his side. He followed her along the way, weeping behind her. Abner finally had to be harsh with him and send him back home.

How willingly had Michal returned to David? Did she still love him, or had she already transferred her affections to her new husband? Would she resent David's other wives?

Ultimately, her feelings were of no concern. Women, even king's daughters, were still traded between kingdoms as kings saw fit. Benaiah was suddenly very happy to be a lowly guard and soldier with only one wife with whom to concern himself. He couldn't imagine Mariah being forced to marry someone she didn't love. An arranged marriage was so much better if there was mutual affection.

Abner bowed low when he approached David. "My lord."

Benaiah shifted his hand to the hilt of his sword as he gave a look of challenge to Abner.

Best to remind him to stay in line. While Benaiah decided to withhold his judgment of whether the man could be trusted until he had heard what he had to say, he would still be on guard. David's safety was his prime concern.

Following the formalities of treaties and covenants, David invited Abner and the elders of Israel to a feast. It was there that David asked Abner the reason he chose not to support Ishbosheth any longer.

"Abner, you've been faithful to Ishbosheth for two years, as you had been faithful to his father, Saul. All these years we've been enemies. Why come to me, and why come to me now?"

Abner signaled for his wine goblet to be refilled. Benaiah saw Joab's men lean closer to hear Abner's response.

"Do you recall a concubine of Saul's named Rizpah?" Abner asked David.

What did a royal concubine have to do with political loyalties? Benaiah didn't understand. Though, hearing the same name of his little sister, now a married woman, caused Benaiah to pause. He wouldn't wish that life on his sister. He couldn't imagine it would be an honor to be a concubine, even of a good king like David. They didn't have the status of a wife, had no marriage contract and no dowry.

But even though the patriarchs had concubines, and his king, David, whom he admired and respected, kept them, Benaiah knew that it was not God's intent. No. For his part, he was happy with the wife so perfectly suited to him. In Hebron, Mariah had given birth to their second son, whom they named Jehoiada, after his father, and a daughter, Maytal, which meant "dew drop."

Benaiah turned his attention back to the conversation between David and Abner.

David tilted his head to the side in thought. "The name sounds familiar. Yes, I think I remember her appearance." Benaiah surmised David probably thought it best not to comment about her appearance one way or another.

"Rizpah became mine," Abner said. He let David consider this for a moment. They would be living together without being married. But, more than that, David would understand what it meant politically to take the concubine of a king. Even if Ishbosheth would not have used her in that way, since she had been his father's concubine, it would be seen as an attempt at the throne. There may or may not have been feelings toward the woman, but Ishbosheth apparently felt threatened by the news and challenged Abner.

"He asked me, 'What makes you think you can take one of my father's concubines as your own?' He was mad, I tell you, just like his father. He thought I wanted his throne!" Abner huffed. "I have no such aspirations. I just wanted the woman, and I know she wanted me too. For years, I've seen the way she looked at me.

"But I was offended that he thought so little of me. I asked him, 'Am I so insignificant and loathsome to you? I've remained loyal to your father, Saul, to his relatives and associates, and to you as well, since you are the rightful heir. I haven't handed you over to David (which I could easily have done, I might have added), and you dare to find fault with me over an insignificant matter like this woman?' I was furious! He didn't appreciate that the only reason he was ruling in any capacity was solely due to me and my support."

"How did he respond to that?" David asked.

Abner laughed. "He seemed to shrink in his throne before my eyes. I said, 'I swear by God that I will help transfer the kingdom from the house of Saul to the house of David, and set up the throne of David over the entire country of Israel and Judah, from Dan in the north to Beersheeba in the south, for God has sworn this to him.' Then what more could he say? I knew he feared me. He knew I could do it, and there was not a thing he could do about it. I left right away, taking Rizpah with me, by the way, and met with the elders of Israel. They all agreed it was finally time for you to be king over all Israel.

"They agreed, acknowledging that, in the past, even when Saul was king, David was really the one who led Israel. They were also aware of God's promise that David would one day be the shepherd and ruler of God's people."

Benaiah smiled inwardly. He truly hoped Abner was sincere. There had been a few years of instability since Saul died. It would be wonderful to have the country ruled by one king. That king should be David! Could the day finally have arrived?

David clasped Abner on the shoulder, "May the Lord make it as you have said, my friend."

Abner stood to leave and promised, "I'll go back to gather the elders of Israel. Then we'll return and make a formal agreement with you to make your reign official."

"Go in peace," David said.

★ ★ ★

Benaiah was in the Guard House when Joab and David's servants returned with much spoil. Abner had already left Hebron in peace to make arrangements for David to take control of the whole country.

Some of the men were dividing the spoil, while others were oiling their leather shields or salting their helmets, when a man Benaiah remembered seeing at the feast told Joab, "You missed seeing your counterpart, General."

"Oh, who would that be?" Joab asked wryly.

"General Abner, son of Ner came, and enjoyed a sumptuous feast." The soldier dropped the news and stepped back, almost as if he knew what Joab's response would be.

"What?" Joab seethed.

"Abner said he defected from Ishbosheth over some woman. He came to the king to inform him that he would help transfer power to David. The king was pleased and sent him away to make it so."

Joab pressed his lips together and snorted through his nostrils. Through clenched teeth he said, "I'll bet David plans to make him head of the whole army as a reward."

"He didn't promise anything like that, but he did seem to trust Abner. What do you think?" Abishai asked his brother.

"What do I think? What do I think?" Joab spat out. "I think Abner can't help but be loyal to the house of Saul. He is spying on our weaknesses so that he and that puppet-boy of a king can rule the whole country, that's what I think!"

"Why would he do that when this way, there is a unified country with no more bloodshed between brothers?" Benaiah asked him.

Joab's face reddened. "You know nothing!" he shouted and then stomped off.

Benaiah followed Joab. He would have liked nothing more than to go home to his wife instead, but Joab was obviously headed to see David. As much as Benaiah knew David was well guarded in his absence, there were times when he didn't trust volatile General Joab, even if he was David's nephew.

Joab hardly waited to be announced before he marched up to David. He made some semblance at bowing, then launched his attack on David.

"What have you done?" he demanded.

David raised his eyebrows at Joab's disrespectful tone. "What does your question concern, nephew?"

"You know! Abner came to you. And you sent him away in peace, and he's already long gone!"

"Yes, he was here. What of it?" David said.

"Surely you must realize that Abner the son of Ner came here to deceive you. He is just spying out your weaknesses. He has no intention to actually hand the kingdom over to you. His loyalties will always be to the house of Saul."

David tilted his head and looked at Joab with what looked like pity.

"Joab," he said gently, "is it so strange to you that Yahweh would soften a man's heart, and order all these events to finally make me king over all Israel, as He promised?"

Joab had no answer. For David to be king over the whole country was something they had talked about for years. It was entirely possible that it was finally happening. But Joab didn't seem to like that it was Abner, and not himself, who would get the credit for it.

Joab stormed out of the room, barely bowing again.

CHAPTER SIXTEEN

"Now when Abner had returned to Hebron, Joab took him aside in the gate to speak with him privately, and there stabbed him in the stomach, so that he died for the blood of Asahel his brother."

—2 Samuel 3:27

David visited Michal in the women's apartments. Benaiah remained on guard outside the room, even though David left the door open. There was a long silence when he first entered the room and Benaiah imagined they just looked at each other after years apart.

"How are you?" Benaiah heard David finally ask.

"I am as well as can be expected, my lord," Michal answered softly.

"Michal, you know I didn't want it to be this way. I would've taken you with me, or come back for you, but your father..."

"I know," Michal answered quietly.

"Then he gave you to another, even while we were still married."

Her voice hardened. "Do not speak of it. I lived it."

"Michal, I can't promise you a relationship like we had in the past. Much has happened; much has changed."

"I know. You have other wives."

"Yes, I do. But your marriage—I can't pretend it didn't happen."

"I can't help that! It's not like my father asked me!" Michal shouted. Benaiah heard her begin to cry.

"Don't cry, love."

"How can you call me that? What am I to you now, David? I have the status of a wife, but not even the privileges of a concubine! I am nothing! At least with Paltiel, I knew I was loved!"

"Do not speak his name," David commanded harshly, but then added, "You are still the king's wife. You will be cared for."

Michal huffed. "I know I'm just here to demonstrate your power over the house of Saul and that pathetic brother of mine."

"Nevertheless, I am glad to have you back, Michal."

Silence.

"I'll give you some time to adjust, but then I want to see you daily at my table."

David was almost out the door when she called his name. He paused, but did not turn back to her. He was facing Benaiah when Michal insisted, "I will not live among these other women. Find me a more suitable place."

David pressed his lips together and loudly exhaled, but didn't respond.

Once they were out of the Court of the Women, David said to Benaiah, "That woman! I can't believe she can bring out so many different emotions in me in the space of a few moments! I missed her so much! I would have held her, as I wanted to do, but I know that wouldn't have been enough for either of us. Then she makes me so angry with her demands, reminding me she is the daughter of a king and therefore deserves special treatment!"

Benaiah wasn't sure if David expected a response. He had none to give. It was just as he suspected: life with more than one wife was bound to have conflict.

"What would you have us do, my lord?" Benaiah finally asked.

"Speak to Ahi, in charge of the Court of the Women. Allow Michal to redecorate her apartment, but she will not live separately from my other wives. She'll have to learn how to get along. We're a family."

★ ★ ★

Soon after David returned to the common room, a messenger arrived with urgent news.

"My lord, Abner, son of Ner—he is dead."

David sighed and rubbed his forehead. "Tell me."

"It was General Joab, my lord. He sent messages after Abner as soon as he left here, asking to meet with him at the city gate. Then he motioned for him to come aside privately. When he did, he stabbed Abner in the stomach. It was horrible. There was so much blood it even spilled over Joab's sandals."

David let out a heavy breath and shook his head in dismay. "Oh, Joab, what have you done?" He said it so quietly that only Benaiah heard him.

Then he stood and announced in a loud voice, "Before God I declare I and my kingdom are innocent of the blood of Abner, son of Ner."

David went further, pronouncing a curse on Joab. "Let the guilt of this crime be on the head of Joab and his father's house and all their descendants. May there always be illness, infirmity, tragedy and deprivation because he has done this thing."

Benaiah thought it was interesting that Joab's father's line was cursed and not his mother's, as that would include David himself in the curse, since Joab's mother was David's sister, Zeruiah.

It was just as Benaiah feared. When it seemed there might finally be peace in Israel with David as king, Joab took this opportunity to take vengeance on Abner for the death of his brother, Asahel. From what Benaiah understood of that unfortunate incident, Abner had killed him in self-defense during battle. Because of that, Joab could not even legally claim to be taking vengeance for the blood of this relative.

No, Joab was just acting out his rash and vindictive nature. Benaiah suspected Joab's murder of Abner was also motivated by his own aspirations of power. He saw Abner as a legitimate contender for the role of general once David was king, and he would not allow it.

Now the future was uncertain. Would the elders of Israel still want David to be king when their representative had been murdered? Would they even believe David's innocence in this matter?

David ordered a state funeral for Abner. He even demanded Joab make an appearance. "Tear your clothes," he ordered them, "and cover yourselves in sackcloth, and mourn for Abner."

Benaiah could see Joab reluctantly going through the ceremony of burial. He apparently had no tears to cry for Abner, unlike David, who followed the procession and wept. They buried Abner in Hebron. At the grave, David's voice rose higher than any other mourners, and all the people wept.

The king even sang a lament over Abner, as he had for Saul and Jonathan:

"Should Abner die as a fool dies?
Your hands were not bound,
nor your feet put in fetters;
As a man falls before wicked men, so you fell."[2]

Benaiah knew David's grief over Abner's death was genuine. But it was only after David refused to eat until after the sun set that the people were finally convinced that he had no part in Abner's murder.

"Today a great prince of a man has fallen in Israel!" David exclaimed before his servants. Benaiah concurred. He had great respect for Abner as a soldier—as a faithful servant and great military leader—even though his loyalties were on the wrong side of the conflict for most of his life. Joab was probably right in fearing that David would set Abner over the whole army of Israel. Abner deserved the position.

"This act has weakened my throne because these men—"he motioned toward Joab and Abishai, but couldn't bring himself to even say their names—"the sons of Zeruiah, are too ruthless for my liking. But I know the Lord will repay wicked men accordingly."

Benaiah wondered at David's inaction to Joab's murder of Abner. Although he denounced the crime, pronounced a guilty verdict on Joab, uttered curses against him and his father's descendants, and separated himself from the crime politically, he failed to punish Joab directly and decisively. He was leaving it to the Lord to repay him, when it was David's responsibility as king to see that justice was done.

Benaiah speculated that the reason for his hesitation to act against Joab was related to Joab's considerable power and reputation in Israel, as well as their familial relationship. But he couldn't help but wonder: would this failure to rein in Joab one day rebound to hurt David's future?

CHAPTER SEVENTEEN

"Now David said, 'Whoever attacks the Jebusites first shall be chief and captain.'
And Joab the son of Zeruiah went up first, and became chief. Then David dwelt
in the stronghold; therefore they called it the City of David."
—1 Chronicles 11:6–7

Nathan, the prophet, was summoned. Benaiah wondered what concerns the king would have that the prophet could help him with.

Nathan entered the dining hall. The man was in his forties, with a full beard and piercing eyes that took in the room. He carried himself with confidence.

"What is troubling you, my lord?" he asked gently.

David's brows furrowed. "Since the Lord established my throne over all Israel and has given me rest from my enemies, I need to consider my dwelling place."

"What of it, my lord?"

"I look around at this opulent palace lined with cedar walls and then I think of the ark of God. It's still inside tent curtains. That does not seem right. I think it's time we had a permanent place of worship."

Benaiah agreed. It had been that way since their sojourn in the wilderness when the children of Israel came up out of Egypt. A proper temple would speak of permanence and better reflect the glory of their great God.

Nathan seemed to consider this briefly, then said, "I'm sure if God has put the idea in your mind, it must be what He desires, since He is with you."

David smiled. "Thank you, my friend. I will begin the designs today."

Nathan bowed before the king and left.

David commanded Shemaiah, the scribe, to come and record his ideas. "I want to use only the best cedars, those from Lebanon. Write letters to King Hiram, asking how many he can provide for us and at what cost."

The scribe dutifully recorded that and David's other instructions. After several hours of dictation, a servant entered and announced, "Nathan the prophet has returned, my lord."

Nathan appeared at the entrance to the common room, wringing his hands.

"What is it, my friend?" David asked. "You seem distressed."

"I spoke before I consulted with the Lord. He sent me back to give you this message: Thus says the Lord to His servant David."

At that, David immediately fell to the floor, prostrate as he heard the pronouncement through the prophet. Shemaiah put his reed pen to the papyrus, awaiting the prophet's words.

"Would you build a house for Me to live in? I haven't lived in a house since I brought the children of Israel out of Egypt. My dwelling has always been the tabernacle. In all the time I moved about with them, have I ever asked anyone from any tribe to build Me a house of cedar?'"

Benaiah also bowed to the ground, amazed at hearing the words of God directly. The Lord was surely with David, as he had been with the patriarchs, and here he was, privileged to witness it.

Nathan continued relaying God's words for David. "I took you from tending sheep to tending my people, Israel. I've been with you wherever you went and have defeated your enemies. I've made your name great among the nations."

How true. The blessing of God on David, and through him to the nation, was evident. "In time, I will appoint a place of their own, and plant them there, so they won't have to move anymore. Nor will they be oppressed as they were during the times of the judges. I have brought you to this time of rest, and I will build you a house."

This confirmed how the family of David had been chosen by God to be the kind of leaders Israel needed.

"When your time has come to rest as your fathers did, I will set up your seed after you, and I will establish his kingdom. He will be the one to build My house, and I'll establish his kingdom forever. I'll be His Father, and he'll be My son. If he sins, I'll chasten him by the hand of his neighbors. But My mercy will not leave him, as I took it from Saul. Your house and kingdom will be established forever."

Such lofty promises! Someone from David's family would sit on the throne of Israel forever? Such a person could only be the Messiah!

Nathan left as quietly as he had arrived. For several moments, David remained prostrate on the floor. Then he rose slowly, as if weighed down by the words pronounced over him.

Benaiah helped David to his feet.

Almost in a daze, David announced, "I must go to the tabernacle."

Benaiah and Shemaiah followed him there and stood at a distance while David sat in the courtyard before the Lord near the altar of sacrifice. It was not usual to sit while praying, but this was not a usual day!

"Who am I, oh God, and what is my family that You've brought me this far?" David cried out.

Benaiah felt as if he were intruding on holiness itself as he witnessed the intimacy of the shepherd-king with his God. But his job was to stay by David's side at all times. He would guard David, even here, where there was an expectation of safety.

"You've given me such promises to generations of my family, and spoken of me as if I'm a man of importance. I don't know what to say, but then, You know me. You've not only done all these things, but You've let me know about them in advance. You are a great God and there is no one like You."

Benaiah shooed away several priests who entered the courtyard.

"Who is like Your people, Israel, the one nation whom God set out to redeem for Himself, in order to make His name great. You redeemed Your people from Egypt and their gods. You've made us Your very own people, and You've become our God."

Benaiah closed his eyes and raised his hands toward heaven, agreeing in his heart with all that David said.

"Now, Lord God, do as You've said, and establish the house of David. Magnify Your name forever."

"Amen," Benaiah agreed.

After David finished praying, he and Benaiah remained there for some time, basking in the peace of the experience.

Benaiah had never seen David so humble before God, and he felt an even greater respect and love toward his friend and king.

Surprisingly, Benaiah felt even more drained by this experience than when he fought against the lion in a pit on a snowy day. He had heard the very words of God! Even if he had become a priest, Benaiah knew he would never have experienced God the way he had this day.

* * *

A commotion at the door of the common room drew Benaiah's attention away from the business of the day. There were at least a dozen cases per day from the people that required David's judgment. The two guards posted at the door glanced at one another, as if unsure what to do.

"We must see the king!" two burly men demanded.

Rarely did anyone demand an audience with King David, but the gift the men brought caused such consternation. They carried a human head between them, dangling it by the hair, the poor man's facial features frozen in fear.

David nodded his approval and the guards allowed the men to enter. A servant shared whispers between them and then announced them as Rechab and Baanah, sons of Rimmon the Beerothite, of the tribe of Benjamin. Benjamin was King Saul's tribe.

They approached the throne where David sat and bowed low to the ground. The gruesome trophy between them thumped on the floor, evoking gasps of shock and disgust from those in the common room. The few women present turned their heads away in horror.

"My lord King David, we are captains of the troops of Ishbosheth, son of Saul. We went to his house in the middle of the day on a pretense of needing supplies. We entered his bedchamber, stabbed him and then beheaded him. Then we escaped and ran throughout the plains all night to come and inform you." Rechab recounted the event in almost one long breath, as though still winded from his journey.

Baanah raised the gory prize for David to appreciate. "Here is the head of Ishbosheth, the son of Saul your enemy, who sought your life. You are now avenged of Saul and his descendants."

Even without a glance at the king, Benaiah knew what David's response would be. He'd spared Saul twice, grieved the king's death, executed the man who claimed to kill him and mourned the deaths of Saul's sons and Abner, Saul's general. David would certainly not praise these men for their treachery. David had made a covenant with Saul and Jonathan, promising he would not execute Saul's descendants when he rose to power.

People would naturally assume David was behind the murder of Ishbosheth. They'd believe he was removing any rivals to the throne of Israel, especially since the killers had made a show of bringing his head to David as a prize, as if he required proof the deed had been done as he'd ordered.

"I swear," David said through clenched teeth, "when someone came and reported that Saul was dead, assuming I'd think it was good news, I had him executed in Ziklag."

Color drained from the men's faces. Baanah released Ishbosheth's head and let it fall to the ground with a wet *thud*. It rolled and glared up at him with open eyes and large, fixed pupils.

"How much worse," David continued, "when wicked men have killed an innocent man in his own house on his bed? His blood is required of you, and you will be removed from the earth!"

Before the sons of Rimmon could protest or beg for their lives, two soldiers seized them, secured their arms behind them, and forced them to their knees. When David nodded to Benaiah, he unsheathed his sword and struck them down with two smooth strokes. The bodies were quickly dragged out of the room, blood trailing behind them.

Servants scurried to remove the evidence of the encounter. When one came to Ishbosheth's head on the floor, he looked to David. "What would you have us do with this, my lord?"

"Bury it in the tomb of Abner in Hebron."

David ran his hand over his mouth and beard and rose. "I need tell Michal about her brother before she hears it from someone else," he whispered so quietly no one but Benaiah could hear.

Benaiah did not envy David that task, especially since their first conversation went so poorly. Would she believe David innocent in her brother's assassination?

★ ★ ★

"How was your day, my love?" Mariah asked as she greeted him at the door.

"The usual." Benaiah removed his sword and placed it on the wall hooks, then picked up little Maytal, kissed her chubby cheek and deposited her back on the reed mat to play.

"How can you say that?" Mariah huffed. "I saw the gruesome bodies hanging by the pool in the center of town, with their hands and feet cut off. Everyone is talking about how these men brought the head of Ishbosheth before David and he had them executed for it."

"If you already know, then I don't need to tell you the details. Where are the boys?"

"They're next door." She followed him to the cooking room, where he took several dates to snack on. "Were you there?"

"Of course. If David is involved, I am as well."

"So were you the one who... killed them?"

"Mariah, I am the executioner. If David gives the order to execute someone, I do it. Then they were publicly displayed to show David's displeasure at the assassination of the prince."

Mariah ladled stew into bowls and placed them on the table. "I don't know how you can bear so much killing. I mean, I know you've killed soldiers in battle, but to take the life of someone who isn't fighting you back doesn't seem fair."

Benaiah took his wife's small hands in his rough, calloused ones. "The fairness of it is not my decision. That responsibility rests with David. Most kings would remove any rivals to the throne and think nothing of it. People wouldn't be surprised if he'd taken revenge on the family of Saul for all the years of trouble he caused, but David didn't. These men confessed, even bragged about their crime in front of witnesses. Executing them was the only thing David could do."

Mariah studied her husband for a moment. "I hadn't thought of that."

Benaiah continued, "He needed to send a strong message to Israel that he wasn't a part of the assassination of Ishbosheth. Israel is still reeling from Abner's recent death, and there are some who still believe David had a hand in it."

Mariah nodded. "It's easier to follow orders when you agree with what he's decided, isn't it?"

That much was true. "Yes. But I respect David. He has proven himself time and again to be the kind of leader our nation needs. He hasn't always done things the way I would have, but Yahweh has honored his obedience. In the same way, I have to obey him. I am his servant. When I do my job well, and obey without questioning, I am serving God as well."

Mariah smiled. "Okay. No more questions. Kiss your wife and call the children for dinner." She winked.

Benaiah sat down and pulled his wife onto his lap. "Now, that's an order I'll happily obey."

★ ★ ★

Ahithophel, David's chief counselor, was summoned to the common room in Hebron to consult with David about matters of state. Benaiah knew David respected the elder man's knowledge and wisdom. He had even said that Ahithophel's advice was as sound as if one had inquired at the oracle of God. He was father to Eliam, who was also one of the mighty men, the thirty soldiers David chose while still on the run from Saul to carry out particular missions. As one of the mighty men himself, Benaiah was in a trusted position to hear about the affairs of the kingdom.

Now that it was determined that Israel and Judah would be united under King David, they needed to discuss the choice of a new capital city.

"To remain in Hebron won't do," Ahithophel stated, as he stood before the king. "Neither will the northern capital of Samaria. Choosing one city over another will upset the image of unity between Judah and Israel that you want to project. There should be no hint of favoritism in either direction."

"What do you suggest?" David asked.

"Perhaps a new capital, one that demonstrates a new beginning, your continuing conquest of the land and defeat of our enemies. Jerusalem would be a fine capital, my lord."

David stroked his beard as he considered it. "The fortress of the Jebusites is highly fortified. No nation has been able to take it because of its great walls and its deep cisterns, which give its citizens the ability to withstand a long siege."

"Perhaps you could present it as a challenge to the military," Ahithophel suggested. "Whoever takes Jerusalem could be commander of the host of the armies of a united Israel."

"I know a certain ambitious general who would pounce on the chance to redeem himself in my eyes," David surmised.

Benaiah had no doubt that Joab would attempt the mission. He was brave, and his ambition was greater still. Joab also knew David had not yet forgiven him for Abner's murder, but the capture of this city would surely please the king.

"Very well, then. I will bring this before the Lord."

Benaiah had no doubt that the city of Jerusalem could eventually be conquered, since the Lord was with them, but would such a conquest be enough to restore David's trust in Joab?

CHAPTER EIGHTEEN

"Jehoiada, the leader of the Aaronites, and with him three thousand seven hundred..."

—1 Chronicles 12:27

Benaiah burst through the door and swept Mariah into an embrace. She giggled even as she protested. "What makes you so joyful today, Husband?"

Benaiah lowered Mariah to the floor and kissed her. "As of today I am David's chief bodyguard!"

Mariah smiled widely. "I'm so happy for you! This is what you've always wanted."

"I suppose it was, before I even knew it."

"But you've been protecting David for years now."

"Yes, he just made it official."

"What will your duties be?"

"I'll help train and organize the new soldiers, under General Joab, of course. I'll continue to be by David's side most days, but I probably won't go out to battle anymore, unless David is going. But now that he's established as the king over all Israel, it's less likely he'll go out to fight. He's too valuable to the nation. Besides, Joab will be anxious to prove himself."

"Is he a good general?"

"I have a lot of respect for him. He didn't get the position just because he's the son of David's sister, Zeruiah. He earned it by taking the stronghold of Jebus, which everyone thought was impossible. So we'll be moving to Jerusalem soon."

Mariah hugged Benaiah again. "I'm so pleased, although I did like it here in Hebron. The children and I will see much more of you. I won't worry so much, and you can watch your children grow up. All four of them." Her cheeks flushed.

"Four?"

Mariah nodded. "I'm expecting again!"

Benaiah spun her around "This is certainly a day of good news!"

"Perhaps this one will be another little girl," Mariah said hopefully, protectively stroking her lower abdomen.

"Then it's a good thing I'm trained to repel unwanted visitors. I'll need to keep the boys away from our precious daughters."

★ ★ ★

Benaiah reveled in the new peace in the land. Word spread all the way from Dan to Beersheba about the deaths of Saul and his sons in battle, as well as the murders of General Abner and Prince Ishbosheth. The men of Israel were finally convinced that David had no part in either General Abner's and Prince Ishbosheth's deaths, and they were eager to see the country finally united under a new king.

As David's coronation day over all Israel drew near, a steady stream of people poured into their new capital city, Jerusalem. David took the fortified stronghold and renamed it the City of David. He ordered enough food to be prepared for three days of festivities. Yet, the guests brought more. Even those from as far away as Issachar and Zebulun and Naphtali led donkeys and camels, mules and oxen, laden with provisions of flour, cakes of figs and raisins, wine and oil. They also brought an abundance of oxen and sheep. Benaiah couldn't imagine how Jehoshaphat, son of Ahilud, the recorder and main palace administrator, managed such details, but he surmised the man had gifts Benaiah did not possess.

Shemaiah the scribe entered the common room to report the numbers of those who were arriving to turn the kingdom of Saul over to David. He unrolled a scroll, cleared his throat, and read, "From the tribe of Judah, the soldiers number six thousand, eight hundred. Of the tribe of Simeon, seven thousand, one hundred mighty men of valor."

Benaiah wondered how the influx of soldiers into David's army would be housed and organized. He would be helping the new General, Joab, who had indeed managed to take the fortress of Jerusalem by climbing up through the water shaft into the city. It was quite ingenious of him, Benaiah had to admit.

Shemaiah continued reading his list. "Of the sons of Levi, four thousand six hundred. Jehoiada, the leader of the Aaronites, and with him three thousand seven hundred priests."

Benaiah's mouth fell open. His father was here in Jerusalem? Benaiah couldn't have been more proud of him for convincing such a great number of priests to show their support for the new king. He must recognize the rightness of David's rule. These were truly glory days.

David held up a hand for Shemaiah to pause, then turned to Benaiah. "Is this your famous father, Benaiah?"

"It is indeed."

"I should very much like to meet him." He nodded to Shemaiah to continue.

Even many Benjamites, relatives of Saul, had chosen to submit to David's rule. These soldiers, who had trained and fought under the leadership of Abner, were dependable, stouthearted men of valor. Skilled with all weapons of war, they knew how to keep battle formation. It would be a pleasure to lead such men.

The sons of the tribe of Issachar were unique in their ability to understand the times and to counsel David. They had two hundred chiefs who were skillful leaders.

So many famous men from prominent tribes had come, all here to proclaim David as king!

When Benaiah first heard that Saul's kingdom would be given to another, many years ago, he assumed it would fall to Prince Jonathan. How like God to do the unexpected and instead take the youngest son of an obscure family. After all, He took David from shepherding sheep to leading people. God had led him from life as a fugitive in the wilderness to a stone palace in the new capital of Jerusalem, where David had the support of the whole country and the blessing of God on his reign.

Benaiah thanked God for placing him with the king at such a glorious time in the life of the nation.

★ ★ ★

The moment Benaiah saw his father in the courtyard of the family home, he rushed toward him and drew him into a long embrace. When had Jehoiada become so thin? His shoulders poked through his skin, his beard had gone completely gray and the furrows on his forehead had deepened, but his eyes still twinkled with the thrill of adventure.

To think Benaiah had once considered his father less of a man because he was a priest rather than a soldier. Jehoiada was one of the wisest, bravest men he had ever known.

"Abba. It's so good to see you." Benaiah remembered when he considered himself too mature to refer to his father as Abba. Now it seemed natural. "How are Ima, Shallum, Rizpah, Jael and Yemima and their families?"

"They're all well. Your Ima would have come to meet you, but she's helping Rizpah with her new baby."

Benaiah shook his head in disbelief. "I still see her as a little girl with pigtails, not as a wife and mother."

"We're all getting older, Son. Look at you. Is that gray I see in your beard?"

Benaiah stroked his chin and grimaced. "I blame the children. I tell them I never had gray hair until they came along."

Jehoiada laughed. "That much is true. Mariah must be happy about settling into a home after those early years on the run from Saul."

"Oh, yes. We did live in homes in Philistia and even Hebron, but that's not the same as being here in Jerusalem." He gazed at his wife, playing with the children in the courtyard of their new home in Jerusalem. Benaiah felt such contentment about so much in his life, yet he needed to talk to his father.

"Let's take a short walk before our evening meal. There's so much to tell you."

As they skirted children playing in the streets, Benaiah said, "I'm so pleased that the priesthood is supportive of David's claim to the throne of Israel."

"I believe that David is the rightful king of Israel. More than once I considered packing up the family and joining you in the stronghold, as you tried to convince me." Jehoiada chuckled. "Can you imagine your mother living such a life?"

Benaiah could not see his mother in any environment she couldn't control. "It was probably best to remain in Kabzeel until the political situation stabilized."

"When we heard of Ishbosheth's assassination and the murder of Abner by General Joab, some of the priests thought David a ruthless man, attempting to grab the throne by whatever means possible, but I suspected he was blameless." A smile tugged at his lips. "I see now that you were right in following Yahweh's lead to the life of a soldier."

Benaiah never thought he'd hear these words from his father. He swallowed the lump in his throat.

"Thank you, Abba. I know you expected me to become a priest, especially after..." Why was it so difficult to speak of his brother after all these years?

Jehoiada laid a hand on Benaiah's arm. "Do not trouble yourself, Son. We still think of him every day, of course, but we know it was the Lord's will to take Ammizabad at a young age. And Shallum, as firstborn, was consecrated to the Lord as priest. As for why your brother died when and how he did, we cannot choose to believe only the aspects of God's sovereignty that suit us. He is either sovereign over all or He is not sovereign at all."

Benaiah thought on his father's words. He supposed it was true that sovereignty could not have degrees, else it would cease to be sovereignty.

"I have tried to live by the words you said to me: 'To obey is better than sacrifice.' I try to be David's most obedient soldier."

"And I am proud of you, Son. So is your mother, though she worries over you, even though you are grown and with a family of your own. You're never far from her thoughts and prayers."

Benaiah's heart swelled at Jehoiada's words. "Thank you for that encouragement. Oh, and the king said he'd like to meet you."

"That would be quite an honor."

He embraced his father again.

"Don't crush me, Son." Jehoiada's eyes glinted with humor.

"Let's get back home. Like Ima, Mariah likes her hot food served hot."

"Well, then, let's not disappoint her."

CHAPTER NINETEEN

"'As for Mephibosheth,' said the king, 'he shall eat at my table like one of the king's sons.'"

—2 Samuel 9:11

The business of the day was completed in the common room. Benaiah commented that there were no more cases for David to judge. David slowly turned his head to Benaiah, as if just hearing him for the first time.

"I'm sorry, Benaiah. I'm a little distracted. What did you say?"

"I said we're through for today, and wondered if you had anything particular in mind." David usually visited the Court of the Women to see his now extensive family after business was completed.

"As a matter of fact, I was remembering my dear friend, Jonathan, just now. I wonder, is there anyone left of the house of Saul that I can show kindness to, for Jonathan's sake?"

In Benaiah's mind, it had been a great kindness to the house of Saul to not execute the whole family when he became king. David would have been content to rule, even knowing Saul's sons, like Ishbosheth, were still alive, since he was sure God had placed him on the throne and it would be secure in spite of them. But then those two scoundrels had assassinated the prince. David was under no obligation to see to the welfare of any rivals to the throne. However, his benevolent character no longer came as a surprise to Benaiah. On days like today, he admired his king more than ever.

Shemaiah the scribe stepped forward. "I am not aware of anyone, my lord. However, you might inquire of Ziba, a servant of the house of Saul. I saw him here in the city just today."

"Bring him to me," David ordered.

Shemaiah bowed and left the room to obey. Soon after, Shemaiah returned, a middle-aged man with him. The man was in his fifth decade, short in stature, with a pronounced nose. His dark brown hair and beard were well trimmed and he dressed in the tunic of a steward or other head servant.

"Are you Ziba?" David asked.

"At your service," he answered with a low bow.

"Tell me. Is there someone of the house of Saul to whom I may show the kindness of God?"

Ziba's eyes flickered with fear. Benaiah wondered if the man was wavering about telling the truth. Did Ziba fear for his own life if he was associated with David's former rival?

"There is a son of Jonathan. His name is Mephibosheth, but he is lame in his feet, sire."

Did the servant assume David wouldn't want a crippled man hobbling through the palace? Ziba didn't know David like Benaiah did.

However, although lame, this man could still pose a threat to David's personal safety. David might let down his guard around such a man, but Benaiah would be vigilant. The king's safety was his primary responsibility.

David sat up straighter. "Where is he?"

"He is staying in the house of Machir in Lo-debar."

David nodded to Benaiah, who dispatched two Pelethite couriers to summon Mephibosheth to the palace.

As Ziba turned to leave, Benaiah excused himself from David's presence and followed him. Halfway down the hall, Benaiah stepped up beside the man. "I need to ask you some questions about this grandson of Saul's."

He squinted at Benaiah. Was he wary for his own sake, or for Mephibosheth? Benaiah wondered. "What do you wish to know?"

"Whatever you can tell me. For example, why is he staying in such a remote place as Lo-debar?"

"He has been in hiding ever since Saul and his father were killed in battle. When he heard that his uncle Ishbosheth was murdered in his bed, he feared vengeance from David on himself as well."

"The king had nothing to do with that!" Benaiah protested.

"Perhaps. Perhaps not." Ziba eyed Benaiah as if testing the truth of his words. "But Mephibosheth isn't taking any chances. He has lived a life of obscurity, even though he is the grandson of the first king of Israel. He hasn't even worked the land he inherited from his forefathers for fear of discovery."

Benaiah didn't appreciate the man's obvious admiration of Saul. Did he not know the man's legacy?

Benaiah crossed his arms and widened his stance, hoping to intimidate the man. "How is it that he became lame?"

"He was five years old when the news came from Jezreel that Saul and his sons were killed in battle. His nurse feared for his life, and as they were fleeing away quickly, he fell and twisted his leg."

Benaiah concluded that perhaps this Mephibosheth wasn't a threat to David after all. If he had been considering an attempt at the throne, or at David's life, would he not have done so by now?

"Thank you. You may go."

Ziba seemed to slink away, casting furtive glances at Benaiah over his shoulder just before he disappeared around a corner.

Benaiah wondered at Ziba's loyalty to his former master's house if he would give up Mephibosheth so easily. Could he be trusted?

* * *

"Mephibosheth, the son of Jonathan, has arrived, my lord," a servant announced. "Along with Ziba, servant of the house of Saul," he added.

David showed no emotion as he watched Mephibosheth approach, while Ziba remained by the large wooden door, but he studied his features as if searching for a family resemblance to his dear friend.

Benaiah's hand went to the hilt of his sword should David require protection against this potential enemy.

A thin, young man hobbled forward, leaning heavily on a hand carved walking stick. A few feet from the throne, he tossed it aside and fell prostrate before the king, his body trembling, no doubt expecting a sword to his neck.

Benaiah kept a wary eye on this descendant of Saul, in spite of his apparent weakness and humility. After all, every child in Israel heard the story of how left-handed Ehud fooled King Eglon of Moab by hiding a sword on his right thigh under his cloaks, only to murder him. Benaiah would not be caught unawares.

David leaned forward and said softly, "Mephibosheth?"

Without looking up, the crippled man answered, "Here is your servant."

David smiled reassuringly. "Don't be afraid. I will treat you kindly because of your father. Jonathan was my dear friend."

Mephibosheth stopped shaking. He dared to raise his head and look at the king.

"And I'll restore all the land that belonged to your grandfather Saul, to you."

Benaiah had grown accustomed to David extending grace and mercy, but this, to give an inheritance to the previous king's only living heir? Astonishing.

Mephibosheth rose to his feet, amazement on his features.

"And you will eat bread at my table every day... like one of my sons."

Benaiah could hardly believe it. A grant of property far from the king was one thing, but to allow him so close to the king on a daily basis meant he trusted him. It was as if the king was adopting Jonathan's son as his own.

Mephibosheth bowed low. "But I'm just a dead dog. Why should the king show such kindness to me?"

A dead dog. Exactly what David had called himself back when he appealed to Saul when he stepped out of the cave they were hiding in to confess he had cut off the king's robe.

"You have a family, I presume?"

"I do, my lord. My wife and I have three sons and one daughter."

"Ziba." David raised his gaze to the back of the room where Ziba stood.

Ziba scurried to Mephibosheth's side and bowed low. "My lord."

"How many sons do you have?" David asked.

Ziba's back straightened with pride. "I have fifteen sons and twenty servants, my lord."

"You and your sons and your servants will work the land for Mephibosheth. And you will bring in the harvest so that your master's children have food to eat."

What a joy to serve such a benevolent, gracious king!

Ziba bowed low. Benaiah felt Ziba overdid it with his fawning and simpering before the king. "I will do all that my lord the king has commanded."

★ ★ ★

As Benaiah walked home, he felt a sudden lightness at his waist. At the same time he heard his club clatter on the stone road and roll away from him with the natural incline of the road.

He'd known this would happen someday. After all these years, the blue-and-white-striped sling at his waist had tattered and frayed to the point that it could no longer support the heavy club.

Benaiah fingered the torn fabric at his waist. In an instant he was a young boy again, begging God to not let Ammizabad die, promising to be a better protector for his brother.

After so much time passed, through many battles, the sling had reminded him that obedience was better than sacrifice. But even the leather reinforcements Mariah had added over the years couldn't forestall this day forever.

With a sigh, Benaiah picked up his club.

When he got home, his children ran to him, arms outstretched.

"Abba!" little Maytal cried.

All he wanted was to be alone with his thoughts. "Wait until I put my weapons away, dewdrop. Then I'll play with you." The words came out more sharply than he'd intended.

Mariah's puzzled look followed him out of the room.

He placed his club and sword on a high shelf in the sleeping room, out of reach of the children. He turned to see Mariah standing in the doorway.

"What's wrong, Benaiah? You never pass by the children or me without a greeting. What happened today?"

He lifted the tattered piece of cloth dangling from his waist.

Mariah's hand covered her mouth. "Oh, Benaiah!" She flew into his arms. "I'm so sorry. I know how much that meant to you."

Unbidden, tears fell from his eyes. Crying over a piece of ripped cloth was silly. Especially for a valiant warrior such as himself.

Yet, he wept harder than he ever had, even when Ammizabad died. His grief went deeper now than when he was a young boy. His inability to protect the cloth sling reminded him of his failure to protect his brother.

Mariah held him and stroked his back, soothing him with soft words he couldn't hear above his sobs.

When he ran out of tears, Mariah said, "I could try to repair it again if you'd like."

Benaiah shook his head. "No. No more."

Mariah's eyes held questions.

"I've been holding on to it, thinking it was the only way I'd remember my brother... and the cost of disobedience, but it became an idol to me."

Mariah pulled back sharply and looked up into his face. "Surely not!"

"In a sense, yes. I was afraid of making the same mistake again." Benaiah wiped at his tears with the back of his hand. "But I will never forget Ammizabad, or the lesson I learned that day." He separated the remaining remnants of the fabric from his waist. "I'm ready to let it go."

Mariah laid a hand gently across Benaiah's face. "I love you so much." She kissed him. "Come out whenever you're ready."

Benaiah squeezed the fabric tightly in his hands. Then, as if in a final good-bye, he tossed it into the woodpile to be burned.

CHAPTER TWENTY

*"It happened one evening that David arose from his bed and walked on the roof
of the king's house. And from the roof he saw a woman bathing, and the woman
was very beautiful to behold."*

—2 Samuel 11:2

B enaiah stood at his post by the door and watched King David pace in his
chambers. Occasionally he would sit, try to read a scroll of plans for the
temple, then roll it up, eat some fruit, unroll another scroll, look out the window,
and then return to pacing.

Spring was the time when kings typically went to battle. But a month ago,
David had sent his troops to fight the people of Ammon under the leadership of
General Joab, besieging the capital city of Rabbah and leaving Benaiah to guard
his restive king rather than fight alongside his fellow soldiers.

"Would you like one of your instruments, sire? Or shall I summon one of
your wives or concubines?" Anything to divert the king's restless energy into a
meaningful use of his time.

David stopped pacing to answer him. "No. I've been trying to work on these
plans for the temple, but my heart is not in it tonight." David screwed up his face.
"Perhaps some fresh air would help clear my mind."

Benaiah opened the heavy wooden door and followed David up the stone
stairs to the roof of the palace. In the spring, and sometimes throughout the fall,
when the nights were especially warm, the king would occasionally sleep on the
roof of the palace in an elaborately decorated tent. He would also conduct some
of his meetings with the political, religious or military leadership of Israel in an
adjacent tent. The sun was low in the horizon, the air was still, and the sounds of
commerce in the city were dying down. Benaiah remained near the door while
David walked the length of the roof, stretching his arms and taking deep breaths.

David stopped and gazed over the west side, which overlooked Jerusalem, the city he loved.

Benaiah wondered if the king regretted staying home while Joab and his army were off fighting the Ammonites. Did he miss the glory days, when he led troops out to battle and returned victorious? Benaiah had mixed feelings. Sure, he was home more with his growing family, and he was in no danger, but he was a soldier in his deepest being. Even when they were on the run from King Saul, they had a purpose.

"Benaiah, come here quickly," David called from the edge of the parapet.

Benaiah was by his side in an instant. "Yes, my lord?"

David pointed to a house below. "Who is that woman?"

Benaiah followed David's lingering gaze to the flat rooftop of a house, where a woman was just stepping out of her bath. Her servant adjusted a sash around her tunic. He couldn't see the woman's face, but he knew her from his many visits to that house with Mariah.

Benaiah recognized the look of desire in David's eyes. He had obviously been staring long before Benaiah saw her with the sash and tunic. It was best to set him straight.

"That is Bathsheba. The daughter of Eliam, the wife of your servant Uriah the Hittite." Benaiah expected to see a look of disappointment in David's eyes when he realized that this woman's father and husband were two of his elite mighty men. But David continued to stare at the rooftop, even after she stepped out of view, as if trying to will her to reappear.

David turned to Benaiah. "Get her for me."

"Excuse me?"

"I'll be in the tent." Without meeting Benaiah's eyes, David flung back a length of tapestried door, strode inside and let the heavy curtain fall back in place.

Benaiah stood motionless, trying to understand what he had just been asked—no, commanded—to do. Benaiah had always obeyed David's commands, following him into fierce battles without hesitation. But having seen the hunger in David's eyes, Benaiah knew the king intended to act on his desire, in spite of her married status.

With leaden feet, Benaiah made his way down the steps and out of the palace. Even without the blue-and-white cloth holding his club in place, he knew he had to obey. He had learned his lesson. Disobedience always led to disastrous consequences.

As chief bodyguard of the king, his job was to do whatever the king asked.

But who would protect the king from himself?

Benaiah ordered another soldier to take his place guarding the king on the rooftop. Then he went to Bathsheba's home. He knocked on the familiar wooden door.

"Who's there?" Bathsheba's servant asked. She opened the door just enough to peer out. Recognition lit her eyes. She opened the door wider, then looked beyond him as if Mariah should be with him.

"I need to speak to your mistress."

His tone must have conveyed urgency, for she turned as she said, "I'll go get her. Come in."

Benaiah stepped into the courtyard of the traditional house, but remained at attention near the door. Such different circumstances for his visit this time.

Bathsheba appeared, her long brown hair still slightly damp, a simple blue gown on her body. "Benaiah! What a surprise. Is Mariah with you?"

"No. This is not a social call. It is a summons from the palace. You are to come with me at once."

Bathsheba looked up at Benaiah with an ache in her eyes. "Is it news of Uriah? Or my father?"

It hadn't even crossed Benaiah's mind that she would think that. But of course she would. Her husband and father were both at war with the people of Ammon, fighting David's battles with the armies of Israel. "No, it's not that."

"Did Grandfather summon me, then?"

Ahithophel, David's chief counselor, was the only person other than himself whom Bathsheba knew from the palace.

"No, not your grandfather. The king wishes to see you." As if he hadn't seen enough of her already. Too much, in fact.

Bathsheba stared. "Why would the king summon me? I didn't think he even knew my name."

He knew now. Benaiah himself had told him.

"Please hurry."

Bathsheba glanced down at her dress. "Please give me a moment to make myself presentable."

"All right," Benaiah conceded, though he knew David wouldn't care what she wore. "But please make it quick."

"Ashima, come help me," Bathsheba said, and the women hurried out of the room.

This was extremely discomforting. Bathsheba would want to look her best for the king, but David already knew what was hiding under her clothes. Benaiah did his best not to think about it.

Bathsheba returned, a new cream-colored gown on, with a light blue veil over her freshly braided brown hair. "I shouldn't be long, Ashima."

"I'll wait for you, mistress," Ashima said as she closed the door behind them.

As Benaiah and Bathsheba stepped out into the warm evening, she asked, "Have you heard any news from Joab about the battle?"

"No." Benaiah did not want to have a conversation right now. He didn't want to be reminded about the circumstances that led to this assignment.

"Do you know why the king wants to see me? Perhaps he has heard something about Uriah or Father that you haven't."

"I assure you, it's nothing like that."

She touched Benaiah's arm to stop him. "What, then?"

"I don't know," he lied.

As they entered the palace, Bathsheba continued her questions. "What's the etiquette for greeting the king? Do I curtsy or bow or fall to the floor before him? How do I address him?"

"You may bow, but you'll find he is very approachable and will set you at ease very quickly." As he answered her questions, his stomach churned at the realization that he was bringing another man's wife to the king's tent. Why was this even happening? The king had several wives and concubines.

As they made their way deeper into the palace past servants, Bathsheba asked, "Is the throne room this way?"

"He's not there right now."

At the door to the roof, Benaiah dismissed the guard who looked quizzingly at Benaiah and the woman at his side. Benaiah wondered how quickly this news would spread. After the guard left, Benaiah escorted Bathsheba onto the roof.

Bathsheba looked around at the scene on the roof. "Benaiah, why are we up here?" Bathsheba looked up at him with innocence, then fear, followed by desperation. He felt as if he were handing over a lamb to a wolf.

Benaiah wished he could protect her. Instead, he announced their presence.

"Enter," David called from inside the tent.

Benaiah felt Bathsheba's questioning gaze, but could not look her in the eye.

Benaiah nodded his assurance and motioned with his head for her to go ahead of him into the tent.

David stood at the back wall of the pavilion, a goblet of wine in his hand. He smiled, placed the goblet on an ornate oak table and walked toward them. "Thank you for coming, Bathsheba."

As if she had a choice. Benaiah took a step back.

"That will be all for the night, Benaiah," David said without taking his gaze off Bathsheba.

As Benaiah let himself out, he heard David offer her some wine.

He took his post outside the rooftop door, feeling as if he were the one betraying his friend Uriah.

He tried to erase the image of Bathsheba's stricken face from his mind. Would he ever be able to look at David without disdain, or at Bathsheba without guilt?

All night, as Benaiah stood watch, he tried not to imagine what was going on in the pavilion behind the door. Was his friend and king really about to do this? David wouldn't physically force himself on her; he knew the king well enough to know that. But would Bathsheba feel coerced into his bed because he was the king?

Back when Abigail, one of David's wives, gave him wise counsel, she managed to make him change course and keep him from shedding innocent blood. Perhaps if Bathsheba reminded David she was married to another man—his friend and a loyal soldier—she could stop him from doing this wicked thing.

"Say something, Bathsheba!" he whispered to no one.

CHAPTER TWENTY-ONE

"The woman conceived; so she sent and told David, and said, 'I am with child.'"
—2 Samuel 11:5

The door at the top of the stairs to the rooftop opened and Bathsheba emerged. She adjusted her pale blue head covering to conceal the lower half of her face. She didn't look at Benaiah.

"See that she gets home, Benaiah," David commanded.

"Yes, my lord."

Benaiah escorted Bathsheba back home in silence, and he noticed that she kept her eyes downcast. Was she ashamed about what had happened?

At the door to her home, she whispered, "Thank you" without looking at him. Benaiah resisted the urge to grunt.

As she closed the door behind her, Benaiah overheard Bathsheba's servant, Ashima, exclaim, "Mistress, I was so worried when you didn't return last night. Were you well?"

He didn't hear Bathsheba's response.

Benaiah turned for home. Had Bathsheba protested? What would it mean if she hadn't? And could he have done something to stop this atrocity? He could have done more than simply tell David she was married. He was David's servant, yes, but he was also his friend. And the son of a priest. He could've tried harder to keep him from this sin.

Eleazar and the other servants of Saul had refused to kill the priests of Nob when ordered. Some had even given their lives in defense of the priests, but Benaiah hadn't even spoken up when David decided to kill the household of Nabal.

Last night he'd had an opportunity to prove he was a man of character. Yet again, he had failed.

Perhaps because he wasn't as righteous as he thought.

What would have happened if the tables were turned and Uriah had been asked to bring Mariah to David instead of him? Uriah was an honorable man. He would have refused, Benaiah was sure of it. He would likely have scolded David for even considering it.

But Benaiah was too worried about the consequences of disobedience. Now he was an accomplice in another man's sin by his silence that night and his inaction since.

Years ago, when Ammizabad died, his father told him, *Being a man is about protecting those you love and value.* He had not protected Bathsheba from David, nor had he protected David from himself.

Benaiah had failed. Again.

* * *

Benaiah drew circles in the packed dirt at his feet. He hadn't even heard his daughters trying to get his attention. His thoughts were on the incident with Bathsheba.

Mariah called his name, set down her needlework and then came over to him. "What's wrong, Benaiah?"

Benaiah upbraided himself for letting his feelings show. He always tried to keep his work and home life separate. "It's nothing."

"You've been moping for days."

Benaiah sighed. Then he regarded his wife, suddenly curious how she would react in Bathsheba's place.

"Mariah, when I was away at war, were you lonely?" He asked the question as if the answer were of no consequence, like the response to what they were having for dinner.

Mariah looked at him incredulously. "Of course I was. What soldier's wife enjoys spending months on end without her husband?"

"What did you do?" Benaiah asked without looking at her. The children continued to play on the ground of the courtyard of their house, unaware of the serious conversation above them.

"The children kept me busy. I had a household to run. And many friends, mostly the other soldiers' wives."

He stood to get closer to his wife.

"But did you feel lonely... as a woman?" he whispered so the children couldn't hear.

Mariah blushed. "Of course I did," she whispered back. "But I spent my solitary times daydreaming of you and imagining our reunion."

Benaiah felt a slow smile spreading, which matched Mariah's. She reached over and stroked his beard, then kissed him gently. "Why all these questions? You know I love you and would never break my vows." She laughed. "Besides, no one who knows you would dare trifle with the wife of Benaiah. You are one of David's mighty men, the captain of his bodyguard. Even the king wouldn't presume such a right."

Benaiah gulped. "Why would you mention David?"

"To point out the very absurdity of the idea. Even the most powerful man in Israel wouldn't be so presumptuous as to take your wife. He has enough wives and concubines to keep him satisfied."

Then Mariah tilted her head and asked, "Benaiah, why are you suddenly insecure after all these years of marriage? Has something happened to make you doubt me?"

Benaiah gazed into her eyes and tucked a strand of her soft, black hair behind her ear. Even with the spray of wrinkles at her temples and the wisps of gray that streaked her ebony tresses, how he loved this woman!

"You've done nothing wrong. I just know these things can happen in marriage, and I'm trying to understand why. I want you to feel so sure of my love that you would never be tempted to stray... even if King David himself desired you."

Mariah laughed out loud. "As if that would happen! I do love you, Benaiah. And I know you love me. I desire no other man but you."

She kissed him then. Not the polite peck of an older couple, but with the passion of a young woman with her lover. Her hands explored his chest and arms as if she were discovering them for the first time, and her touch inflamed his desire, as it had always done over the years.

The sound of their servant, Milka, humming as she prepared food in the cooking room carried to his ears. Benaiah nodded toward the back rooms of the house. "Perhaps we could sneak across the hall for a little *reassurance*?"

"Benaiah! It's the middle of the afternoon!" The sparkle in her eyes belied her words of protest.

"We can pretend it's our wedding week."

Mariah squealed as Benaiah chased her into their sleeping room.

* * *

It had been two months since the incident with Bathsheba and David, and Benaiah felt no less guilt over it. He felt more in fact, as he anticipated the day when the battle for Rabbah would be over and the mighty men and the rest of the army would return to Israel. How could he look into Uriah's face without shame and pity?

As Benaiah neared the palace, Bathsheba's servant, Ashima, stopped him by calling his name.

"I have an urgent message for the king from my lady." She thrust a sealed papyrus into Benaiah's hand. "You must give this to the king personally and immediately."

Benaiah felt annoyance at her demand. A love note, no doubt, from David's new mistress. The Pelethites were the official royal couriers, but since Benaiah was in charge of them, he took it. "Very well. I'll see that he gets it."

She let out a breath. "I knew I could trust you."

Benaiah continued on his way. How would David respond? Would he be secretive about it? Would he send it back unopened, as he should, and end this?

★ ★ ★

Benaiah accompanied David from his apartment to the common room, ready to begin the day's business in the kingdom. The spacious room held David's throne, seats for some of his counselors and administrators, and guards by the door who ushered individuals in to beseech the king for judgment in their cases. The recorder, Jehoshaphat, screened them in advance so that David only had to deal with the most serious or urgent matters.

David relaxed into his throne. Benaiah approached him before the first supplicant was announced and handed him the note. He whispered that it had been sent by Bathsheba, feeling like he was a part of their deception.

David hesitated, glanced briefly at Benaiah, then broke the seal, unrolled it and settled back to read it.

Benaiah took his place at David's side, awaiting orders. He stole glances at the king.

David crumpled the note in his hand. Not a love note then, Benaiah concluded. Could it be a scathing diatribe against his actions? Had she finally found the courage to let him know that he had abused his power in summoning her, making her feel pressured to give into him? Was she demanding he never do so again? Benaiah hoped it was so.

Benaiah wanted to believe that night with Bathsheba was a single incident, an example of a momentary lapse in judgment on David's part. He wanted to think the best about this man whom, up until this point, Benaiah had admired. Had David repented of it and learned his lesson?

But what of the law? Adultery was not the type of offense that could be atoned for with sacrifice. The penalty was death by stoning, of both guilty parties.

"Benaiah, send a message to Joab." David's voice brought him out of his musings. "Command him to send Uriah the Hittite to Jerusalem to report to me immediately."

"Yes, my lord." Benaiah wondered what possible connection could exist between a note from Bathsheba and an urgent summons for Uriah? But his job was not to question, merely to obey. He motioned for a Pelethite runner to take the dispatch to the battlefield.

CHAPTER TWENTY-TWO

"In the morning it happened that David wrote a letter to Joab and sent it by the hand of Uriah."

—2 Samuel 11:14

"The land will pass to the daughters, as there is no male heir," David determined in the case before him.

"Thank you, my lord," the woman said with a bow.

As she left the room, one of the guards at the door announced, "Uriah the Hittite, sire."

David looked up, perhaps surprised that Uriah had arrived within the week. "Approach," the king said.

Uriah bowed to the ground before David. Benaiah fixed his eyes forward, glancing only occasionally, wanting to avoid any eye contact with the man. He had been dreading this day for two months.

"Uriah, old friend, it is good to see you. You may stand."

Uriah straightened. Benaiah was surprised that the king would refer to him as an old friend. They had great comradery back in the wilderness days, but even then, everyone understood David was superior to them. How much more was he now that he was king?

"How are you?" David asked.

"I am well, my lord."

"And how is my nephew Joab?"

"He is leading well, as usual."

"And how is morale among the troops?"

"Morale is always high when we are defeating my lord's enemies." Uriah smiled.

David seemed not to hear the answers to his questions. "So there is good progress in the battle?"

"We have besieged Rabbah and have destroyed all Ammonites who have come against us. General Joab doesn't anticipate it will be much more than a month before they surrender."

"Good. Good. Yes, very good."

Could this report not have been sent as a missive rather than delivered in person by a top soldier? Or a less valuable soldier could have been sent to relay the information.

David looked around the room as if searching for another topic of conversation. "Any losses on our side?"

"None, my lord." Benaiah was not surprised at that. The Lord was with them.

"Thank you for the report."

"My lord." Uriah bowed again.

"Since it's too late to travel back to the battlefield tonight, why don't you go to your home and see your wife? What was her name, again?"

"Bathsheba, my lord."

"Ah, yes. Bathsheba. Relax, enjoy yourself with Bathsheba. Get a bath to wash off the grime of battle. Sleep in your own bed."

"Yes, sire." Uriah snapped to attention, turned sharply and left the common room.

As soon as Uriah left the room, David summoned another servant forward. "Go to the kitchen and have the cooks prepare a basket of whatever is on the menu for dinner tonight. Include a bottle of my best wine and flowers. Send it to the home of Uriah the Hittite. Quickly!"

What was that about?

★ ★ ★

As Benaiah arrived at the palace, the sun had just risen behind him. He saw a group of four soldiers, including Uriah, at the guard house, leaning against the wall. Their bedrolls beside them, their untrimmed beards and remnants of the breakfast that had been delivered to them on the ground all testified that they had not even gone inside to sleep in the guard house outside the palace. Benaiah stopped to speak to them and was not surprised to learn they were itching to be dismissed by David so they could return to their fellow soldiers and the battle for the town of Rabbah.

"Why would the king single me out to bring a battlefield report in person, when General Joab has been sending written accounts periodically already?" Uriah asked Benaiah pointedly.

Benaiah wondered the same thing, but instead he answered vaguely, "The king doesn't inform me of his reasoning for his actions." How true that was! "Ours is not to question orders, but to follow them." These were the words he lived by, but did he have no obligation to think things through? How much responsibility fell on his own shoulders when he obeyed wicked commands? If the circumstances were different, would he want someone to tell him if something similar had happened with the king and his wife? Or would he prefer never to find out? He had no answers. These were the thoughts that stole Benaiah's sleep. But Uriah knew nothing of his struggles, and Benaiah determined it would remain so.

Benaiah changed topics and inquired after his friend, Mikhael, and asked them to inform him that his newest son was now walking. How he missed his childhood friend and that life and the fellowship of other soldiers. They were like brothers to him, more so even than his elder brother Shallum, the priest. He and Benaiah were such opposites in every way, you'd never know they had the same parents.

Benaiah found it hard to talk to Uriah, knowing what he knew. Seeing him now, part of him wanted to blurt out what had happened between Bathsheba and David, confess it. He hadn't done enough to stop it on his part. Benaiah had often wondered if he should inform him, but quickly concluded that no good could come of it, other than perhaps an easing of his guilty conscience.

Besides, it was David's sin to confess.

Benaiah tried to understand David's rationale in summoning Uriah. At first he hoped it would be to confess their sin in person. But that didn't happen. What then? Restitution perhaps? Did David desire to do something positive for Uriah to make up for what he did with his wife, without revealing the reason for it? Was David attempting to placate both Bathsheba and Uriah by allowing the two of them some time together? That would explain the special meal, wine and flowers.

Had David recognized that Bathsheba probably missed her husband and needed to see him, and his guilty feelings caused him to want to solidify their marriage? After all, they had no children yet to take up her time while her husband was away.

Yes, that would have made Benaiah feel better about his king. David sinned, and grievously so, but at least he felt bad about it. Didn't he? And he was doing something to try to make it right.

But now Benaiah realized that neither confession nor restitution was on David's heart.

So why had he summoned Uriah?

Did David's interest in Uriah have anything to do with Bathsheba?

When Benaiah reported to David that he had seen Uriah that morning, David snapped, "Have Uriah the Hittite report to me right away."

Uriah arrived soon after, his appearance not much different than the day before, no freshly washed hair, fresh tunic or trimmed beard. He bowed deferentially.

"Uriah, my friend," David said, his voice taking on an obvious note of concern. "You've made a long journey from a fierce battlefield. You must be tired of sleeping on the ground. Why did you not go down to your house last night?"

Uriah's mouth fell open, then he quickly closed it, thinking for a moment before he spoke.

"The ark and Israel and Judah are out under shelters in the field," he answered slowly. "And General Joab and your other servants are camping out in the open field. Should I go to my house, to eat and drink and to lie with my wife? I could not do such a thing!"

Benaiah heard a slight gasp from David. Was he surprised by Uriah's resolve? He shouldn't be. Had David forgotten the solidarity between soldiers? Had he already forgotten the rough life of a soldier since he had traded it for cushioned couches and musical performances? Apparently.

David was not deterred. "Very well. Remain here one more day and I'll send you back tomorrow. Dine with me tonight. We'll talk about old times." David attempted a smile, but it lacked sincerity. What was going on in the king's mind?

That evening, during the lavish meal of venison and fowl, Benaiah stood by the door. David repeatedly motioned for Uriah's wine glass to be refilled, while he made only a pretense of drinking his own. If Benaiah didn't know better, he'd conclude that David was trying to make Uriah drunk. But why would he do that?

Before long, Uriah was bleary eyed and staggering.

David draped an arm across Uriah's shoulders, as if they were old friends, rather than king and subject. "Go on home now. Get some sleep, Uriah." He led the drunken soldier to the door where Benaiah was stationed.

"Benaiah, walk Uriah home to make sure he gets there safely. Then go home yourself. I'll see you both tomorrow morning."

David glanced at Benaiah as he gave the order, but then quickly looked away. Was he remembering the last time he sent Benaiah to escort someone to that house? Benaiah remembered, and the memory burned his conscience.

As Benaiah began to lead Uriah to the street that led to his home, Uriah brushed him off. "Leave me, Benaiah. I'm not going there."

"But the king..." Benaiah began.

"The king..." Uriah sputtered, then thought better of finishing his sentence in front of David's loyal soldier. "Never mind." Then Uriah turned and walked back toward the guard house where he had spent the previous night.

* * *

The next morning, Benaiah passed the same group of soldiers outside the palace, and again saw Uriah among them.

When he arrived in the common room, Benaiah reported that Uriah refused to go home again the second night as well, but was outside at the guard house. David scowled, then told Shemaiah he desired to send a written message.

The scribe readied his reed pen and a papyrus scroll.

"Address the message to General Joab," David began.

The scribe wrote, and then looked up expectantly for more.

Instead, David suddenly got up and pushed him aside with his elbow. He took the pen and scroll from him. "I'll do it myself."

Shemaiah's questioning gaze fell on Benaiah, who raised a shoulder in response.

David wrote furiously, then ordered Shemaiah to seal the message with the royal seal. The scribe took the scroll back to his table and used the king's signet ring to impress the symbol of the lion of Judah into wax.

"Summon Uriah the Hittite at once." David ordered no one in particular, but it was carried out regardless.

David said he would not commence the day's work of hearing cases from the people, until he had spoken with Uriah.

When Uriah the Hittite was announced, he bowed again, but not as deeply. Was he tiring of these useless exchanges?

David addressed his soldier. "You may return to the battlefield."

Was that relief on Uriah's face?

"And please deliver this message to General Joab for me." David handed the note to Benaiah, who placed it in the hand of his friend. Uriah took the scroll, bowed low before David and left.

The king was certainly exhibiting some odd behavior. The events of the past two days were inexplicable. Israel had already endured one moody sovereign in King Saul. What was it about power that changed men's behavior?

CHAPTER TWENTY-THREE

"And he wrote in the letter, saying, 'Set Uriah in the forefront of the hottest battle, and retreat from him, that he may be struck down and die.'"

—2 Samuel 11:15

A month later, during the daily business in the common room, Shemaiah announced, "A messenger from Joab, sire."

"Approach. What news?" David asked.

Shemaiah approached, unrolled the scroll, skimmed it and handed it back to the soldier, who read: "From General Joab to King David. Battlefield report fifteen: sixth day of the month of Abib: Battle with the people of Ammon. We encountered fierce fighting. The men of Rabbah gained an advantage over us and came out against us in the field. We drove them back to the entrance of the city gate. Their archers shot at your servants from the wall. Some of the king's soldiers were killed, ten in all. Uriah the Hittite is dead also. Names recorded below."

Benaiah's mouth fell open in shock. He heard gasps from the advisers in David's council. God had protected them in all their recent battles to the extent that they had no losses. He felt as if he had a blow to his midsection. He wanted to sit down to process this horrific news. Uriah, his friend and fellow soldier, with whom he had fought for years and who was the first man he and Mikhael met when they joined with David all those years ago, was dead.

Benaiah was devastated, wondering which of his friends might be on that list. Ten soldiers fallen. So many families would mourn this week.

Benaiah looked over at the king, expecting a similar reaction, but was stunned to find there was no look of shock. There wasn't even concern or grief. David didn't tear his robes, as he had when he heard the news of Saul and Jonathan. He looked no different than if he'd received an invitation to dine with a friend. The messenger handed David the scroll, who motioned toward Benaiah to take it. What was he to do with it?

David straightened. "Shemaiah, send a reply. Tell Joab, 'Do not let this matter trouble you, for I do not hold you responsible for this setback. The sword devours one soldier one day, another the next. Get back to the business at hand, attack the city and overthrow it.'"

How could David consider the death of ten of his most trusted soldiers a mere setback? He'd always cared for his men, had borne the loss of each soldier keenly, and felt personally responsible for their deaths, even though it was the enemy's doing. He had even mourned his adversary, King Saul!

Now to hear him dismiss the deaths of several loyal soldiers, including Uriah, one of his mighty men, in so callous a fashion was unlike him, and very disappointing to witness. Had David forgotten the value of his soldiers while he relaxed here in his royal palace?

All of Benaiah's emotions about David's wrongdoing with Bathsheba came flooding back.

After David's night with Bathsheba, everything changed. Benaiah found he was losing respect for David, something he thought would never happen. But then he felt guilty for his feelings of disrespect. He convinced himself he was David's most loyal soldier, that nothing the king could ever do would alter that.

But something had altered it.

Benaiah snapped out of his musing. Someone needed to inform Bathsheba that her husband was dead. There would be an official messenger from the palace, but Benaiah felt he should be the one to notify her in this case. He asked permission from David, who absentmindedly agreed.

Benaiah took the note with him. When he stepped outside the common room, he unrolled the scroll and read the list of fallen soldiers. The third name was Mikhael ben Kenan, his childhood friend from Kabzeel. Benaiah threw back his head and cried out in grief.

As a boy, Mikhael had dreamed of fighting for Israel. As a young man, he joined David in the wilderness, eager to serve under the shepherd-warrior of Israel to avenge the slaughter of the people of Nob and to see David installed as king on the throne of Israel. He joined the army and fought alongside Benaiah and the other mighty men.

Now he was dead. And Benaiah hadn't been there with him to comfort him as he died, to grieve over him, to bury him. How had he fallen? How long did he suffer?

Benaiah stepped into a nearby unoccupied room and sat down on a bench. How could he comfort others when he was reeling from the news himself? He needed to compose himself before he would go to Mikhael's and Uriah's families. He'd delegate the others to another palace official, some of his Pelethites. He didn't regret his impetuous offer to be the bearer of bad news. It should be him, but it would be the hardest thing he'd done in this role.

Benaiah wiped away his tears with the back of his hand, stood up, took a deep breath and pushed open the door of the private room.

CHAPTER TWENTY-FOUR

"When the wife of Uriah heard that her husband was dead, she mourned for her husband. And when her mourning was over, David sent and brought her to his house, and she became his wife and bore him a son. But the thing that David had done displeased the Lord."

—2 Samuel 11:26–27

Benaiah had left Mikhael's wife—correction, widow Netaniah—and was now standing awkwardly by the door after informing Bathsheba of Uriah's death. Bathsheba wept at her table.

She was incredulous. "No. It can't be true. Uriah is a valiant warrior."

She referred to her husband as if he were still alive. A common occurrence.

"He promised to come back to me."

Benaiah regretted not bringing Mariah along with him to both homes. She was better at dealing with tears. She'd also think of something comforting to say. Benaiah couldn't even offer any information other than the fact that they had fallen in battle. He had no details about how it had happened, although he was sure they had fought valiantly.

As was the custom, the bodies would have been buried within a day because of the heat. It would not comfort the widows to know they were buried in enemy territory and would have no permanent marker in Israel.

Benaiah stepped forward and kneeled down near Bathsheba. "Would you like me to contact your family?"

"Ashima can go for them." She nodded toward her servant who was standing wide-eyed in the hallway. As she left the home, Bathsheba suddenly sat up straight. "Father! How is he?"

How thoughtless of him. Of course she'd worry about her father's welfare, as he was also one of David's mighty men. "There was no news that Eliam was among the fallen."

Bathsheba exhaled loudly. "Praise be the Lord. I wouldn't have been able to bear it if I lost them both."

Benaiah couldn't imagine even one loss, let alone two in one family.

Bathsheba looked up at him. "Benaiah," she whispered, "Do you think this is a result of what happened?"

Normally, he would not attribute the loss of a soldier in battle to God's punishment on a person. But in Bathsheba's case, he had to admit the thought had crossed his mind. He knew better than most that disobedience could result in the death of a loved one.

"I can't say," he hedged.

A fresh round of sobs told him she feared the same.

"I didn't deserve Uriah. Not after what happened. So God took him. And now I'll be alone."

★ ★ ★

A week later, Mariah challenged Benaiah. "My husband works in the palace, in the very presence of the king, and I'm always the last person in Jerusalem to know what's happening!"

Benaiah gave her a sharp look.

"This isn't even private news. Everyone knows the king is taking another wife. As if six weren't enough! And Bathsheba! The poor girl was just widowed, and he only gave her a week to mourn before taking her to live in the palace. It's disgraceful. Couldn't you have talked some sense into him?"

"My job is to guard the king's person. His marriages are none of my business."

"Strange. Kings often marry for political reasons. But Bathsheba's not from any famous family, other than the military connection. I didn't even realize the king knew her. Did you?"

Oh, he "knew" her, all right. But he couldn't tell Mariah about that.

"Yes, of course. He wouldn't have married her if he hadn't met her before. Perhaps he feels he needs to take her in as she has no children, unlike the other soldiers who fell," Benaiah surmised.

"I can't believe my friend and neighbor is married to the king."

Benaiah did not want to talk about this. He wondered at the suddenness of the marriage as well—just another example of the king's strange behavior this past year. Mariah didn't seem to need any acknowledgment to continue her musings.

"And it wasn't even a large public event, which is rather odd don't you think?"

"I need to get to the palace."

★ ★ ★

A month later, Mariah was still curious about palace news.

"Did you know that Bathsheba is expecting?" she asked him privately after dinner.

"Yes, the king told me last week. He's very proud."

Mariah sat up straighter. "Last week? And you didn't tell me?"

"You mustn't gossip," Benaiah chided.

"It's not gossip when her pregnancy is plain for all to see."

That much was true. Benaiah noticed that Bathsheba was already showing. He was beginning to put two and two together. It took nine months to make a baby and David and Bathsheba had only been married less than two months.

"Strange that she never conceived while she was married to Uriah, but with David she gets pregnant right after the wedding."

"What are you saying?" What *was* she saying?

Mariah huffed and crossed her arms across her chest. "Just that God must be blessing their union."

As Benaiah thought of it, he understood that Bathsheba must have conceived that night in the spring. Was that why David called Uriah back from battle? He didn't need a firsthand report; he was trying to cover up his sin. Did he hope Uriah would sleep with his wife, so he wouldn't have suspected her guilty of adultery when the news came that she was pregnant?

That must have been the intent of the note Bathsheba sent. The one that made David angry, and caused him to send for Uriah. This pregnancy was not a result of God's blessing on their marriage, but the result of their adultery.

Benaiah couldn't keep his anguish to himself any longer.

"Mariah, I need to tell you something about David and Bathsheba's marriage, but you must keep this between us."

"Of course. What's happened that has you so upset?"

Benaiah shared the whole incident, including his feelings of guilt and shame for his inaction that night.

"I know I should've refused. I should have challenged him, protected her. But I feared disobeying more than anything else."

"I'm just shocked that David would do such a thing. He has wives and concubines." Mariah responded. "Why would he do this?"

"I've wondered that myself. It's never just one factor. Lust? Restlessness? Abuse of power? But, no matter the reason for his behavior, at the time I hoped Bathsheba would speak up and change his mind."

Mariah stood and challenged her husband. "Did it ever occur to you that if you couldn't refuse the king without fear of repercussions, then maybe Bathsheba couldn't either? Especially since she had no one to stand up for her with her husband and father away at war?"

Benaiah dropped his head. "I was hoping she could persuade him, like Abigail had."

"That was a different situation, before he was a powerful king, and in public, where David was surrounded by his men. Those factors influenced his behavior as well, not just Abigail's words. But now, in private, a powerful king summoned his subject, a woman, who was alone. She must have felt she could not refuse him."

"But he didn't force her, of that I'm sure. He wouldn't do that."

"You weren't there, Benaiah. Even if he didn't physically force her, he coerced her as a powerful man over a woman who couldn't say no."

"But if she felt that way, why didn't she cry out?"

"Benaiah, she may have been terrified. You said yourself that she didn't seem to know why she was being summoned. She may have frozen with fear. Poor girl."

Benaiah raked his fingers through his hair. "I know! I feel ashamed for my lack of resolve. And now Bathsheba feels that Uriah's death is somehow a result of that night."

Mariah sank back into her chair. "Oh, my dear friend! Do you want me to speak with her?"

"No! You mustn't say a thing. I'll trust that David will make it right, somehow."

Benaiah reached across the table and took Mariah's hand, thanking her for listening. He hadn't realized how much he had needed to unload his heart to his wife and the relief that came with just acknowledging everything that had been burdening him over the past months. But could such a situation be made right?

★ ★ ★

"Benaiah, come with me. I want to show you my new son."

David and Benaiah walked to the Court of the Women, as David did every afternoon to see his family. But this time, his first stop was to see Bathsheba and the son she bore him.

David approached Bathsheba. The child was wrapped in a blanket in the crook of her arm. David and Bathsheba shared a smile.

"How are you feeling, my love?"

"I have quite forgotten my ordeal now that I can hold him in my arms. He was worth all that pain."

David tilted his head sympathetically.

"I do appreciate what you have endured. But what a reward for your labor!" David reached forward for the child. "May I?" he asked.

"Of course."

David took the child from his mother very gently, laid him on the bed beside her, and opened up the blanket so he could take a better look at him. The cooler air startled the child and he began to cry.

"There, there, now little one. You can't let a little draft scare you. You're going to be a brave warrior one day."

David turned the child over, picked up his feet in turn and announced, "All is well. Ten fingers and ten toes. And look at the strength in his legs! He'll be a fine soldier."

Bathsheba laughed. "Can I have him for a few years first?"

"I suppose," David conceded, then pronounced, "He is perfect, my love. Well done."

CHAPTER TWENTY-FIVE

"So David said to Nathan, 'I have sinned against the Lord.' And Nathan said to David, 'The Lord also has put away your sin, you shall not die.'"

—2 Samuel 12:13

On their return from the Court of the Women to see the baby, David and Benaiah prepared to review some plans for the temple and hear updates on the accumulation of supplies. But then a servant announced that the prophet Nathan had arrived.

Benaiah knew David respected Nathan and hoped that he would make a positive pronouncement that would lift David's spirits. In spite of his joy at the birth of their son, David had been out of sorts. He didn't show the same enthusiasm when he went to the house of the Lord, he hadn't written any psalms in months, and he barely picked up his instruments anymore. Was he becoming as melancholy as his predecessor Saul? Back then, it was David who would be called whenever Saul was plagued by a distressing spirit. He would play the harp before the king, and the distressing spirit would leave him.

But who would comfort David?

Nathan offered no greeting, nor did he bow before the king. His brow was furrowed, as if he had a heavy burden on his mind.

"What's wrong, friend?" David asked.

Nathan approached David. After seeing the look on his face, David shooed away the servants entering with arms laden with scrolls.

"We'll deal with that later." They turned on their heel and departed.

"Sire, something has happened in your kingdom that I feel I must report in order to get the king's desire on how it should be resolved."

Shemaiah the scribe, Jehoshaphat the recorder, Ahithophel, David's chief counselor and some of the other counselors and advisers remained in the common room. Perhaps they could help the king with whatever judgment he would make.

Nathan's presence in this setting was indeed strange. Prophets didn't usually have dilemmas. Benaiah assumed they took any concerns straight to God and He would advise them. What could David possibly help him with? Benaiah was curious. So, apparently, was David, who motioned for Nathan to speak.

Nathan began his report of the situation that had him so distressed.

"In a city, there were two men who were neighbors, one rich and the other poor. The rich man had many flocks and herds, whereas the poor man had only one little ewe lamb. He treated it kindly, allowing his children to play with it as a pet. He even kept it in his home and fed it and treated it like one of his children."

David listened intently. Benaiah imagined that since David had been a shepherd in his youth, he could relate to the tenderness shown to such a helpless animal. Benaiah had no such understanding.

"Then a traveler came to the rich man's home. But instead of feeding the man from his own flock or herd, he took the poor man's only lamb and slaughtered it to for his guest."

David leaped out of his throne. "I swear that the man who has done this is worthy of death!" Then he added a further punishment of restitution. "And he must restore four times as many lambs to the poor man, because he did such a thing and showed no pity."

With a steady finger, Nathan pointed at him. "You are that rich man!"

Benaiah's heart almost stopped. This was a judgment on David for his adultery. *The lamb is Bathsheba!*

David's mouth fell open, and he stumbled back into his throne.

Benaiah half expected Nathan to wheel around and point at him too. He felt guilty for his complicity in the sinful act. He should have spoken up—king or no king.

And he'd kept silent all these months, playing along, as if Bathsheba and David had only fallen in love after Uriah's death.

Nathan came closer to the king, emboldened in his pronouncement. "This is what the God of Israel says to you, 'I chose you to be king over Israel, and kept you safe from Saul time and again. I gave you the house of Saul and put you over Israel and Judah. And, if that wasn't enough, I would've given you even more.'"

Benaiah's knees weakened. Although the admonishment was meant for David, it could have been for him as well. He too had been blessed beyond measure.

He saw their miraculous deliverance from Saul's hand time and again in the wilderness: when David and Abishai went into the midst of the camp; when three of his mighty men broke through enemy lines to get David a drink; when their families were captured by the Amalekites. Yet he had treated the blessing of God as if it were a trifle, by being an accessory in David's crime, and then by not exposing it or challenging David himself.

The prophet's voice softened when he saw David's grief. "Why did you disobey God and do such a horrible thing?"

Benaiah knew this was about the adultery. He had always known that God could see all of His creature's thoughts and actions. He knew that no one really could hide anything from Him. David himself had written a psalm that said, "The Lord is sitting in His sacred temple on His throne in heaven. He knows everything we do, because He sees all." David was a man after God's own heart, and yet even he was being judged for his sin.

"You have taken Uriah the Hittite's wife." At this, Ahithophel, Bathsheba's grandfather and David's chief counselor, grasped behind him for a chair and sank into it, mouth hanging open, head slowly shaking from side to side in disbelief. Benaiah could only imagine the betrayal he felt.

But it was out in the open now. As horrible as this moment was, Benaiah also felt a great sense of relief. It wasn't his burden to carry alone anymore.

"And you've murdered Uriah by having the Ammonites kill him, so you could take his wife."

A collective gasp rose from those in the common room.

Shemaiah the scribe stopped writing and looked up, no doubt wondering if he should continue. David buried his face in his hands.

Benaiah had figured out Bathsheba was pregnant with David's child when they married and that the reason he sent for Uriah was to try to cover up the pregnancy by making him think the child was his. But what he hadn't imagined was that, since Uriah didn't do as David expected, he went to the next step and put him in mortal danger. He committed the sin of murder, even murder by proxy, in order to conceal his sin of adultery.

So Uriah's death was not a normal consequence of war? He was killed by the enemies of Israel at King David's order? Benaiah both could and couldn't believe it. David was desperate. He was mad with desire for Bathsheba and obviously intended to have her one way or another. He thought it would not be unheard of for a soldier to die in battle, and then his widow would be free to marry him.

But what of the other nine soldiers who died that day? Like his best friend, Mikhael. Peripheral damage? Killed for nothing?

"'Now,' the Lord says, 'because you wouldn't obey me and took Uriah's wife for yourself, your family will never live in peace. I'll bring trouble against you from someone in your own family, and I'll take your wives and give them to another man before your very eyes. He'll sleep with them in the open. Your sin was done in secret, but the punishment will be out in public, for everyone in Israel to see.'"

Such a punishment! But it was a mercy that David wasn't sentenced to death, as the law required. David slowly raised his head. He looked at Nathan with tears in his eyes. He threw back his head in anguish and admitted, "My sin is against the Lord."

Benaiah breathed a sigh of relief. He was so glad David didn't try to justify himself or make excuses. Benaiah looked over at the advisers. Ahithophel's expression had changed from shock to anger and disgust.

Nathan nodded slowly. "The Lord will forgive you, even for this sin. You will not die."

Benaiah had feared the coming punishment. According to the law, anyone guilty of either adultery or murder was to be put to death. Other sins could be forgiven if the proper sacrifice was provided, but there was no prescribed sacrifice for either of those heinous acts.

David had broken four of the commandments: coveting, adultery, lying and murder. How could God forgive him? And yet, He had. Nathan confirmed it.

"Nevertheless..." the prophet began.

Oh no! What more? What would the consequences be for David? And for his family?

"Since your actions have given the enemies of God opportunity to honor Him less, and even to malign Him, your new baby son will die."

David doubled over as if physically struck.

The child Bathsheba just delivered would die? How would she bear it? Benaiah couldn't imagine. He and Mariah had never lost a child in infancy, although it happened frequently in some places.

Having completed his pronouncement, Nathan turned and left the room. As he walked, Benaiah noticed he stood less erect, almost as if delivering the news had emptied him. Benaiah admired him. It couldn't have been easy to confront a powerful king. Had he been able to sleep since God gave him the message? And yet, by using a parable, it had disarmed David. He didn't know until it was too late that a dagger was at his own throat.

"Leave me!" David shouted.

The servants quickly cleared the room, no doubt to spread word of the scandalous behavior of their king and the prophet's pronouncement of judgment.

Ahithophel narrowed his eyes at David accusingly, then left the room.

As Benaiah turned to leave, assuming the king wanted complete privacy, David whispered, "Not you, Benaiah. Please stay."

CHAPTER TWENTY-SIX

Blessed is the one whose transgression is forgiven,
whose sin is covered.
Blessed is the man against whom the Lord
counts no iniquity,
and in whose spirit there is no deceit.

For when I kept silent, my bones wasted away
through my groaning all day long.
For day and night your hand was heavy upon me;
my strength was dried up as by the heat of summer. Selah

I acknowledged my sin to you,
and I did not cover my iniquity;
I said, "I will confess my transgressions to the Lord,"
and you forgave the iniquity of my sin. Selah

—Psalm 32:1–5, ESV

With the common room cleared, Benaiah stood alone while David sat on his throne, his head in his hands. The prophet's words kept ringing in his mind. *He took the poor man's lamb.* When Benaiah brought Bathsheba to David that night, he had indeed felt like he was bringing a lamb to be slaughtered. It was Benaiah who took the poor man's lamb and delivered it to the rich man. And now the poor man, Uriah, was dead, along with eight other soldiers and Mikhael.

Benaiah wanted nothing more than to flee the palace. To talk to God and beg His forgiveness. But as David's bodyguard, he was still on duty. So he stayed.

Although doing his duty was what got him in this predicament in the first place.

He just hoped David didn't expect him to provide comfort.

The only comfort he felt for himself came from the words, "The Lord will forgive you, even for this sin. You will not die." If there was forgiveness for the man who sinned, perhaps some of that mercy would spill over and cover the sin of the accomplice? *Please, God, be merciful to me.*

Benaiah sensed David staring at him, so he turned to face him.

"You know, I actually feel relieved that it's finally out in the open." David tipped his head back and let out a long breath, as if exhaling the worries of the past year.

While he was glad David felt relieved, as he himself did, Benaiah wondered if the weight of the prophet's words were truly appreciated yet. Or was he still reeling from the emotional hit? There were consequences yet to be felt, both to him and his family. No one knew what that would entail other than the first hammer blow: the death of Bathsheba's newborn son.

"For months, I haven't been able to sleep. Or worship God with a clear conscience."

Benaiah was not surprised. For a man like David, who was so close to God, having this come between them was unavoidable. Benaiah had noticed David either decreasing the number of times he went to the tabernacle, which he used to love to do, or else worshiping half-heartedly. There seemed to be no joy when he sang. And he hadn't been composing psalms for some time.

Benaiah nodded. "I noticed, my lord."

David put his head in his hands. "I'm so sorry. Especially for the deaths of my valiant soldiers."

He had to ask. "How? How did they die?"

David looked up and scrubbed his hands down his face. "The simple truth is that I ordered it. I sent a message to Joab to set Uriah in the forefront of the hottest battle..." David paused and looked over at Benaiah, as if he hated to say the next words. "And then I ordered him to retreat from him, so that he'd die at the hands of the Ammonites." David exhaled loudly as if sending the last horrid details out of his mouth.

Benaiah supposed David expected him to console him since he'd been forgiven. But he couldn't get the image out of his mind. "My lord, did the other mighty men know about this plan? Did they take part in it as well?" He couldn't imagine the betrayal if that was the case.

"Not as far as I know. I only told Joab."

"But we always look out for each other. What must Uriah have felt to see his brothers retreating from him, leaving him to be attacked by the Ammonites? What must he have suffered? Why? He would have died alone. They might not even have been able to retrieve his body for burial. The enemy may have done anything to him before he died or to his body afterwards." Benaiah couldn't stop the horrible images of Uriah's last moments. Nor could he stop himself from voicing them to David, king or not.

"And the other men, my friend, Mikhael. They all had families, all widowed and fatherless now."

David took the verbal assault from Benaiah, no doubt feeling it was justified. It didn't make Benaiah feel any better to say it, or to know it hurt David, but he had to help him understand just how horrible this action was. Uriah may have been the only intended target of David's wicked plan, but nine other soldiers were dead, ten women were widowed and many children were fatherless. Benaiah felt so angry at David—angry and disappointed.

"All of this started because of my desire for Bathsheba."

"It wasn't just that you desired her. You used your power to take her."

David nodded. "You tried to warn me."

Benaiah finally looked David in the eye. "Bathsheba was my friend's wife. I should have protected her. Even from you."

"You are not to blame, Benaiah. It was me that the prophet confronted. I sinned against Uriah, and Bathsheba, and all those other people. Every part of this sin rests on my shoulders alone. As do the consequences. Our son will die and Bathsheba will suffer yet another loss."

"I don't understand how God works, or how the death of this baby boy is somehow just. I'm sorry for all the consequences of this whole mess." Benaiah said.

"I've made a decision," David said. "I know it won't undo what I've done, but I've no wish to add hardship to the families of the fallen soldiers. Their widows will be exempt from taxes for life, even if they remarry. As will their children. And their wages will continue to be paid to the widows for life, to support them and their children. Moreover, this will be the policy in Israel for any fallen soldier from now on."

Benaiah felt some relief at this pronouncement. True, it may have arisen from his guilty conscience, but it was the right thing to do. It also gave some comfort to Benaiah to know that if he was killed in battle, his family would not suffer undue privation in his absence.

David sighed heavily as he rose from his throne. "I need to speak with Bathsheba."

Benaiah did not envy David that task.

* * *

Benaiah followed David to the Court of the Women. As they left the common room, a few advisers who had been ordered out were waiting outside the door, no doubt watching to see how he'd react to Nathan's parable and pronouncement. David breezed past them, intent on seeing his wife and new son.

Benaiah heard the high-pitched cries of the infant even before David entered Bathsheba's apartment. David flung open the door and rushed in. Benaiah took a post just inside the open doorway.

Bathsheba was pacing with the baby, trying to get him to stop crying. "I don't know what's wrong with him. He had no signs of illness all day. Now he's burning up."

David stormed back out of the room, sent someone to bring his personal physician, then went back inside and fell to his knees near the baby.

It was apparent that no one had yet told Bathsheba about Nathan's prophecy. David took the child from his mother, looked at him for a long moment, then placed him in his cradle. He pulled Bathsheba into his arms.

As David held her, he locked eyes with Benaiah over her shoulder, determination in his eyes. He didn't tell her about Nathan's prophecy, nor did he assure his wife that the baby would recover.

Was it the best decision? Benaiah couldn't tell what he would have done in that moment.

* * *

That evening, Benaiah relayed the events of the day: God's judgment pronounced by Nathan, and the child's illness and imminent death.

"Oh, how dreadful! I can hardly believe it: the other soldiers and their families, Uriah's murder, the poor baby. And Bathsheba! How is she?"

"David hasn't told her yet why the baby is sick," Benaiah said softly.

Mariah folded him in her arms and held him for a long while. She didn't say anything else. But her touch, her prayers and her listening ear gave him all the comfort he needed right now.

★ ★ ★

When Benaiah returned to the palace the next morning, one of the guards at the door to the common room informed him that David was still in Bathsheba's apartment in the Court of the Women and no cases would be heard that day. None of the advisers were there either. Benaiah wondered where Ahithophel was and how angry he was that the king had committed adultery with his granddaughter. The mood in the palace was somber. Benaiah was sure there was gossip over what had transpired yesterday, but his concern was with the king and the unfolding drama with his ill son.

The guard inside the door of Bathsheba's apartment reported, "The child is no better. The doctor has offered treatments, but to no avail. The king's wife is distraught. The king has eaten nothing at all since yesterday afternoon."

"What has the physician said?" Benaiah asked.

"He said he doesn't know what the source of the illness could be. He's tried cooling baths, but the fever remains. And now the child's breathing is becoming labored."

Benaiah peered into the room and noticed the attendants, the doctor and Bathsheba around the cradle. He knew the physician would not be able to do anything. The king was prostrate on the floor. Benaiah motioned to the king, eyebrows raised.

"He's been praying all night."

Benaiah turned back to the guard. "I'll take over now." The guard straightened, turned on his heel and left the room.

Bathsheba looked up from the couch next to the cradle and their gazes met. She reached in and picked him up. Was that look of anguish just because her child was ill, or had David told her he would not survive?

Benaiah approached the king on the floor. He knelt down near his face. "My king," he said softly. "You must eat something."

David did not respond. Benaiah stood and returned to the doorway.

Benaiah imagined the agony and helplessness he and Mariah would feel if one of their children were dying in their arms. But David's torture was worse, since he knew this suffering was a direct result of his own selfish actions.

Benaiah walked over to Bathsheba and the infant. The rise and fall of his chest indicated that each breath required great effort. "My lady, you too should rest and eat."

P. H. Thompson

Bathsheba shook her head. "If he will only be with us a short time, he will be in his mother's arms, knowing he is loved." She stroked the boy's hair, still damp from his latest cooling bath, and sniffled.

Benaiah wished he could escape this heartbreaking scene. But his job was to guard the king. Even if that meant spending the day watching desperate parents see the life ebbing away from their son.

How long would the boy suffer? *Please, Adonai, take him soon.*

★ ★ ★

For six days, Benaiah watched the child struggle to breathe, Bathsheba become more despondent and David continue to plead for the life of their baby boy. *Why, Lord? Why should this innocent infant be made to suffer for the sins of his parents?*

He would never understand the judgments of God. But, as with the king, it was not his place to question.

On the seventh day of the child's illness, God mercifully took him. Bathsheba laid the baby in his cradle so calmly and quietly, Benaiah wouldn't have known he was dead. Then she kissed his tiny forehead, her tears splashing on his motionless chest. She stood and walked past Benaiah, without looking at him, her back straight and chin high.

Benaiah was always amazed at the different ways people expressed their grief. Mariah wailed, some cried quietly, others searched for activities to do so they wouldn't have to think about it. Bathsheba had probably shed all her tears and was numb.

After she left the room, two servants approached Benaiah. "What should we do with the baby's body?"

"Do nothing until after the king has been informed," he whispered. David was still face down on the floor, arms outstretched.

"He's been like that for days. How can we tell him such news? He may seek to harm himself. You tell him."

David raised himself off the floor. He turned to the three men huddled together. "Is he dead?"

The two servants looked at each other and then at Benaiah.

"He is, my lord," Benaiah said. "I'm sorry."

David walked over to the cradle, gazed on the baby's still form and then left the room. Benaiah followed, worried he may very well do as the servants feared and harm himself.

168

The king went to his chambers, called for a bath and clean clothes, then made his way to the house of the Lord. Benaiah wondered if this was how David grieved. He followed David into the tabernacle courtyard. David brought a lamb as an offering. Benaiah watched as David laid his hands on its head and confessed his sins over it, ceremonially transferring his sin to the sacrifice about to be killed, reminding himself that sin results in death.

After the lamb was killed by Abiathar the priest, David joined others in singing psalms of worship to God. As Benaiah watched David with his hands lifted and his eyes closed as he sang, Benaiah tried to reconcile it with the man who had spent a week prostrate on the floor in prayer, crying out to God.

Afterward, David made arrangements with the priests to bury his unnamed son. Benaiah was more than a little surprised at the calm David exhibited.

Then David returned to his house and requested food. As David ate, the servants cast questioning glances at one another over the table.

When David had taken his last bite, he walked to the common room. It was empty, the counselors awaiting word that business would again resume. David took his seat on the throne. Benaiah finally questioned David's strange behavior.

"My lord, you fasted and wept for your son while he was alive. But when he died, you arose and ate food. It's hard to understand."

David smiled indulgently. "I suppose it would seem as if I did things backwards. But while the baby was still living, I cried and refused to eat because I thought, 'Who knows? Maybe the Lord will feel sorry for me and let the baby live.' But that didn't happen, so why should I fast any longer? Can I bring him back to life again? No. Someday, I'll go to him, but he cannot come back to me."

Benaiah had to admit that David's behavior showed his great faith in God's mercy. Even though David knew that God said the child would die, he still believed that God was merciful and would possibly spare him. Yet when that didn't happen, he entrusted the child into God's loving hands, believing he would see him again one day. That's why he was able to worship. Like Job of old, he could say, "When I was born into this world, I was naked and had nothing. When I die, it will be the same. The Lord gives, and the Lord takes away. Praise the name of the Lord."

★ ★ ★

The baby was buried the next day. He was as yet unnamed because he was only a week old, and he would have received his name when he was circumcised on the eighth day. Yet he was known to God.

Bathsheba's grief was revived when the tiny body, wrapped in a shroud, was lowered into the ground. It was heartbreaking to watch. David wrapped his arm around his wife. His whole family, along with the palace servants and multitudes from Jerusalem and the surrounding area who had heard the news, were in attendance.

Benaiah trudged to the common room at the start of the day. For the first time since he started working in the palace, he wanted to leave. Perhaps he could go back to Kabzeel and find work in some profession that didn't face life and death on a daily basis.

He shared his thoughts with Mariah. He was again amazed at her empathy. She said she knew this had been a hard year for him, and if he felt he needed to do something else, she would be supportive. He appreciated it, but he told her he would probably get over it soon, so not to pack yet.

Bathsheba continued to live in the Court of the Women with David's other wives and children. Benaiah imagined that she was not well received by the others because of the circumstances of her sudden marriage, which was probably the reason David went out of his way to spend more time with her after the baby died.

One day a few months later, Benaiah overheard Bathsheba tell David she was expecting again. He kissed her and told her he was happy, but she burst into tears.

"What's wrong, love?" David asked. "Aren't you pleased?"

"What if this child dies, too?"

David stroked her hair. "Don't cry, Bathsheba. I'll ask Nathan."

Benaiah remembered that in Nathan's parable, he had pronounced judgment on the rich man, saying he should pay fourfold for his sin. Did that mean that four of David's children would die? Would they all be Bathsheba's? Benaiah had no answers. Who knew the ways of God?

And would the forgiveness David experienced extend to her as well?

When David was anointed by Samuel, he said, "The Lord doesn't see as man sees; because man looks at outward appearances, but the Lord looks inward, at the heart."

What did God see when He looked at Benaiah's heart? Did He recognize his remorse, his guilt, his repentance? Did He see that Benaiah wanted only to please Yahweh?

Ever since the death of Ammizabad, Benaiah had determined to always obey. If he did that, he was sure there would be no death.

But disobedience had brought death. and now so had obedience.

How could he continue to do this job when every action and inaction led to disastrous consequences?

CHAPTER TWENTY-SEVEN

"For You do not desire sacrifice, or else I would give it; You do not delight in burnt offering. The sacrifices of God are a broken spirit, a broken and a contrite heart—these, O God, You will not despise."

—Psalm 51:16–17

After his daily visit to the Court of the Women to see his family, David asked Benaiah to accompany him to his quarters before they headed back to the common room. "I've composed a psalm for worship that I plan to sing the next time we go to the house of the Lord. May I play it for you?"

"Of course, my lord."

As David sat down and stroked his harp of cypress wood, Benaiah wondered how David could be such a rough, even ruthless soldier at times, and a gentle, creative musician at others. There was no one like him.

He sang,

"Have mercy upon me, O God,
according to Your lovingkindness;
according to the multitude of Your tender mercies,
blot out my transgressions.
Wash me thoroughly from my iniquity,
and cleanse me from my sin.

"For I acknowledge my transgressions,
and my sin is always before me.
Against You, You only, have I sinned,
and done this evil in Your sight—

> *That You may be found just when You speak,*
> *and blameless when You judge."*

Benaiah understood that, even though David had been assured of God's forgiveness by Nathan, he still felt the need to cry out to God.

> *"Behold, I was brought forth in iniquity,*
> *and in sin my mother conceived me.*
> *Behold, You desire truth in the inward parts,*
> *and in the hidden part You will make me to know wisdom.*
>
> *"Purge me with hyssop, and I shall be clean;*
> *wash me, and I shall be whiter than snow.*
> *Make me hear joy and gladness,*
> *that the bones You have broken may rejoice.*
> *Hide Your face from my sins,*
> *and blot out all my iniquities."*

Benaiah desired that kind of cleansing too. He wanted to feel joy again. Could it be possible that God would blot out David's horrific sins... and his as well?

> *"Create in me a clean heart, O God,*
> *and renew a steadfast spirit within me.*
> *Do not cast me away from Your presence,*
> *and do not take Your Holy Spirit from me."*

Could Benaiah dare to hope that both he and David could have a clean heart before God?

> *"Restore to me the joy of Your salvation,*
> *and uphold me by Your generous Spirit.*
> *Then I will teach transgressors Your ways,*
> *and sinners shall be converted to You."*

Could Almighty God actually use the awful things that had happened to be a testimony to those who didn't know Him? What an amazing God!

"Deliver me from the guilt of bloodshed, O God,
the God of my salvation,
and my tongue shall sing aloud of Your righteousness.
O Lord, open my lips,
and my mouth shall show forth Your praise.
For You do not desire sacrifice, or else I would give it;
You do not delight in burnt offering.
The sacrifices of God are a broken spirit,
a broken and a contrite heart—
These, O God, You will not despise."

For You do not desire sacrifice, or else I would give it, Benaiah repeated to himself. Although David did bring sacrifices, he understood that God also desired a broken spirit and a contrite heart, and that He wasn't concerned with only outward observances and empty ritual. It was like the words he lived by: *To obey is better than sacrifice.*

It was becoming apparent to Benaiah that the king did have a broken and contrite heart. Benaiah's heart was broken and contrite as well, which, according to David's song, meant there was hope for both of them after all.

"Do good in Your good pleasure to Zion;
Build the walls of Jerusalem.
Then You shall be pleased with the sacrifices of righteousness,
with burnt offering and whole burnt offering;
Then they shall offer bulls on Your altar."[3]

David stilled the quivering harp strings with his palms and looked up from his harp. "What do you think?"

Benaiah wiped away a tear that had escaped in spite of his effort to keep it reined in. "Do you think it could be true, my lord? Can a man's sins be covered simply because he is repentant? Will God forgive... even me?"

David set aside his harp, approached Benaiah, and put a hand on his shoulder.

"Oh, my friend, I am so sorry my sins spilled over onto you. So many people were hurt by my selfish actions that night. Yet I do believe the Lord is pleased with a broken and contrite heart."

The sacrifice on the Day of Atonement forgave the sins of the people during the previous year, but sin was never fully and permanently dealt with. What kind of sacrifice could possibly cover all the sins committed in the past, even those presumptuous sins that were unforgivable under the law?

How could God be just in judging people's sins and yet forgive them?

He would have to ask his father.

Oh, what joy would be his if he could know for certain that the Lord was not going to impute this heinous sin to his account.

★ ★ ★

As the battle for Rabbah raged on, Bathsheba bore David another son. They named him Solomon.

Benaiah recalled the day several years earlier, when Nathan visited David with the comforting promise that David would always have a descendant to sit on the throne and that his son would reign after him. God even revealed to David that the son's name would be Solomon, meaning "peaceful," because God would give peace and quietness to Israel in those days. He would also be the one to build a house to God's name.

David practically skipped as they went to the Court of the Women to see his whole family, but in particular Bathsheba and the new baby, Solomon. David's exuberance was encouraging to Benaiah and so different from his recent mood. He really did seem to revel in the joy of knowing his sin was forgiven.

David knocked on the closed door of Bathsheba's apartment and called her name. She told him to enter. As they stepped in she finished adjusting her clothing. The child was on her lap. Benaiah guessed she had been nursing him.

The wife of a king did not normally nurse her own child, whose care was normally tasked to a wet nurse. But Benaiah assumed she must be fearful of losing this child, so she didn't allow him to be farther than arm's reach away from her.

David picked up the little one to burp him. He inquired after Bathsheba's well-being, and then he handed the child back to his mother, who placed him in his cradle.

A Pelethite messenger arrived and handed Benaiah a scroll. He bowed to the king and his wife.

"The prophet Nathan sent me, sire," he said to the king. "He is not well enough to come to greet the new babe in person, but he wanted this message to be delivered immediately."

David took the scroll from Benaiah and dismissed the messenger, who bowed again before he backed out of the room. Benaiah went to stand inside the door to give the family some privacy.

David didn't seem to notice that Bathsheba flinched at the sound of the prophet's name. Did she fear he would always bring a word of condemnation?

As David read the message silently, Benaiah wondered what this message from Nathan might say... and how it might affect the king. Should David perhaps have waited to read the message until after leaving his wife's apartment, in case it was bad news?

When David looked up, he smiled at Bathsheba. "It says, 'Fear not, for this child, Solomon, is beloved of the Lord. He will sit on the throne of his father, David.'"

Bathsheba burst into tears.

David reached out to her and stroked her back. "Why are you crying, my love? This is good news. Nothing will happen to this son of ours. He will follow me on the throne."

Benaiah understood now one of the reasons the first son died. Because he was conceived while they were unmarried, some might protest his legitimate claim to the throne. That was not the case with this new son.

Bathsheba wiped at her tears with the veil over her shoulders. "For so long, I've feared that I would never be forgiven for what we did. The prophet said God forgave you, but he said nothing of me."

That was true. Benaiah could understand how she could fear that forgiveness didn't extend to her.

"I felt certain God would take this child as well."

David sat down next to her, a hopeful expression on his face.

"Instead of the judgment I deserved, God promised not just life for my son, but also the throne. The result of our union is the one God chose to succeed me. It's more than I ever expected. That's beyond mercy. It's unmerited grace and favor."

Bathsheba exhaled and smiled, and David continued.

"The sins I committed were worthy of death. Yet the prophet told me that I would not die. I don't understand how God can cover my sin without my having to pay for it. But I take Him at His word, and I rejoice in His forgiveness."

Bathsheba closed her eyes and inhaled deeply, as if drinking in the comfort of her husband's words. Then she kissed David over their sleeping child and caressed his bearded face. "My two greatest loves," Bathsheba whispered.

"Mine as well."

Benaiah wondered if he would live to see the day when this boy ascended to his father's throne. He longed to see the blessing of God on Israel.

Oh, Lord, make it so!

★ ★ ★

"A military report from General Joab, sire," the servant at the door to the common room announced. He took the scroll from the Pelethite courier and brought it to Shemaiah the scribe, who unrolled it and read it before the king.

"From General Joab to King David. Battlefield report twenty-two: twelfth day of the month of Elul. Battle with the people of Ammon. I have fought against Rabbah, the royal city, and have taken the city's water supply. Now bring the rest of the army together and attack Rabbah. Capture this city before I do, or else it'll be called by my name."

David tensed and pressed his lips together. Then his features suddenly brightened, and he smiled at Benaiah.

"Benaiah! How do you feel about doing some old-fashioned soldiering?"

Benaiah smiled back. He would love to experience that feeling a few more times in his life. As much as he appreciated the safety and routine of his current role, he was a soldier at heart. "My sword is already sharp, my lord."

"Very well. Assemble ten thousand soldiers and ready them. We march on Rabbah at dawn."

Benaiah hurried to do the king's bidding, energized by the prospect of battle. Yet he wondered at the bold tone of Joab's note. His words were practically a threat to David, challenging the king to at least make a show of being the leader of the armies of Israel. A popular military man could sway a country away from a king under the wrong circumstances; he had witnessed that with General Abner and Saul's son, Ishbosheth. Benaiah resolved to be watchful of Joab. After all, he was quite willing to obey David's order and allow Uriah to be killed on the battlefield. And he had murdered his rival, Abner, for his own personal revenge and advancement in rank.

No, Benaiah did not trust Joab. Not one bit.

★ ★ ★

The walled city of Rabbah, the capital of the people of Ammon, east of the Jordan, had already been secured by Joab and the Israelite soldiers. It remained only for David to make it official and gather the spoils.

David and his men met up with Joab and his men. Benaiah realized this was the first time David and Joab had seen each other face to face after David sent the death warrant by the hand of Uriah himself. Had Joab heard anything about the aftermath of that event: David's marriage to Bathsheba, the death of their child, the birth of Solomon?

Benaiah asked the other mighty men about the fateful battle where Uriah lost his life. The men told Benaiah they were ordered by General Joab to retreat from Uriah. It went against everything they had ever done and been trained to do to leave one of their own in such a situation. They confided to him that they felt guilty about it, and wondered at Joab's indifference when he saw Uriah fall. It made them feel insecure about his leadership. Would he do the same to them?

Good question, Benaiah thought.

The city was in ruins, and many parts burned. The Ammonite king was kept alive until David arrived. He was brought before David and forced to kneel before the king. Then David pushed him over and placed his foot on the man's neck, symbolizing the king's defeat.

"Praise be to the God of Israel, who has this day given us victory over our enemies!" David shouted. Cheers rose from the ranks of Israel's soldiers. David himself dispatched the Ammonite king.

Joab brought David the king's crown, studded with jewels. It looked heavy, possibly a talent of gold in weight, Benaiah guessed. He noticed Joab paused for a moment before placing the crown on David's head, as though hesitant to part with it. Was he imagining it on his own head instead? Or had he already tried it on? Did the man have aspirations beyond his station, even to the throne?

With the crown on David's head, Benaiah breathed a sigh of relief. It set off another round of cheers. It had been a long, hard battle, and Benaiah couldn't forget this was where ten soldiers had been lost, including Uriah and Mikhael.

There was such great spoil, it took two days to bring it all out of the city. There was gold and silver, jewels, garments, farming implements, wagons, horses and livestock. The people were rounded up and organized into groups for forced labor in brickwork and forestry.

The sight of this victory almost made Benaiah forget the ugly business with Bathsheba.

Almost.

CHAPTER TWENTY-EIGHT

"After this Absalom the son of David had a lovely sister, whose name was Tamar; and Amnon the son of David loved her."

—2 Samuel 13:1

There was no end to palace intrigue. Just as Benaiah had supposed, having more than one wife led to strife among the king's children. Now, twenty-five years later, although Israel had been at peace with their neighbors most of that time, those adorable little children had grown up and David's wives fought to have their own children as his favorites. Two of David's children were born to Maacah, the princess of Geshur: his daughter, Tamar and her brother, Absalom, who were both very attractive. Absalom had flawless features and he carried himself with a princely bearing.

As Benaiah made his way through the halls of the palace to meet with the Pelethites and Cherethites under his command, he saw twenty-five-year-old Absalom skittering down the hallway with his cousin, Jonadab. He carried a bag of rich tapestry with his arms straight down in front of him, as if it was very heavy.

The king's children had the finest tutors and access to any number of adventures and experiences, yet Benaiah noticed that, instead of taking advantage of these privileges to become men and women of character, most of them spent their days indulging themselves at the expense of the people. This was especially true of Absalom. He was handsome and he knew it. He couldn't pass a brass mirror without stopping to admire himself. He was especially proud of his thick, shiny black hair, of all things.

Benaiah stopped when they met up. "May I help my lord, the prince?"

Absalom giggled.

Benaiah inwardly rolled his eyes at the young man's silliness, but maintained a neutral expression. What man giggled like that?

"Yes, Benaiah, you may. We're transporting some of the most valuable assets in my father's kingdom, and we must hurry to secure them in the king's treasury."

Why would the prince be in possession of any spoils? And why would he be conveying them anywhere himself? The prince never performed manual labor of any sort.

Benaiah reached up to relieve him of his burden. As he took the parcel, it felt empty.

When Absalom saw his puzzled features, he and Jonadab burst out laughing, then opened the tapestry bag to reveal what looked to be a mass of black curls. Benaiah reached in to see if something precious was hidden in the unique packaging, but Absalom flicked at his fingers as if he were a naughty boy sneaking dates before mealtime.

"Ah-ah-ah! Don't touch, Benaiah. You'll mess them up."

Benaiah held his anger at the insolent young man in check, if only for David's sake. David had fallen into the trap of favoritism, and he seemed to see only Absalom's external qualities and ignored his appalling lack of character. Benaiah couldn't understand how this fawning, arrogant young man could possibly be David's favorite son.

"I had them brushed just so before they were cut off." Absalom pawed at his neck, now lightened of his long, full locks. He tipped his head from side to side. "I feel so much lighter!"

"What are you saving it for?" Benaiah asked. No one kept their hair after they'd cut it.

"I just couldn't bear to part with it after I worked so hard at its production."

Benaiah thought he'd heard everything in his field of responsibility, but to imply that growing hair was hard work? That was ridiculous. Next he'd be hoarding the clippings from his beard.

"I weighed it so it can be included in the king's treasury. Guess how much it weighed, Benaiah. Guess!"

Benaiah would not play this foolish game. He crossed his arms across his chest.

"I cannot imagine," he said dryly.

Absalom pouted. Actually pouted. "Oh, you're no fun.

"According to the king's standard, it weighed over two hundred shekels!"

"You are very fortunate to have such a treasure that automatically replenishes itself," Benaiah remarked sarcastically.

Absalom started to smile in agreement, then narrowed his eyes as if suddenly questioning Benaiah's sincerity. He snatched the treasure from Benaiah's hands and pulled it into a protective embrace.

"Never mind. I'll see to it myself." Absalom thrust his nose in the air.

"Of course, my lord. If you're sure you don't want me to make certain it arrives safely in the treasury."

Absalom turned with a sneer, pulling his cousin in his wake. As they left, Jonadab whispered, "Some people just don't appreciate how exquisite your hair is, cousin."

Benaiah walked away, shaking his head at the absurdity of Absalom's actions. These princes had no worthwhile pursuits. They'd been born into this life of privilege, hard-fought and won by David and his men. And David's nephew, Jonadab, the son of his brother, Shimeah, was flattering the prince, but to what end? To win his favor? Did he anticipate great things from Absalom in the future because of David's obvious favoritism?

Absalom's pursuits were even more self-indulgent than his siblings. He showed no interest in politics and seemed resigned to accept the idea that his elder brother, Amnon would succeed David as king; Benaiah supposed it was not common knowledge that Solomon would be the next king. Absalom's vanity earned the disgust of most of the soldiers, who would often complain in the guard house about the arrogant young prince.

His one redeeming quality was his fierce loyalty to his mother and sister. That was because, in spite of David thinking he had only one family, he in fact had at least seven factions because of his seven wives. The children of the concubines had no real power or future, but they tried to win his favor nonetheless.

One day, Absalom burst in the common room and interrupted the business of the day, causing David to postpone the case to the next day. After the room was cleared of all but essential staff, David asked the reason for his son's sudden appearance.

"I knew this would happen! That son of yours has been drooling over my sister for years!" Absalom stormed.

David descended from his throne to stand face-to-face with his favorite son, no doubt to calm him so he could make sense of his outburst.

"What has happened? Which son?" David asked.

Absalom growled. "I shouldn't be surprised that you didn't even know what was going on. It's Amnon! He tricked Tamar into coming to his home to care for him because he feigned illness. Then he sent everyone else out and forced himself on her. She begged him not to do it! She even tried to put him off by telling him to ask you for permission to marry her instead, but he wouldn't hear of it!"

David's mouth fell open. "I... how could he do that? And lie to me? I went to see him because I heard he was sick, and he convinced me to send Tamar to him to bake some cakes for him. So I did. I never suspected he was pretending to be ill or planning such a thing!"

Benaiah could see David felt guilty for his part in this horrific act.

"Where is Tamar now?" David asked.

"She is at my home, where she will remain. We will care for her." David seemed to know better than to protest.

"She came to me directly, her robe of many colors torn, ashes on her head in mourning. I couldn't console her. She knows this means she will never marry. Amnon has seen to that. I knew right away what had happened. But it was even worse because after he attacked her, he despised her, as if she was the guilty party, and he put her out of the room and ordered his servants to bolt the door behind her."

"What of Amnon? Did you confront him?" David asked, but grimaced as if he feared the answer.

"Of course I did! He tried to divert the blame to your nephew, Jonadab. Amnon claimed it was he who suggested the ruse in the first place, when he saw how distressed over her he was. He was getting thinner because he wasn't eating." Absalom looked ready to spit. "Poor little prince!" he added sarcastically.

"You didn't hurt him, did you?"

Absalom was incredulous. "I should have, but I didn't. I have control over my emotions, unlike Amnon. Besides, I expected that you would find a suitable punishment once you heard about it. That's why I came to you."

David seemed to be considering his options.

"Take me to Tamar. I'll see her first."

Benaiah accompanied the king and prince to Absalom's home, where David consoled Tamar. Then he went to see Amnon. He heard the prince try to defend his actions. Benaiah was not convinced, but David seemed almost sympathetic to the scoundrel.

Benaiah was shocked at the story itself, because such a thing should not happen in Israel, and the royal family should be examples of righteousness. But more than shock; it was disappointment he felt towards David. He expected that when the news came about what his eldest son had done, he'd act decisively. But there was no action against his son except a tongue lashing. He didn't even consult the priests about it, perhaps because he didn't want to hear the answer.

David's feelings of entitlement as a man in a powerful position had clearly passed on to his son.

David's indulgent attitude toward his children and his leniency in punishing them may have been in part due to lingering guilt over the incident with Bathsheba, which no one seemed to forget. They were all waiting for the other consequences that Nathan the prophet assured them were to come.

Benaiah wondered if, after his sin with Bathsheba, perhaps David didn't feel he had the right to judge his children. But as a king and as a parent, it was his responsibility to set standards and uphold them.

Nothing good could come from letting such a transgression pass.

Benaiah also worried about Absalom. He had expected the passionate young man to retaliate against Amnon, but as he remained calm in the following weeks and months, almost indifferent; it gave Benaiah pause. It was so unlike him. In fact, he acted almost like it had never happened, and went back to planning parties, measuring the weight of his haircut and indulging himself with all the privileges of royalty.

★ ★ ★

Two years later, a herald burst into the common room. The guards stopped him with spears crisscrossing his chest.

"I have an urgent message for the king!" he cried.

"Speak," David said.

"Absalom has killed all the king's sons, every one of them!"

The king stood, cried out and ripped his outer robe. He stepped down from his throne and fell prostrate on the floor. He had seventeen sons.

All of his servants likewise tore their clothes and lay face down, except Benaiah, who remained vigilant. Could the king's life also be threatened?

He recalled Nathan's words, when he announced the punishment that was to come upon David because of his sin with Bathsheba: *Your family will never live in peace.*

But to lose all of his sons in one day! It was unthinkable.

Jonadab, David's nephew, burst into the common room. "Permission to approach the king?" he asked.

Benaiah put his hand on his sword and stepped forward, glaring at the young man.

185

"What is this about?" Benaiah demanded.

"I have news for the king."

"If it's about his sons, we already know," Benaiah replied dismissively.

"My lord the king," he addressed David, ignoring Benaiah. "It's not true that Absalom has killed all of the king's sons, for only Amnon is dead."

David slowly raised his head. Tears streaked his face, and his eyes were red and puffy.

"They're not all dead?" he asked weakly.

Jonadab smiled and repeated himself, as if it was good news that any one of the king's sons should be dead. "Absalom has been planning this since the day Amnon forced himself on his sister, because he hated him for it and wanted to see justice done."

Benaiah knew Absalom's cool response was not in character. But for him to wait this long as he planned his revenge? The man was calculating and devious, not unlike Jonadab. And how was it that Jonadab had become so close to Absalom now as to know what he was plotting? This was the same man who had convinced Amnon to rape his half-sister. And now his allegiance was with the brother of Amnon's victim? What kind of game was he playing?

David sat up. A watchman near the window, exclaimed, "My lord, a crowd of men on mules are coming from the hillside in the direction of Absalom's home. They are dressed like the king's sons."

Jonadab's eyes sparkled. "See? The king's sons are coming! They are well, just as I told you!"

The king's sons arrived and came straight into the common room, where David embraced them. They all wept and spoke at once to tell David what had transpired.

David asked Shephatiah, his son by Abital, to speak on behalf of the group.

"Oh, my king! We were drinking wine. Everyone was joyful. Absalom practically made Amnon the guest of honor, lavishing all the best food and wine on him. Then suddenly he shouted to his servants, 'Strike Amnon!' Before anyone could blink, he was stabbed in the back. I hadn't even seen a weapon. When our brother fell over dead, we feared we were next, so we fled for our lives. Oh, Father, it was horrible!"

"How could he do such a thing to his own brother?" David exclaimed. Then he embraced his sons again. "I'm so thankful you are all safe."

Perhaps from now on David would be more active in his sons' lives, control them more firmly. After all, they were no longer children fighting over toys in the courtyard; they were young men who would be soon be involved in leading the nation.

Benaiah sighed. It was unlikely that the way David behaved toward his sons would really change. He wondered how much more devastation and grief lay in store for the king from his own household.

"Where is my son, Absalom?" David asked, his voice hoarse.

"He has fled to his mother's family in Geshur," Jonadab announced.

Geshur was across the Jordan and on the north east side of the Sea of Chinnereth. Absalom's grandfather was King Talmai of Geshur. Benaiah was relieved to hear that at least he didn't try to flee to a city of refuge; those six cities were only for people who were guilty of manslaughter, not premeditated murder, like Absalom.

Benaiah wondered how Jonadab already knew where Absalom had fled. Had he been in on the planning for this murder all along? Benaiah would investigate.

"I don't want Absalom back in Jerusalem so I can punish him. In spite of all he has done, he is still my son."

David's pronouncement so soon after the murder shocked Benaiah. David's lack of justice after a crime was what led to Absalom taking matters into his own hands in the first place. Now he was going to let Absalom get away with premeditated murder?

He was again showing his weakness in the area of parental discipline by favoring one son over the others.

CHAPTER TWENTY-NINE

"Now a messenger came to David, saying, 'The hearts of the men of Israel are with Absalom.'"

—2 Samuel 15:13

For three long years, Absalom remained with his grandfather, Talmai, the king of Geshur. Although David mourned for his son every day, often wondering aloud how long he planned to stay away, Benaiah appreciated his absence. Benaiah didn't trust him.

In fact, David spoke more of Absalom, the murderer, than Amnon, the murdered son. While Amnon was no upright character, considering he had raped his half-sister, he didn't deserve to be murdered by his own brother..

Absalom returned to Jerusalem after Joab hatched a plan to ingratiate himself to the king, because he perceived that David longed for Absalom to return. Benaiah was surprised by this, since he knew Joab cared for Absalom least among all the king's sons. But if something would be expedient for himself and his future, he'd even do something as distasteful as this.

David didn't know it at the time, but one of the daily cases he judged had a hidden meaning. Joab had paid a woman of Tekoa to dress in mourning apparel and come before the king with a made up story.

She cried out, "My king, please help me!"

The king said to her, "What's the problem?"

She answered, "I'm a widow, alone with two sons. They were fighting out in the field, and because there was no one to break them apart, one son was killed by the other."

A sad story indeed, Benaiah thought.

"Now the whole family is against me. They told me to hand over the son who killed his brother, so that they can put him to death for murder, since they are the avengers of blood in our family. But that would mean that my late husband will have no heir, and the flame of life will be extinguished. No one will be able to care for my husband's property, and it will pass to a stranger. My husband's name will pass into obscurity."

David said to the woman, "Go home, and I'll take care of things for you." He needed time to consider the matter and possibly consult with his advisers.

But then the woman of Tekoa said to the king, "Let the blame be on me, my lord and king. You and your kingdom are innocent."

David nodded. "If anyone speaks against you, bring him to me. They won't bother you again." He was offering his protection while the matter was sorted.

The woman clasped her hands. "Please promise me by God that you won't let them take the life of my other son." She had a legitimate fear that one of her relatives would come after her son in the meantime.

"As God is my witness, no one will harm even a hair on your son's head," David promised.

Then the woman was emboldened to say, "May I say one more thing to the king?"

David nodded his assent for her to proceed.

"Why has the king done the same thing? By saying these things, you show you are guilty because you've not brought back the son who you forced to leave home."

Understanding lit David's eyes. She was speaking about Absalom, but making it seem like Amnon was killed unintentionally like the brother in her fictional story. Surely David would see that!

"We will all die and be like water spilled on the ground, unable to be gathered up again. You know God forgives people and provides a place of safety for them to flee to. I knew you would be able to help me, because you are like an angel of God, discerning between truth and error.'"

David leaned forward and said to the woman, "You must answer truthfully the question I ask of you."

"Please ask the question, my king."

"Did Joab put you up to this?" David said.

The woman answered, "You are right, my lord. General Joab did tell me to say these things, hoping to bring about a change of affairs if you saw this situation from a different point of view. But you have the wisdom of God and will no doubt do the right thing."

Then the king summoned Joab and said to him, "All right, I'll do it. Go and bring back the young man, Absalom."

Benaiah was surprised when proud Joab fell to the ground on his face and thanked the king.

Joab said, "Now I know you're pleased with me, because you've done as I asked."

Benaiah was perplexed at David's image of his son, Absalom. He still referred to him as a young man, even though he was already thirty-one. At what point would David see him as a man, responsible for his own actions? And what did Joab have to gain by encouraging David to end his estrangement with Absalom?

So Joab traveled to Geshur and brought Absalom back to Jerusalem. However, the king stipulated, "Absalom must go back to his own house. He cannot come to see me." So Absalom remained on house arrest.

This didn't sit well with Absalom though, and after a time, he tried to talk with Joab, but he wouldn't come when called. So Absalom ordered his servants to set one of Joab's barley fields on fire. When Joab challenged him about his rash decision, he said, "I wanted to send you to the king to ask him why he even bothered to have me return from Geshur. I can't see him, so I might as well have stayed there. I demand to see the king. But if he thinks I'm guilty of some crime, let him execute me himself."

When David heard that, he allowed Absalom to come to the palace. Benaiah didn't trust the prince. He still wasn't sure he hadn't also intended to assassinate the king that day when he murdered his brother, and was only hindered because David refused to go.

Absalom made a great show of obeisance to the king, bowing low before him with his face to the ground. Then the king kissed him and welcomed him back.

But Benaiah regarded Absalom with suspicion.

★ ★ ★

Soon Absalom, his father's favorite son, became the people's favorite as well.

David remarked how there seemed to be fewer cases to judge lately. Benaiah didn't think there had ceased to be strife in the country, so he decided to investigate.

As Benaiah arrived at the palace, he passed by the city gate where business was conducted. As people passed by there on their way to see the king for his judgment in a dispute, Absalom, who had arrived early, would intercept them, find out the details of the case and reassure them that they had a legitimate claim.

Benaiah overheard him say, "Look, you all have legitimate concerns, but the king is far too busy and distracted with other affairs to see to the issues of the common man." Then he sighed dramatically.

"I wish someone would make me a judge in this country! Then I could help everyone who comes to me with a problem. I would be able to get them a fair solution to their concern."

When the people began to complain about the king being too busy to hear them, he'd say, "I would be honored to hear your civil cases."

So the people brought their cases to Absalom.

Benaiah would have liked to challenge Absalom publicly about his behavior, but for David's sake he refrained and instead reported it to the king. But again, no action was taken.

Absalom's wife had borne him three sons and a daughter, whom he named Tamar after his sister, but, tragically, all of his sons died at a young age. Since he would never have any heirs to carry on his branch of the family line, he commissioned a monument to be built to commemorate his life. It was set up in the King's Valley and was known as Absalom's monument.

When Benaiah heard where it was placed, he thought, *How arrogant of Absalom to assume he'll be king!* Benaiah suspected that becoming the next king had been in his mind from an early age, but more so once he murdered his eldest brother. The second son, Daniel, sometimes called Chileab, who was David's son by Abigail, was sickly, and not likely to survive. That left Absalom next in line to the throne. He must not have heard that God ordained Solomon to follow David. Perhaps it was for the best, so the young prince Solomon would remain safe.

Rumors reached the palace that the populace had turned from David to Absalom. That was concerning enough, and David had been warned earlier, but now talk of conspiracy was confirmed. David changed from thinking only the best about Absalom to fearing him. He didn't even dare to confront him, which fell in line with David's manner of dealing with family disputes. Instead, he gave the order, and he and the royal family and all the palace household staff fled for their lives from Absalom. Joab, the mighty men, and hundreds of soldiers also followed David. He only left behind ten of his concubines.

Absalom knew better than to try to usurp power in Jerusalem where the king dwelt. Instead, he gathered a large group of important people to Hebron, where David reigned seven years, and then sounded a trumpet and had people shout, "Absalom is king in Hebron!" The original group of two hundred went along innocently, but because they were men of influence, it attracted more and more people to the conspiracy. Absalom had even managed to draw away Bathsheba's grandfather, Ahithophel, who had turned against David because of David's adultery with Bathsheba.

Because of the large number of people who fled and the haste required, David told them only to take the essentials. David had encouraged his loyal friend Hushai the Archite to stay behind and act as a spy and tell Absalom, "'My king, I am your servant. I am faithful to whomever the people of Israel choose. As I served your father, now I will serve you.' By being close to him, you may be able to disagree with any advice from Ahithophel and make it useless." He then arranged for him to relay information to David through the sons of the priests. It was through Jonathan and Ahimaaz that David heard what happened after they left.

At the advice of Ahithophel, David's once loyal adviser, Absalom set up a tent on the palace roof. He took each of David's remaining concubines into the tent, one at a time, and slept with them. What a disgusting way to send a message that David's kingdom was now his.

David ran his hands through his wavy hair. "Is this not what Nathan told me would happen because I took another man's wife?"

Benaiah recalled the prophet's words clearly, as they had rung in his head every day for the past ten years, pondering their meaning. *I'll bring trouble against you from someone in your own family, and I'll take your wives and give them to another man before your very eyes. He'll sleep with them in the open. Your sin was done in secret, but the punishment will be out in public, for everyone in Israel to see.*

Now he understood.

★ ★ ★

The whole country wept as the royal family fled for their lives. The king himself crossed over the Brook Kidron, and all the people crossed over toward the way of the wilderness.

The priests, Zadok and Abiathar, and the Levites fled with them, bearing the ark of the covenant of God.

David said to Zadok, "Take the ark of God back into Jerusalem. If God shows me favor, He'll bring me back to see the tabernacle and it again. But if not, then let Him do whatever He wants to me." So Zadok and Abiathar carried the ark of God back to Jerusalem and remained there.

After two days' travel, David's company was running out of supplies. Then they saw Mephibosheth's servant Ziba approach with saddled donkeys, loaded down with about two hundred loaves of bread, clusters of raisins, summer fruits, and skins of wine.

David eyed Ziba with suspicion. "What do you intend to do with these provisions?"

Ziba bowed low before the king. "The donkeys are for the king's household to ride on. The bread and fruit are for the servants to eat, and the wine is refreshment for whoever begins to feel weak in the desert."

While not a lot, it would sustain them for the day at least.

David looked beyond Ziba, as if searching for someone. "Where is Mephibosheth, your master? Why is he not here with you?"

Ziba looked to the ground, but Benaiah thought it was because he didn't want to look David in the eye as he lied to him. "He is still in Jerusalem. I heard him say, 'Now the Israelites will give my father's kingdom back to me,' so I fled to find you, my king."

David reeled back in shock. Benaiah could hardly believe it either. This was Jonathan's son, the one David had taken into the palace and cared for as his own. Had he really defected to Absalom, hoping to turn the kingdom back to the descendants of Saul? It didn't seem likely. Not from what he knew of Mephibosheth's character all these years. He was loyal to David. If anyone was not to be trusted, it was Ziba.

Ziba had always seemed self-serving. Even now, he was giving up Mephibosheth's location and speaking disparagingly of him to the king while building himself up, as though he were being generous.

In spite of the fact that there was no evidence to support Mephibosheth's defection other than Ziba's testimony, yet David surprised him by saying to Ziba, "All right, I'll give you everything that belonged to Mephibosheth."

Ziba said, "I humbly bow before you. I pray I'll always be able to please you."

When Ziba caught Benaiah's glare, he quickly averted his eyes. Benaiah didn't care. Let Ziba know he was watching him.

CHAPTER THIRTY

"And David said to Abishai and all his servants, 'See how my son who came from my own body seeks my life. How much more now may this Benjamite? Let him alone, and let him curse; for so the Lord has ordered him.'"

—2 Samuel 16:11

A s David and his household trudged along the countryside, fleeing from Absalom, they came to a point where they had to pass through a valley bracketed by high cliffs. Without warning, rocks landed around them: not a landslide, but well-aimed projectiles. The mighty men closed in around the royal family to absorb the blows; they held up their shields to deflect the rain of heavy rocks.

Then a voice called out to David from above them on the cliff.

"Get out, get out, you no-good murderer! The Lord is punishing you for killing the people in Saul's family. You usurped Saul as king, but now the same bad things are happening to you, and you deserve them. God has handed over the kingdom to your son, Absalom, because you're a murderer."

"Who is that?" Benaiah asked David.

"I know him. His name is Shimei, a Benjamite from Bahurim. He's a relative of Palti, the man my father married Michal off to." He added, "He must be doubly angry. First as a Benjamite from the same tribe as Saul. He no doubt assumed I was responsible for the deaths of Abner and Ishbosheth, so he called me a murderer. And then because Michal was taken from his relative and returned to me."

Abishai, Joab's brother, said to David, "Who does this dead dog think he is to curse the king? Let me go over and remove his head."

But the king said, "What am I to do with you? Both you and your brother are always quick to use your swords to solve problems. Perhaps Shimei is cursing me because God put it into his mind to curse me."

David addressed everyone else who was present. "Look, if my own son is trying to kill me, should I be surprised to hear curses from this man from the tribe of Benajmin? Let it go. If God has ordered him to curse, who am I to stop him?"

David hung his head and walked on in silence. Shimei continued to curse, and David nodded as if he agreed with all that the scoundrel said.

Benaiah knew David must be so discouraged to be on the run again after so many years of stability. He was not pleased to be here either; he'd had to send for Mariah and the younger children to meet them as they fled.

And now David felt he deserved the curses. "Perhaps the Lord will see all my troubles and repay me with something good in place of everything this man is saying."

It was true that the Lord had brought this suffering on David because of his sin, but it was his sin against Bathsheba and Uriah that caused it, not any injustice to the house of Saul.

The rocks continued to rain down on them while they walked swiftly. After they passed out of range, they refreshed themselves in the Lord. He would see them through in spite of their many enemies. That much they learned from their previous wilderness experience.

Benaiah had never seen David so broken. Not even during that horrible week when David and Bathsheba grieved the loss of their first son. Or when David heard about the rape of Tamar, the murder of Amnon, or Absalom's banishment and subsequent rebellion. Not even with the public humiliation of David's concubines. To bear the cursing of one man as he fled in disgrace must have seemed a small thing to David in comparison to what he had already suffered.

Joab approached David. "I know we have women and children with us, but we must hurry, my lord. Absalom will no doubt send his troops after us as soon as he learns we've gone. Ahithophel will advise him that way, no doubt."

David smiled. "I have no fear in that regard. I planted a spy in Absalom's court; my loyal friend, Hushai the Archite. He will report any news back to us through Jonathan and Ahimaaz, sons of the priests, Abiathar and Zadok. And I've prayed that God would confound the advice of Ahithophel."

That evening as they stopped to eat, the two spies arrived at David's camp.

"Come, sit. Would you like some water?" David offered. They shook their heads.

"We were almost discovered, but a servant girl hid us in a dry well and spread a blanket and ground grain over it so we were concealed while soldiers searched for us. We came to inform you that Ahithophel has advised against you. He offered to lead a troop of twelve thousand men to pursue you this very night. By coming on your company when you were weak and weary from your flight, he was sure the people would flee, and then you could be struck down. Then the people would be returned to Absalom and there would be peace."

Ahithophel's plan was sound and would most certainly have ended in success. Twelve thousand troops against their small number were sure to succeed. If that was the case, they'd best flee or be ready to fight. Benaiah would prefer the former, since they had women and children with them.

"At first the elders were pleased with the advice. But then Absalom summoned Hushai the Archite." Jonathan continued, out of breath. "Hushai contradicted Ahithophel's advice without disparaging him, who understood David's strategies, strengths and weaknesses better than anyone. He merely stated, 'The advice that Ahithophel has given is not good *at this time*.' He reminded Absalom that David and his men were valiant warriors and the situation would enrage them, much like a bear robbed of her cubs. He suggested David would not even be in the midst of his people, but would be encamped elsewhere. He also proposed that even the smallest losses from Israel would be inflated to sound like a resounding defeat.

"As an alternative plan, Hushai suggested mobilizing a huge, country-wide army, from Dan in the north to Beersheba in the south, with the inspiring presence of Absalom himself at the lead, and then search David out, falling on him with even more overwhelming numbers. This way, not only would David be destroyed, but all the valiant men with him."

"Hushai added that if David were to take refuge in some city, its walls could be taken down stone by stone," Ahimaaz said.

Amazingly, Absalom and the elders of Israel agreed, and one elder said, "Hushai's advice is better than Ahithophel's."

It most certainly wasn't. But Hushai's eloquence and dramatic flair convinced Absalom that he should personally head a large, victorious army. They also pandered to Absalom's pride that he should personally lead the search for David. Absalom's men became convinced that David and his men, who were too valiant to overthrow at the beginning of his speech, would be trapped by superior numbers and easily defeated. David's prayer that God would confound the advice of Ahithophel, had been answered.

Nevertheless, Hushai's misdirection had given David's small company time to escape, recover their strength and choose the best terrain in which to fight.

The messengers encouraged David to flee immediately and cross the river Jordan. "There is still a possibility that Absalom will change his mind."

Once David reached the Jordan, Absalom's army would lose the advantage of surprise. Then they'd surely turn back from their pursuit.

They picked up their pace and headed east to the Jordan River. Thanks be to God, they'd be safe tonight.

CHAPTER THIRTY-ONE

"And Absalom made Amasa captain of the army instead of Joab…"

—2 Samuel 17:25

The next news David received after they crossed the Jordan regarded Ahithophel.

When Absalom took Hushai the Archite's advice over his, Ahithophel must have realized that there would be no future for him if Absalom were defeated. Aware of what was at stake, he traveled to his home in the country, set his affairs in order and hanged himself. When David got the news, he went to inform Bathsheba of the death of her grandfather. Then David told Eliam, who was Ahithophel's son, and one of his mighty men.

Benaiah had always admired Ahithophel. He'd been a wise counselor and an invaluable member of David's court. But his anger at David over his treatment of Bathsheba had simmered over the years, until he could no longer respect the king. Benaiah had long wondered why David kept him as part of his inner circle.

They also learned Absalom made his cousin Amasa, son of Jether, captain of the army in place of Joab. Amasa was Joab's cousin. Their mothers, Abigail and Zeruiah, were David's half-sisters. These cousins now commanded opposing armies. Benaiah wondered how Joab would feel when he heard the news, considering how he treated his rival, Abner. Would Amasa's life be in danger, too?

When David and his company came to Mahanaim, beyond the Jordan River, three men approached them with wagons loaded with bedrolls and basins, earthen vessels for cooking and washing, and supplies of wheat, barley and flour, parched grain and beans, lentils and parched seeds, honey and curds, sheep and cheese. The Lord provided for His people in the wilderness yet again. It was probably even better tasting than manna, Benaiah concluded.

One of the men was Machir, son of Ammiel, from Lo Debar—who had sheltered Mephibosheth in the years before David sought him out—and the other was Barzillai the Gileadite. The third man was Shobi, the son of Nahash, from Rabbah in Ammon, east of the Jordan, and the son of a former enemy of David.

In the evening, after the children were all settled, Benaiah searched for Machir to speak with him privately. He relayed Ziba's version of what had happened when they were forced to flee, and what he claimed about Mephibosheth's loyalties transferring to Absalom in hopes that the house of Saul would regain power.

Machir shook his head. "I don't believe that. Mephibosheth was terrified of David when he lived with me. But once he was received, cared for and sustained by the king, he had nothing but respect and honor for him. He was astounded that the lands owned by King Saul were restored to his descendants. But he did not aspire to the throne of Israel in any way; he would never do that."

"What could Ziba gain, then, by lying and misrepresenting Mephibosheth?"—Then it dawned on him—"Other than Mephibosheth's land, which David has already given him."

"The estate is quite large, and that scheming servant would rather own it than just work it. I never trusted him, and now it seems he has David's trust and favor. He has made Mephibosheth appear to be a deceitful opportunist instead of himself."

Benaiah clapped him on the shoulder. "Thank you for your opinion."

He would have to watch Ziba carefully and keep him away from David.

★ ★ ★

David numbered the soldiers who were with him and set captains over the hundreds and thousands. He divided them into thirds under the command of Joab, his brother Abishai, and Ittai the Gittite.

David girded on his sword.

"No, no, no, my lord." Benaiah said. "You cannot go out with the soldiers. If the rest of us flee away from Absalom's army, they won't care about us. Even if half of us died, they wouldn't care. But you are worth ten thousand of us. Besides, you're of more value to us here."

David sighed and removed his sword. "Whatever seems best to you I will do."

Perhaps the thought that he might come face-to-face with his son was not something he wanted to experience.

Instead, David observed the troops as they marched out, encouraging them by his presence. As they prepared to move out, David spoke with Joab, Abishai and Ittai.

"Deal gently with the young man, Absalom, for my sake." The commanders responded affirmatively, except for Joab, who appeared to only move his lips.

CHAPTER THIRTY-TWO

"Then the king was deeply moved, and went up to the chamber over the gate, and wept. And as he went, he said thus: 'O my son Absalom—my son, my son Absalom—if only I had died in your place! O Absalom my son, my son!'"
— 2 Samuel 18:33

The armies of father against son engaged in battle in the forests of Ephraim. Before long, the smaller force of David's men had killed twenty thousand of Israel's troops under Absalom. It was bittersweet, since these were formerly their fellow soldiers and citizens of Israel, but they were part of the rebellion that had to be put down.

Joab was overjoyed when he learned they were near Absalom's troops, but what he really wanted was to run into the man himself. Then run him through. Though he had been the one to suggest David receive Absalom back to Jerusalem after the murder of Amnon, he only did that to try to get back into David's good graces. He felt the king still hadn't forgiven him for the murder of his rival, General Abner.

But now he wanted nothing more than to dispatch that simpering upstart who had caused them to run for their lives. He had had enough of that in his younger days, when David was on the run from Saul. Now he wanted to live in Jerusalem with his family and his fields, command a peacetime army and live in ease.

Absalom had changed all that. Yet in spite of his treason, David was still going easy on him. "Be gentle with the young man, Absalom, for my sake." Joab spat in disgust. He'd be gentle all right, just a few gentle jabs with his sword.

One of his soldiers ran up to him and reported that he saw Absalom caught in a low-hanging tree branch by his hair as he was trying to ride under it on his mule. The mule rode on and Absalom was left hanging.

"You just saw him? And you left him there? Why did you not run him through with your sword? I would have rewarded you with silver and a belt."

"Even if you were to give me a thousand pieces of silver, I wouldn't raise my hand against the king's son. We all heard the king give explicit instructions to the generals regarding him. I would have been gambling with my own life. For the king would hear of it and then you would set yourself against me and deny ever giving such an order."

Joab couldn't argue that what he said was probably true.

"I won't waste my time here with you! Where was he?" he demanded.

The soldier pointed to the forest directly behind him. Joab motioned to his armor-bearer and nine other soldiers to follow him. He found his cousin, Absalom, suspended above the ground, caught by the very object of his vanity, his hair. He was well within reach. Close enough to taunt.

"Well, well, well. Lost your mule, I heard?" He laughed, as did his soldiers.

Absalom's wide eyes darted between the men beneath him. He didn't beg for mercy, which made Joab admire him just a little bit. But, maybe he didn't beg because he already knew he wouldn't receive any compassion.

"So, you fancy yourself a king, do you? Did you think you'd be able to wear a crown on that mane on your head? Do you think because your tribe's symbol is the lion of Judah that you have to look like one?"

He circled Absalom.

"You seem a little stuck there, young man. It doesn't look comfortable."

Joab was enjoying this. He despised him.

"Shall we put you out of your misery, then?"

Absalom whimpered.

"What's that?" Joab cupped his ear as if he cared to hear what the man had to say.

He was done. He cast the first spear himself, relishing the sound it made as it pierced Absalom's mid-section. He was still alive, and the second spear hit his heart. There was no more whimpering, but Joab took a spear from his armor-bearer and sent it into his chest for good measure.

"Don't worry," he said to the armor-bearer, "you'll get it back."

Satisfied that Absalom was dead, but now thinking his men might feel left out, he held out his arm to present the object at hand.

"Have at him."

The ten soldiers took turns hurling spears, thrusting swords, swinging clubs and doing whatever came to their minds to do to the corpse dangling from the tree.

Eventually, Joab said, "Enough. Cut him down."

He looked around in the forest and saw a natural pit about three feet deep.

"He should be buried. Toss him in there and cover him with rocks. It should keep the animals away for a while at least. He is a prince, after all."

Joab walked out of the woods and blew his trumpet, halting the battle. Without a leader, Israel was essentially defeated by David's forces.

★ ★ ★

Benaiah saw two runners approach. When the first one, Ahimaaz, son of Zadok, arrived, David asked how the battle was.

Still panting, he bowed down with his face to the earth before the king, and said, "Praise the Lord God! He has brought about the defeat of the men who rose up against you."

The king asked, "But is Absalom still safe?"

Ahimaaz hesitated, then answered, "When Joab sent us, I saw a great commotion, but I'm not sure what it was about."

Benaiah wondered why Ahimaaz hesitated when a moment before he seemed eager to share the news. Did he fear David's response? Was it bad news?

David looked beyond him and then said, "Wait here."

Just then another runner, a Cushite came, and he said, "I bring good news, my lord. Today the Lord has punished all those who were against you!"

And the king asked the Cushite, "But how is Absalom?"

So the Cushite answered, "May whoever tries to hurt you suffer the same end as he did!"

Then Benaiah knew that Absalom had been killed in battle. David tore his robe and cried out, "Oh, Absalom, my dear son! I wish I had died instead of you!"

Really? Why were they on the run then, if David didn't care about saving his life? If he would've been as happy if Absalom took the throne and had David's family and followers executed. Benaiah understood David was grieving his favorite son, but this was too much!

★ ★ ★

Joab returned to the city gate where David waited in the room suspended between the two gate posts. He and his men were shouting and celebrating their victory as they arrived, but they were shushed by Benaiah, who stood guard.

"Why do we need to be quiet? We just won! It's over now. The usurper is dead and we can get the king back to Jerusalem and life as usual."

Benaiah answered, "The king has just heard the news and is weeping and mourning his son."

"His son? As in, Absalom, his son?" Joab asked, incredulous.

Benaiah nodded. Then Joab looked up at the open window when he heard it for himself.

"Oh, Absalom, my dear son! I wish I had died instead of you! Oh, Absalom, my son, my son!"

Joab pursed his lips and pushed past Benaiah. He stomped up the steps and pushed open the door to David's room, Benaiah following close behind him.

David turned at the sound of the open door, his eyes red. Joab placed his clenched fists on his hips.

"Today, you have humiliated all of the men who just saved your life and the lives of your sons and daughters. Instead of celebrating a great victory over that usurper that caused us to flee Jerusalem, we had to steal back here in silence, as if we had something to be ashamed of."

He let that sink in, then added, "You have made it clear that the commanders and their men mean nothing to you. Apparently you would be pleased if Absalom were alive today and all of us were dead."

David's mouth fell open, no doubt shocked at Joab's sharp rebuke.

Joab pointed to the door. "Now, go out there and encourage your men. Because if you don't, I swear by the Lord that not a man will be left with you by nightfall, and it will be worse for you now than it had been all the years from your youth."

David rightly recognized there was truth to what Joab said, so he went out and sat by the gate.

But Benaiah wondered if Joab's threat about David losing all his soldiers implied that it would be Joab, himself, who would draw them away.

CHAPTER THIRTY-THREE

*"And say to Amasa, 'Are you not my bone and my flesh? God do so to me, and more
also, if you are not commander of the army before me continually in place of Joab.'"*
—2 Samuel 19:13

*"But Amasa did not notice the sword that was in Joab's hand. And he struck him
with it in the stomach, and his entrails poured out on the ground; and he did not
strike him again. Thus he died."*
—2 Samuel 20:10

With Absalom dead and the revolt quashed, David sent messengers ahead to
Amasa, and promoted him to command the whole army of Israel in place
of Joab. Since he had been appointed by Absalom he had the respect of half of
Israel. It would be a good way to begin to heal the country.

Benaiah wasn't sure if David suspected Joab had a hand in Absalom's death.
He himself knew it to be true because Joab boasted about it. But Benaiah thought
it best not to tell David, unless he asked directly. Yet it was hard to imagine that
Amasa's promotion over Joab was only for political advantage, and not to spite
his nephew. David must at least have suspected that Joab killed his son against
his direct orders. It would be a way to punish him indirectly, which seemed to fit
David's non-confrontational way to deal with conflicts and difficult personalities.

Was David's lack of resolve to stand up to Joab partially because he feared
Joab's volatility and his sway over his army? Did he think Joab capable of a military coup like General Abner had done to Saul's son, Ishbosheth? Perhaps.

When Joab did finally hear he had been replaced as general, he stormed
through the House of the Mighty Men, kicking over helmets and shouting that
David rewards rebellion and punishes loyalty. There was some truth to that, since
he was so quick to flee from Absalom, basically handing the kingdom over to him,

and then grieving his loss rather than celebrating their victory. And demoting Joab after his great victory over Israel, was yet more proof.

But Benaiah was concerned about Joab's anger. Might he direct it at the king if he was angry enough?

Once David heard that the people of the land were with him again, he returned to Jerusalem with his family. As the king neared the Jordan, a group of about a thousand men came up to the troop and offered to ferry the king's household across the river.

Once they crossed the Jordan, Benaiah recognized Shimei, Ziba, Mephibosheth and Barzillai approach, along with whom he guessed to be Ziba's fifteen sons and twenty servants. Shimei, son of Gera, was the Benjamite who had cursed David and tried to stone him as he fled from Absalom.Benaiah wondered why Shimei and Ziba would be allied together. Apparently self-serving people often found one another.

Benaiah kept a close eye on Ziba, whom he didn't trust. When the king approached the ferry, Shimei hurried forward and fell down before him in obeisance. "My lord and king, don't think about the wrong things I did when you left Jerusalem. I know that I sinned by my rash behavior."

Was Shimei implying that he didn't mean what he said when he cursed the king and assaulted their company with stones? Or that David shouldn't be too offended by it?

"That's why I'm here today, representing the tribe of Joseph by being the first to welcome you back to Israel, where you belong."

Unbelievable! Now he was claiming to be the king's most loyal servant just because he was the first one to acknowledge David's right to the throne? And, by aligning himself with Joseph, Benjamin's famous brother, he seemed to be wanting David to forget he was a Benjamite, like his enemy, Saul.

Abishai pushed through the crowd, drew his sword and advanced toward Shimei.

"Shouldn't he be put to death for cursing the king and trying to kill him?"

David reached out his hand to stay his impetuous soldier. "Abishai, put away your sword! No one will be executed today, because this is a day of celebration. I am once again king over Israel."

Benaiah thought that although David's words are triumphant, there was a sadness in his eyes.

David nodded to Shimei. "I swear to you by God that I will not put you to death."

Shimei's shoulders slumped forward in relief. He groveled on his knees, as if he would attempt to kiss the king's feet if allowed, but Benaiah hauled him up and sent him on his way.

Mephibosheth approached next, tossing aside his walking stick and falling prostrate before the king. His clothes were soiled, his feet unshod and his beard untrimmed. Normally Benaiah would turn away any man who did not properly prepare himself to approach the king, but he was eager to hear Mephibosheth's version of events, as David undoubtedly was as well.

David studied him for some time before asking gently, "Why did you not go with us when we fled Jerusalem, Mephibosheth?"

Mephibosheth looked up at the king. "My king, my servant deceived me. I asked him to saddle my donkey and load it with provisions for you and your family, but he left without me."

Benaiah recalled Ziba's generous "gift" to David. He should have known the man was being deceitful.

Mephibosheth continued, "He has no doubt slandered me to you. But you are wise. Do whatever you think best. I know you could have killed everyone in my grandfather's family, but you didn't. Instead, you included me among the people who eat at your own table. So what right do I have to complain about anything?"

Ziba, standing nearby, gave a slight shake of his head as if to refute Mephibosheth's testimony, but said nothing. Would David be swayed by the word of this deceitful servant over the son of his old friend Jonathan?

David's gaze moved between the two men, uncertainty in his eyes. Finally he said, "Say no more about it. This is my decision: the land will be divided between the two of you."

Could David not tell which one was telling the truth? Now Mephibosheth would have only half of his land returned to him! And Ziba would be rewarded for his deception and greed.

Mephibosheth shook his head. "No. It is enough of a blessing to see that the king has returned safe and sound. Let Ziba take the land."

Ziba didn't even try to hide a self-satisfied smirk.

Was Mephibosheth really willing to hand over all of his lands to this treacherous servant? Surely David could see now that Mephibosheth had no desire for his throne.

Yet David said nothing else, except to dismiss both men.

The next person to speak with the king was Barzillai the Gileadite, one of the men who had brought food and necessities to them when they first fled from

Absalom. He was a tall, gray haired man, well dressed as accorded his station. David embraced him warmly. "My friend," he said, "my company and I greatly appreciate your very generous provision during our flight from Jerusalem. I would like to take you and your family with me to Jerusalem so you can all be under my care."

Barzillai bowed. "My king is beyond generous, but why should he repay me with such a reward? The honor was mine to share the Lord's blessing with my king, but my age precludes me from enjoying the privileges of life in the palace. Can my palate discern the quality of the food I eat? Can I even hear the sound of the singers at court? Why should I be a burden to the king? No, no, I will accompany the king's company a little while further and then return home. I'm sure I don't have long to live. I am already eighty years old, and I wish to die near the graves of my parents."

He turned behind him and motioned another man forward. "However, if it pleases the king, perhaps my son, Chimham could go with the king in my place, to serve you."

"I would be honored to care for Chimham, as you request."

The group then proceeded to Jerusalem with their escort. There was great joy on their return to the palace. David resolved to take the ten concubines who had been humiliated by Absalom, and care for them for the remainder of their days as widows. He did not sleep with them again.

★ ★ ★

They had no sooner returned to Jerusalem and resettled into the palace, when word came of a new revolt led by a man named Sheba, son of Bicri. To add to Joab's demotion, David excluded him from his plans to put down the insurgency. He instead assigned the task to the new general, Amasa.

David ordered Amasa to summon the men of Judah and come to fight within three days. But when, for some unknown reason he failed to arrive in the time allotted to him, David feared more upheaval than Absalom had caused. So he assigned leadership of the task to Abishai, Joab's brother, and another of his loyal commanders.

But then word came that Amasa had been killed. This time, David didn't even bother to ask what happened. Abner had been killed by Joab soon after he transferred his allegiance from Ishbosheth to David. And now, clearly, Joab had removed yet another rival, even though they were cousins.

Benaiah investigated the matter and learned it was as David suspected. He learned that Joab had approached Amasa at the stone landmark in Gibeon. He reached for Amasa with his right hand to kiss him in greeting while, with his left hand, retrieving his sword and stabbing Amasa in the stomach. His body was left to wallow in his own blood in the middle of the highway.

Benaiah could understand David's frustration with his nephews, Joab and Abishai. They were both uncommonly bloodthirsty.

Benaiah recalled a story he'd heard from his father about left-handed Ehud, who, during the time of the judges, had requested an audience with the Moabite King of Eglon in private, then surprised him by pulling out a sword with his left hand and burying it in his ample abdomen up to its hilt. Ehud was considered a hero because he killed a foreign oppressor to liberate their nation.

But this situation was entirely different. Joab killed strictly for his own advantage. He sacrificed the interests of the king and a peaceful kingdom in favor of personal revenge and ambition. Also, Amasa was not killed in battle by an enemy, but in peacetime, by a fellow soldier of Israel, and with premeditation. The timing of it, so soon after Absalom's revolt and murder, couldn't be worse.

Benaiah returned to the palace and reported what he'd learned to David.

"I don't know what to do with Joab," said David. "When I promote him, he does what he pleases, and disobeys direct orders. When I replace him with someone more worthy, he kills them. Yet if I anger him too much, he may well use his authority and popularity against me, as Abner did against Ishbosheth."

David looked intently at Benaiah.

"I fear I'll have to keep him close and let him think he is in my favor. But watch him, Benaiah. He can't be trusted."

Once again, David had failed to implement justice. Joab should have been punished for murder according to the law. But David seemed to have a blind spot where family members were concerned, seeing only what he wanted to see, like in the case of Absalom. He always assumed the best of them and defended them in spite of tremendous, obvious evidence to the contrary. Or if he did see their faults or crimes, like Joab, he let them get away with it.

CHAPTER THIRTY-FOUR

"The third captain of the army for the third month was Benaiah, the son of Je-hoiada the priest, who was chief; in his division were twenty-four thousand. This was the Benaiah who was mighty among the thirty, and was over the thirty; in his division was Ammizabad his son."

—1 Chronicles 27:5–6

Benaiah's current mission was not as dangerous as some he'd been tasked with, but it was no less important.

His daughter's betrothed, Jair, sat across from him at their dining table, squirming as he poked at his food. Although he'd consented to the marriage of his youngest daughter, Sela, to Jair, the son of one of his close friends, Benaiah felt he had to establish his protectiveness of her. So over their bowls of venison stew, he occasionally eyed his future son-in-law with probing looks.

"Shall I tell you about the Moabite ariels I fought single-handedly?" Benaiah asked, breaking the uncomfortable silence. He never boasted about his military accomplishments. They were well-established facts, as was his reputation as one of David's mighty men and his personal bodyguard.

Sela rolled her eyes. "That's not necessary, Abba. Everyone already knows."

Benaiah would not be deterred.

"Jair, did Sela tell you that her brother Ammizabad is under my command now? And he is with my division of 24,000 soldiers?"

"Yes, I'd heard that, sir." Jair's Adam's apple bobbed as he swallowed hard. "You must be very proud." His voice rose an octave at the last word.

Benaiah crossed his arms across his muscular chest. It wouldn't hurt for the boy to know that his future wife's father and brother were both able military men.

Mariah huffed and rose from the table. "Dear one," she said with a false smile, "would you please come with me?"

"I'm not finished eating." Benaiah dipped his spelt bread into the stew.

Mariah stretched out her hand toward him. "I have something important to show you."

Her look gave him little choice but to follow her. He placed the bread back on the plate. Sela stifled a laugh behind her hand, no doubt amused that her father was on the receiving end of discipline.

As soon as they reached the rooftop, out of earshot of the rest of the family, Mariah turned to him and scowled. "Why are you so hard on poor Jair? He has nothing to prove to us. You shouldn't try to intimidate him so."

"I wasn't trying to intimidate him," Benaiah huffed. "Okay, well, maybe a little bit. But I didn't say anything that wasn't true." Why did he feel so defensive with this petite woman?

"Making him call you sir is ridiculous. You are not his commanding officer. As your son, he should be calling you Abba."

Benaiah recalled his own experiences with Mariah's father, Tirhanah, and his struggles with the concept of adopting a second Abba. "But she's my baby. Our last child to get married. I just want to make sure he'll treat her right."

Mariah stepped into his arms, and he wrapped them tightly around his wife of many years. Her hair had more gray than black now, and lines etched her face, but her eyes still sparkled with the fire of the beautiful young woman he married.

"Oh, my love, I know it's hard to let go. Soon our house will be empty of our own children. But we'll get to see our grandchildren daily. And we have each other."

Benaiah kissed the top of Mariah's head, then looked down into her eyes. "Were we ever that young and awkward?"

Mariah laughed. "I'm sure we were. You must remember what it felt like to be young and in love."

Benaiah pulled back from her. "That's exactly what I'm trying not to think of. I know what thoughts men have of women!"

Mariah tipped her head to one side. "You need to make an effort at being more welcoming and less threatening so they'll come around after they're married. I'll want to see all of my grandchildren."

Benaiah straightened. He did enjoy being a grandfather. "I'll try to do better."

Mariah kissed him. He followed her back down the stone steps.

Sela and Jair glanced up nervously when they returned. Benaiah said nothing as he resumed his meal. He broke off another hunk of spelt bread from the loaf. Noticing that Jair had cleaned his plate, Benaiah handed him the piece.

"Thank you, sir."

"Call me Abba." Benaiah said it more harshly than he intended, making it sound more like a command than a request, so he softened his tone. "After all, you're my son now."

Jair's mouth dropped open. "Yes, sir. I mean, yes, Abba."

"This afternoon, if you'd like, I'll show you and Sela around the House of the Mighty Men and some parts of the palace."

Jair glanced between his betrothed and Benaiah, as if unsure whether this abrupt change of character was some kind of test or a new reality. "I'd like that... Abba," he finally squeaked out.

Benaiah grumbled a response as he pushed a piece of bread into his mouth.

* * *

Dressed in his peacetime tunic, Benaiah stood in a corner of the palace rooftop. David had called a meeting with the captains of his army and General Joab. They had assembled in the outdoor pavilion, which was cooler than inside the palace due to the autumn breezes. Benaiah wondered what kind of military plans David would discuss with these men today.

To his surprise, Benaiah overheard the king say, "I want you to conduct a census of Israel and Judah."

Benaiah heard a grunt of protest from Joab and stepped closer to the tent.

"Go throughout all the tribes of Israel, from Dan to Beersheba, and count the people, making note of those men over the age of twenty. I specifically want to know how many fighting men I have."

What could David's motive be for such an act? Was he planning to raise taxes? Draft more soldiers? Plan an offensive to take more land than Yahweh had already granted them?

Joab said, "May the Lord add a hundred times more people than there are, and may it happen in your day." It was not like the general to flatter. "But why do you want to do this? What purpose could it possibly serve?" His tone was conciliatory, almost fawning. Joab was loyal to David, but he never fawned.

Benaiah awaited the king's answer to the question he himself wondered.

"I do not need to explain myself to you, nephew," David growled. "I want to know what resources I have in my kingdom. Since we are not currently at war, the soldiers have time to conduct this worthy mission. I want it commenced immediately. I anticipate the assignment taking about three quarters of a year to complete. I'll leave it up to you to divide up the task. You are dismissed."

After the others departed, Benaiah assigned another soldier to his place, left the rooftop and went to seek out Abiathar the priest.

"I seem to recall something in the law of Moses about the correct way to take a census," he said, wondering if his childhood training might prove useful after all.

The priest nodded slowly. "There are instructions in the law about how a census should be conducted," he agreed. Abiathar dug through the wall of scrolls, reverently pulled one out and spread it across the table. Bending over it, he read, "Every time the Israelites are counted, each man over twenty must make a payment for himself to the Lord. This must be done every time so there will be no plague among the people. All men must make this same offering of half a shekel each as a payment for his life to the Lord. The rich must not give more, the poor must not give less."

"The king has just ordered a census be taken. He said nothing of a ransom offering." Benaiah shuddered at the thought of the Lord sending a plague.

The priest straightened. "I will discuss this with Zadok. Together we will decide how to handle this."

Benaiah chafed like a bridled horse. "And what shall I tell the king?"

Abiathar patted his shoulder. "You needn't concern yourself with religious matters, my son. In spite of your famous father, we priests are able to advise the king."

What an odd comment. Did he think Benaiah was overstepping his role as David's bodyguard? Was Abiathar jealous of his father, Jehoiada?

Benaiah would never understand the aspirations of men in power.

★ ★ ★

Almost ten months after David called his meeting with his captains, they again assembled on the roof of the palace. Benaiah lingered in a shaded corner, taking a respite from the summer heat while he could.

"Do you think the king will question our numbers?" Abishai whispered to Joab.

The general scoffed. "I saw no reason to add the Levites or the Benjamites into the total. The Levites are not eligible for military service. And the temple is in Gibeon, with the tribe of Benjamin."

"And you will explain this to King David?" Abishai asked.

"Only if he asks. Which I doubt he will."

The two men fell silent as they joined the other captains in the pavilion, clearly unaware that Benaiah had overheard their conversation.

While Joab's reasoning had merit, Benaiah suspected the real reason for the general's half-hearted obedience was his disdain toward David's order.

Inside the tent, Joab sat on the king's right side, Abishai on his left. Benaiah stood directly behind David, not wanting to miss a moment, nor a word, of this conversation.

"We have done as you asked, my lord" Abishai announced with a mix of pride and dread.

"Very good. And what are your findings?"

"In total, sire, Israel has eight hundred thousand valiant men over the age of twenty able to fight in the army, and five hundred thousand in Judah."

David smiled, clearly pleased that his men had followed his orders and returned with encouraging numbers. He dismissed his generals. After they left, he walked to the edge of the roof and looked out over the city he loved.

"I fear I have behaved foolishly, Benaiah," the king said with a sigh.

"My lord?"

"I shouldn't have conducted that census. I did it for the sake of my pride, so I could see what I've accomplished in the years since I began to reign. As if any of this"—he waved a hand around him—"was the result of my efforts."

Benaiah had wondered what his motive had been.

"The Lord saw me when I was merely a shepherd boy and elevated me to this high position. He has blessed me beyond measure and given us rest from all our enemies."

David clenched his teeth and shook his head in disgust at his actions. "But I just had to know how many troops I had at my disposal. As if the Lord wasn't the one responsible for our victories. I speak of trusting the Lord, but ordering a census proves that I trust more in the arm of man."

He buried his forehead in his hands. "Benaiah, I have sinned yet again."

"Perhaps the Lord will forgive you, if you ask," Benaiah said hopefully. "He's done it before."

David attempted a weak smile. "I hope you're right, my friend."

Benaiah hoped so as well.

★ ★ ★

Soon after Benaiah took his position in the common room, a messenger announced the arrival of the prophet Gad. Benaiah had first seen the now elderly man back when David was on the run from Saul and he often advised David on spiritual matters over the years.

The prophet approached David's throne with confidence. The look of resignation in David's expression indicated that he knew the news would not be good.

Benaiah wondered if this prophet would tell David a story, as Nathan had, to illustrate the king's condemnation. But Gad didn't waste any time explaining the problem. "Thus says the Lord." His deep voice echoed throughout the room, causing a hush.

David threw himself on the floor before the prophet, ready to accept his punishment.

"Thus says the Lord, 'There are three ways you can be punished. Choose one.'"

Benaiah gulped. Would it be worse to choose one's own punishment than to merely take whatever the Lord decided to send?

"Will you choose seven years of famine for you and your country? Or will you be chased by your enemies for three months until they defeat you? Or will there be three days of plague in your land?"

Famine, enemies or plague. The usual punishments for disobedience since their nation began. But how to choose? Any of them would result in much death.

"What answer should I take back to Him who sent me?" Gad asked dispassionately.

All eyes focused on David, who remained on his face for some time. Finally he raised himself slowly off the floor. "This is a terrible choice to make. But it would be better to be punished by the Lord than anyone else, because He is merciful."

So, David chose either famine or plague. After all those years in the wilderness running from Saul, and more recently on the run from his son Absalom, David must have been overwhelmingly distressed at the thought of fleeing from his enemies again. And this time falling by the sword. Benaiah wondered if there was some measure of selfishness in David's choice. Perhaps this old warrior-king preferred the idea of dying in his bed.

But then Benaiah chastised himself for being too harsh in his thoughts toward his king. David had learned how great the Lord's mercies were when He forgave his grievous sins.

Benaiah had experienced the mercies of God as well. Yes, David had chosen wisely.

★ ★ ★

As Benaiah approached his home, the sound of wailing came from behind nearly every door. How weary he had grown of death. How many would die this night as a result of David's actions?

He took a deep breath before opening his own door. What would he find waiting for him inside?

As he entered the courtyard, Mariah ran to him, deep sorrow in her eyes.

"There is a plague upon Israel," Benaiah told her, "sent from the Lord."

His wife's hand flew to her mouth.

Benaiah embraced her and stroked her hair. "How are the children?" he choked out, dreading the answer.

"Maytal and Sela are fine, so far as I know, as are their families."

Benaiah released a pent-up breath.

"But I haven't heard about Ammizabad or Jehoiada's families yet," she added, distress in her features.

"I saw Ammizabad today, training his soldiers in the field. He's well." For now.

"Oh, Benaiah, I don't know what I'll do if we lose someone in our family." Her eyes widened. "Or if I lose you!" She wept into his shoulder.

Benaiah held her, unable to find words to reassure her. There were none. His children were well today. But this plague would last three days. He had no idea how it would end. Or who would remain standing when it was over.

"Why is this happening?" Mariah asked, lifting her face to him.

"The Lord is punishing the people because of David's sin in numbering the people with a census."

Mariah blanched. Benaiah led her to a bench. After settling her onto it, he took her small hands in his.

"How do you know this?"

"I was there when the prophet Gad confronted David."

Benaiah had witnessed God's supernatural power over events in David's life many times, always in his favor. Yet he knew, this time, God's punishment would happen just as the prophet said. There would be no reprieve.

Like the judgments on ancient Egypt in the day of Moses, God was revealing His mighty arm. He would do as He wished in the affairs of men. He had discerned what was in David's heart, what motivated him to order the census.

"Why must the people suffer for the king's folly? It's not fair."

Mariah had voiced his own tortured thoughts. "I don't know, my love. If the king was motivated by pride in the military power of his people, perhaps the Lord is taking away from our number to show him that He alone is the cause of blessing or cursing, mercy or judgment."

"But what's so wrong about a census?" Mariah asked, her face etched with confusion.

"Often the sins we think are small are offensive to God because he knows our motives."

Benaiah's conscience smote him. Yet again he had failed to properly counsel the king. Immediately after hearing David give the command, he had inquired about the regulations for taking a census, but he didn't tell David. He'd left it in the hands of the priests, whom he assumed would do as they promised. He hadn't even followed up to make sure they told the king.

And now a plague was upon the nation. How many of his countrymen would die? How many in his own family? He had failed to protect them, yet again. When would he ever learn?

"But if he repents, won't God forgive him, like before?"

Benaiah stroked her hair, comforting himself in the process. "He has repented. I heard him confess last night, before he knew the prophet would come to him."

"But isn't that enough?"

"Perhaps, even when we are repentant, God forgives us, yet the consequences still come. David was forgiven for his sins against Bathsheba and Uriah, yet their child still died."

Thoughts of his little brother rushed in. Benaiah had regretted the way he mistreated Ammizabad, but God still took him. "Who can understand the judgments of God?"

"If David offers the sacrifice for willful sin, do you think God will relent?"

Benaiah thought about that. "The law commands a sacrifice before a census, not after. And when the prophet pronounced the judgment, it didn't come with options to avoid it."

Mariah wept afresh. "Will every family lose someone—like in the plague in Egypt?"

Benaiah hadn't considered such a scenario. "I don't know, my love. I don't know."

★ ★ ★

In spite of the death all around him, and his concerns for the safety of his own family, Benaiah returned to the palace the next morning and resumed his position at David's side. He couldn't stop the judgment of God any more than David could. Yet all day he feared that a messenger would arrive at any moment with terrible news about his loved ones.

Reports arrived throughout the day of thousands of dead throughout all Israel, from Dan in the north to Beersheba in the south. The greatest number of deaths seemed to be here, in Jerusalem, the city that bore Yahweh's name.

How were his relatives in southern Judah? His brother, Shallum and his family, his sisters, Rizpah, Jael, and Yemima and their families? His parents? Mariah's family?

For three long, dreadful days, all business was suspended. The whole country was either trying to flee from the plague in a panic or caring for the dead and dying. David and all the elders of Israel wore the sackcloth of mourning from sunrise to sunset.

At the end of the first two days, Benaiah went home to his family, relieved that they had not succumbed to the plague... and wondered why his family had been spared.

On the evening of the third day, Benaiah followed David to the rooftop. Even from this height, the cries of mourning could be heard in the streets below. Heartache clouded David's eyes as he looked out over the balcony.

"Do you see that?" David said, pointing at the eastern sky.

Benaiah followed his gaze. Dark clouds clearly formed in the shape of a man with his sword drawn and outstretched over Jerusalem, the city David loved.

The king fell to his face. "I'm the one who sinned!" he cried out. "These people only did what I told them—they followed me like sheep. They did nothing wrong. Please let Your punishment fall on me and my family instead."

Although he was angry at David that this punishment had come upon them, Benaiah couldn't imagine, if he were in the king's position, wishing curses on his own family in the place of others. David had already seen much suffering in his family as a result of his actions, and now he was willing to take on even more, to spare his people. He was truly a shepherd of his people, concerned for their welfare over his own.

In their ceremonial sacrifices, the life of an innocent animal took the place of a guilty person. But David, the guilty man, offered himself in place of his innocent sheep. How different was this king now than he was that night on the roof all those years ago, when he abused his power to take another man's wife? The consequences of that one sin had truly humbled David.

The prophet, Gad, came up behind them on the roof. When David raised his eyes, Gad proclaimed, "The Lord has relented of the disaster and has restrained the hand of the destroying angel."

David looked back into the sky and saw the sword extended in the hand of the angel had been withdrawn. He exhaled with relief.

"Now go and build an altar to the Lord on the threshing floor of Ornan the Jebusite," Gad said.

How odd that the Lord would direct David to a place of worship other than the tabernacle in Gibeon, a short walk from Jerusalem. But the king did not question the prophet's command. He hurried to observe the word of the Lord, perhaps thinking to spare even one more person if he obeyed quickly.

Benaiah, Zadok the priest and several guards followed David as he climbed into his covered chariot and traveled in the direction of the vision he had seen in the sky over Jerusalem. Benaiah was glad Zadok had come rather than Abiathar, the other high priest. He was still angry at him for not informing David about the proper way to perform a census, mostly out of spite against Benaiah.

As the royal chariot passed by, the citizens of Jerusalem exclaimed, "The king has come down to see our suffering!"

David turned away in anguish. Many did not know he was the cause of the plague. When they learned of it, they may well curse him instead.

When the chariot neared Mount Moriah, Benaiah asked a man walking with his son for directions to the home of Ornan the Jebusite. When they arrived, an old man looked up from his threshing, clearly startled to see the king and his servants on his property.

David exited the chariot and walked up to the man, who bowed before the king with his face to the ground.

"Are you Ornan the Jebusite?" David asked.

He raised his head slightly and nodded, then asked, "Why has my lord and king come to me?" Ornan's voice trembled. The man must have feared for his life.

"I came to buy the threshing floor from you. Then I can build an altar to the Lord, so this plague will stop."

Ornan lifted his head, relief and surprise in his eyes. "My lord and king, you may take anything you want for a sacrifice." He motioned to a yoke of oxen nearby. "Here are oxen you can use as a burnt offering, and the threshing boards and yokes can be used for wood. I gladly give all these things to you." Then, with a bow, he added, "May the Lord your God be pleased with you and your offering."

David helped Ornan to his feet. "Your generosity is appreciated. However, I will buy these things from you for full price. For I will not take what belongs to someone else and give it to the Lord. Nor will I offer burnt offerings to the Lord that cost me nothing."

David ordered one of his servants to bring money, and then he counted out a generous sum of silver and paid Ornan.

Brushing away the help offered by his servants, David set about building the altar himself. When Benaiah joined him, intending to carry some of the rocks to the raised section of earth, David touched his forearm. "No, my friend. I must do this myself."

As Benaiah and the other guards watched, the king placed each stone, one by one, on the growing altar. When it was done, David offered sin offerings and peace offerings through the priest, Zadok, acknowledging God's righteous judgment and mercy.

When the ox had been laid on the altar, David fell to his knees and cried out, "Oh gracious and merciful Lord. You do as You please in the affairs of men, for You are sovereign. You take down one king to raise up another. All blessings come from Your hand alone. You have no need of armies, as You are able to save apart from them. Every one of our victories is Yours. Our strength is not in our numbers, but in the sure mercies of God. You reveal Your arm, and the nations tremble."

David beat his breast. "I have done wickedly. My pride motivated me to number the people. Because You hate haughty thoughts, You abased me. Now I see myself as I truly am in Your sight, and I repent of the evil I have done.

"Now, Lord, be pleased to accept this sacrifice. I acknowledge my guilt before You and plead for peace between us. Please reconcile me to Yourself, O Lord my God. Look upon Your people, whom You have chosen, with favor."

David rose and faced Zadok. "Proceed with lighting the burnt offering."

As Zadok prepared to strike the flint to burn the sacrifice, fire fell from heaven directly onto the altar, consuming the ox.

The guards around Benaiah fell backward. Some cried out in fear. David fell on his face to the dry ground.

Benaiah stared in wonder as the flames from heaven engulfed the sacrifice. He felt the heat as the fire completely consumed the animal in a matter of moments.

The Lord had answered David's prayer and accepted his sacrifice. If the plague had been a supernatural occurrence, this was far more so. God's judgments were just, but even greater was His mercy toward His people.

God's anger had been spent. The avenging angel had sheathed its sword, near Mount Moriah, the same place where Abraham's hand was stayed from killing Isaac so long ago.

It was over. There would be no more deaths from this plague. God was faithful.

David had been humbled by this event, perhaps even more so than after his sin with Bathsheba. He'd ordered a census because of his pride. Now he realized he was no greater than the poor farmer whose land he'd purchased. He had finally seen that true worship was costly—just as his disobedience had been costly.

★ ★ ★

A week after David's confession and offering, a messenger arrived in the palace with word that seventy thousand men had perished throughout Israel. He used the military term "fallen," as if they had died in battle. Indeed they had, for God Himself had fought against His people.

David had originally thought to encourage himself by knowing the strength of his army. Instead, the Lord reduced that number, teaching him that the battle was the Lord's.

Mariah's sister's husband was among the dead. Even as Benaiah traveled with his wife to Kabzeel, to comfort her sister in her loss, he thanked the Lord for sparing all of his other loved ones.

He even thanked God for sparing Jair... his soon-to-be son.

CHAPTER THIRTY-FIVE

"But Noah found grace in the eyes of the Lord."

—Genesis 6:8

The day after Benaiah's brother-in-law died, he traveled with his wife and children to his family home for the memorial, as Merari had already been buried the next day, as was the custom. They stayed with Jehoiada and Dinah for two days.

Benaiah's childhood home seemed empty and quiet compared to the days of his youth, when it was full of children and activity. His mother could no longer see well enough to do her needlework, so she kept her hands busy preparing more food than they needed.

Benaiah felt his father's gaze on him, so he suggested a walk. As much as he appreciated seeing his family, the town of Kabzeel held many painful memories, even after all this time. As he passed through the streets, thoughts of Ammizabad threatened to drown him in despair, and he didn't have the strength to fight them.

They strolled to the edge of town, away from the noises and smells of everyday life, to a quiet stream. It had been many years since Benaiah had come to Kabzeel, the last time probably for one of his sisters' weddings.

Jehoiada plucked a leaf from an overhanging tree and rubbed it between his fingers. He motioned for Benaiah to sit near the stream, and they sat in silence for a few moments.

Jehoiada laid a hand on Benaiah's shoulder, conveying comfort and strength. He heaved a heavy sigh.

"How are you, my son?"

It wasn't just a casual question.

How was he? Depressed. Discouraged. Uncertain whether God was pleased with him, even after a lifetime of service. But how could he communicate that to his father? Should he even try?

Gazing at the ground, Benaiah asked, "Do you remember what you said to me after Ammiz' funeral, about Saul's disobedience and the words of the prophet to him?"

Jehoiada nodded. "'To obey is better than sacrifice.' What of it?"

Benaiah swallowed hard. "I tried, Abba. After Ammiz died, I swore it would be my life's mission to obey God and those in authority over me, and to protect those entrusted to my care."

"And you've done that. You fought alongside David, championing his cause, guarding him and your family and obeying as a soldier. So what concerns you?"

Benaiah hung his head. "My disobedience caused my brother's death. But when I sought to obey, that resulted in death as well."

"How could that be, son?"

Benaiah told his father about David's orders to kill Nabal, which he would have blindly obeyed if Abigail had not intervened. "A woman had to step in and save me from following that wicked order. I didn't have enough strength of character to question David or even appeal to him as a friend. I was so afraid of disobeying that I would have spilled the innocent blood of a family in Israel."

"But God spared you."

"Yes, that time. But then I failed to protect Mariah. I assured her father that she would be safe with me. But when the Amalekites raided Ziklag, they took our families captive. Ammiz was just a year old. They trusted me, and I let them down."

"But God kept them all safe and secure. You told me nothing was lost."

"It's true, but that's not the worst of it." Benaiah hesitated. "I... I played a part in David's adultery with Bathsheba."

His father sucked in a sharp breath. "How could that be, Son?"

Benaiah shared how he had followed the king's command to get the wife of Uriah for him.

"David was responsible for his own sin. And you did try to warn him."

"It wasn't enough! I should have refused. Or told him he shouldn't do this wicked thing. I should have stood up to him. But I was so sure that obedience was what the Lord expected of me, I said nothing." Benaiah closed his eyes in an attempt to block out the painful memories. "I could have prevented it."

Jehoiada offered no words of comfort. What could he say?

"Then when David wrote the orders for Uriah to be abandoned on the battlefield, I passed the note to Uriah myself! Several others died in that battle, including my friend Mikhael. Then the son of David and Bathsheba died as well. All because I delivered Bathsheba to David that night."

Jehoiada stroked Benaiah's back. "Did you know what was in the note?"

"No, but so many people have suffered and died because of me."

Jehoiada lowered his head, and Benaiah knew he was praying.

Finally he looked up. "I am proud of you, my son. You have a heart to serve and please God. He led you into this vocation, so far removed from what I expected and yet so perfectly suited to you. He put you into the life and times of our nation for a reason."

Could his father truly be proud of him? Surely he still held some disappointment in his chosen profession,

"God is not pleased with only outward signs and ceremonies, because He sees our motives and thoughts. It is not obedience in itself that is the path to life."

His father could have just as well slapped him in the face. This was a complete contradiction of what he'd believed all his life, that only obedience pleased God. "Well, what is it then?"

"It's grace."

"I don't understand."

Jehoiada stroked his beard, a move Benaiah always associated with an impending lecture when he was young. "Do you remember the stories I told you over the years about our forefathers, Abraham, Isaac and Jacob? And Noah and Joseph? About the wilderness wanderings and God's provision of food and water?"

"Of course."

"Those stories reveal the character of our God. The failures of our people are meant to show that none of us can fully keep God's law."

"But if can't keep the law, why did God give it to Moses?"

"To drive us to call out to Him for mercy. He doesn't bless us because we please him by our actions. That would be like an employee receiving his wages. Scripture says Abraham believed God, and it was counted to him as righteousness. It was his faith in God, not his actions, that caused God to declare him righteous. Scripture also says that before the flood the Lord saw that the wickedness of man was great, and that every intent of the thoughts of his heart was only evil continually. But then it says that Noah found grace in the eyes of the Lord. That was before he built the ark in obedience to God's command."

Benaiah contemplated his father's words. How had he never seen it that way before?

"We priests are careful to observe the law and strive to keep God's ordinances—all six hundred and thirteen of them. But fully keeping the law is impossible. Only God is holy. And unless He shows us grace, we are all lost.

"Remember how the children of Israel grumbled about the manna God provided? He sent fiery serpents among them and many died. And when Moses interceded for them, God told him to fashion a bronze serpent on a pole."

"I've always thought that odd. Why would the Lord order Moses to make an idol of any sort, let alone one of a creature that would remind people about the sin of our first parents in the Garden of Eden?"

"The people were not to worship it, merely to look at it. When they gazed upon it in faith, they were healed."

"It must have seemed an absurd command, to merely look," Benaiah mused.

"The image represented their problem—which was, on one level, deadly snakebites, but on a deeper level, deadly sin. In the same way, our problem is not just physical death, but our potential for being separated from God forever."

"Isn't that why we strive to obey God, to please Him?" Benaiah asked earnestly.

"Indeed. And yet, all He wants us to do is look to Him in faith and believe that He will make a way for us, even when we continually fail."

"Are you saying we shouldn't strive to keep the law?" Benaiah was incredulous.

"Of course we should. That is what sets our nation apart from others. But He did not choose us because we were greater in number than any other people. He chose us because He loved us, and because He was keeping the oath that He swore to our fathers when he brought them out from bondage under the hand of Pharaoh in Egypt.

"We have nothing to boast about, in spite of our many blessings. It's faith in God's promises that sets apart those who believe from those who trust in their own goodness or in their lineage or tribe. We do not earn God's favor by keeping His laws perfectly. Our blessings are the response of a loving God who chooses to show us His grace."

Could this be the answer to his search for redemption and acceptance with God?

"Son, you need to cease striving and rest in God's grace. Have faith that He will teach you."

"I have seen God blessings many times in my service to David. Once, a word came to him from the Lord promising that He would build David an enduring house and that someone from his lineage would sit on the throne forever."

"That prophecy refers to the Messiah. Who else could have an eternal kingdom and live forever? King David is blessed indeed if the Messiah is to come through his family line. And you are blessed to be in his presence and witness the unfolding purposes of God."

"The king himself demonstrated that kind of grace when he showed kindness to one of Prince Jonathan's descendants because of his covenant with Jonathan. He spared Mephibosheth, gave Saul's lands to him as an inheritance, and took him in as one of his own sons, providing for him every day at the king's table and offering him fellowship."

"And just as Mephibosheth accepted these undeserved gifts from David, I pray you will be able to rest in God's grace as your faith in His promises grows."

They rose to leave, and Benaiah embraced his father.

"Thank you, Abba. You've given me much to consider."

As they returned home, Benaiah's heart felt lighter. Could it really be that easy? Just trust in the word of God and rest in His grace?

Why didn't I find this out sooner?

CHAPTER THIRTY-SIX

"After Ahithophel was Jehoiada the son of Benaiah, then Abiathar. And the general of the king's army was Joab."

—1 Chronicles 27:34

It pained Benaiah to see his former king and friend reduced to such frailty. David was not yet three score and ten, and only ten years older than Benaiah, yet his hard life had taken its toll.

He was completely bedridden, and despite the many covers on him, he could not seem to get warm. Someone suggested a young virgin be found to warm him. The king responded favorably to the idea, so Abishag the Shunammite was brought to him. She was a beautiful young woman, and she served David and cared for him, but David was not intimate with her.

★ ★ ★

In the House of the Mighty Men, Rei, one of David's other bodyguards, said, "Did you hear what Adonijah has done?"

Benaiah shook his head, wondering what else the sons of the king had found to do to stir up trouble in the kingdom. Adonijah, David's fourth son, and now eldest to survive, had won the hearts of the people in southern Judah, just as his brother Absalom had done years ago. Adonijah was also handsome, like his late brother, so people stared in admiration when he spoke to them. He convinced them he cared about them and their concerns more than the king, when in reality he only loved the adoration of the people.

"He got himself a chariot and horses."

"What?" Was this the treachery of Absalom all over again? They begin with self-importance and moved to treason. Benaiah couldn't bring himself to imagine that yet another son of David would attempt to take the throne. In some cultures, when a king lost his virility, it was seen as a sign that he could no longer lead the nation. Had word of his chaste treatment of Abishag become common knowledge?

"Not only that, but fifty men to run before him."

A royal bodyguard? For what purpose? "Why would Joab release David's soldiers from their regular duty to make such a pretense of importance and power for the prince?"

"Apparently Joab supports him."

Benaiah's jaw slackened. "Surely not! Joab has been loyal to David through-out his life, even during Absalom's rebellion. I can't believe he would turn on the king now."

Oh, why hadn't David officially named his successor? Most knew he was partial to Solomon because he was beloved of the Lord, according to the pro-nouncement of Nathan the prophet. Because of it, David favored him shamelessly before his other sons.

David also acknowledged Bathsheba as his favorite wife. And through Na-than, the Lord had named Solomon as the son who would reign after David.

How could there be any opposition to the appointment?

But the history of his people had proven that they were constantly chal-lenged by the enemies of God, within and without the country.

"I don't know, but I suspect trouble." Rei said. "The people know David isn't long for this world. They want a king who is visible, powerful, popular. I've heard Adonijah has even publicly declared that he will be the next king."

"What of Abishai and the other mighty men? Are they also in his camp?" Benaiah asked, half afraid to hear the answer.

"None, other than Joab, from what I've heard."

Surely David had heard of the public claim to the throne and was even now planning to put down another rebellious son. This time he wouldn't turn and run, as he had with Absalom. Not that he had the strength to run anymore.

Benaiah hurried to the palace, eager to find out what David's plans were for quelling the rebellion and naming his successor. When he arrived, he was told, "No business will be conducted today. Adonijah is sacrificing sheep, oxen and fattened cattle by the stone of Zoheleth, by En Rogel. He has invited all the king's sons, and all the leading men of Judah, to attend."

This sounded terribly familiar to Benaiah.

The area was in a somewhat secluded place near the convergence of the Hin-nom and Kidron valleys. The perfect location for a clandestine purpose. When

Absalom decided to kill Amnon in retaliation for the rape of Tamar, he invited all the king's sons to a sheep shearing as a pretense. It couldn't be happening again!

Benaiah had to tell Nathan. As if summoned by his thoughts, the prophet appeared from the stone stairwell at the end of the long hallway. His age had not diminished his erect stature or noble bearing, although his receding hairline and graying beard announced his six decades of life.

Benaiah hurried toward him and relayed the information he had heard. "Did you know about this?"

Nathan shook his head. "I was not invited. Surely if he was planning to show he had a legitimate claim to the throne, he would have invited both of us."

"Is Solomon in danger?"

Nathan laid a hand on Benaiah's arm. "For now, he is safe. I just left him. He was not invited either, it would seem."

Benaiah let out a relieved breath. "Thank God."

"I must find Bathsheba." Nathan said. "You go to David's side, as usual. I will send Bathsheba in to give him the news, then I'll follow to confirm her words. Perhaps we can stop this rebellion before it starts."

Benaiah hurried to David's chamber, where he found Abishag the Shunammite pouring water into a basin to bathe the king. David was on his bed. His face was pale.

Benaiah bowed before the king. "How does my lord fare today?"

David attempted a smile. "Not sure I would have the strength to hold up a sword."

Bathsheba was announced by the guard at the door. She rushed to the king's bedside and bowed before the king. David smiled at his wife. Abishag withdrew towards the back of the room.

He reached up to stroke Bathsheba's hair. "What is your wish, my beloved?"

Bathsheba drew in a deep breath. "My lord, you swore to me in God's name that our son Solomon would be the next king after you."

David nodded. "I remember. I am not that feeble of mind."

Bathsheba took his hand. "You don't know this, but Adonijah has made himself king."

David propped himself up on one elbow, his features strained. "How do you know this?"

"He is hosting a large fellowship meal with many oxen, cattle and sheep. And he has invited all of your sons to the meal, along with Abiathar, the priest, and Joab, commander of the army. But he did not invite your faithful son, Solomon."

David's head fell back against the pillow. "My nephew has sided with him against me?" Benaiah could only imagine the sense of betrayal David felt.

"Yes," Bathsheba said.

Benaiah could see how the three conspirators had arranged to share power. Adonijah would get the throne, supported by the priesthood represented by Abiathar, and the military, led by Joab. It would appear, to those who didn't know David's true intent, that this was legitimate and that Adonijah, as the eldest living son, would become the next king after David.

"My lord and king," Bathsheba said, "all eyes in Israel are on you, watching to see who you decide will be the next king after you. If you don't decide, then after you're buried, these men will say that Solomon and I are criminals, and will have us executed."

David lay back and covered his eyes with his hand. Benaiah wondered if it was too late to make his succession announcement, now that he was too ill to go out in public.

A servant appeared in the doorway and announced. "Nathan, the prophet is here."

The prophet approached the king's bedside and bowed down with his face to the ground. Bathsheba stepped to the back of the room.

"What news, friend?" David asked, his voice wavering.

Nathan rose and told the king about Adonijah's plot to take the throne, including the fact that it was reported they were shouting, "Long live King Adonijah!" And that neither Solomon, Zadok the priest, Benaiah the son of Jehoiada, nor he had been invited.

David turned to Benaiah. "Is Solomon safe?"

"Yes, my lord. I have him guarded by six of the mighty men," he reassured the king.

Nathan asked, "My king, did you do this without telling us? Please tell us who you plan to make king after you."

David summoned all of his remaining strength to sit up in his bed. Abishag rushed forward to help prop him up, and he called for Bathsheba.

David's vitality seemed to return to him. "As surely as the Lord lives, who has saved me from every danger, I will fulfill the promise I made to you, and Solomon, your son will take my place on the throne. I will keep my promise this very day."

Bathsheba bowed with her face to the earth. "Long live King David!"

"Summon Zadok the priest to join us," David commanded. "Then have him go with Nathan, the prophet, and Benaiah, son of Jehoiada and my officers." When the priest arrived, the three stepped forward and David continued, "Put my son, Solomon, on my own royal mule and take him to Gihon Spring. Anoint him, blow the horn and announce, 'This is the new king, Solomon!'"

How confused the people would be to hear such a contradictory pronouncement on the same day as Adonijah's claim. But the detail of Solomon on the king's mule would add legitimacy to the second proclamation.

"Then come back here with him. He will sit on the throne and rule in Israel and Judah in my place even now while I live."

Joy at having lived to witness what David had pronounced at Solomon's birth gave Benaiah courage to cry out, "Amen! May God make it so! As the Lord has been with you, I pray that He will also be with Solomon and make his kingdom even more powerful than yours has been."

"Amen!" cried Nathan.

David and Bathsheba both smiled contentedly. David said, "Praise the Lord God of Israel. He has put one of my own sons on my throne, and has let me live to see it done!"

As Solomon rode to Gihon, a great multitude of Cherethites and Pelethites joined the procession. When they arrived at the tabernacle, Zadok took a horn of oil from the priest's chamber and poured the oil over his head to anoint Solomon.

They blew the ram's horn and all the people who had followed them repeatedly shouted, "Long live King Solomon!" The crowd rejoiced and played instruments. The earth seemed to split with the joyful sound.

Benaiah had felt this happy and content only a few other times in his life: on his wedding day, at the births of his children, and on David's coronation day.

★ ★ ★

When Adonijah's guests heard the sound of rejoicing, Joab asked, "Why is the city in such a noisy uproar?"

Jonathan the son of Abiathar reported, "King David has made Solomon the king."

With Jonathan's news, the guests departed, afraid, and Adonijah fled to the tabernacle for fear of Solomon. In distress, he took hold of the horns of the altar, praying that Solomon would not put him to death.

When all this was reported to the new king, the company turned to Solomon, waiting to see what manner of person he was. Would his first order as king be for revenge or mercy? He had a legitimate responsibility to protect his throne from all threats, and Adonijah, Joab and Abiathar were very real threats.

Solomon said, "If my brother can prove he is a worthy man, I promise I won't hurt a hair on his head. But if he does anything wrong, he will die."

Would Adonijah prove himself "a worthy man" and renounce all claims to the throne? Time would tell.

"Bring Adonijah here from the altar."

When he came, flanked by two guards, he fell down trembling before the new king.

Solomon ordered Adonijah, "Go to your house and remain there."

Benaiah didn't trust Adonijah. In his opinion, Adonijah should be imprisoned at the least, instead of given freedom and opportunity to gather support again and oust the new king. But Solomon showed more grace than he himself likely would have received if Adonijah's treasonous attempt had been successful.

CHAPTER THIRTY-SEVEN

"So David rested with his fathers, and was buried in the City of David. The period that David reigned over Israel was forty years; seven years he reigned in Hebron, and in Jerusalem he reigned thirty-three years. Then Solomon, his son sat on the throne of his father David; and his kingdom was firmly established."

—1 Kings 2:10–12

"So King Solomon sent by the hand of Benaiah the son of Jehoiada; and he struck him [Adonijah] down, and he died."

—1 Kings 2:25

As David's breathing became labored, Abishag helped him sit up. She adjusted pillows behind his back for support.

"Benaiah, call Solomon to me," David rasped.

When they reached David's side, Solomon knelt at his bedside, kissed his father's hand, and touched his forehead to it. "What does my lord the king desire?"

"I am about to die, as all men must. But you are growing stronger and becoming a man. You must carefully obey all the commands and laws of the Lord your God, everything written in the Law of Moses. If you do this, you'll be successful at whatever you do and wherever you go. And if you remain faithful, the Lord will keep His promise to me that if my sons carefully live the way He instructs, sincerely, with all their hearts, the king of Israel will always be a man from my family."

David took a deep breath, the effort almost too much for him.

"My son, I wanted to build a temple for the Lord God, one that would be famous among the nations. But the Lord denied me, saying, 'You have fought many wars and shed much blood, so you cannot build a temple to My name. But you will have a son who will be a man of peace, and I will give him rest from all his enemies. His name will be Solomon, and I will give Israel rest and quietness in his days. He will build a house for My name. He will be My son, and I will be his Father, and someone from his family will rule Israel forever.

"Now, my son, may the Lord be with you and give you success as you build this temple, as He said you would. You are now the king of Israel. May He give you wisdom and understanding so that you can lead His people. Be strong and brave, and do not be afraid."

David moved up in the bed, and continued with an urgency that suggested he knew he didn't have much time left.

"You remember what Joab did to me, by killing two of the commanders of Israel's armies, Abner, son of Ner, and Amasa, son of Jether. He killed both of them during a time of peace. I should have punished him then. But use your wisdom and don't let him die peacefully of old age."

Solomon nodded. "Yes, my king."

"Show kindness to the children of Barzillai from Gilead. Befriend them and let them eat at your table, because they provided for me when I fled from your brother, Absalom.

"And remember that Shimei, the son of Gera, is still around. He is the Benjamite from Bahurim who cursed me as I fled. But when he came down to meet me at the Jordan River, I made a promise to him in the name of the Lord that I wouldn't kill him. Now you are a wise man, and you know what you must do. Don't leave him unpunished or let him die in peace."

David leaned his head back on the pillow, physically and emotionally spent by the effort required to charge his son.

"Yes, father."

Solomon dropped his head onto the bed near David's chest and wept.

David stroked his curly hair. "You will be a fine king if you continue to serve the God of our fathers."

Solomon sat up and wiped his tears. He stood, gazed at David for a long moment and then left the room.

★ ★ ★

Once the greater business of the kingdom was settled, and Solomon was officially reigning over Israel David seemed to relax. Even though he knew death was imminent, he didn't seem to fear it. In fact, one of the many psalms he had written revealed his assurance that he would soon see the God he loved all his life. One verse of the psalm said, "As for me, I will see Your face in righteousness; I will be fully satisfied when I awake to find myself seeing Your face."

He and Benaiah reminisced about the good and bad of their many years soldiering together: the way God was always faithful to protect them from their enemies and from King Saul. They recalled the joy of David's throne being established, first in Hebron for seven years, and then in Jerusalem over all of Israel for thirty-three years. There were many battles, and their fallen soldiers were grieved. David's wives and concubines had borne him many children.

"Benaiah," David said one afternoon from his bed.

"Yes, my lord?"

David smiled. "Benaiah, of all my mighty men, you have been by my side the most. As chief of my bodyguard, you've seen all the goings on of my kingdom and my family. My nephews, Joab and Abishai, although loyal, have been so bloodthirsty and harsh."

Benaiah wasn't sure how to respond, so he just repeated, "Yes, my lord."

"In fact, I'd venture to say that not only were you my most loyal servant, but I like to think you are also my friend." David looked up at Benaiah expectantly, even hopefully.

Benaiah relaxed. "I do feel that way, as well, sire. I respect and love you. I just wish I had been a true friend when it mattered."

"Now, now, Benaiah, we've been over that. I wouldn't have listened at the time anyway."

"Then, yes, I do feel we are friends," he admitted.

"Then can you oblige me just once, and call me David? Especially now when no one else is here?" His smile held a hint of challenge.

"I don't know if I can. You've always been my superior and then my sovereign."

David shifted in bed and sat up. "Please try."

Benaiah screwed up his face. This didn't come naturally.

"David... you have a fine son on the throne." Benaiah squirmed. He meant the words, but the manner of speech was foreign to him. "He may be young, but he is teachable and humble. I believe he will make the nation even greater than it has been."

David reached out to grasp Benaiah's hands.

"Thank you, my friend. Thank you."

King David died soon afterwards, and Benaiah felt privileged to be at his side when his friend and king passed to his reward. He was remembered as a man after God's own heart, and the sweet psalmist of Israel. Benaiah recalled another psalm David had written that said, "The death of one of the Lord's loyal ones is precious in His eyes."

Truly this time period was a fulfillment of the promises God made to the patriarchs Abraham, Isaac and Jacob. The nation that Moses had led out of Egypt centuries earlier was now settled, established and growing. The times of the judges were over and, although still a theocracy in one sense, they had a king, like the nations around them. Wealth was pouring into their country. God was truly blessing them. They were now in the land flowing with milk and honey, as God promised.

The whole nation mourned for the king a full month. Even foreign kings sent messages of condolence to the new king. One of them was Hiram, king of Tyre in the north. He had always loved David and had supplied cedar trees, carpenters and masons to help build David's house when they moved from Hebron to Jerusalem. He rejoiced to know that Solomon was now on the throne of his father David. His message read, "I praise the Lord for giving David a wise son to rule this great nation in his place."

The change in government from King David to King Solomon passed without incident. Solomon had been content with the shared power of the co-regency while his father David lived, and let his time to reign come to pass as God planned. Yet once his father died, he moved swiftly to establish his rule.

Benaiah found it no hardship to serve the son as he had his father. Solomon was even-tempered and sober. Not as joyful as his father was, but not as prone to bouts of melancholy either, perhaps because he had no reason to be sad. This was a rare time of peace in Israel. Solomon had inherited a stable kingdom—if one didn't count the usurpers within the palace walls.

"The queen mother would like a word with her son," a servant announced at the door.

Bathsheba entered the common room, graceful and beautiful as ever even in her sixth decade.

Solomon rose from his throne and bowed to her, then sat back down.

"Another throne for the queen mother," Solomon ordered. "Quickly."

When it was set in place near Solomon's right hand, she took her seat on it.

Solomon reached out and kissed his mother's hand and smiled at her. "What can I do for you, Mother?"

Bathsheba smoothed out nonexistent wrinkles from her luxurious gown. "I have one small thing to ask of you." She took a deep breath. "Please don't refuse me."

Solomon looked at her in disbelief. "Ask anything, my mother."

"Let your brother Adonijah marry Abishag, the woman from Shunem."

Benaiah stifled a gasp at the implications of this request. Adonijah's machinations had not ceased. First the royal body guard and chariots, then the pronouncement that he was king. And now he was attempting to take a royal wife or concubine as a method of legitimizing his claim to the throne. Absalom had done so with David's concubines, and Abner with Ishbosheth's concubine, Rizpah.

A storm flared behind Solomon's eyes. He rose slowly from his throne. "Why would you request such a thing, Mother? Why don't you just ask me to give him the whole kingdom as well! After all, he's my older brother, and both Abiathar, the priest, and Joab support him."

Bathsheba seemed not at all shocked by her son's heated response. Perhaps she was looking out for the security of her son's kingdom by posing a seemingly innocent question that was meant to raise Solomon's awareness of an imminent threat.

"By God, I swear I'll make Adonijah pay for this treason with his life! God has established me as king of Israel on the throne of my father, David. It was promised to me and my descendants. Adonijah will die today!"

Solomon nodded to Benaiah. In obedience to the unspoken order, he left the common room and ordered another soldier to take his place at the king's side so he could go and execute Adonijah.

He took with him two other soldiers, although they would not be necessary. Benaiah knew how to do his job.

Benaiah wondered if Bathsheba harbored any feelings of jealousy for Abishag, and if that's what prompted her to agree to Adonijah's request to approach Solomon. With so many women in David's harem, there was bound to be some rivalry. Was Bathsheba upset that David sought out a younger, more beautiful woman to keep him warm in his old age, rather than his favorite wife? In bringing Adonijah's request to her son, she must have suspected what his response would be. If Abishag's loyalty to David and Solomon could be brought into question, perhaps Bathsheba hoped she'd be banished.

Benaiah searched for Adonijah, expecting him to be in hiding. Instead he found him in his quarters. Did he really expect Solomon to just hand Abishag over to him, like when they were boys and Solomon gave his older brother a prize to console him for losing a fight?

Benaiah ordered the two soldiers to escort Adonijah's guards out of the room, which they did... at the points of their swords.

"I take it my little brother denied my request?" Adonijah laughed mirthlessly. "Too bad. I did find the girl somewhat appealing."

So he wasn't sincere in his request? Benaiah advanced toward the king's brother and drew his sword. "Kneel," he commanded.

Adonijah hesitated, then lowered himself in front of Benaiah. "What is my sentence?" he asked, as if he didn't know.

Benaiah grasped Adonijah's hair to expose the man's neck.

"For treason against the Lord's chosen, King Solomon, you are found guilty. The punishment is death."

"At least assure me your sword is sharp, Benaiah," Adonijah said.

"It is," Benaiah answered evenly, then dragged it across the traitor's throat with a swift stroke. The body dropped to the floor. Assured that Adonijah was dead, Benaiah ordered his servants to come back inside. "Arrange for his burial."

As Benaiah returned to the palace, he reflected on all the prophecies he had seen come to pass. Solomon, the son of David, was reigning in Israel, just as the prophet Nathan had told David long before that evening with Bathsheba. Solomon's son, Rehoboam, was born a year before Solomon took the throne, so the Lord was establishing Solomon's house by already providing an heir to the newly crowned king.

And now the prophetic judgment from David's own lips, against the fictional man who had acted wickedly by stealing his neighbor's ewe lamb, had also come to pass. David had demanded that the thief restore fourfold what he had unlawfully taken, not realizing that he was the perpetrator in this tale. He had now lost four sons: the newborn, unnamed son; Amnon, killed by Absalom for the rape of Tamar; Absalom killed by Joab, against David's orders; and now finally Adonijah, for his treasonous request.

Could it be that the consequences of that fateful night were finally at an end?

Benaiah still carried guilt for his part in the sinful act that had led to this moment. He felt responsible for the death of David's first son, and now directly for this fourth son. He never imagined that it would be his own hand that took the life of one of David's sons.

But the Lord had called him to this profession, at this time, for His glory.

★ ★ ★

"Summon Abiathar the priest to me," Solomon ordered.

When Abiathar was brought before the king, he bowed low to the ground, trembling. "My lord." He gulped, no doubt expecting to hear a certain death sentence.

"Where are you living, Abiathar?" the king asked.

"In Anathoth, my lord," he squeaked out.

"Go back to your fields there," Solomon ordered.

"Sir?"

"You well know that you deserve death for your part in Adonijah's treason." Abiathar hung his head in agreement.

"But because you were the mediator between my father and the Lord when he was on the run, and you shared the hard times with my father, I won't put you to death."

The elderly priest let out the breath he'd been holding.

"Yet you will no longer be a priest to the Lord."

Abiathar nodded in acceptance of his judgment. "Thank you, sire, for your great mercy."

CHAPTER THIRTY-EIGHT

"But if a man acts with premeditation against his neighbor, to kill him by treachery, you shall take him from my altar, that he may die."

—Exodus 21:14

"Joab!" Abishai shouted as he entered the courtyard of Joab's home. "You must flee!"

Joab stumbled out of the house. His gray hair was unkempt, his eyes puffy, worry etched on the deep lines of his face. "What has happened, brother?"

"You are not safe here! Now that Solomon is established on his throne, he is quashing any rivals to his kingdom. Adonijah's bold request for Abishag was viewed as treason, so Solomon had Benaiah execute him."

Joab sank down onto the wooden bench, his head in his hands. "It's only a matter of time before they come for me. All my years of loyalty mean nothing since I sided with Adonijah against Solomon. I intended no disloyalty to David by it, but with Amnon and Absalom dead, Adonijah is the rightful heir."

Abishai would have reminded him that David often said Solomon was his choice to succeed him, but he kept silent. What's done was done.

"Solomon knows nothing about me. I took this fortress city from the Jebusites before he was even born! I was in charge of the entire army of Israel. I fought alongside his father, my uncle. Yet now I will likely be executed as a traitor." Joab wept.

Uncomfortable with the uncharacteristic display of emotion in his elder brother and unsure of how to console him, Abishai placed a hand awkwardly on his shoulder.

"Perhaps it will go well with you after all, brother. Solomon was lenient with Abiathar the priest, in spite of his support of the treason. He only removed him from the priesthood and exiled him to his own home and fields. It's possible he'll recognize your loyalty to David all these years. You are his cousin, after all."

Joab wiped his eyes with the palms of his large hands. He looked up at his brother and shook his head. "I appreciate your optimism, but I know this shrewd king better than you do. What would it matter that I'm his cousin if he'd execute his own brother? Besides, I hold sway over the army. The men respect me, and Solomon can't take the chance that I'll lead them away from him."

Abishai's mouth fell open. "You wouldn't do that! Would you?"

"No, brother. But that will not matter to the king."

"Perhaps I can speak to him on your behalf," Abishai offered hopefully. "Appeal for mercy."

Joab looked at the darkening sky over the courtyard and sighed. "There's a new king on the throne. He will establish his kingdom by removing all pretenders to the throne... and their supporters."

Joab stood and awkwardly embraced his younger brother, unable to find words to comfort him. Abishai pulled back and looked into Joab's eyes through his own tears. "Where will you go, brother?"

"I will flee to the tabernacle of the Lord in Gibeon." Joab laughed mirthlessly. "Imagine that, Abishai! I, who never took this religious business seriously, now seek to extend my life by seeking refuge there."

Joab's expression softened at Abishai's obvious pain. "Do not grieve long, brother. I have lived well. I don't regret my decisions to kill Abner, Amasa or Absalom. And I would still choose Adonijah over Solomon if I had it to do over again."

Joab left Abishai in the courtyard. Even in the face of imminent judgment, Joab was a proud, obstinate man.

Within the hour, soldiers arrived to search Joab's home and questioned Abishai about his brother's whereabouts.

"What do you want with him?" he asked, even though he knew the answer.

"King Solomon has summoned him."

Abishai dropped his head. "He has fled to the tabernacle."

★ ★ ★

"Joab has fled to the tabernacle of the Lord in Gibeon," a messenger reported to Solomon.

The king motioned to Benaiah. "Go strike him down."

As Benaiah marched to the tabernacle in Gibeon, northwest of Jerusalem, he remembered David's instructions to Solomon from his deathbed: to make sure that Joab paid for his wickedness in murdering his rivals. It didn't seem right that David would ask Solomon to carry out a sentence he himself was unwilling to do. But then, that was his non-confrontational way to deal with difficult situations in his family.

Benaiah was convinced of Joab's guilt. Although Joab had been loyal to David most of his life, he had only a grudging respect toward him, often berating David publicly or secretly disobeying him. He was jealous for Abner's and Amasa's positions of power. He murdered Absalom contrary to David's orders. And he refused to number the Levites or Benjamites when he disagreed with David's plan for a census, to say nothing of his part in the death of Uriah the Hittite, Mikhael, and eight others during the battle for Rabbah.

Yet Benaiah had a grudging admiration for Joab. He'd been Benaiah's commanding officer for many years, had fought alongside him in military battles and camped with him when they were on the run from Saul. He spoke up if he disagreed with David, something Benaiah should have done on more than one occasion. In the years when he had fought alongside Joab as one of David's elite soldiers, or followed the orders of Joab as general of the army, Benaiah never imagined that he would one day be called upon to end the man's life.

When Benaiah arrived at the tabernacle, he asked Zadok about Joab. The priest said, "He is inside. He has taken hold of the horns of the altar." This was the sign of great distress and an appeal to the mercy of God.

Zadok leaned close to Benaiah. "I think it has less to do with his appeal to God for mercy and more to do with the fact that he knew you'd be the one coming for him."

Even now, at the end of his life, Joab was scheming. He was well aware that Benaiah would be chosen to execute him, which is why he came to the tabernacle for sanctuary. Yet Benaiah was confident in who he was: the son of Jehoiada. In spite of the fact that he was a lifelong soldier, he was always remembered in connection with his valiant father, the priest of Yahweh. Benaiah was never prouder to be his son than when Jehoiada led three thousand and seven hundred priests to Jerusalem to show their support of the new king, David.

Joab knew that Benaiah had been taught the law, so he would understand that a person should not be killed within the tabernacle, for it was a holy place.

Another thought struck Benaiah. If Joab were not currently in charge of the army, then he himself might be considered for the position. Perhaps Joab considered Benaiah as another rival, like Abner and Amasa. Would Joab try to deceive Benaiah and stab him when he lowered his guard, as he had the two generals?

Benaiah shook off the thought. Joab must know his days of scheming were over. This would be his last stand.

Benaiah asked Zadok, "Did he have any weapons with him?"

"He did." Zadok pointed to the ground, where a sword and club lay on the ground. "I told him he must surrender them if he was claiming refuge."

Benaiah noticed Joab's favorite dagger was not with the other weapons. Did Joab still have it? Would he try to fight Benaiah?

Benaiah drew close to the tent of meeting and called out in a loud voice, "Joab! The king orders you to come out of the tabernacle!"

After a long silence, Joab squeaked out, "No, I choose to die here instead."

Benaiah could hardly believe the weak, frightened voice belonged to the once-strong general of Israel's army.

Benaiah sighed. Joab was right about him. He could not murder a man at the altar of the Lord. Yet Solomon had issued a just order, and he had to obey it.

After a lifetime of hard lessons, Benaiah understood that it was not obedience that pleased God, but a broken and contrite heart, as David said.

Still, Benaiah had also learned that to obey was better than sacrifice. Uzzah's sin in handling the ark of the covenant was a sobering reminder that the Lord took the manner of worship seriously. The ark was being returned from the land of the Philistines, who had captured it in battle. But instead of carrying it on the shoulders of the Levites, as prescribed, they put it on a cart. Then when it got jostled along the way, a man named Uzzah reached out to steady it, and as soon as he touched it, God struck him dead. From this event they learned things had to be done in the way God required. He was not to be trifled with.

As God told Samuel, "The Lord doesn't see as man sees; because man looks at outward appearances, but the Lord looks inward, at the heart." Benaiah was now faced with a just order to execute a wicked man. He wanted to obey. Yet he also wanted to uphold the sanctity of this place, where God chose to meet with His people.

After a lifetime of following orders, this old soldier would no longer obey blindly.

Feeling confident that Joab would not venture from his place of refuge, Benaiah made his way back to the palace. He recalled the words from one of the psalms of David:

Behold, You desire truth in the inward parts,
and in the hidden part You will make me to know wisdom.[4]

He would tell the king. Solomon was wise. He would know how to solve this dilemma.

When Benaiah returned to the palace, he informed Solomon of Joab's answer and his dilemma.

The king replied, "Then do as he said, and kill him and bury him. By doing so, I will be free of guilt from the innocent blood shed by Joab. He killed two men who were much better than he was: Abner, the commander of the army of Israel, and Amasa, the commander of the army of Judah. He did both of those things without my father's knowledge. But now the Lord will punish Joab for his crime, and the guilt of their deaths will forever be on his descendants. There will be peace on David's house and kingdom forever."

Benaiah bowed. "Yes, my lord."

Yet as he made his way back to Gibeon, he found himself conflicted. Solomon didn't give clear directions. But Benaiah was no longer a rough soldier who followed orders and killed without thought. He was also a follower of Yahweh, who must one day answer to Him.

He was Benaiah, son of Jehoiada, and he knew the law. He called to mind the Scriptures regarding punishment for murder.

"Whoever plans to kill someone out of anger or hatred must be punished. Take them away from my altar and kill them."

Joab did kill with premeditation and treachery in both cases. He was truly guilty. Benaiah repeated the verse.

"Whoever plans to kill someone out of anger or hatred must be punished. Take them away from my altar and kill them."

He laughed. Was the answer to his conflict contained in the law itself?

Thank you, Lord!

CHAPTER THIRTY-NINE

"So Benaiah the son of Jehoiada went up and struck and killed him [Joab]; and he was buried in his own house in the wilderness. The king put Benaiah the son of Jehoiada in his place over the army, and the king put Zadok the priest in the place of Abiathar."

—1 Kings 2:34–35

As Benaiah approached the tabernacle, another priest pushed aside the heavy linen curtain embroidered with blue, purple and scarlet thread at the entrance to the court. Soon after, Zadok the high priest emerged.

"Is he still there?" Benaiah asked.

"Yes. What do you plan to do?" Zadok looked at Benaiah, wariness in his eyes.

"The king has ordered his execution."

Zadok grasped Benaiah's arm. "You can't do it in there!"

Benaiah shook off the man's hand. "I know that. But he has no right to claim refuge at the altar. He is guilty of premeditated murder."

"He's a broken man, Benaiah. Perhaps you can convince him to come out."

Benaiah pressed his lips into a grim line. "Get everyone else out of there," he ordered.

Zadok disappeared behind the curtain and emerged with three other priests. They stole nervous glances at the resolute warrior as they exited the tabernacle.

Benaiah would normally have his sword drawn and ready, but since he was entering the tabernacle, he kept it sheathed. His club dangled from his waist, held there now by a simple leather strap. He no longer needed the blue and white striped cloth to be reminded of his brother.

Benaiah drew in a deep breath, prayed for strength and wisdom and lifted the heavy curtain to the inner courtyard. Joab clung to the horns of the bronze altar, seemingly contrite. His head rested on top of the altar, his face turned away from the entrance, giving the appearance of resignation and remorse.

Benaiah approached warily. Knowing Joab's history of craftiness and deception, Benaiah did not trust him. After all, he'd made the pretense of embracing both Abner and Amasa before he killed them.

"General Joab, you must come with me."

Joab lifted his head slowly. His eyes were red from weeping. "So is this to be my end?" he asked weakly.

Benaiah merely nodded. He wasn't going to explain. Joab didn't need to be convinced of his own guilt. "I never took you for a coward, General."

"It was not unreasonable that I should side with David's eldest son."

Benaiah shook his head. Did he think this sentence was only the result of his latest treachery? Did he see no connection between his punishment and the murder of his two rival generals?

Joab narrowed his eyes at his would-be executioner.

Benaiah shouldn't have been surprised by the defiance he saw in Joab's eyes, yet he had hoped the general wouldn't fight the inevitable. "Yet you came here hoping to escape the punishment you deserve."

Joab smirked. "What are you going to do, Benaiah, son of Jehoiada?" he taunted. "Would you kill a man in the midst of worship? In this holy place?"

Benaiah knew Joab cared nothing for worship, or holiness or true repentance. His presence here was an act of cowardice, not an appeal to the mercy of God.

"Come out!" Benaiah commanded.

"I am a warrior," Joab said through clenched teeth. "I do not submit. I will die in battle, even if it means that battle is to be here, with you." Joab's earlier weariness was now replaced by an eagerness for battle.

Joab's insolence and lack of respect for this place inflamed Benaiah's anger. It was time to act.

Benaiah approached with slow, cautious movements, his hands out before him. Circling behind Joab, his plan was to pin his arms so he could drag him out. He observed Joab carefully, lest he reach for the dagger Benaiah knew he kept concealed beneath his right shin guard.

Before Benaiah could secure the general's arms, Joab swung around to face him. For a man in his sixth decade, he was surprisingly fast, fear and anger fueling him in the final fight of his life.

Benaiah would not draw his sword until he was outside the walls of the tent. He trusted that God would help him remove the man from His holy premises so he could follow the king's orders and still maintain his integrity.

Joab backed away from Benaiah. The men crouched and circled the altar, looking for an opportunity to capitalize on some weakness in the other. They had been fighting side by side for so long, they knew each other's fighting style. Yet other than practice wrestling, they had not truly tested their strengths against one another, never in a fight in which one of them would surely die.

Joab suddenly bolted to his right, indicating he might escape. Benaiah was so surprised by the unexpected move that he hesitated. Joab exploited the indecision to punch Benaiah across the jaw. He staggered back a step. As he recovered, Joab pulled his dagger out of its sheath. The general obviously had no qualms about using a weapon in the tabernacle.

Joab lunged toward Benaiah with the dagger, a look of desperation in his eyes. Benaiah ducked out of reach. Joab lunged again, but this time Benaiah was quicker and grabbed the general's wrist. He bent Joab's wrist backwards, waiting to hear the sound of a snap as the bones broke. Joab fought to escape, clawing at Benaiah with his left hand, grunting as he twisted his body in an attempt to escape the inevitable.

The dagger fell to the ground just as Benaiah heard the small bones of his wrist snap. Joab cried out and fell to his knees. Benaiah kicked the dagger out of reach. He secured both arms behind Joab's back and pulled him to his feet.

The men now stood eye to eye. Joab dropped his head in resignation to his fate. Then a hint of a smile crossed his face.

"Well done, soldier. I taught you well."

Benaiah couldn't make sense of the man. Was he now proud of Benaiah for besting him in battle?

As they pushed through the heavy curtain, Benaiah motioned for the priests to go back inside the tabernacle. They didn't need to witness the execution.

Benaiah pushed Joab to his knees as he drew his sword. Now standing at his side, Benaiah said, "General Joab, for the murders of General Abner and General Amasa, and for your part in the treachery of Adonijah's attempt to take the rightful throne of David from King Solomon, you are sentenced to death."

Benaiah expected a final protest, a sneer or spitting at the pronouncement. Instead Joab raised his head proudly and fixed his eyes forward, seeming to have finally found the courage to face death.

P. H. Thompson

Benaiah felt a sadness he had never before experienced. With a strong stroke of his sword across Joab's neck, he released the man's soul and let his body fall to the ground.

The curtain of the tabernacle wavered. The priests had been watching. The heavy drape opened a little wider and a hand appeared. It tossed Joab's dagger onto the ground, where it clanged across the stones and landed near the dead general's broken wrist.

Zadok emerged from the tabernacle and into the outer courtyard, inquiring about the body at his feet.

"Cover it up," Benaiah instructed. "I'll send soldiers to transport it to his house. His family can arrange for burial." Joab would not receive a hero's funeral like Abner or Amasa had, but even criminals deserved to be buried. Benaiah picked up the dagger and laid it next to Joab's sword and club. "Make sure these are sent with his body."

EPILOGUE

"And all Israel heard of the judgment which the king had rendered; and they feared the king, for they saw that the wisdom of God was in him to administer justice."
—1 Kings 3:28

"How do you like your new position?" Mariah asked as she and Benaiah sat in the rooftop garden of their home one evening.

He considered a moment. Being head of the entire army of Israel was more time-consuming than the job of personal bodyguard. Since he wasn't in the palace on a daily basis, he didn't see his son, Jehoiada as much. The day their youngest son, Jehoiada was promoted to the position of chief counselor to the king in place of Bathsheba's grandfather, Ahithophel, Benaiah had nearly burst from pride.

"I enjoy getting to see Ammizabad regularly." Since his son was in charge of his own soldiers now, he reported directly to Benaiah. It was a surprise to Benaiah that neither of his sons went into the priesthood either.

"There's more organizational and administrative work." He hadn't thought he could learn to do such sedate labor, but as age crept up on him, he'd found he missed the action of being a warrior less and less.

"How does Solomon compare to David?"

"He inherited an established kingdom at peace, given by the grace of God, and he kept it by that same grace. But his devotion to God is as strong as David's."

Solomon had proceeded with his father's plans for the temple in the location where David offered up his sacrifice after the unlawful census. Many expected him to build it in the high place of Gibeon, where Saul had originally placed the tabernacle. But David chose the threshing floor of Ornan the Jebusite to worship since that time. He felt that was the site chosen by God when He answered his prayer by fire. He never returned to the tabernacle after that.

David's final instruction to Solomon was fulfilled when Shimei, the man who cursed him as he fled from Absalom, was executed by Benaiah for breaking the terms of his house arrest. With this final rebel dealt with, Solomon's reign was firmly established.

"Sometimes God seems like a capricious judge." Mariah shuddered and pulled her shawl more tightly across her shoulders.

"Do you mean because of the plague?"

Mariah nodded.

"Do you not see His many mercies to us as a nation?" Benaiah asked.

"When I think of all the times He showed His care of us in the midst of trouble, I see His mercy. Like when we were taken away in the Amalekite raid. Or as the kingdom was being established. Or when David and his family fled from Absalom, and we went along with him. But many others have suffered more than we have. Like Mikhael's family. Or my sister's family when Merari died. It's hard to see the goodness of God in evil events."

"Job suffered more than anyone. Yet in the midst of his troubles, he said, 'When I was born into this world, I was naked and had nothing. When I die and leave this world, I will be naked and have nothing. The Lord gives, and the Lord takes away. Praise His name!'" Benaiah took his wife's hand. "I think suffering reveals to us who God is—that He is holy and not to be trifled with. He sets the standard for righteousness. We need to be reminded that we are His creatures and He is our Creator."

Mariah tilted her head up and smiled. "You certainly are your father's son, Benaiah ben Jehoiada."

He returned her smile. The other soldiers typically referred to one another by their given names, but he was always Benaiah ben Jehoiada. There was a time when he didn't want to be associated with his father. He didn't think the profession of priest served a useful purpose for the nation. Soldiering seemed a far more worthwhile way to spend a life. But God intruded into all aspects of his life. Benaiah couldn't escape Him or go about as if his actions had no consequences.

"God raised up David for His own glory, not for David's fame. And He has established David's son Solomon on the throne of Israel for His own glory as well. In fact, I had an opportunity to see how God had blessed the new king yesterday, when I arrived in the throne room to report on the army. Just then the king was judging a unique case that reminded me of the time David had to decide if Mephibosheth or Ziba was telling the truth."

"What happened?" Mariah asked.

"Two women stood before the king. The first woman stepped forward and presented her case. She said, 'Sir, this woman and I live in the same house. We were both pregnant at the same time. I gave birth to my son first, and she had her son three days later. We were alone in the house. One night, her child died. While I slept, she came and took my son, and replaced him with her dead son. In the morning when I woke up to nurse him, I saw he was dead. But when I looked closely, I recognized he was not my son, but hers.'"

"How dreadful! How could she possibly prove he was her son?" Mariah exclaimed.

"That's when I saw the wisdom God had given Solomon. It seemed like an impossible dilemma. Especially when the second woman denied she had done such a thing. So the two women argued in front of the king.

"Finally the king mused aloud, 'Each of you claims the living baby is your own and that the dead baby belongs to the other woman.' After looking intently at the women, and briefly closing his eyes, no doubt in prayer, the king ordered his chief bodyguard to draw his sword. Then he ordered, 'Cut the living baby in two and give one half to each woman.'"

"What?" Mariah cried. "How could that be a solution?"

"That's the amazing thing. It was the best decision. As the servant stepped towards the women and child, the second woman said, 'Yes, cut him in two. Then neither of us will have him.' But the first woman, the real mother, appealed to the king for her son's life, and said, 'Please, my king, please don't kill the baby! Give him to her instead!'

After that the king announced his decision. 'Stop. Don't kill the baby. Give him to this woman. She is the real mother.'"

Mariah sat in astonishment for a few moments, then she slowly shook her head. "Benaiah, that's an incredible story. What insight and wisdom the king has, to suggest such a test. Only the real mother would care more about the life of her child over her own demands."

Benaiah agreed. "Yes, it was wonderful to see the real mother gather up her son in her arms. The servants who daily hear King Solomon's wisdom are truly blessed. God has shown His great love for our nation by answering David's prayer and giving us such a king after him."

Mariah slid closer to him and nestled under his arm. "What a great privilege you've been given, to witness so much, both with David and now with King Solomon."

"You are an even greater privilege." He gazed into her eyes. "If you've found a wife, you've found something good. She shows that the Lord is pleased with you."

Mariah's eyes registered astonishment. "That's the first time I've ever heard anything close to poetry from your lips."

Benaiah smiled. "Like his father, Solomon composes songs and proverbs—including that one. But when I heard it, I thought of you." He squeezed her hand. "You are the best thing in my life. And you were right all those years ago when you said you'd still be here even when my days of soldiering were over. I'm so thankful to God for that."

Mariah looked deep into his eyes. Evening sounds filled the air—families closing up their garden doors for the night, frogs croaking, crying babies being soothed to sleep.

She pushed up from the bench to stand in front of him and brushed a tender kiss across his forehead.

Benaiah nodded toward the stairs, his eyebrows raised. "The king wrote a song for his new bride, Abishag. He called it the Song of Songs. I think it will surprise you. I'll read it to you in our bedroom."

Mariah laughed.

Some things never changed.

The End

ENDNOTES

1. 1 Samuel 19–27.
2. 1 Samuel 3:34.
3. Psalm 51.
4. Psalm 51:6.

QUESTIONS FOR REFLECTION
OR GROUP STUDY

1. Benaiah used the blue-and-white-striped cloth to remind him of his brother and of his need to obey at all costs. Do you have an object that holds that kind of significance for you? What are the benefits of such an object? Are there any dangers to such a practice?

2. David felt guilty about cutting the corner of Saul's robe in the cave because the robe symbolized the office of the king, and David took it with violence. Do you think David was being hypersensitive or do you think, like Benaiah, he understood the truth behind the symbolism?

3. After reading this book, has your understanding of Benaiah's three heroic deeds, or your appreciation of him as a person, changed?

4. Jehoiada said, "We cannot choose to believe only the aspects of God's sovereignty that suit us. He is either sovereign over all or He is not sovereign at all." How much does the knowledge of God's sovereignty comfort or concern you when unexplained or tragic events occur in your life?

5. Benaiah lived during the glory days of Israel, and no doubt witnessed many things in his various roles. But it was a time of war until Solomon's reign and, like David, he spilled much blood. His wife, Mariah didn't really understand how he could do some of the things he did, like execute people.

    In the New Testament, when asked by soldiers what they should do to show their faith, John the Baptist did not tell them to stop being soldiers, but only to not abuse their power: "...*So he said to them, 'Do not intimidate anyone or accuse falsely, and be content with your wages'*" (Luke 3:14). Do you think there is a tension between being a believer and a soldier?

6. How much blame rests with Bathsheba for the adultery? No protest is recorded, as in other cases, like David's daughter Tamar (2 Samuel 13:12–13) or Joseph (Genesis 39:7–10). Nor is there any indication he physically forced her, as in the case of Dinah (Genesis 34:1–2) and Tamar (2 Samuel 13:14). What are your thoughts? Is she completely innocent, like David's daughter, Tamar? Do you think she had the power to say "no" or, as a subject, was she expected to follow the orders of the king? Does your understanding of the story change in light of our contemporary views on consent and sexual assault?

7. Do you think Bathsheba suspected that David had anything to do with Uriah's death before it was revealed by the prophet? Scripture doesn't tell us, but how do you think she felt about David once she found out?

8. Do you think Uriah suspected David had slept with his wife? What reasons do you have for this view?

9. Bathsheba was the wife of Uriah the Hittite and the daughter of Eliam, who was the son of Ahithophel. That makes David triple guilty as Bathsheba was both a wife and daughter of two of his mighty men, and the granddaughter of one of his most trusted counselors.

   Though our culture downplays the seriousness of adultery, our sin is never secret or without consequences. Why do you think God was so angry about this sin, since He seemed to look the other way when David took many wives and concubines, contrary to His instructions?

10. According to the Mosaic Law, "*The man who commits adultery with another man's wife, he who commits adultery with his neighbor's wife, the adulterer and the adulteress, shall surely be put to death*"(Leviticus 20:10). Both Bathsheba and David should have been be put to death, but God forgave them. Think about that! David broke four of the commandments: coveting his neighbor's wife, adultery, murder and lying. But he could rejoice and say, "*Blessed is he whose transgression is forgiven, whose sin is covered. Blessed is the man to whom the Lord does not impute iniquity, and in whose spirit there is no deceit*" (Psalm 32:1–2).

    Since we live on this side of the cross, we know that the reason God could forgive David was because Jesus would pay for his sin. All Old Testament saints were, in a sense, saved on credit. They knew the Messiah was coming, but how much do you think they understood of what that would be like, in regards to a final payment for sin?

11. When David pronounced judgment on the scoundrel in Nathan's story, he was passing judgment on himself, which would be fulfilled in the death of four of his sons: the first unnamed son by Bathsheba, Amnon, Absalom and Adonijah. The violence in his family, the rebellion of Absalom, and Absalom's rape of David's concubines were also part of the judgment that God pronounced on David through Nathan. He would feel the guilt of this one event many times throughout his life. Do you feel God punished David enough or that he didn't have to personally feel the punishment because it fell on his family members?

12. Even though he was forgiven by God, David still received the consequences of his sin. God said there were two reasons for this: *"For you did it secretly, but I will do this thing before all Israel, before the sun"* (2 Samuel 12:12) and *"However, because by this deed you have given great occasion to the enemies of the Lord to blaspheme, the child also who is born to you shall surely die"* (2 Samuel 12:14). This shows us that nothing we do is hidden from God, that He will judge, and His judgment is according to righteousness. We can also see that He is concerned with the glory of His reputation, which David dishonored. Have you seen an example of God forgiving a person, yet still making them feel the consequences of their sin?

13. Although the story of David and Bathsheba's adultery is more of a cautionary tale of what not to do, it is nevertheless an encouragement to those who feel their sins are beyond the reach of God's forgiveness. David is told God forgives him. What about Bathsheba? Could she ever move past this event? She suffers the death of their first child. She must deal with the gossip and disdain of the rest of David's family, his wives and grown sons.

Does God forgive her? In 2 Samuel 12:24–25, Bathsheba is comforted by David, and she is referred to as David's wife, rather than Uriah's. God grants her conception and she gives birth to Solomon. God also sends Nathan the prophet to encourage her by saying his name is Jedidiah, which means "the Lord loved him." Further, of all of David's sons, Bathsheba seems to instruct Solomon in his faith, as he mentions many times in Proverbs, and it is Solomon who succeeds David on the throne (1 Kings 1:25–35). But her ultimate blessing is to be recorded in the genealogy of Jesus Christ (Matthew 1:1–16). Have you ever felt that you'll live with the stigma of some sins throughout your whole life?

14. Although Scripture is silent on the issue of what happens to infants who die, as to their eternal destiny, some use the example of the death of David and Bathsheba's first son to infer that they go to heaven. David said, *"I shall go to him, but he shall not return to me"* (2 Samuel 12:23). Some think he is talking about heaven, but he could just mean the grave. When Scripture is silent we mustn't presume. Where it stops, we mustn't proceed. Yet it is enough to say, with Abraham: *"…Shall not the Judge of all the earth do right?"* (Genesis 18:25). It's God's definition of right that matters, not ours. What are your thoughts? Does the fact that David's first son was uncircumcised, and therefore un-named, affect your views at all?

15. Benaiah felt like an accomplice to David's sin of adultery for bringing Bath-sheba to him even though she was married. Then he felt responsible for all the fallout as well. Do you think there is any justification for his feeling this way? How much of an excuse is, "I was just following orders"? Paul tells Timothy, *"Do not lay hands on anyone hastily, nor share in other people's sins; keep yourself pure"* (1 Timothy 5:22). Was Benaiah sharing in David's sin by his actions and subsequent inaction?

16. Throughout his whole life, and at key moments of crisis, Benaiah made the wrong decision and then felt he wasn't pleasing God. As a result, Benaiah struggled with guilt for much of his life, until his father reminded him of God's grace. This changed his feelings about how much his behavior af-fected God. He knew he couldn't obey his way into God's favor or disobey away His mercy, even though his actions were not unimportant. Do you ever feel God is not satisfied with what you do? How much does grace fac-tor into the equation?

17. Benaiah failed to counsel David about the proper way to do a census to avoid a plague, and then he again felt the weight of the consequences of his inac-tion. Even though he wasn't David's spiritual adviser, he knew, as the son of a priest, he should say something to the king when the high priest failed to

do so. What is the balance between doing what we know is right and remaining in our prescribed roles? Was Benaiah wrong to keep silent?

18. How do you feel about David's choice to accept famine or a plague among the three options offered to him in 2 Samuel 24? Do they reveal selfishness or faith?

19. Benaiah's hesitation to kill Joab in the tabernacle is understandable. As a believer, and the son of a priest, he would know such a thing should not be done. He had an ethical dilemma, but this time, he went back to Solomon to receive further instructions. It would seem that he did kill him in the tabernacle, but perhaps Benaiah dragged Joab away from the altar to do it. This was his moment of redemption: he no longer blindly obeyed if he didn't agree. Were you surprised to learn that Scripture recorded this seemingly insignificant conversation between Benaiah and Solomon?

AUTHOR'S NOTE

In historical fiction, it is the author's duty to be true to the events that happened, and then to use poetic license to fill in the gaps. I feel the standard is even higher with biblical, historical fiction. With a more obscure biblical character like Benaiah, I used the few verses where he is named or quoted and incorporated them into the story. I also included the relevant Scripture verses at the beginning of each chapter.

Because he was known as one of David's Mighty Men, his chief bodyguard, and then head of the army of Israel under Solomon, I feel it is safe to assume he was present during many key events in Israel's history and privy to many conversations in the palace, as well as David's personal actions. Many of the stories in this novel are familiar, but they are told from Benaiah's point of view.

What do We Know about Him?

We know he was from Kabzeel, in the south of Judah near the border of Philistia. His name is pronounced be-naw'yaw, and it means "Built by Jehovah."

We know Benaiah was promoted by David over his bodyguard of Cherethites and Pelethites. Cherethites were those tribes of the Philistines who dwelt in the southwest of Canaan. Cherethites and Pelethites was a collective term for David's personal bodyguard. The words indicate a rank: literally executioners or couriers who would convey the kings orders to distant places. At a later date, they were called the captains and the guards. So Benaiah would have been a Captain and executioner. We see this role especially under Solomon, when he was sent to execute Adonijah, Shimei and Joab.

We know he was a valiant man, with exploits against both men and beasts. He is known for three heroic deeds that lead to his appointment in the elite force of David's Mighty Men: aggressively going down into a pit on a snowy day to kill a lion; fighting two Moabite ariels; and challenging a giant Egyptian, armed with only a staff and killing him with the man's own spear (2 Samuel 23:21; 1 Chronicles 11:22).

We know he was David's chief bodyguard and then head of the army of Israel in place of Joab, during the reign of Solomon.

We know he was married and had at least two sons: Ammizabad, who was a soldier (1 Chronicles 27:6) under Benaiah's command, and Jehoiada, named after his grandfather, who became an adviser to the king after Ahithophel's suicide (1 Chronicles 27:34).

Since Benaiah was so well respected, it is not unreasonable to assume that his sons would also be men of honor. The unique name of his son prompted me to extrapolate backwards and name his brother Ammizabad.

We know he is almost always mentioned in connection with his father, Jehoiada, who was a priest. He was an Aaronite who led three thousand seven hundred priests in support of David when he took the throne in Hebron over a united kingdom (1 Chronicles 12:27).

What don't We Know about Him?

We don't know why he became a soldier instead of a priest. As a Levite, and particularly an Aaronite, he would have been expected to be a priest. Why didn't he? I decided to explore that question. I added in an older brother who was already a priest so it wouldn't be too scandalous for him to not do as expected.

We don't know about his early life and family before he was married. We don't know anything about his wife, so I filled in the gaps with my imagination.

We don't know how he felt when asked to follow commands he knew to be wrong, like the proposed attack on the family of Nabal and Abigail, or to summon the wife of his friend and fellow soldier, Uriah.

We don't know at what point Benaiah joined David, but I inserted him into the story while David was on the run from Saul. I had him as a mercenary soldier when he did his famous three deeds that eventually earned him a spot among David's Mighty Men. I also made him about ten years younger than David, so he would have been about sixty when David died and he was promoted to head of the army.

I wondered about the soldier at David's side that evening on the roof. It's not unlikely that it was Benaiah. When asked the identity of the woman bathing, he told David who she was, so he must also have been one of the Mighty Men in order to know that. Then he was ordered to get her for him. **We don't know** how he felt about that. How did he feel afterwards, when he knew the part he played in David's sin and saw the repercussions of it?

Benaiah killed two Moabite ariels according to early translations. My research led me to question the retranslation of the word "ariels" to "lion-like men." The problem is no one knows what an ariel is. In Hebrew, it sounds like "lion" so they translated it as "two lion-like men of Moab." The original readers would have known what it was so it was not explained. But others believe ariel is actually a military term, possibly meaning a group of soldiers, like a platoon. A single platoon can consist of twenty to forty soldiers. If Benaiah fought two against one, it would have been impressive, But, if he fought two platoons single-handedly, Benaiah is even more awesome. I chose the latter option.

If I was naming the characters, I would not have chosen so many names beginning with A, because it can be confusing to readers, especially those unfamiliar with biblical names. I also included a cast of characters to help the reader make sense of who is who. This is especially helpful to anyone unfamiliar with Bible stories or names.

I hope you learned to appreciate Benaiah by reading about him as much as I did by research. I have a few favorite Bible characters that I'm looking forward to talking with for quite a while in Heaven: Jesus, of course, and Hezekiah, Abigail and Benaiah, among others.

I'd encourage you to read 1 and 2 Samuel, and the first few chapters of 1 Kings with fresh eyes, imagining Benaiah there to witness the events firsthand.

ABOUT THE AUTHOR

P. H. Thompson is a former oncology nurse, turned writer. When not writing, she leads women's Bible studies, speaks at women's conferences, spoils her active grandchildren and takes long naps to recover. She and her husband live near Toronto and have two adult daughters.

She is a member of The Word Guild, Canada; ACFW, the American Christian Fiction Writers; and ALLi, the Alliance of Independent Authors. You can find out about upcoming projects at her website, phthompson.com, her Facebook page, P.H. Thompson, Author, or her blog, the-scarlet-thread.com.

CPSIA information can be obtained
at www.ICGtesting.com
Printed in the USA
LVHW092314130819
627584LV00002B/281/P